About

Rebecca Winters lives [in] canyons and high alpine [...] she never runs out of pl[...] favourite holiday spot[...] backgrounds for her romance novels because writing [is] her passion, along with her family and church. Rebecca loves to hear from readers. If you wish to e-mail her, please visit her website at: cleanromances.net

Patricia Thayer was born in Muncie, Indiana, the second of eight children. She attended Ball State University before heading to California. A longtime member of RWA, Patricia has authored fifty books. She's been nominated for the Prestige RITA® award and winner of the RT Reviewer's Choice award. She loves travelling with her husband, Steve, calling it research. When she wants some time with her guy, they escape to their mountain cabin and sit on the deck and let the world race by.

Approaching fifty Mills & Boon titles, **Dianne Drake** is still as passionate about writing romance as ever. As a former intensive care nurse, it's no wonder medicine has found its way into her writing, and she's grateful to Mills & Boon Medicals for allowing her to write her stories. 'They return me to the days I loved being a nurse and combine that with my love of the romance novels I've been reading since I was a young teen.'

The Forever Family

COLLECTION

A Forever Family: Reunited by their Baby

REBECCA WINTERS

PATRICIA THAYER

DIANNE DRAKE

MILLS & BOON

First Published in Great Britain 2020
By Mills & Boon, an imprint of HarperCollins*Publishers*
1 London Bridge Street, London, SE1 9GF

A FOREVER FAMILY: REUNITED BY THEIR BABY © 2020
Harlequin Books S.A.

Baby out of the Blue © 2013 Rebecca Winters
Her Baby Wish © 2009 Patricia Wright
Doctor, Mummy...Wife? © 2016 Dianne Despain

ISBN: 978-0-263-28075-3

0120

MIX
Paper from
responsible sources
FSC™ C007454

This book is produced from independently certified FSC™ paper to ensure responsible forest management.

For more information visit: www.harpercollins.co.uk/green

Printed and bound in Spain
by CPI, Barcelona

BABY OUT OF THE BLUE

REBECCA WINTERS

CHAPTER ONE

FRAN MYERS' GAZE fastened on the scenery unfolding at every bend along the coastal road. Against the azure blue of the Aegean, the miles of white beaches with their background of deep green pines didn't seem real. Dark, fast-moving clouds swirled overhead, adding a dramatic aspect to the landscape. The panorama of colors was quite spectacular.

"I didn't know the Greek Riviera was this beautiful, Kellie. I'm in awe. It's so unspoiled here."

"That's why my husband had built the resort where we'll be staying for the next few days. The Persephone is the latest getaway for the very wealthy who can afford to have peace and quiet in total luxury."

It was such a fabulous area, the news didn't surprise Fran. "Is that why you've brought me all the way from Athens? Because you think I need peace and quiet?"

"Exactly the opposite. Many royals come here to vacation. I'm hoping you'll meet one who's unattached and gorgeous. You two will take one look at each other and it'll be love at first sight."

"That'll never happen, not after my bad marriage."

Fran's best friend since childhood flashed her a searching glance.

"Don't look so surprised, Kellie."

"I'm not surprised. What I see is that a vacation for you is long overdue. Every time I've called since your divorce, you've been at the hospital doing your patient advocacy work all hours of the day and night, and you couldn't talk more than a few minutes. You need a passionate romance to bring you back to life!"

"You're hilarious. It's true I've buried myself in work to keep me from thinking, but it's been a year. I'm doing a lot better now."

"Liar. I don't need your mom to tell me you don't have a life and need to take a break in completely different surroundings. I intend to see you're pampered for a change. We'll laze around, swim, sail, hike, do whatever while we scope out eligible men."

"You're incorrigible, but I love you for it. You know very well that when I told you I would come, I didn't expect you to go to this kind of trouble for me. I thought we'd be staying in Athens to see the rest of the sights I missed when I flew over for your wedding. That was too busy a time to get everything in. Besides, your adoring husband couldn't be thrilled with this arrangement."

Kellie waved her hand in the air in a dismissive gesture. "July is Leandros's busiest time. He's off doing business in the Peloponnese and looking for new resort sites in other places. This is the perfect time for me to spend with the person who's been the sister I never had. That's why I called you to come now and wouldn't take no for an answer. We have a lot of catching up to do."

"Agreed."

The two women had been friends since they'd attended the same elementary school in Philadelphia. They could read each other's moods. Having gone through the good and the bad of their lives together, they'd become closer than most sisters.

When they'd been planning this trip, they'd talked about September. But Kellie had changed her mind and was insistent on Fran coming as soon as possible. Something was going on; normally her friend traveled everywhere with her husband. It sounded as though she needed to talk to Fran in person.

Two years ago Kellie had married millionaire Greek business tycoon Leandros Petralia in Athens. Fran had been the matron of honor at her wedding. Though they'd talked on the phone and emailed since then, they'd only seen each other the half a dozen times Kellie had flown home to Pennsylvania to be with her family for a few days. On those short visits Fran could tell her friend was so crazy over her exciting husband, she couldn't bear to be gone from him longer than a few nights.

But clearly that wasn't the case today. Kellie seemed wired, and her show of gaiety was somehow artificial. Physically she was thinner than the last time Fran had seen her. On their five-hour drive to the resort south of Thessolonika, Kellie's glib responses throughout their conversation weren't at all like her.

Fran decided to hold off until tomorrow to have a heart-to-heart with her golden-blonde friend. Right now she wanted Kellie to concentrate while she drove the fabulous slate-blue luxury saloon—too fast for Fran's liking. As they whizzed along, Fran's eyes darted to the stormy sky. "Have you noticed how black those clouds ahead are?"

"Yes. It's almost spooky and so windy, it's buffeting the car. That's very strange. This place is legendary for its sunshine. Wouldn't you know it would choose today to cloud up for your arrival?"

"Maybe it's a bad omen and your hubby came back to Athens early only to find you missing."

"Don't be absurd—" Kellie answered with uncharacteristic sharpness. "He's got his secretary with him. Maybe they're really somewhere in the Dodecanese Islands, a favorite place of his when he wants to relax."

With Mrs. Kostas? She was in her late forties.

Her friend's emotional outburst took Fran by surprise. "I was just having some fun with you." She'd never seen Kellie explode this way before.

"I'd rather talk about you. Has Rob called yet, wanting you two to get back together?"

"No. In fact, I've heard he's involved with someone at his work."

"He'll soon realize he's lost the best thing that could ever happen to him."

"Spoken like my best friend."

Kellie had been the maid of honor at Fran's wedding. Four years ago Fran had married Rob Myers after meeting him through mutual friends in Philadelphia. He was an upcoming estate-planning attorney working for a prestigious local law firm. On their third date she'd told Rob that she could never conceive, so if he didn't want to see her again, she'd understand.

He'd told her he didn't have a problem with adoption. It was a great option for childless couples. Besides, he was interested in *her*, and he had proven it by marrying her. After a year passed, she'd brought up the idea of putting in adoption papers, but he'd said it was too soon to think about and kept putting her off.

Eventually she realized he had issues and she suggested they go for counseling so they could talk about them in depth. But the counseling revealed that with the busy law practice thriving, he no longer had the time or the interest to enlarge their family, especially when the child couldn't be their own flesh and blood. Fran was enough for him.

But she wanted children badly. After three years of a married life no longer happy or fulfilling for either of them, they'd agreed to divorce. It was the only way to end the pain. Since then Fran had decided marriage wasn't for her. Kellie scoffed at such nonsense and told her she would find the right husband for her no matter what.

"Kellie? I don't know about you, but I'm thirsty. Let's stop at the village I can see up ahead and get ourselves a drink at one of those cute hotel bars."

"It's only twelve more miles to the Persephone," her friend responded in a clipped tone. "We'll order room service and have dinner in our suite where we can relax. But, of course, if you can't wait…"

"I hope you don't mind."

Kellie's hands tightened on the steering wheel, further proof her friend was barely holding herself in check. "Of course not."

There was no softening of her tone, or a reassuring smile. Right now, Fran was more concerned with Kellie, who'd been driving over the speed limit. She never used to drive this fast. After they stopped for a soda maybe Fran could prevail on her friend to let her drive the rest of the way. She'd use the pretext that she'd never been behind the wheel of a Mercedes before.

Fran wanted both of them to arrive at the resort in one piece. With this wind, the driving could be dangerous. To her alarm, the idea came into her head that Kellie wasn't even seeing the road. Intuition told her the once flourishing Petralia marriage was having problems.

Not Kellie, too.

By the time they reached the village proper the wind was so powerful there was actual debris in the air. "Stop in front of that hotel on the corner, Kellie. It's starting to hail. Let's make a run for it."

The small ice balls pounded down, emptying the street of people rushing to take cover. All the shops and cafés had taken their display items and tables inside. When Fran entered the hotel bar with Kellie, tourists and staff alike were huddled in groups talking and gesticulating while they brushed themselves off.

"Kellie? You understand Greek. What are they saying?"

"I don't know, but I'll find out."

Fran followed her friend over to the counter where Kellie got a waiter's attention. He rattled off an answer to her question. She turned to Fran. "Someone in the back was listening to the radio and heard that tornado-like winds have swept through the area. There's no television reception right now. The police have issued a warning that everyone should stay indoors until the danger has passed. It's a good thing you wanted to stop here."

Considering the violence of the elements, it was providential they'd been passing by this village. "Let's get a drink and find a place to sit down while we wait this out."

After being served, they carried their sodas to an

unoccupied bistro table. By now the hail had stopped and a heavy downpour had descended.

Kellie frowned. "I can't believe this weather."

"Since it made the six o'clock news, maybe you ought to call and let Leandros know you're all right."

Her jaw hardened. "He knows. Whenever I leave our apartment, my bodyguard Yannis follows me. If my husband is interested, he'll phone me." She pulled out her cell and checked everything. "Nope. No calls yet. See?" She showed her the screen. "No messages."

"Kellie—" Fran put a hand on her friend's arm. "Tell me what's going on. I'd planned to wait until morning to ask you that question, but since we won't be leaving here any time soon, I'm asking it now. I want to know what's happened to the happiest wife I've ever known. Where did she go?" The reason Kellie had wanted Fran to come to Greece was no longer a mystery.

Kellie averted her soulful brown eyes. "Maybe you should be asking Leandros that question."

"He's not here. *You* are. What's wrong?"

Kellie's face was a study in pain. "I'm losing him, Fran. In fact, I've discovered I never really had him and I can't stand it."

Her friend's emotions were so brittle they'd crack if Fran pushed too hard. Instead of arguing with her that it couldn't possibly be true, she took a deep breath before saying, "Does this have anything to do with the fact that you haven't gotten pregnant yet? You're probably putting too much pressure on yourself to give Leandros a child. These things take time."

"Since I've been diagnosed with seminal plasma hypersensitivity, that's the understatement of the year.

I've never wanted to talk about it, but you deserve an explanation.

"Our marriage took a crushing blow when I discovered that the painful itching and hives I experienced after intercourse was because my body is allergic to Leandros's sperm. When the doctor told me twenty thousand-plus women suffer from it in the U.S. alone, I couldn't believe it."

Fran shook her head. "I had no idea."

"I know. Growing up, I never knew such a problem existed. Leandros had to have been devastated, but he was wonderful about it. He's worn a condom every time, but I *know* deep down he must hate it.

"The doctor knew we wanted a baby and said we could try artificial insemination with a good hope of success. They have to wash his sperm of the proteins first before the procedure is done. We've been trying that method since last year, but unfortunately it hasn't worked for us. He said he's willing to adopt. How's that for irony after what you've lived through? At this point I'm thinking it's just as well," came the bleak admission.

Fran couldn't believe what she was hearing. "What do you mean?"

"I'm talking about Karmela Paulos. She came to work for Leandros a month ago as part of the typing pool."

Ah. Karmela. The woman couldn't get to him by other means, so she'd insinuated herself into the office. Now things were starting to make sense.

Karmela Paulos was the gorgeous, raven-haired younger sister of Leandros's first wife, Petra. Petra had been pregnant when she'd died in a helicopter crash over the Ionian Sea.

Two years later Leandros had met Kellie by accident at the Cassandra in Athens, one of the famous Petralia five-star hotels. It hadn't taken long before he'd married her, but it seemed that since his late wife's funeral, Leandros had acquired a constant companion in Karmela who was always around.

Fran had met her at the wedding and hadn't liked her proprietorial behavior with Leandros either. Though he was now a husband for the second time, it seemed Karmela had won herself a position that placed her closer to Leandros than before. This was foul play at its best. Being her brother-in-law, he could hardly turn her down.

"It was clear to me at the wedding that your marriage had thwarted her dreams to become the next Mrs. Leandros Petralia." Whatever subterfuge was going on here, Fran was positive Karmela was behind it in order to break them apart. She clearly still wanted Leandros for herself.

Too bad. Fran intended to make sure this was resolved before she went back to Pennsylvania in two weeks.

"Tell you what, Kellie. You heard the warning from the police, so I have an idea. Since we're not supposed to be out on the street, how about we get a room for tonight right here?"

"That sounds good."

"I think so, too. It'll be fun. How long has it been since we hung out in some cozy little hotel like this?"

"I don't remember."

"We'll watch the news on TV when it comes back on, and we'll get some food. Then we can talk all night if we want. I've got an idea about how to thwart Karmela without your husband realizing what's happening."

"I don't know if that's possible."

Fran smiled. "You haven't heard my plan yet." She got up from the table. "I'll talk to the proprietor and arrange a room for us. When the rain stops, we'll go out to the car for our luggage."

By now Fran figured Kellie's bodyguard would have contacted Leandros wherever he was and told him his wife was safe and sound. She hoped Leandros would call her soon. The problems in their marriage were tearing her best friend apart. No one knew what that felt like better than Fran.

Nik Angelis had just entered his Athens penthouse when one of his brothers phoned him. He clicked on. "Sandro? What's up?" They'd already spent part of the day in a board meeting at the Angelis Corporation. Nik had recently taken over for his father who'd retired.

"Turn on your television. The news about the tornado is on every station."

"I was in it, remember?" It was the only talk at Angelis headquarters. After he'd seen his sister and her family off to Thessalonika early that morning on the company jet, Nik had headed over to the international air cargo station to check on some shipments. While he was talking business with one of the staff, a funnel had dropped down from clouds descending on Athens. It had swept through in a northwest direction and headed straight for the air cargo station.

After a few minutes it dissipated, but in that amount of time, it had caused damage to the constructions in its path and left a trail of destruction. Fortunately everyone involved had escaped injury, including Nik. Before he instructed his limo driver to take him to his office, he'd made contact with his pilot.

Relief had filled him to learn they'd been at cruising speed and out of range of the severe turbulence of the weather pattern before the tornado had formed. Knowing his sister's family were safely on their way north for a vacation, he'd been able to relax.

"No, no," Sandro cried anxiously. "Not that one. I'm talking about another one that touched down near Thessalonika a few minutes ago."

Another one?

"Let's pray Melina and Stavros are safe."

Nik's heart had already received one workout this morning, but now it almost failed him. "Hold on." He raced into his den and clicked on the TV with the remote. Every station was covering the news using split screens to show the funnel clouds of both tornadoes.

...and then another tornado struck a part of the Greek Riviera at 5:13 p.m. this evening. It was reported as a T-4, and has since dissipated, but we won't know the true extent of the damage for a while. Word has already reached the station that a dozen villas and some private suites at the world-famous Persephone Resort owned by the Petralia Corporation, have been destroyed.

Nik felt as if a grenade had blown up his insides. The Persephone was where Melina, Stavros and their infant daughter were going to stay for the first two nights of their vacation. Nik's good friend, in business and socially, Leandros Petralia, was the owner of the resort.

"I called Melina on her cell, but there's no phone service." Sandro sounded frantic.

The knowledge sent ice through Nik's veins.

So far twenty people are unaccounted for. We re-peat, it doesn't mean those are fatalities. Relief is pouring in from all over. We ask people to stay away from the area and let the police and search-and-rescue workers do their job. Cell phones are not working. We've posted a series of hotline numbers on the screen in case you have or need information about a loved one.

Pure terror seized his heart. "Do you think Cosimo is home from the office yet?"

"I don't know, but I'll try to reach him."

"Tell him to meet us at the airport, Sandro." He wanted both his brothers with him. "We'll fly to Thes-salonika."

"I'm on my way!"

Nik clicked off, then phoned his driver and told him to bring the car around. On his way out the door he called his pilot and told him to ready the jet for another flight to Thessolonika. In a little over an hour Nik and his brothers could be there. They would need a car.

En route to the airport he phoned his parents at the family villa on Mykonos. They'd just heard the news and were in total anguish. "Our precious Melina, our Demitra," his mother half sobbed the words.

"Their suite may not have been among the ones af-fected, *Mana*. In any case, Stavros will have protected them. We have to have faith. Sandro and Cosimo are going to fly there with me now. You get on one of those hotlines and see what you can find out! Call me when you know anything. Let's pray phone service is restored there soon. I'll call you when I know anything."

A rap on the hotel-room door the next morning brought both girls awake. With the TV knocked out last night, they'd talked for hours about Karmela. Before falling asleep, Fran had made sure her friend was armed with a firm plan in mind for once their vacation was over.

Kellie lifted her head and checked her watch. "It's ten after ten!"

"Maybe it's one of the maids waiting to make up our room. I'm closest." Fran jumped out of bed in her plaid cotton pajamas. "Who is it?" she called through the door.

"Yannis."

"I'll talk to him," Kellie murmured. In an instant she slid out of her bed and rushed over to the door. The dark-haired bodyguard stood in the hall while they spoke in Greek. The conversation went on for a minute until Kellie groaned and closed the door again. Her face had turned ashen.

Fran thought her friend was going to faint and caught her around the shoulders. "What's wrong? Come sit down on the chair and tell me."

But Kellie just stood with tears gushing down her pale cheeks. "A tornado touched down twelve miles to the north of here last evening, killing nine people. Among them were five guests staying at the P-Perse-phone."

They stared at each other in disbelief. "I can't credit it," Fran whispered in shock. "If we hadn't pulled over when we did…" They could have been among the fatalities. She started to tremble.

"Yannis said Leandros heard about it on the television, but he was almost a thousand miles away in Rhodes. He flew here immediately, but even with his own jet and a police escort, he had trouble getting into the site until the middle of the night. Three of the twelve individual suites were demolished. There's nothing left of them."

Fran gasped. "On top of the human tragedy, your poor husband is having to deal with that, too."

"Leandros told Yannis it's a nightmare, and there's still no phone, internet or television service to that area. He got hold of him through the help of the police to let me know what has happened. I've been asked to stay put here until he joins us. Yannis said it shouldn't be long now." Kellie's teeth were chattering.

"Come on. We need to get ready and go downstairs. Knowing your husband, he must be absolutely devastated and is going to need you more than he's ever needed anyone in his life." Now would be the time for Kellie to draw close to Leandros and put the plan they'd talked about last night into action.

Both of them showered and dressed in a daze. Fran put on white linen pants with a spring-green-and-white-printed top. She tied her dark honey-blonde hair back at the nape with a white chiffon scarf. After slipping on white sandals, she announced she was ready. Nothing seemed real as they packed up and carried their bags downstairs to wait for Leandros.

To Fran's surprise, the main doors of the hotel were open for patrons to walk out and enjoy coffee at the tables set up in front of the building. Warm air filtered inside and a golden sun shone out of a blue sky. Up and down the street, life appeared to be going on as usual. You would never have known there'd been a natural disaster twelve miles away from here last evening.

A waiter approached them. "The tables in front are full. If you'll walk around to the patio in back, we'll serve you out there."

"Thank you," Fran said before taking Kellie aside. "Yannis is sitting outside in his car by yours. Let's stow our luggage and then tell him we'll be in back of the hotel. We need breakfast with our coffee. He can show Leandros where to come. I feel like soaking up some sun until he arrives. Don't you?"

"I guess so," Kellie answered in a wooden voice.

They walked over to their car and put their cases in the back. "This hotel seems to be a popular place. Go ahead and talk to Yannis while I get us a table before they're all taken."

"Okay."

Fran followed the stone pathway to the rear of the hotel where blue chairs and tables were set with bright blue-and-white-check cloths. There was an overhang of bougainvillea above the back door, and further on, a small garden. Too bad the wind had denuded most of the flowering plants. There were only a few red petals left.

She took a seat in the sun while she waited, thinking she was alone. But all of a sudden she heard a strange sound, like a whimper. Surprised, Fran looked around, then up. Maybe it was coming from one of the rooms on the next floor where a window was open.

Again she heard the faint cry. It didn't sound frantic and it seemed to be coming from the garden area. Maybe it was a kitten that had been injured in the storm.

Poor thing. She jumped up and walked over to investigate.

When she looked in the corner, a gasp escaped her lips. There, on its back in the bushes, lay a dirty black-haired baby with cuts from head to toe—

Fran couldn't fathom it. The child was dressed in nothing more than a torn pink undershirt. The little olive-skinned girl couldn't be more than seven months old. Where in heaven's name had she come from? A groan came out of Fran. She wondered how long the child had been out here in this condition.

Trying to be as gentle as possible, Fran lifted the limp body in her arms, petrified because the baby had to be dying of hypothermia. Her pallor was pronounced and her little lids were closed.

"Fran?" Kellie called out and ran up to her. "What on earth?"

She turned to her friend with tear-filled eyes. "Look— I found this baby in the garden."

A gasp flew from Kellie's lips. "I can see that, but I can't believe what I'm seeing."

"I know. Quick—get me a blanket and drive us to the hospital. I'm afraid she's going to die."

Kellie's eyes rounded before she dashed through the back door, calling in Greek for help. Within seconds, the staff came running out. One of them brought a blanket. Fran wrapped the baby as carefully as she could and headed around the front of the hotel. Kellie ran ahead of her to talk to Yannis.

"He'll drive us to the hospital."

He helped Fran and the baby inside the backseat of his car. She thought he looked as white-faced as Kellie, who climbed in front. She looked back at Fran. "What do you think happened?"

"Who knows? Maybe the mother was on the street around the corner when a microburst toppled the stroller or something and this dear little thing landed in the garden."

"But she's only wearing a torn shirt."

Both of them were aghast. "I agree, nothing makes sense."

"Do you think she could have been out there all night?"

"I don't know," Fran's voice trembled. "But what other explanation could there possibly be, Kellie? The baby has superficial cuts all over."

"I'm still in shock. You don't suppose the mother is lying around the hotel grounds somewhere, too? Maybe concussed?"

"It's a possibility," Fran murmured. "We know what tornadoes can do. The one in Dallas tossed truck rigs in the air like matchsticks. Sometimes I feel that's all we see on the news back home. I just have never heard about a tornado in Greece."

"They get them from time to time. Leandros told me they usually happen near coastal waters."

The baby had gone so still, it was like holding a doll. "Tell Yannis to please hurry, Kellie. She's not making any more sounds. The police need to be notified and start looking for this baby's parents."

Once they reached the emergency entrance, everything became a blur as the baby was rushed away. Fran wanted to go with her, but the emergency-room staff told her they needed information and showed her to the registration desk.

The man in charge told them them to be seated while he asked a lot of questions. He indicated that no one had contacted the hospital looking for a lost baby. Furthermore, no mother or father injured in the storm had been brought in. So far, only a young man whose car had skidded in the downpour and hit a building had come in for some stitches on his arm.

When the questioning was over he said, "One of our staff has already contacted the police. They've assured us they'll do a thorough investigation to unite the baby with her parents. An officer should be here within the hour to take your statements. Just go into the E.R. lounge to wait, or go to the cafeteria at the end of the hall."

When they walked out, Kellie touched Fran's arm. "I think we'd better eat something now."

"Agreed."

After a quick breakfast, they returned to the E.R. lounge. "If the baby lives, it will be thanks to you and your quick thinking. Had you been even a couple of minutes later arriving at the patio the baby might not have had the strength to cry and no one would have discovered her in time."

Hot tears trickled down Fran's cheeks. "She has to live, Kellie, otherwise life really doesn't make sense."

"I know. I've been thinking the same thing." They both had. Kellie had been praying to get pregnant and it had been Fran's fate not to be able to conceive. What a pair they made! She found two seats and they sat down.

"I wish Leandros would get here. After seeing this baby, I'm worried sick for what he's had to deal with. Lives were lost in that tornado. He'll take their deaths seriously."

"It's too awful to think about. I'm still having trouble believing this has happened. When I saw her lying in those bushes, I thought I was hallucinating."

Before long, two police officers came into the lounge to talk to them. There was still no word about the parents. After they went out again, Fran jumped up. "I can't sit still. Let's go into the E.R. Maybe someone at the desk can tell us if there's been any news on the baby yet."

Kellie got to her feet. "While you do that, I'm going outside to talk to Yannis. Maybe he's heard from Leandros."

Quickly, Fran hurried through the doors to the E.R. and approached one of the staff at the counter. "Could you tell me anything about the baby we brought in a little while ago?"

"You can ask Dr. Xanthis, the attending physician. He's coming through those doors now."

Fran needed no urging to rush toward the middle-aged doctor. "Excuse me—I'm Mrs. Myers. I understand you might be able to tell me something about the baby my friend and I brought to the hospital." Her heart hammered in fear. "Is she going to live?"

"We won't know for several hours," he answered in a strong Greek accent.

"Can I see her?"

He shook his head. "Only family is allowed in the infant ICU."

"But no one has located her family yet. She's all alone. I found her in the bushes in the garden behind the hotel."

"So I understand. It's most extraordinary."

"Couldn't I just be in the same room with her until her parents are found?"

The man's sharp eyes studied her for a moment. "Why would you want to do that?"

"Please?" she asked in a trembling voice.

"She's a stranger to you."

Fran bit her lip. "She's a baby. I—I feel she needs someone," her voice faltered.

All of a sudden a small smile lifted one corner of his mouth. "Come. I'll take you to her."

"Just a moment." She turned to the staff person. "If my friend Mrs. Petralia comes in asking for me, please tell her I'm with the baby, but I'll be back here in a little while."

"Very good."

The doctor led her through the far doors to an elevator that took them to the second floor. They walked through some other doors to the nursery area where he introduced her to a nurse. "I've given *Kyria* Myers permission to be with the baby until the police locate the mother and father. See that she is outfitted."

"This way," the other woman gestured as she spoke.

"Thank you so much, Dr. Xanthis."

His brows lifted. "Thank you for being willing to help out."

"It's my pleasure, believe me."

CHAPTER TWO

FRAN FOLLOWED THE NURSE to an anteroom to wash her hands. She was no stranger to a hospital, having worked in one since college to follow up on patients who needed care when they first went home.

When she'd put on a gown and mask, they left through another door that opened into the ICU. She counted three incubators with sick babies. The baby she'd found in the garden was over in one corner, hooked up to an IV. She'd been fitted with nasal prongs to deliver oxygen. A cardiopulmonary monitor on her chest tracked the heartbeat on the screen.

She was glad to see this hospital had up-to-date equipment to help the baby survive, yet the second she spied the little form lying on her back, so still and help-less, she had to stifle her cry of pain. The precious child had cuts everywhere, even into her black curls, but they'd been treated. Mercifully none of them were deep or required stitches. With the dirt washed away, they stood out clearly.

The nurse pulled a chair over so Fran could sit next to the incubator. "Everyone hopes she will wake up. You can reach in and touch her arm, talk to her. I'll be back."

Finally alone with the baby, Fran studied the beautiful features and profile. She was perfectly formed, and to all appearances had been healthy before this terrible thing had happened to her. All the cuts and hookups couldn't disguise her amazingly long black eyelashes or the sweetness of her sculpted lips.

With such exquisite coloring, she looked like a cherub from the famous painting done by the Italian artist Raphael, but this cherub's eyes were closed and there was no animation.

She put her hand through the hole and touched the baby's forearm. "Where did you come from? Did you fall out of heaven by accident? Please come back to life, little sweetheart. Open your eyes. I want to see their color."

There was no response and that broke her heart. Even if the baby could hear her, she couldn't understand English. "Of course you want your mommy and daddy. People are trying to find them, but until they do, will you mind if I stay with you?"

Fran caressed her skin with her fingers, careful not to touch any cuts. "I know you belong to someone else, but do you know how much I'd love to claim a baby like you for my own? You have no idea how wonderful you are."

Tears trickled down her cheeks. "You can't die. You just can't—" Fran's shoulders heaved, but it wouldn't do for the baby to hear her sobs. By sheer strength of will she pulled herself together and sang some lullabies to her.

After a time the nurse walked over. "I'm sure you're being a comfort to her, but you're wanted down in the E.R. Come back whenever you want."

Fran's head lifted. She'd been concentrating so hard

on the baby, she hadn't realized she'd already been up here several hours. "Thank you."

"Leave everything in the restroom on your way out."

"I will." With reluctance she removed her hand and stood up. "I'll be back, sweetheart."

A few minutes later she reached the E.R. lounge and discovered Kellie talking quietly with Leandros. Her attractive husband had arrived at last, but he looked as though he'd aged since Easter. When he'd flown to Pennsylvania with Kellie in the Petralia company jet at that time, the three of them had gone out for dinner and all had been well.

The second her friend saw her, she jumped up from the chair and ran across the room to meet her. Leandros followed. "Is the baby going to make it?" Kellie cried anxiously.

"I don't know. She's just lying there limp in the incubator, but she's still breathing and has a steady heartbeat. Have the police found her parents yet?"

"There's been no news."

Leandros reached for her. "Fran—" he whispered with a throb in his voice. It revealed the depth of his grief. They gave each other a long, hard hug.

"It's so good to see you again, Leandros, but I wish to heaven it were under different circumstances. I'm so sorry about everything," she told him. "I'm sure you feel like you've been through a war."

He nodded, eyeing his wife with pained eyes. Something told Fran the pain she saw wasn't all because of the tragedy. She could feel the negative tension between Kellie and her husband. Her friend hadn't been exaggerating. In fact, their relationship seemed to be in deeper trouble than even Fran had imagined.

"Five guests at the resort died," he muttered morosely. "We can thank God the honeymoon couple weren't in their suite when the tornado touched down or there would have been two more victims. Unfortunately the other two suites were occupied. Mr. Pappas, the retired president of the Hellenic Bank and his wife, were celebrating their sixtieth wedding anniversary."

"How terrible for everything to end that way. What about the other couple?" Fran asked because she sensed his hesitation.

Leandros looked anguished. "The sister of my friend Nikolos Angelis and her husband had only checked in a few hours earlier with their baby."

"A baby?" she blurted.

"Yes, but when the bodies were recovered, there was no sign of the child. The police have formed a net to search everywhere. You can imagine the anguish of the Angelis family. They're in total shock. People are still combing the area."

"Nik is the brilliant youngest of the Angelis brothers," Kellie informed her. "He's the new CEO of the multimillion-dollar mega corporation established by their family fifty years ago. He was out of the country when Leandros and I married, or he would have been at the wedding."

"I remember seeing some pictures of him in a couple of magazines while I was on the plane flying over." *Gorgeous* was the only word to come to mind.

Leandros nodded. "We've both put up money for volunteers to scour the region, but so far nothing. His parents are utterly devastated. They not only lost their daughter and son-in-law, but their little granddaughter."

Granddaughter?

The mention of a baby girl jolted her as she thought of the baby upstairs fighting for her life.

"How old is the baby?"

"Seven months."

"What color is her hair?"

"Black."

A cry escaped her lips.

Maybe she hadn't fallen out of heaven.

Was it possible she'd been carried in the whirlwind and dropped in the hotel garden? Stranger things had happened throughout the world during tornadoes.

"Kellie?"

"I know what you're thinking, Fran—" Kellie cried. "So am I." The two women stared at each other. "Remember the little girl in the midwest a few years ago who was found awake and sitting up ten miles away in a field after a tornado struck, killing her entire family? We both saw her picture on the news and couldn't believe it."

"Yes! She was the miracle baby who *lived*!"

"It would explain everything."

Leandros's dark brows furrowed. "What are you two talking about?"

"Quick, Kellie. While you tell him what we're thinking, I'm going back upstairs to be with the baby. Maybe she has come to by now. After hearing from Leandros that their baby is missing, I think she could be that lost child! She *has* to be! There's no other explanation. She *has* to live." Those words had become Fran's mantra.

The police had made a grid for the volunteers to follow. Nik and his brothers had been given an area to cover in the pine trees behind the resort. They'd searched for hours. Separated by several yards, they walked abreast while looking for any sign of Demi.

Debris had been scattered like confetti, but he saw nothing to identify their family's belongings. The tornado had destroyed everything in its path, including lives. Pain stabbed him over and over.

Where in the hell was the baby? How could they go home without her body and face their parents? The grief was beyond imagining.

Each of his brothers had two children, all boys. Their wives and families, along with Stavros's family had flown to Mykonos to join Nik's parents. He knew Sandro and Cosimo were thanking providence that their own children hadn't been anywhere near either tornado, but right now their hearts were so heavy with loss, none of them could talk.

Demi was the only little girl in the family, so beautiful—just like her mother. Not having married yet, Nik had a huge soft spot for his niece. She possessed a sweetness and a special appeal that had charmed him from the moment she was born.

Melina's baby was the kind of child he would love to have if he ever settled down. But that meant finding the kind of woman who could handle what he would have to tell her about himself before they could be married.

Up to now he hadn't met her yet and was forced to put up with the public's false assumption about him. Throughout the last year, various tabloids had put unauthorized pictures of him on their covers with the label Greece's New Corporate Dynamo—The Most Sought-After Playboy Bachelor of the Decade. He was sickened by the unwanted publicity. But this tragedy made the problems in his personal life fade in comparison.

Just two weeks ago he'd bought Demi a toy where you passed a ball through a tube and it came out the other end. She loved it and would wait for it to show up, then crawl on her belly after it. She could sit most of the time without help and she put everything possible in her mouth. Her smile delighted him. Never to see it—or her—again…he couldn't bear it. None of them could.

Hot tears stung his eyes at the thought that the seven-month-old was gone, along with her parents. It was a blow he didn't know whether he could ever get over. He and Melina had shared a special bond. She'd been there for him at the darkest point in his life. A grimace broke out on his face as he realized he couldn't even find her baby. He felt completely helpless.

Sandro caught his arm. "We've finished this section."

"Let's move to the next grid."

"Someone else has done it," Cosimo muttered.

"I don't care," he bit out. "Let's do it again, more thoroughly this time. Examine every tree."

They went along with him. Maybe five minutes had gone by when his cell phone rang. He checked the caller ID. "It's Petralia."

Their heads swiveled around, as they prayed for news that some volunteer had found her body.

"Leandros?" he said after clicking on. "Any word yet?"

"Maybe. If you believe in miracles."

Nik reeled. "What do you mean?"

"I'm with my wife at the hospital in Leminos village. It's twelve miles south of you. Come quickly. This morning her best friend Mrs. Myers from the States, who's staying with us for a few weeks, found a baby girl, barely alive, in a hotel garden."

Nik's hand tightened on the cell phone. "Did I just hear you right?"

"Yes. If you can believe this, she was lying in some bushes at the rear of the hotel. On their drive to the Persephone yesterday, the storm got so bad, they ended up staying in Leminos."

"You mean your wife and her friend—"

"Could have been among the casualties," he finished for him. The emotion in Leandros's voice needed no translation. "Fran went out to the back patio to get them a table for breakfast when she heard some faint cries and walked over to investigate."

"What?"

"It's an absolutely incredible story. The child is cut up and bruised. All she had on was a torn undershirt. They brought her to the hospital and Fran has been staying in the infant ICU with her in order to comfort her. So far no parents have shown up yet to claim her."

"You've *seen* her?" Nik cried out.

"Yes. She's about seven months old, with your family's coloring. She's alive, but not awake yet. So far that's good news according to the doctor who thought at first they were going to lose her. Come as fast as you can to the E.R. entrance. We'll show you to the ICU."

He eyed his brothers. "We're on our way, Leandros— My gratitude knows no bounds."

"Don't thank me yet. This child might not be your niece."

"I have to believe she is!"

Nik clicked off and he and his brothers started running through the forest. On the way he told them the fantastic story. Before long they reached the rental car at the police check point. Nik broke every speed record getting to Leminos while they all said silent prayers.

Once they reached the village, he followed the signs to the hospital. Leandros and his wife were waiting for them in the lounge of the E.R. His lovely wife, Kellie, was in tears over what had happened to Nik's family. He was deeply moved by her compassion. She, in turn, introduced them to the doctor who was taking care of the baby.

"Come with me and we'll see if she belongs to you." On the way upstairs the doctor said, "I'm happy to report that a half hour ago, the baby opened her eyes for the first time and looked around. I think that had something to do with *Kyria* Myers who's been singing to her and caressing her through the incubator. She's the one who first heard the baby cry and found her before she lost consciousness."

Nik couldn't wait to see if the baby was Demi, but he understood they had to wash their hands and put on masks and gowns. It took all his self-control not to burst into the ICU. If it wasn't their niece lying in there it would kill all three of them to have to return to Mykonos without her.

When they were ready, the nurse opened the door and beckoned them to follow her to the corner of the room. A woman gowned and masked like themselves sat next to the incubator with her hand inside the hole to touch the baby. With her back to them, he could only glimpse dark honey-blond hair tied back with a filmy scarf. She was singing to the child with the kind of love a mother might show for her own flesh and blood.

Touched by her devotion to a child she didn't even

know, Nik had a suffocating feeling in his chest as he drew closer and caught his first sight of the baby.

"Demi—"

His brothers crowded around, equally ecstatic at discovering their niece lying hooked up to machines, but squirming as if she didn't like being trapped in there. She kept turning her head. Sounds of joy and tears escaped their lips as her name echoed through the ICU. But Demi took one look at them and started crying. With their masks on, she was frightened.

The woman caressing her limbs spoke in soothing tones and soon calmed her down. Nik could hardly believe it. Those words might be spoken in English, but Melina's baby responded to the tender tone in which she'd said them.

After a minute, the woman pulled her hand through and stood up. Nik noticed she was of medium height. When she turned to them, he found himself staring into eyes a shade of violet-blue he'd only seen in the flowers that grew in certain pockets on Mykonos. They were glazed with tears.

"Mrs. Myers? I'm Nik Angelis," he spoke through the mask. "These are my brothers Sandro and Cosimo. I understand you're the person we have to thank for finding our niece before it was too late to revive her."

"I just happened to be the first guest to walk out to the back patio of the hotel to be served," came her muffled response. "When I heard her crying, I thought it was a kitten who'd been injured by the storm. I almost fainted when I saw her lying there face-up in the bushes." Her eyes searched his. "What's her name?"

"Demitra, but we call her Demi."

"That's a beautiful name." He heard her take a deep

breath. "There's no way to express how sorry I am for the loss of your sister and her husband, Mr. Angelis. But I'm thankful you've been reunited with their daughter. She's the most precious child I've ever seen," she said with a quiver in her voice. Nik happened to agree with her. "If you could remove your masks, I'm sure it would make all the difference to her."

"Demi doesn't seem to have any problem with *you* wearing one."

He saw a distinct flush creep above her mask. "That's because I've been talking to her since we brought her here. I couldn't stand it that she didn't have anyone to give her love. Babies want their mothers. Her experience had to have terrified her."

Not every woman had such a strong maternal instinct as Melina's, but being a married woman, he had to assume Mrs. Myers had children of her own. "Leandros told me you're here on vacation. For you to forget everything except taking care of Demi constitutes a generosity and unselfishness we appreciate more than you could ever know. She'll be the reason our parents can go on living."

"It's true," his brothers concurred before expressing their gratitude.

Nik moved closer. "I hope you realize our family owes you a debt we can never repay."

She shook her head. "What payment could anyone want except to see that sweet little girl reunited with her family?" Her eyes still possessed a liquid sheen as they played over him. "Anyone can see she's an Angelis from head to toe. Of course I don't know about the noses and mouths yet." Her husky voice disturbed his senses in ways that surprised him.

In spite of the horrendous grief of the past twenty-four hours, her comment made one side of his mouth lift. Until he'd entered the ICU and watched the loving way she was handling Melina's daughter, he couldn't imagine ever having a reason to smile again.

She took a step back. "Well—I'll leave you gentlemen alone to be with your niece. When you speak to her, your voices will be blessedly familiar and will reassure her."

Nik wasn't so certain Demi wouldn't start to cry the second Mrs. Myers left the room. "Where are you going?"

"Downstairs to join Kellie."

"Don't leave the hospital yet. We need to talk."

"Since I'm their guest, I'm not sure what our plans are now."

Making one of those decisions on sheer instinct in case she got away, he said, "In that case, I'll go downstairs with you. I need to call our parents and give them the kind of news that will breathe new life into them. Above all, they'll want to thank you." He turned to his brothers and told them his plans before he left for the anteroom with her.

Once inside, he removed his mask and gown while she untied hers. Though she was married, he was a man who enjoyed looking at a beautiful woman and was curious to see what she looked like unwrapped.

Once she'd discarded everything, he discovered a slender figure clothed in a stunning green-and-white-print outfit. She had classic bone structure and a face that more than lived up to the beauty of her eyes. In a word, she stole his breath.

"What's the verdict?" he asked after she'd studied him back.

Again, he saw warmth enter her cheeks, but she didn't look away. "I happened to see your picture on the cover of a magazine while I was reading on the plane." Nik's teeth snapped together at the mention of it. "If you want honesty, then let me say I'm glad your niece received all the feminine features of her parentage."

He'd been expecting her to say something about his reputation. Instead her thoughts were focused on Demi. Her surprising comment lightened his mood,

"Your sister must have been a real beauty to have produced a daughter like Demi."

Nik reached for his wallet and showed her a picture. "This was taken on Melina's thirtieth birthday two months ago. She and Stavros had been trying for four years for a baby before one came."

Kellie needed to hear that. Not every woman conceived as quickly as one hoped.

Fran studied it for a moment. "What a lovely family." Her voice shook. "I see a lot of your sister in her."

His throat swelled with raw emotion. "Yes. She'll live on through Demi." He opened the other door. "Shall we go downstairs?"

"I'll ride down with you," Dr. Xanthis said. "We'll need confirmation of your relationship to the baby with a DNA test."

"Of course. I'll ask the hospital in Athens to send my information so you can run a test."

"Excellent. I'll tell the lab to expedite the process."

Fran wondered what condition had been serious enough to put Nik in a hospital and to have provided a

DNA match, but it was none of her business. She wished she weren't so aware of him.

Though she'd always thought Leandros was a true hunk, Nikolos Angelis was in a class by himself. Despite the grief lines etched in his striking Greek countenance, he was easily the most attractive male she'd ever met in her life. The photos of him didn't do him justice.

Besides his masculine appeal, he had the aura of a man in charge of his life—one who could accomplish anything. Kellie's hope that Fran would meet some gorgeous royal on this trip and fall instantly in love was still laughable, but she had to admit Nik Angelis was a fabulous-looking man.

Standing next to him, Fran thought he must be at least six feet three of solid lean muscle. She wasn't surprised he was still wearing soiled suit trousers and a creased blue shirt with the sleeves shoved up to the elbows. All three brothers had arrived in clothes they'd worn to work when they'd heard about the tornado. Naturally they'd dropped everything to fly to Thessalonika to search for their family. None of them had slept.

He needed a shave, but if anything, his male virility was even more potent. She noticed he wore his black wavy hair medium length. It had such a healthy gloss that it made you want to run your hands through it. Before the door opened, Fran gave him another covert glance.

Brows of the same blackness framed midnight-brown eyes with indecently long black lashes like Demi's. Between his hard-boned features and compelling mouth, she had to force herself to stop staring. Until now, no men she'd worked around for the last year had made any kind of an impact.

To be singling him out when he'd just been hit with the loss of his sister and brother-in-law made her ashamed. She rushed from the elevator ahead of him. But just as she was about to turn toward the lounge, he grasped her elbow. A warm current passed through her body without her volition.

"Come outside with me where my cell phone will work better. My parents will want to ask you some questions."

"All right."

They walked through the sliding doors into the late-afternoon sun. It was quarter to five already. She watched and listened as he communicated in unintelligible Greek with his parents. During the silences, she read between the lines. Her heart went out to all of them.

After a few minutes his penetrating gaze landed on her. He handed her the phone. "They speak English and are anxious to hear anything you can tell them."

Fran took the cell phone from him and said hello.

"We are overjoyed you found our Demitra," his mother spoke first in a heavy Greek accent. In a voice full of tears she said, "Our son tells us you've been at the hospital with her the whole time."

"Yes. She's the sweetest little thing I ever saw. A cherub. And now that she's awake, she seems fine."

"Ah... That's the news we've been waiting to hear," Nik's father broke in. "We want to meet you. I told him to bring you and the Petralias to Mykonos when Demitra is released. After the funeral, you will stay on as our guests for as long as you wish. He tells me you've just started your vacation. We'd like you to spend it with us. Because of you, a miracle has happened."

"Someone else would have found her if I hadn't, Mr.

Angelis, but thank you very much for your kind words. Here's Nik." She handed him the phone. "I'm going to the lounge," she whispered.

"I'll be right there." His deep voice curled through her as she walked back inside the building.

Once again she found Kellie and Leandros seated on one of the couches. You didn't have to be a mind reader to guess they were having an intense conversation that wasn't going well. Judging by Kellie's taut body and his grim countenance, they were both in agony. But when they saw Fran, they stopped talking and stood up.

Kellie rushed over to her, as if she were glad for the interruption. "Dr. Xanthis came to talk to us a minute ago and said he'll release the baby tomorrow once the DNA testing is done. I was just telling Leandros that since she's been reunited with her family, you and I can continue on with our vacation while he flies back to Rhodes."

Obviously Kellie wanted Fran to fall in with her wishes despite anything Leandros had to say. But her comment caused his firm jaw to tighten, making Fran uncomfortable. "My project supervisor can finish up the work there. I have a helicopter waiting to fly the three of us back to Athens. One of my employees will drive the car home."

Kellie tossed her blond head. "Don't be silly, Leandros. I don't want to interfere with your work. Besides, Fran and I want to sightsee in places where we've never been before."

"Where exactly?" he demanded quietly. Fran had never heard him so terse.

"We're going to do some hiking, but haven't decided

all the details yet. After dinner, we'll get out the map to plan our next destination."

Just when Fran didn't think she could stand the tension any longer, Nik entered the lounge and walked up to them. He darted her a searching glance. "Did you tell them about my father's invitation?"

The girls exchanged a private look before Fran said, "I haven't had time yet." Kellie's troubles with Leandros had weighted them down.

In the next breath Nik extended them all a personal invitation to fly to Mykonos in the morning and spend a few days with his family. "My parents insist."

"I was planning to pay them a personal visit anyway, Nik. We'd be honored to come," Leandros spoke up before Kellie could say anything. "Under the circumstances, I'll drive us back to Athens in Kellie's car. Tomorrow we'll fly to your villa."

Uh-oh. That meant a lot of hours for them to talk, but Fran decided that was a good thing. Kellie could approach him with the plan they'd talked about last night.

"Excellent." Nik shot Fran a level glance. "I realize you came here on vacation, but if it wouldn't inconvenience you too much, would you mind staying with me at the hospital overnight?

"Between the two of us taking turns, we ought to be able to comfort Demi while my brothers arrange for Melina's and Stavros's bodies to be flown home on our company plane. I'd very much like your help when we take Demi in the helicopter to Thessalonika airport in the morning. From there we'll fly on the plane to Mykonos."

Her heart thudded. Nik honestly wanted her help with his niece? He couldn't know she wasn't ready to say goodbye to the adorable child. Another night to hold her thrilled Fran to pieces.

Trying to sound in control she said, "If you feel it's necessary, I'd be glad to help." She looked at Kellie, knowing her friend didn't want to be left alone with her husband right now. The situation was precarious. "What do you think, Kellie? Would it be all right with you?"

Fran knew Kellie was stuck in a hard spot. She couldn't say no to Nik who'd already lost part of his family, but that meant she'd have to face Leandros sooner than she'd expected. It was providential they'd come up with an idea last night. *It had to work!*

"Of course. I'll see you tomorrow and we'll resume our vacation."

If Kellie worked things out with Leandros, maybe she wouldn't want to go on a trip after all. Fran was hoping for that outcome. "All right then."

The news seemed to relax Leandros a little. No doubt he was thankful for this much of a reprieve so he could talk to his wife. "Fran? I'll bring your bags in from the car."

Nik shook his head. "Don't bother, Leandros. I'll come with you and put them in my rental car." He turned to Fran. "I'll be back in a minute."

After the two men walked out of the lounge, Fran put an arm around Kellie's shoulders. "I'm sorry about this. I had no idea Nik would ask me to stay on. Frankly, I didn't know what to say."

"Neither of us had a choice. It would have been churlish to refuse him."

"If I stay overnight with the baby, are you going to be okay?"

Her friend took a shuddering breath. "I thought I'd

have two weeks to be away from Leandros, but this situation has changed things for the moment and can't be helped. Wish me luck broaching your suggestion to him," she whispered in a pain-filled voice.

"Kellie, last night we talked a lot about Karmela, but I sense there's still something you haven't told me. What is it?"

Her head was bowed. "I was afraid to tell you. N-night before last, I told him this vacation was more than that. I wanted a separation."

Fran groaned. "No wonder he looks shattered." Fran was aghast that their marriage had already broken down to that extent.

Her friend's lips tightened. "He said I wasn't thinking clearly before he stormed out of the bedroom angrier than I've ever seen him. On our drive back to Athens, I'm going to do what you said. I'll tell him that since I haven't gotten pregnant, I need something substantial to do and want to work with him in his private office. I'll remind him I was once a part of an advertising agency and am perfectly capable.

"But if he turns me down flat, and I'm afraid he will, then he needs to hear what I think about the sacred Karmela. Up until now I've been careful about saying anything negative, but no longer. I might as well get everything out in the open right now."

Fran would have told her not to plunge in with Leandros where Karmela was concerned yet. Let the idea of his wife working with him take hold first. But both men came back in the lounge, preventing further conversation.

Leandros put his arm around his wife. "It's going to be a long drive. We need to get going."

"I'll see you tomorrow." Fran hugged her. "Tell him you love him so much, you want the opportunity to work with him," she begged in a quiet whisper. "I don't see how he can turn you down."

When Kellie let her go without an answer, Leandros grasped his wife's hand and they walked out of the lounge.

She felt Nik's gaze on her. "We need a meal. Let's drive to the hotel where you stayed last night and get a couple of rooms so we can shower and have dinner. By then we'll feel much more prepared to spend the night with Demi."

"That sounds good to me." She would have said more, such as the fact that he hadn't had any sleep last night, but she'd bring it up to him later.

He walked her out to the parking lot and helped her into the rental car. His dark eyes noticed every detail, and she was glad she was wearing her linen pants. Once he got in the driver's side he said, "You'll have to guide me to the hotel."

"It's on the southern end of the village near the main highway." She gave him a few directions, not quite believing that he was taking her to the place where she'd found his niece. "There on the corner," she said. He flipped a U-turn and pulled up close to the front entrance where people were dining. "Before we go in, I'll show you the garden out in back."

"Good. I want to take pictures while there's still some light."

She got out of the car before he could help her and they walked around the side to the rear of the hotel where more customers were enjoying their evening meal. Fran kept going until she came to the garden.

"I found her right there." She pointed to the bushes in the corner. "There's no indication she lay there all those hours. It's still totally unbelievable to me. Finding her alive so far away from the Persephone is one of those inexplicable miracles."

Their eyes met. "Finding her alive in time to *save* her constituted another miracle. That's *your* doing," Nik said in a deep voice full of emotion.

He hunkered down to examine the spot, fingering the bushes. After he stood up, he pulled out his cell phone and took several pictures. Before she could stop him, he took a picture of her, then turned and snapped a few more of the back of the hotel. "When Demi is old enough to understand, I'll show her these pictures."

"Let me get one of you standing there," she said on impulse. "Demi will be thrilled to see her uncle in the very place she landed. She'll always be known as the Greek version of Dorothy Gale, the girl from Kansas in *The Wizard of Oz.* But instead of being blown to Oz, Demi was caught up in a tornado and deposited in a Grecian garden miles away. What a ride she must have had," her voice throbbed.

Something flickered in those black-brown depths. "Amen," he said before handing her the phone. His fingers overlapped hers, conveying warmth. She backed away far enough to get his tall, hard-muscled frame in the picture with the garden just behind him.

As she finished and gave the phone back to him, the proprietor approached. "You're the one who found the miracle baby!"

"Yes. And this is Nikolos Angelis, the baby's uncle. I was just showing him where I discovered her."

The owner stared at Nik. "You are the new head of

the Angelis Corporation. I saw your picture on television."

"That's right," he murmured.

Fran said, "His sister and her husband were killed in the tornado, but the baby survived and will be leaving the hospital tomorrow. I'll ask them to return the blanket to you."

"Not to worry about that. We are all very sorry about this tragedy, *Kyrie* Angelis."

Nik shook the man's hand. "Thank you."

"Can we serve you dinner? It will be our pleasure."

"We'd like that, wouldn't we, Mrs. Myers?" The way he included her as if they'd been friends a long time seemed to come out of the blue. Her pulse raced for no good reason.

"Come through to the front desk and everything will be arranged," the owner said.

"We'll need two rooms to change in. Later my brothers will be arriving to stay the night."

"Very good."

Nik ushered her inside the rear door. His touch might be impersonal, but she felt it in every atom of her body.

Once behind the desk, the owner gave them each a key. "The rooms are on the second floor."

"Thank you." Nik turned to her. "Why don't you go on up while I bring in our bags? I always keep one onboard the plane in case of an emergency. With a change of clothes and a good meal, we ought to be set to spend the night with Demi."

She nodded and hurried up the stairs. It was hot out and she was eager for another shower. He wasn't far behind with her suitcase. After walking into her bedroom, his gaze found hers. "I'll meet you in the back of the hotel in half an hour. After we eat, we'll take our bags out to the car and leave for the hospital."

"Demi must be so frightened."

He grimaced. "My brothers promised to stay with her until we get there. She knows and loves them. That ought to help."

Her eyelids stung with unshed tears. "But she'll still be looking for her mommy and daddy."

He lounged against the doorjamb. "Of course, but I wouldn't be surprised if she isn't looking for *you* too. See you shortly."

Fran averted her eyes. *He was too striking.*

Physical attraction was a powerful thing. Under other circumstances, she could be swept away. Thankfully she'd learned her lesson with Rob. Though he'd been conventionally handsome, she'd discovered good looks weren't enough to hold a relationship together, let alone a marriage.

For him to have said he'd be willing to adopt and then change his mind had inflicted indescribable pain. Fran had not only lost hope of being a mother, she'd lost the ability to trust.

CHAPTER THREE

AFTER A PHONE CALL to the hospital in Athens, Nik showered and shaved. Once they'd eaten a good meal, he felt restored and imagined Mrs. Myers did, too. He'd almost slipped and called her Fran in front of the proprietor, but realized he needed to keep thinking of her as Mrs. Myers, a married woman.

En route to the hospital, he phoned Sandro who told him the doctor had moved Demi to her own room in the pediatric wing. They didn't have to wear masks and gowns any longer and were able to hold her.

"That's wonderful," Fran declared when he'd conveyed the good news to her. "After what she's been through, she needs to be cuddled."

Nik's thoughts exactly. He parked around the side entrance to the hospital with easier access to the pediatric unit.

On the drive over he'd inhaled his companion's flowery fragrance. By the time they got out of the car and entered the hospital, he could hardly take his eyes off her stunning figure clothed in a summery print skirt and white blouse. She wore white leather sandals. With her hair flowing to her shoulders from a side part, she made an enticing vision of femininity he doubted she was aware of.

He thought about her being in Greece on her own. American women had a tendency to be independent. For her and Leandros's wife to be traveling alone shouldn't have surprised him. But he thought Fran's husband a fool to let his attractive wife vacation in a foreign country without him.

He wondered how Leandros handled being apart from his wife, but he had no right to speculate. The media had painted Nik to be the most eligible playboy in Greece, a label he was forced to wear. But it would do as a cover to hide his real reason for not being married by now. Therefore he wasn't in any position to judge what went on in another man's life or marriage.

In truth he felt shame for having any of those thoughts where Mrs. Myers and Kellie Petralia were concerned. If the two women hadn't been out together, Fran wouldn't have spotted their precious Demi. That was a miracle in and of itself. So was her desire to make sure the baby hadn't been left alone at the hospital.

Interesting that it had been Fran, not Kellie, who'd planted herself next to Demi in the ICU. He wondered why…

For a moment Nik's thoughts flew to Lena, the last woman he'd dated. After two dates she'd suggested they move in together. She was a desirable woman, but he didn't believe in living together. Because of a painful issue from his past that had prevented him from proposing to any woman yet, he didn't want to encourage her. In order not to be cruel, he'd stopped seeing her.

In truth, none of his romantic relationships had ever gotten past the point where he'd felt he could take the next step. As for Lena, he couldn't help wondering what would have happened if she'd been the one who found Demi. Would she have dropped everything and changed her plans in order to comfort the baby? Would she have shown such a strong maternal instinct?

He doubted it, yet the minute he'd posed those questions, he chastized himself. It wasn't fair to compare any of the women in his past to Fran. The moment she'd discovered Demi in that garden, she'd felt a special responsibility to care for her. The whole situation was unlike any other. She was unique, but his thoughts had to stop there. She was another man's *wife*. He needed to remember that before he got in real trouble.

What did he mean by *before?* He already was in trouble, because deep in his gut, he felt she was the kind of woman he might trust enough to reveal his painful secret to. Why her and why now?

Following his brothers' directions, he found Demi's room. When he walked inside with Fran, he saw an exhausted-looking Cosimo walking around holding the baby, but she was fussing. Sandro had passed out in an easy chair brought in for them.

Nik nodded to his brother and walked over to take the baby from him, needing to nestle her against his chest. He was still incredulous she was alive. She recognized him, but there was no accompanying smile because she wasn't herself. Her world had literally been blown apart.

"It's me, Demi, your Uncle Nikolos. I'm here." He kissed her neck and cheeks, careful not to hurt the cuts that were already healing. "Where's my little sunshine girl? Hmm?" But she still seemed restless, the way she'd been with Cosimo.

Fran walked up next to him and touched her black curls. "Hi, Demi. Do you remember me? It's Fran."

The baby heard her voice and turned her head to focus on her. All of a sudden she started to cry and held out her arms to Fran, almost leaping to get to her. Nik couldn't believe a bond had formed so fast that his niece would go to Fran with an eagerness that was astonishing. Even more amazing was the way Demi settled down and buried her face in Fran's neck, reminding him of the way she always was with Melina.

Fran rocked her and sang a little song. Nik took advantage of the time to take Cosimo aside and talk to him. "I've got rooms for you and Sandro at the hotel where Fran found the baby." He gave him the directions. "Take Sandro with you and get some sleep. Come back here tomorrow morning and we'll use the hospital helicopter to get to Thessalonika before we fly home. The bodies should be loaded on the plane by then."

Sadness filled Cosimo's eyes. "You're sure you won't need help?"

"Positive. Fran and I will take turns tonight."

"She's willing to stay?"

Nik nodded. His brother looked relieved. "But you haven't had any sleep."

"I'll get it now."

"I'm afraid Demi hasn't slept. She's looking for Melina. I've never felt so helpless in my life."

"I have a feeling she might get her rest now that Fran is here. You two go on."

Cosimo nodded and woke up their brother. Nik walked them out of the room and down the hall. After saying goodnight, he went to the desk where he asked for a cot to be brought in.

Within a few minutes, housekeeping delivered one and left. Finally he was alone with Fran and turned off the light. Though he was beyond tired, he still wanted to talk to her before he got some sleep. Heaving a deep sigh, he sank down in one of the chairs and sat back, marveling over her rapport with his niece.

"I think you've gotten her to sleep."

"Yes," she whispered. "The dear little thing must be so tired and bewildered."

"With you holding her, it's apparent she'll get the rest she needs. When you're too tired, I'll take over."

"I'm not desperate for sleep like you. Kellie and I slept in until ten this morning. Why don't you undo the cot and lie down? I'll waken you when it's your turn."

"Promise?"

She gave him a half smile. "Believe it."

In the semidarkness, her generous mouth drew his attention, spiking his guilt for having those kinds of thoughts about her. "Where did you come from?"

"Not from the whirlwind, if that's what you mean," she drawled.

He crossed his legs at the ankles. "You might as well have. Earlier today my brothers and I were combing through the pines behind the resort, dying a little with every step because there was no trace of Demi.

"Then the call came from Leandros telling us to get to the Leminos hospital as fast as possible because a miracle may have happened. Suddenly, out of nowhere, I find this American woman taking care of my niece as if she were her mother. I'm still not sure if I'm dreaming this or not."

Fran kissed Demi's curls before sitting down in the other chair. "Then we're both having the same inexplicable dream. Day before yesterday I flew from Philadelphia to Athens to spend my vacation with Kellie. Leandros had already flown to Rhodes on business.

"At six yesterday morning, she and I left the city because we knew we had a long drive ahead of us. We'd planned to drive around new areas of Greece neither of us had visited before. She wanted me to see the Petralias' latest resort, so we decided to stay a night at the Persphone before moving on.

"But by late afternoon a fierce storm arose and I suggested we pull off the highway in Leminos to find shelter. Kellie wanted to keep going because the resort was only twelve miles farther, but then the hail started, so we hurried inside the first hotel we came to.

"When we learned from the staff that a tornado had destroyed some suites at the Persephone, we both fell apart. Not only because we realized we might have been caught and lost our lives, too, but because she knew Leandros would be devastated to think such a thing had happened to the guests staying at the resort. He would take it very hard and he was so far away on business. There was no way to reach him by phone."

Nik sat foward. "For a while it was chaos. Do you know about the other tornado?"

Her beautiful eyes widened. "What are you talking about?"

"There was one at the airport yesterday morning."

"You're kidding!"

He shook his head. "I came close to being affected. After seeing my sister and her family off around 6:30 a.m., I went over to the air cargo area to do business when a funnel cloud struck. No one was injured, but it was terrifying to see how much damage it did in the space of a short time."

"Now I understand why it was so windy when we left, but we haven't had any news here."

"That's not surprising. I was just leaving my office at the end of the day when my brother phoned and told me about a second tornado."

"We get so many in the States, but I didn't realize you got them, too."

"Once in a while," he murmured, "but yesterday's phenomena probably won't happen for another couple of decades or more."

"Let's pray not."

"When I turned on the TV, what I heard was enough to make my blood run cold." Just the way he said it made her chill. "My brothers and I took off in the plane for Thessalonika. By the time we reached the resort, we learned that Melina and Stavros were two of the victims. To our horror, there was no sign of Demi."

"I don't know how any of you are holding up." The sadness in her voice touched him to the core.

"It's our parents we're worried about. That's why it's so important you come to the villa with me tomorrow. They love their grandchildren, but Demi has a special place in their hearts because she's the only girl."

"I can understand that." Fran looked down at Demi who was cuddled in her arms, fast asleep. "This little child is too precious for words. She'll always be a special joy to them."

"And to me."

A tremor rocked his body. On Melina's birthday, she'd taken Nik aside and asked him to be Demi's guardian if anything ever happened to her and Stavros.

Without hesitation he'd told her yes, but he was unable to entertain the thought of anything ever happening to his sister and her husband. Remembering her request, the hairs lifted on the back of his neck. Had she asked him because of a premonition?

"Demi's blessed to have such loving family."

Nik eyed Fran speculatively. "Since you're married and have such a close rapport with my niece, I'm wondering if you have children."

She didn't meet his eyes. "No."

No?

"How does your husband let you leave him for such a long time?" The question he'd sworn not to ask left his lips before he could stop it.

"We're divorced."

His thoughts reeled. "How long ago?"

"A year."

What husband in his right mind wouldn't have held on to a woman like her? Nik sensed he'd be wandering into forbidden territory with more questions, yet he was intrigued by her. Now that he knew those pertinent facts, he was determined to learn more and no longer felt guilty about it. With time and patience, he'd get his answers. "Are you ready to let me hold her now?"

"I'm fine. I was going to suggest you go to sleep."

"Maybe I will for a little while."

He got to his feet to undo the cot. After taking off his shoes, he stretched out. Another heavy sigh escaped him. "This feels so good, I fear I might never get up again. You're sure you don't mind?"

"Positive. Holding this angel is a joy. You need sleep or you won't be any good to your family tomorrow."

"You're right. If I haven't said it already, I'm grateful you're here for Demi."

"*I'm* the one who's grateful."

His instincts told him those weren't empty words. He needed to find out what emotions were driving them, but before he could ask, oblivion took over.

The next time he was aware of his surroundings, it was morning.

Nik sat up and got to his feet, removing the blanket Fran must have thrown over him. His gaze shot to her. She was asleep in the easy chair while Demi slept in the hospital crib.

He had no idea how long Fran had stayed awake, but she'd chosen not to disturb him for any reason. Unable to help himself, he looked down, studying her facial features. With no makeup and her dark blond hair somewhat disheveled, she was lovelier than most women who worked at it all day.

Since Demi was still asleep, he tiptoed out to the hall to phone his brothers. They were on their way over with a new outfit for the baby. As he talked with them, the doctor slipped inside the room. By the time Nik hung up and returned, he discovered Fran standing by the crib talking to the doctor. She'd brushed her hair and applied lipstick, looking amazingly fresh for someone who'd probably been up most of the night.

The doctor turned to him with a smile. "The lab has confirmed she's your niece. I'm happy to say her cuts are starting to heal. She's doing fine in every regard and can be released. Keep her hydrated. What she needs now is the love of her family which I can see isn't going to be a problem. Just so you know, the media has been inundating the hospital for information.

"In order to make them go away, I gave a statement that I hope will satisfy them and give your family a chance to breathe before they descend on you. When you're ready to leave, come to the desk and someone will escort you to the roof where the helicopter is waiting."

Nik shook his hand. "Thank you for everything you've done, doctor. The Angelis family is indebted to you."

The older man's eyes flashed. "And no doubt to *Kyria* Myers who made the baby feel safe and loved until you arrived. We could use more like her around the ICU." He eyed Fran. "Are you a nurse?"

"No. But I work in a hospital for patients' rights and make certain they get the follow up care they need after they go home."

"You wouldn't like a job with us, would you?" he threw out.

"I've already got a position in mind for her," Nik inserted, flashing her a glance. She looked at him in confusion. "Of course I haven't discussed it with her yet."

The thought had been percolating in his mind since yesterday, but until he knew she was divorced, he'd kept it at bay. Before he could explain more, the doctor said, "I'll be at the desk. When you're ready to leave, I'll escort you to the private elevator that will take you to the roof." He left as Nik's brothers arrived with a new quilt and stretchy suit they'd purchased.

All the talking woke up Demi who turned to the bars and tried to get up. She babbled and looked longingly at Fran, asking to be rescued. Everyone chuckled as Fran leaned over and plucked her from her prison. Giving her a kiss on both cheeks she was rewarded with a smile on Demi's face that had been missing until now. That happy countenance cemented the idea Nik planned to propose to Fran when the time was right.

She spoke to the baby. "Look who's here—your favorite uncles!"

He was witnessing another kind of miracle, one of communication despite the fact that Fran didn't understand Greek, nor did the baby comprehend English.

Nik and his brothers took turns kissing her, but the baby clung to Fran. The nurse came in with a bag of diapers and enough formula to satisfy the baby until they reached home. Fran changed her and put on the new pink outfit, then looked around. "Who wants to feed her?"

Sandro took Demi from her arms, but the baby wanted none of it. "Well, that settles it." He kissed her curls before returning her to Fran's arms. "I'm afraid you're stuck, *Kyria* Myers."

"Call me Fran, and I don't mind at all."

The nurse handed her a bottle. Soon Demi had settled down to drink, content for the moment. She eventually burped a couple of times, announcing she'd drained it. More chuckles ensued from everyone. Despite the sadness ahead when they returned to Mykonos, Demi was the bright light that kept them all from sinking right now.

Nik walked over to Fran. "We're ready to go. I'll carry Demi to the helicopter. After we're onboard the plane, we'll eat breakfast." He relieved her of the baby and wrapped her in the quilt.

"Come on, *Demitza*. We're going for a ride."

Fran followed him from the room with his brothers. Once they rode the elevator to the roof, they helped her into the helicopter while he climbed in with Demi. He handed her over to Cosimo who strapped her in the infant seat next to Fran. His brothers sat on the opposite side.

When everyone was settled in, Nik noticed Fran reach for Demi's little hand before he took his place in the copilot's seat. The gesture touched him and told him even more about the compassionate woman who'd put her vacation plans aside to make Demi secure. Again he wondered how many other women he'd known would have done that.

In a few minutes they lifted off and made a beeline for the airport. He heard his brothers talking to Fran. "We want to thank you again for all your help so far. Demi hasn't been around other people besides family, so it's a real surprise that she's taken to you."

"I'm sure it's because I was the one who found her in the garden. She'd been lying there helpless all night."

"I think it's more than that," Sandro confided. "You have a loving way with her like our sister."

"Well, thank you. It's been my pleasure to stay with her, believe me."

"How long will you be in Greece?"

"I fly home in less than two weeks."

Maybe not, Nik mused. Before he introduced Fran to his parents, he needed to have a private talk with her. The best place to do that would be aboard the jet in the compartment he used for his office.

"I guess you know our parents would like you to stay with us on Mykonos for part of the time."

"That's kind of them, Cosimo, but it's really up to

my friend Kellie Petralia who invited me here. She'd
planned this time for us to be together."

"She and her husband are welcome to stay with us,
too," Sandro chimed in.

"Your parents told me as much on the phone."

"That's because we're all grateful to you."

Grateful didn't exactly cover Fran's deepest feelings.
She'd been empty for too long. To suddenly be taking
care of a baby who was content to be in her arms made
her feel whole for the first time in years. Even though
she would have to relinquish Demi tomorrow, she would
savor this sweet time with her today and tonight.

In her teens she'd been told she couldn't have children. It had been like a light going out, but over the
years she'd come around to the idea of adoption.

During the short flight to Thessalonika, Fran looked
out the helicopter window at the sparkling blue Aegean
below, wishing she could concentrate on the spectacular panorama. Instead she found herself reliving the
painful moment when Rob had shattered her dreams
of being a mother.

Even if it were possible to love another man again,
the idea of meeting one who said he'd be willing to
adopt wasn't an option for her. Maybe one day she might
meet and fall in love with a widower who had a child or
children. At least then she could take over the mother
role to help fill that empty space in her heart.

She simply couldn't see it happening, but Kellie
wouldn't let her think that way. Dear Kellie... Her
friend was in turmoil right now.

Her eyes strayed to Demi who was wide awake for
the trip. She made sounds and was growing restless at

being confined. In order to placate her, Fran got out another bottle of formula to keep her happy. Demi held it and mostly played with it, only sucking on the nipple without absorbing a lot of liquid. Her two bottom teeth had come in, helping her to tug on it.

Fran was amused to see the funny behavior coming from this child who could win the most beautiful baby of the year award. That was because she had the classic features of her mother and glossy black hair like Nik's... and his brothers, Fran hastened to remind herself.

But Nik possessed an unconscious sensuality and sophistication that stood out from his siblings. She put her head back for a minute and closed her eyes so she wouldn't keep staring at the back of his head where a few tendrils of black hair lay curled against his neck. Once in a while he turned to say something to his brothers and she glimpsed his striking male profile and chiseled jaw.

Dressed in the light brown sport shirt and dark trousers he'd changed into at the hotel last night, there was no man to match him. The celebrated bachelor's appeal went far beyond the physical. He was warm and generous. She doubted he had a selfish bone in his body. Nik was so different from Rob....

Before long the helicopter landed, and they were driven to the Angelis Corporation jet, the size of a 727, waiting on the tarmac. While Sandro and Cosimo helped her and Demi onboard, Nik excused himself to talk to the people who'd taken care of putting his family's bodies in the cargo area.

A few minutes later he walked down the aisle toward her. After speaking to his brothers on the way, he came to sit on the other side of her and Demi. His half smile turned her heart over.

"The flight to Mykonos won't take too long. Then it's just another short helicopter ride to the villa. After we reach cruising speed, we'll eat breakfast, then I'd like to have a private talk with you in the compartment behind the galley. My brothers will entertain Demi."

She nodded, but couldn't help but wonder what was on his mind. He'd said something about a position in front of the doctor. What exactly had he meant?

She strapped herself in, and the jet took off. Like clockwork, the minute the Fasten Seat Belt light went off, the steward started serving their food. Fran needed a good meal, if only to brace herself for their talk.

Once the steward removed their trays, she undid Demi long enough to change her diaper. Nik got up from his seat and reached for another bottle in the hospital diaper bag. Once Demi was strapped in again, he kissed her and gave her the bottle to keep her occupied.

Touching Fran's elbow he whispered, "Follow me."

She did his bidding, but it was but a few seconds before they could hear Demi cry. Fran felt like the biggest meanie on earth, but she kept going. Once inside the compartment set up as a den with a computer, Nik closed the door and invited her to sit in one of the club seats opposite him. They could still hear Demi's cries though they sounded fainter. Fran knew the baby's uncles would take care of her, but the sound of her distress tugged at her.

Nik sat back in his club chair with that unconscious aura of a CEO at home in his world. His dark eyes seemed to scrutinize her as if he were looking for secrets she might be hiding. Her pulse quickened in response.

"Before we reach Mykonos, I wonder if you'd answer some personal questions for me."

Personal? "If I can."

"Are you a full-time employee at the hospital?"

"Yes."

He cocked his head. "What would happen if you needed more time off? Would they give it to you without it causing you problems?"

"I think so, but it would have to be because of an emergency."

"Of course. One more question. Are you involved with another man right now?"

She blinked. He obviously had a reason for all this probing. "No."

"And your friend Kellie. Would it disappoint her terribly if you didn't spend your vacation with her?"

"Yes," Fran answered honestly. "Why?"

Her question caused him to lean forward with his hands clasped. His intelligent dark eyes fused with hers. "Because I have a great favor to ask of you. I know I don't have the right, but Demi's needs are going to be top priority for my family in the days ahead."

"I can understand that."

"Judging by her behavior around you in the hospital, and including the fact that she started crying the minute we walked away from her a few moments ago, it's clear Demi has formed a strong attachment to you. I dread what things are going to be like when you leave on your vacation with Kellie. She'll not only be looking for her parents, but for you. That's what's got me worried."

Fran had been worried about it, too, but she would

never have brought it up. "Surely when she's surrounded by your family again, she'll get through the transition."

He inhaled sharply. "I would have thought her seeing me and my brothers would have been all she needed. We're a close family and get together often. But this experience has traumatized her in some way we don't understand. If she isn't clinging to us, then I don't expect she'll want anyone else, not even the staff who are familiar to her."

"What about your parents? Your mother? Does she look like Melina?"

"They shared certain traits." His eyes stared into Fran's. "But I don't know if Demi would cling to them the way she does to you. I'm very interested to see what happens when she's with them again. Something tells me it won't be enough to make the baby feel secure."

"You'll have to give Demi time."

"That goes without saying. Nevertheless, I plan to consult a child psychiatrist after the funeral is over. Depending on what he or she says, I'll go from there. But for the time being, I'd like to hire you to take care of Demi until you have to get back to Philadelphia. By then I'll have some idea of how to proceed."

Fran stirred in the chair. While trembling with excitement at the prospect of loving that little girl for a while longer, she knew how painful it would be when she had to say a final goodbye. She'd known a lot of pain in her life. First the death of her brother, then the death of a dream that had ended in divorce. She might not have lost Rob in death, but it felt like one.

No brother, no husband, no child of her own after three years of marriage. Fran knew herself too well. Another twenty-four hours taking care of that precious baby would be hard enough. But ten more days? She couldn't risk the inevitable pain. It would come and she wouldn't be able to stop it.

"When she's been with your parents, or one of your brothers' families, she'll eventually adapt."

One black brow dipped. "I don't know. It's too soon to work all that out and I want a doctor's opinion first. The one thing I do know is that Demi wants *you.* If you could bring yourself to help us out here, you'll be handsomely compensated. Anything you want."

She shook her head. "That's very generous, Nik, but I wouldn't do it for the money."

He sat back again. "If Kellie doesn't mind a change in your plans, would you consider it? You'll stay in an apartment at the villa. There's a guest room and another smaller room we'll set up as a nursery. Kellie is welcome to be with you any time you want. But I guess I haven't asked the most important question. Is this something you wouldn't mind doing?"

Mind? If he had any idea... Demi had climbed into her heart where she would always stay. Discovering the baby in that garden was as if providence had set the baby down in those bushes at the precise moment for Fran to find her.

But the flags had gone up, warning her that if she told him she wouldn't mind at all, she could plan for rivers of anguish down the road when she had to tear herself away from that baby. It was a trauma she'd never get over.

"Fran?" he prodded. His smoky-sounding tone defeated her.

Although the youngest, Nik clearly carried the weight of the Angelis family on his shoulders. She had noticed how his brothers looked to him. This was a problem none of them had faced before. At the moment she recognized he needed a different kind of help and wanted Fran's.

But for her own self-preservation, she needed to remain firm. "It isn't a case of minding. It's just that I know what Kellie's answer will be when I ask her. We've been planning this trip for a long time. It will upset her too much and I can't disappoint her. I'm sorry. But until the funeral is over, I'll be happy to help out."

"Then I'm grateful for that much." He got to his feet. "Shall we get back to Demi before my frantic brothers come bursting in here with her?"

Fran had hated disappointing him, but her first priority had to be to herself.

CHAPTER FOUR

AT THREE THE NEXT afternoon, Nik left Fran holding the baby while he walked out to meet Leandros and his wife at the helicopter pad behind the villa. They'd been paying their respects to the other family, the ones who had lost their parents in the tornado and who couldn't get away before now.

"Fran will be relieved you're here now. It's all that matters." He led them out to the patio of the Angelis family villa where everyone had congregated to talk and eat. More tears ensued while Leandros and Kellie commiserated with his family.

Incredibly, the pain of losing Melina and Stavros was softened by the joy of having found Demi alive, a blessing no one had expected. Nik was heartened to see his family's spirits had lifted despite their loss.

"It's all over the news," Sandro spoke up. "Demi is known as the Miracle Baby. Did you know the hotel in Leminos has become famous overnight?"

"So has the hospital," Cosimo declared. "They even interviewed Demi's doctor on the noon news."

Though the whole family was eager to hold her, Demi clung to Fran just as Nik had suspected she would. The only time she didn't cry was when his parents held her.

But after a few minutes, Demi was looking for Fran and making sounds that indicated she didn't want to be with anyone else.

Nik knew his parents were hurt, but they hid it well. When they had issued her an invitation over the phone to be their guest for as long as she wanted, they had had no idea they would need her on hand to keep Demi happy. He smiled to himself. Though Fran had turned him down about staying on, she didn't know this story wasn't over yet.

His father eyed Fran who was holding Demi against her shoulder. The baby looked around chewing on her teething ring. "Tell us what you thought when you found her. We want details," he beseeched her.

Fran broke into a tender smile. Once more she repeated her amazing tale. "The hotel is situated on a corner of the street. My first thought was that her mother or father had been walking her in a stroller on the other side of the hotel when those gale-force winds drove Kellie and me to run inside for shelter.

"It seemed more than possible she'd been blown into the garden at the rear of the building. But if that were true, then where were her parents? I was in shock to think she'd been exposed to the elements all night. Honestly, she looked like she'd been dropped from the sky."

Nik's sisters-in-law made moaning sounds to think such a thing had happened.

Kellie sat forward. "I came around back and saw Fran holding a limp baby who was wearing only a torn shirt. I thought I was hallucinating."

"You weren't the only one," Fran added. "When neither the police or the hospital staff had heard of anyone looking for their baby, I began to think that's exactly what had happened, that she'd been carried by the wind and deposited in a cushion of bushes."

"But twelve miles—" Nik's mother cried out and put her hands to her mouth. "God wanted her to live." His father nodded his silver head and wept.

"Nik?" Fran eyed him from her place on the swing. "Has your family seen the pictures you took with your camera?"

He'd been planning to show them later. "Let's do it right now," he said, but he had difficulty talking because of the lump in his throat. After pulling out his phone, he clicked on to the picture gallery and handed it to his parents. "Slide your thumb across to see all of them. I took a few pictures in the hospital, too." He'd made certain he'd gotten some shots of Fran.

For the next little while his family and the Petralias took turns viewing them. Nik's six- and seven-year-old nephews were eager to look at them, too. The younger three- and four-year-olds had no idea what was going on and played with their toys. In the quiet, Fran's eyes met his. They were both remembering that surreal moment when she'd showed him the now-famous spot.

While everyone was talking, he walked over to her. "Do you think she's ready for something besides a bottle?"

"I hope so. She needs the nourishment."

"That's what I'm thinking. I'll tell cook to get out a jar of her favorite fruit and meat."

Fran hugged the baby. "You'd like some food, wouldn't you, sweetheart?"

Whether she wanted it or not, she needed it. Having made up his mind, Nik left the patio and headed for the kitchen. In a minute he returned with the food and the high chair that had been in use for several years.

He put it in front of Fran, then plucked the baby from her arms and set her inside it. The cook had given him a bib that he tied around her neck. Both Fran and Demi looked up at him in surprise.

Nik shot them an amused glance. "We'll both feed her," he explained and sat down on the swing next to her. "You take the turkey." He handed her the jar and a spoon. "I'll give her some plums."

"Coward," she whispered. Her chuckle filled him with warmth.

To his relief the baby began to eat, which meant her initial trauma had passed and she was relaxed enough to want her semi-solid food again. Once she'd been put in a private room at the hospital, the nurse hadn't been able to get her to eat anything. Fran had to see the transformation and think twice about turning him down when he asked her again.

"Well, look at you," she said to Demi with a big smile. "I didn't know you were such a good eater."

Demi beamed back at both of them. Nik had never actually fed Demi before. Aided and abetted by Fran, he found himself having more fun than he could remember. Some turkey clung to the baby's upper lip, making her look adorable. Both he and Fran chuckled in delight to see her behaving normally.

Soon she finished her food while the family looked on in varying degrees of interest and curiosity. They weren't used to seeing Nik feed her. But most of all, they were shocked at the way Demi responded to Fran. The hurt in his parents' eyes had intensified. It didn't surprise him when Nik's father eventually got up from his chair and walked over to give his granddaughter a kiss on the cheek.

"One would never know what you lived through, Demi," he spoke in Greek. "Come to your grandpa." He wiped her mouth with the bib, then untied it and picked her up to take her over to Nik's mother.

Demi adored her grandfather, but the further he took her from Fran, the more she squirmed and kept turning her head to find her. Nik's mother got to her feet and held out her hands to Demi, but the baby started to cry.

"What's wrong, darling?" his mother talked to her in their native tongue, attempting to cuddle her. "Tell me what's the matter."

Nik knew the answer to that. She wanted Fran. It really was astonishing to see that even with the entire family surrounding her, Demi wanted a stranger if she couldn't have her own mother and father. He eyed Fran covertly, daring her to close her mind and heart to what was going on here.

His stomach muscles tightened as he watched the looks of surprise and confusion from everyone, but especially at the pain on his parents' faces when Demi started crying in earnest.

They'd lost Melina, but it had never occurred to anyone that Demi wouldn't soak up the love they were ready to heap on her. Nik believed it was a passing phenomenon. It *had* to be. But right now something needed to be done to calm the baby down.

"You know what I think?" he said in English. "Demi's barely out of the hospital and needs to go to bed." So did his parents who needed to rest to get through this ordeal.

"Of course," his mother concurred.

"Fran and I will take her and put her down, then we'll be back."

He clutched the baby to him and started for the villa. Fran got up from the swing and followed him to the apartment. Earlier he'd asked the housekeeper to get it prepared. With the help of the staff, they'd moved the crib and other things from the nursery in Melina's apartment to the spare room. For now it would serve as a nursery while Fran took care of Demi.

Together they got the baby ready for her afternoon nap with a fresh diaper and a white sleeper with feet.

"You look so cute in this," Fran said, kissing her cheeks several times. Once again Nik marveled how natural she was with Demi, almost as if the baby were hers. Neither of them were bilingual, but it didn't matter. They spoke a special language of love that managed to transcend. Watching Demi, you'd think Fran was her mother. How could that be? Unless…

Was it possible that the baby's head had suffered an injury when she hit the earth and she'd developed *amnesia*?

Were there cases of such a thing happening to an infant? Amnesia might explain her connection to Fran. She'd been the first person Demi saw when she'd awakened in the hospital.

But if that were true, then why did she respond to the family, to Nik? Though it was half-hearted, she did recognize everyone. He was baffled and anxious to talk to a doctor first thing in the morning.

Nik drew a bottle of premixed formula from the bag. When Fran put the baby in the crib, he handed Demi her bottle. Speaking Greek to her, he told her he loved her and wanted her to go to sleep.

Before she started drinking, the baby made sounds and stared up at the two of them with those dark brown eyes that could have been Melina's.

"Come on, Fran," he whispered. "Let's go."

"See you later, sweetheart." Fran patted her cheek, then started to follow Nik out of the room. They'd no sooner reached the door than Demi burst into tears.

Fran looked at him with pleading eyes. "I can't leave her yet."

Nik had been counting on that. "She loves you."

Again Fran averted her eyes because she knew what he'd just said was true. "You go on and be with your family, Nik. I'm sure you have things to discuss before the funeral tomorrow. Tell Kellie to come and keep me company while Demi falls asleep."

"I will. Maybe when she sees how much the baby wants you, she'll tell you the vacation can wait a few more days."

"I—I don't think so." Her little stammer indicated she wasn't quite as confident as she'd been on the plane.

"We'll see," he murmured.

She gripped the bars of the crib. "The baby's worn-out from all the excitement, but still needs time to settle down and get sleepy. I'll join you on the patio later."

This extraordinary woman was right on all counts, but if the truth be told, Nik would rather stay in here with her. "All right, but I'll be back soon to relieve you if she proves too restless."

He strode swiftly through the villa to the patio and sought out Kellie. "Fran wants to talk to you. I'll show you to the nursery."

She spoke to Leandros who nodded his head, then she followed Nik through the house. Before they entered the apartment he said, "I'm not sure there wouldn't have been a catastrophe tonight if Fran weren't here to take charge of Demi."

Kellie smiled at him. "After college she went into hospital administration, but they soon found out she's a remarkable people person for the young and the old. That's why they put her in the position she holds now. I wager she's sorely missed already. I'm lucky she could take off these two weeks for our vacation."

Having seen her in action with Demi, Nik agreed. He also got the message from Kellie not to count on Fran's generosity beyond tonight. In fact, he was sure he'd been warned off, in the nicest way possible. While cogitating on that thought, he was more determined than ever to prevail on Fran to remain longer.

They reached the door to the apartment. "Come find the family after my niece has fallen asleep."

A half hour later Fran tiptoed out of the nursery with Kellie and they went into the bedroom. "I think she'll stay asleep now. Tell me what's happened with Leandros?"

"If anything, things are worse. But before we get into that, tell me what's going on with Nik."

"What do you mean?"

Kellie sat down on the side of the king-size bed. "He has you ensconced in this fabulous apartment with the baby in the adjoining room, almost like you're a permanent fixture."

"I told him I'd help out until after the funeral tomorrow."

"But he'd like it to be longer, right?"

Nothing got past Kellie. Fran nodded. "On the flight

to Mykonos, Nik asked me if I would stay on to tend Demi until she's comfortable with the family again. He hopes I'll remain here until I have to go back to Philadelphia. I told him no because you and I were on vacation."

"Are you hoping I won't hold you to it?"

She shook her head. "No, Kellie. I only told him that as an excuse. This has nothing to do with you or our trip. I need to leave tomorrow before I find myself wishing I could take her back home with me. If it were possible, I'd like to adopt her."

"Adopt an Angelis?"

"I know how outrageous that sounds. That's why I'm glad we're leaving tomorrow."

Looking haunted, Kellie got up from the bed. "I know how attached you are to the baby already and would love to say yes to him."

"Actually, I wouldn't."

"You must think I'm being difficult, but it's because I'm afraid to see you get hurt again. When I think what you went through with Rob…"

Fran sucked in her breath. "Believe me, I don't want that kind of pain again either. When I found Demi in that garden, I felt like I'd been handed a gift. I wanted her to be mine. But she isn't! If I stayed here ten more days, it would kill me to have to walk away from her, traumatizing her once again. I refuse to put myself or her in that position. I've had too many losses in my life."

"Oh, Fran—" Kellie gave her a commiserating hug.

She wiped her eyes. "I'm glad we're leaving after the funeral. I need to put this experience behind me and forget Demi exists. It has dredged up too many painful memories. I need to move on."

By now Kellie's eyes were wet. "That makes two of us. Leandros doesn't want me working in his office."

"He wouldn't even consider it?"

"No. He says he wants to be able to come home to me after a hard day's work, but the reason is crystal-clear. Though he hasn't come right out and said it, our love life has never been satisfactory to him.

"How could it have been with a bride who was in terrible pain the first time he made love to her? His marriage to Petra was nothing like ours. They were expecting a baby when—when—" She couldn't go on. "That's why I have to put some real distance between us. Karmela can supply him what's missing. Our marriage is over."

"I can't bear it, Kellie."

"It's for the best. Like you, I refuse to wallow in any more pain. As for the Angelis family, they need to hire a nanny as soon as tomorrow after the funeral and get her installed right away."

"Agreed. I know Demi will miss me, but she'll get over it. She'll *have* to. I made that clear to Nik."

"For your sake, I'm glad." They eyed each other for a long moment. "Even though I'm nursing a horrendous headache, what do you say we put on our best smiles and go out to the patio as if nothing in the world is wrong? After we've mingled for a while, I plan to have an early night."

"So do I. Demi will be needing another bottle before sleeping through the night."

They reached the door. "Leandros will cover for me until he's ready for bed. It's what he's good at. You might as well know we haven't slept together for the last month."

Fran understood her pain. She hadn't slept with Rob for the three months leading up to their separation. It had been the beginning of the end.

The day was winding down. Nik's mother and sisters-in-law spoke together while he talked with the men. But they all stopped long enough to admire the two American beauties who'd just stepped out onto the patio.

At the first sight of Fran, Nik felt an unwanted quickening in his body. The same thing had happened at the hospital when they'd been removing their masks and gowns. In a very short time she'd grown on him despite the pain he was in.

Most of the Greek women he'd known and dated were more chatty and conscious of themselves, famous for drama on occasion. His sisters-in-law were like that. Fiery at times—beautiful—and they knew it. Melina hadn't been quite so theatrical. That's probably why she'd appealed to the quietly spoken Stavros.

Fran was an entirely different kind of woman. She seemed comfortable in her attractive skin, reminding Nik of still waters that ran deep. Did her calm aura hide unknown fires within? He felt in his gut this woman could become of vital importance to him.

After some soul-searching, he recognized his motivation to keep Fran in Athens wasn't driven exclusively by Demi's best interests. Already he was trying to find a way to persuade her to stay on for his own personal reasons. But he feared that if he lowered the bars to let her inside his soul and she couldn't take what he would be forced to tell her, blackness would envelop his world. He faced a dilemma he'd never experienced before.

Should he run from what he feared most? Or did he

reach out for the one thing that might bring him the greatest joy?

On impulse he turned to the others. "If you'll excuse me, I need to talk to *Kyria* Myers."

By now Kellie had joined her husband, leaving Fran alone. He watched her wander to the wall at the edge of the patio and look out over the water. Her violet-blue eyes flicked to his when she saw him approach. "I can't imagine gazing out on this idyllic view every night of your life. All the stories about the Greek Islands are true. You live in a paradise, especially here on Mykonos."

"I agree there's no place on earth quite like it. On the weekends, I look forward to leaving the office in Athens and coming home. The temperature of the air and the sea turns us into water babies around here."

She smiled. "There's an American artist who has done some serigraphs of Mykonos. He's captured the white cubic style of a villa like your family's to perfection."

"I know the artist you mean. I'm fond of his artwork, too, particularly several of his Italian masterpieces."

"Aren't they wonderful?"

He nodded, enjoying their conversation, but was impatient to get down to business. "How long did it take Demi to finally fall asleep?"

"Um, maybe ten songs," she quipped. Her gentle laugh found its way beneath his skin.

"Let's go for a walk along the beach." He took off his shoes. "Be sure to remove your sandals. You can leave them here by mine."

"All right." Together they walked down the steps

to the sand. From there it was only a few yards to the water. "Oh. Lovely. It warms my toes."

Nik chuckled. "Twilight is my favorite time to swim. If you wait a while, the moon will come up. Then everything is magical."

"It already is."

They walked in companionable silence for a long time. Unlike most women he knew, she felt no need to fill it in with conversation. That was a quality he liked very much, except for tonight. At the moment he had the perverse wish she would speak her mind. Fran knew he was waiting to hear she'd changed her mind.

Taking the initiative, he said, "Are you and Kellie still intent on leaving tomorrow?"

She slowed to a stop. In the dying light, she looked straight at him. "Yes. Much as I'd like to help you out, I'm afraid I can't. But I'll have you know it has been my privilege to take care of Demi over the last few days. If it's your wish, I'll stay with her until the funeral services are over. Then I'll fly back to Athens with Kellie and Leandros."

His heart clapped to a stop. She'd turned him down flat. Over his years in business, he'd made a study of people to find out what made them tick. Before Kellie Petralia had spent time alone with her in the bedroom, he could have sworn Fran was considering his proposition. He rubbed the back of his neck. Leandros's wife had a definite agenda and Nik's appeal to Fran had gotten in the way.

Trying a different tack he said, "Could you possibly wait another day? With the funeral tomorrow, I won't be able to do anything about Demi's care until the next day.

What I'd like to do is interview some nannies for the position. It would be a big help if you were there, too.

"Your hospital work makes you somewhat of an expert in reading people. If we both come up with our own questions, I'm sure we'll be able to pick the right nanny for her."

"I'm sorry, Nik, but I promised Kellie we'd leave as soon as you all came back from the interment. Surely your own mother and sisters-in-law would be the perfect ones to help out?"

Disappointed by her noncapitulation, he bit down hard on his teeth. "They would if Demi would let them hold her. I'm afraid a hysterical baby could put off a potential nanny."

"If that's the case, then you need to keep looking for one who can handle the situation, no matter how difficult."

Damn if beneath that ultra-feminine exterior she didn't think like a man....

He felt a grudging respect for her, but this battle was far from over and he was determined to win. "What if I offered you the job of permanent nanny? It's what I'd been thinking about all along after I saw how you cared for her in the hospital. No one could have been more like a mother. That's why she responded to you."

"Thank you for the compliment, but I already have a career," she came back without blinking an eye. "As much as I love that little girl—and who wouldn't?—it's a job, and the last one I'd want."

Nik was dumbfounded. "Are you so enamored of your hospital work, you can't imagine yourself leaving it for a position that could pay you an income to set you up for life in surroundings like this?"

"Actually, I can't, and I don't want that kind of money."

Then she belonged to a dying breed.

"Let me ask you the same question, Nik. Do you love what you do to make a living?"

His eyes narrowed on her appealing features, particularly her generous mouth. "What does one have to do with the other?"

"I was just thinking of a way to solve your problem. In the hospital, you treated Demi like a father would. Maybe you ought to become her nanny and give your brothers more responsibility for running the Angelis Corporation. Your sister Melina and Stavros would look down from heaven and love you forever for making such a great sacrifice."

Fran didn't know he'd agreed to be Demi's guardian if anything happened to them. Her comment found his vulnerable spot and pierced the jugular. He could feel his blood pressure climbing.

"Then again," she said softly, "you could find a wife who would love Demi and make a beautiful home for the three of you. That would take care of every problem. Your parents must be worried sick you haven't settled down yet."

Adrenaline pushed his anger through the roof. "Now we come to the crunch. After reading the tabloids on the plane, is it possible you're offering to become my bride and bring an end to my wicked ways? Is that what this verbal exercise has all been about?"

Her gentle laughter rang out in the night air. "Heavens, no. You're no more wicked than the next man."

While he digested that surprising comment she said, "I've been through marriage once and have no desire to be locked in that unhappy prison again. I was only teasing you, Nik, but it was wrong of me to try to lighten your mood on the eve of the funeral. Forgive me for that. I can see why you're such a powerhouse in business. You make it impossible to say no."

"Yet you've just said no to me." The nerve at his temple throbbed. This woman was twisting him in knots.

She eyed him critically. "You've told me you value what I've learned from my hospital work. If that's true, then listen to me. Demi's going to be all right. I promise. For a while we know she'll grieve for her parents, but in time she'll respond to your loving family.

"They're wonderful and they're all here willing to do anything. Let them help. Don't take it all on by yourself or you'll burn out."

"What are you talking about?" he growled with impatience.

"I'm talking about *you.* Leandros sings your praises as the new brains and power behind the Angelis Corporation. But you can't be everything to everyone every minute of the day and night the way you've been doing since you heard about the tornado. You remind me of Atlas carrying the world on your shoulders."

Atlas?

"I've seen it happen in families once a patient goes home from the hospital. There's always one person like you who carries the whole load, whether because of a greater capacity to feel compassion or a stronger need to give service. Who knows all the reasons? But the point is, this develops into a habit, and you're too young for this to happen to you."

Without question Fran Myers was the most unique

individual he'd ever met. No woman had ever confounded him so much before.

He sucked in his breath. "Let's go back, shall we? On the way, I want to hear about the reason why your marriage failed you to the point that you no longer believe in it."

Slowly they retraced their footsteps. "In a couple of sentences, I can tell you why it didn't work. He was the live wire at his law firm trying to make it to the top. Furthermore, he didn't feel he had the time to be a family man. He was too consumed by his work."

"What vital ingredient have you left out?"

When Fran almost stumbled, he knew he'd hit a nerve. "I'm afraid we both fell out of love. It happens all the time to millions of people."

"But not to someone like you. If he didn't have an affair, then what's the real reason it failed?"

"I'd rather not discuss it."

"Since you pretty well laid me out to the bare bones a little while ago, how about some honesty from you in return?"

"I suppose that would only be fair." She tossed her head back, causing the dark blond mass of gleaming hair to resettle on her shoulders. "You could say that when he didn't live up to the bargain we'd made before we married, there was nothing to hold us together any longer."

"Then he lied to you."

"I wouldn't say it was a lie… More of a human failing. When faced with the reality of what he'd committed to while we were dating, he couldn't go through with it. I didn't blame him for it, but my disappointment was so profound, my heart shut down."

"I'm sorry. How long were you married?"

"Three years."

And no children.

He wanted to know more. "Was he your first love?"

"No. Over the years I met and dated several men I thought might be the one. I'm sure the same experiences have happened to you."

"It's true I've enjoyed my share of women and still do. All of them have traits I admire."

"But so far none of them has delivered the whole package. At least that's what the tabloids infer," she added in a playful tone. "It was the same for me until Rob came along. He had everything that appealed to me and I didn't hesitate when he asked me to marry him."

Nik's dark brows lifted. "And once you'd each said I do, the one essential element to make your marriage work wasn't there after all, and it drove you apart."

"Precisely."

She was good at maintaining her cool, but every so often when their arms or legs brushed while they were walking, he could feel her trembling because she was holding back critical information. Her friend Kellie could enlighten him, but he knew deep down that wasn't the route to go. He'd find Leandros.

As if thinking about him conjured him up, they discovered him taking a swim. Like Nik, he'd been born on an island in the Aegean and found the water the ideal place to wind down at the end of the day. But Nik had to admit surprise his wife hadn't joined him.

"Hey, Leandros—" Fran called to him. "Where's Kellie?"

When he saw them, Leandros swam to shore. After picking up a towel he walked toward them while he dried himself off. "She had a headache and went to bed."

"After the horror of the last few days, I'm not surprised," she said in a quiet tone. "I'm ready to turn in myself." She glanced at Nik. "Thank you for your hospitality and the privilege of taking care of Demi one more night. I'll see you and your family in the morning before the funeral. Goodnight."

She gave Leandros a hug before she started for the steps leading up to the patio. Once at the top, she waved to them before disappearing inside the villa.

"Would you mind leveling with me about something?"

Leandros's gaze switched to Nik. "Not at all."

"I asked Fran if she'd be willing to stay on for another week to help while our family tries to find the right nanny. Because she looked after Demi from the moment she found her, I thought she might be willing. But when I asked her this evening, she indicated she's planning to travel with your wife and can't change her plans."

A grimace broke out on his face. "My wife's mind is made up."

There was a lot Leandros wasn't saying, but it was none of Nik's business until his friend chose to tell him.

"Then that relieves my fear. I thought maybe she'd said no to me as an excuse because of something I may have said or done to offend her. In my attempt to compliment her for the way she took care of Demi by asking her to stay on for a while longer, I may have accomplished the opposite result.

"As you saw earlier, my little niece clings to her and is unhappy with anyone else. When I told Fran she'd be well paid for her sacrifice, I think she took it as the final insult, which was the last thing I meant to do."

Leandros shook his head. "Not Fran. She stayed with your niece at the hospital because she wanted to. I'm sure she would have agreed to help you if Kellie weren't so insistent on their taking this trip."

"Where are they going?"

"On a driving trip to see other parts of Greece and do some hiking."

"I see."

"Fran's first marriage didn't work and Kellie has worried about her ever since. Just between us, my wife is determined to find Fran a husband."

That was an interesting piece of news. "Does she have someone particular in mind?"

"I doubt it. I think she's hoping they'll meet some unattached American over here on holiday with the right credentials who will sweep Fran off her feet. In the meantime, rest assured Fran's decision has nothing to do with you or the baby. I happen to know she's as crazy about kids as Kellie is."

Finally Nik had his answer though he already had proof how much she loved children by her attachment to Demi.

He patted Leandros's shoulder. "Thanks for the talk. You've relieved my mind in more ways than you know. See you in the morning. If I haven't told you yet, my family and I are honored that you'll be here for us."

"It's the least I can do for a good friend," Leandros's voice grated. "I plan to attend the services for the other family this weekend."

But Leandros's wife wouldn't be with him. Something was wrong and it gave him an idea.

"Leandros? Before you go to bed, there's something else I'd like to talk to you about it if you don't mind. I've been trying to think of a way to reward Fran for all she's done and would like to run it by you."

"Go ahead. I'm not ready for bed yet."

CHAPTER FIVE

THE ANGELIS FAMILY lived on a private part of the island overlooking a brilliant blue sea. Fran found the dazzling white villa with the main patio as the focal point for the family to congregate, an architectural wonder. She could see why the Cyclades was the desired vacation spot in Greece, especially this portion of the renowned Kalo Livadi Beach where she'd walked with Nik last night.

Their conversation had created a tension that had still gripped her after she'd gone to bed, making her sleep fitful. She'd never been so outspoken in her life with anyone, but fear of being in pain again had driven her to say those things to him.

While some of the staff came out to get things ready for the meal to be served when the family got back, Fran's gaze lit on the beautiful child whom she'd put in the high chair to feed her a midafternoon snack. She'd placed Demi beneath the shade of the umbrella while Fran sat in the sun to soak up what she could. Pretty soon everyone would return. After that, she and Kellie would leave for Athens.

Out of deference to his family, she'd dressed more formally in a light blue summer suit and white high heeled sandals. Beneath the short-sleeved jacket she wore a white T-shirt. After applying her lipstick, she'd fastened her hair back with a tortoise shell clip. She often wore it this way to work.

Rob had said he preferred it back because it made her look more sophisticated. For him, the right look was everything. But Fran had chosen to wear it this way today because Demi liked to pull on it and she was strong.

"Do you know you're the best eater?" Though the seven-month-old couldn't possibly understand her, she smiled and opened her mouth for more peaches. "You like these better than plums, don't you. Two more bites and you're all finished." She moved the spoon around to bait her before putting it in her mouth. Demi laughed, encouraging Fran to do it again.

As the baby laughed harder, a shadow fell over her. It couldn't be a cloud. She turned her head in time to see a somber-faced Nik staring down at her from those dark eyes she couldn't read. Standing there so tall and hard-muscled, he looked incredibly handsome in the midnight-blue mourning suit and tie he'd worn to the funeral.

"There's nothing like Demi's laughter to dissolve the gloom, is there?" he murmured before bending down to kiss his niece on both cheeks. "Sorry we're late, but there was a huge crowd at the burial and many people who wanted to express their sympathy."

Fran nodded, feeling his pain. Demi's parents had been laid to rest. She would never know them. The enormity of raising this little girl who would need the Angelis family from here on out settled on Fran like a mantle.

She could only imagine Nik's feelings of love mixed with inadequacy right now. Their whole family had to

be weighted by the new responsibility thrust upon them.
Moved with compassion, Fran got to her feet and wiped
Demi's mouth with her bib. Driven by her own heart-
felt emotions, she picked up the baby and handed her
to Nik, who must be feeling empty inside.

"Demi's going to need all of you now. If you'll excuse me, I have to go finish the last of my packing."

She practically ran inside the villa so she wouldn't
hear the baby start to cry. Nik was a big boy now. He
would deal with this crisis in the expert way he handled
all of his business transactions.

Fran had done her packing early, but she'd needed
the excuse to tear herself away from Demi. To be sure
she hadn't left anything behind, she made one more trip
into the bathroom.

"Fran? Are you about ready?"

"Whenever you are." She came back out to find Kellie who'd changed from her black dress to white pleated
pants and a watermelon-colored top.

"I asked Leandros to tell the family the three of us
couldn't stay to eat. We've already said our goodbyes
to them. I'll help carry your cases out to the helicopter pad." She took the big one while Fran reached for
the smaller bag.

Halfway down the hall they met Leandros, whose
drawn features aged him. He gave Fran a hug. "You
look beautiful."

"Thank you," she whispered.

There was an ominous quiet as he took the suitcase
from Kellie and they walked through the villa to the
rear entrance. Neither of them had another word to say.
Fran was so uncomfortable, she could scream.

When they stepped into the sunlight, Fran could see

the helicopter waiting for them in the distance. She almost ran toward it, but as she drew closer, she saw a tall figure talking to the pilot. It was Nik!

Her heart missed a beat because she'd thought she'd seen the last of him. When she'd handed Demi to him on the patio, she'd intended that to be her own form of goodbye.

"Here. Let me take your bag while you climb inside."

Fran had no choice but to give it to Nik before he helped her up. The touch of his hand sent fire through her body. No sooner had she found a seat than he joined her in the one next to her. Behind him came Kellie. Apparently their luggage had been put onboard ahead of time. Then Leandros climbed in next to the pilot and shut the door.

She turned to Nik in shock. "You're not staying with your family?" But her question came too late because the rotors whirred and they lifted off.

He gave her a ghost of a smile. "Last night after I went to bed, I thought about our conversation and decided to take your advice. Everyone who loves Demi is there to take care of her. I'm going to let them, and give myself a vacation. In another week they'll have sorted out what's best for her without my taking charge."

Guilt smote her for having been so outspoken. "You're joking…aren't you?" she blurted in consternation.

"Not at all. You made perfect sense. I'm afraid I have a tendency to do everything myself. Thanks to you, that's a flaw I'm going to work on. A vacation from my problems is exactly what I need. I haven't had a real one in over a year."

She blinked. "Where will you go?"

"Well, I was hoping you'd let me and Leandros drive you and Kellie around. I talked to him about it last night. I never drive anywhere anymore. Believe it or not, driving used to be one of my great passions. Not only would it be a great pleasure, but it would make me feel like I'd paid all of you back for everything you did for Demi and my family."

Kellie looked even paler than she had earlier in the morning. She shot Fran a private message before she looked at Nik. "That's very thoughtful of you, but Fran and I have decided to fly back to the States in the morning and vacation in California."

Uh-oh. For Kellie to have made a decision like that, the situation between her and her husband had reached flashpoint.

Nik's piercing gaze shot to Fran. "I haven't been there in years. How would you feel about having a third party along?"

Fran had no choice but to back up her friend. "I had no idea you could be such a joker."

"It turns out we make a good pair." His comment was meant to remind her of the way she'd talked to him last night. "But if you're not going to take me seriously, at least agree to have dinner with me this evening. I refuse to let you leave the country without enjoying a night out in the Plaka. I owe you a great deal for all you've done."

Afraid he would be unstoppable until she gave in, she decided to capitulate to that extent. "Your invitation sounds delightful, but if I say yes, it will have to be an early night."

"Good. In that case I'll ask Leandros to drop us off at my apartment. You can change clothes there. We'll go casual and play tourist while we walk around and eat what we want."

In the next instant he spoke to Leandros who nodded and gave instructions to the pilot. Soon Fran saw the glory of Athens spread before them in the late afternoon sun. The magnificent Parthenon, one of the most famous landmarks in the world, sat atop the Acropolis.

Seeing this sight from the air with Nik gave it special meaning. Just when she thought she'd figured him out, he did something unexpected that illuminated other appealing facets of his intriguing personality. She had to admit she wanted to spend the rest of the day and evening with him.

Right now his spontaneity thrilled her down to her toenails. With Rob every move had been calculated and planned out. She didn't want to compare the two men, but she couldn't help it. Rob wasn't unkind, but he'd expected her to conform. When she didn't, he went into a private sulk until she ended up being the one to apologize.

Nik, on the other hand, wouldn't know how to pout. He had hidden depths. Already she'd learned that his way was to zoom in and change the game plan if necessary to achieve the desired outcome. If he ever settled down, it would have to be with a woman who was even more unpredictable than himself. His psyche required a challenge.

Unfortunately Nik occupied too many of her thoughts and was becoming important to her. Any woman who became involved with him would know joy for a time, but in the end she'd pay for it. Wasn't that what Kellie had been saying about Leandros? The thought was terrifying.

Her mind was still full of him when the helicopter set down on the helipad atop his apartment building. She had to look away so she wouldn't get dizzy. This form of transportation was as natural as breathing to businessmen like him and Leandros, but for Fran it would have to become an acquired taste.

She turned to Kellie. Close to her ear she said, "I'll see you later tonight."

"Be back before the clock strikes twelve," her friend responded without mirth. Something dark was on Kellie's mind, leaving Fran troubled.

"I promise."

Nik grabbed Fran's bags. As they started for the stairs, the helicopter lifted off, creating wind that molded her skirt to her shapely legs. She caught at it with her hands, but she was too late. When they entered the elevator, he could see the flush that had crept into her cheeks. How nice to be with a truly modest woman. It made her more enticing to him.

"Here we are." The doors opened on his glassed-in penthouse.

She stepped into the entrance hall. For a full minute she appraised his fully modern apartment. "If I didn't know better, I'd think I was in the control tower at the airport."

He burst into laughter. Fran Myers was a breath of fresh air. "I pretend Athens is the sea I miss when I'm working in the city."

"The view is spectacular." She darted him a mischievous glance. "I'd say Atlas has it pretty good splitting his time between here and Mykonos."

"There's no Atlas here today. Haven't you noticed I'm not carrying the world on my shoulders?"

She studied him rather intently. "How does it feel to have all that weight removed for a little while?"

"I'll let you know later. First I'm sure you'd like to freshen up and change. The guest bedroom is down this hall." He set her bags inside the room. "Come into the living room when you're ready."

After closing the door, he walked to his bedroom for a shower. The idea of mingling with the crowds like any foreigner visiting Athens appealed to him. In deference to the heat, he changed into a well-worn pair of jeans and a linen sport shirt. Once he'd slipped on his sandals, he was ready to go.

The funeral had robbed him of an appetite, but the thought of being with Fran for the rest of the evening had brought it back. In fact, he was starving, and he wagered she was hungry, too.

More pleasant surprises greeted him to discover she was waiting for him at the window overlooking Stygmata Square. She'd put on a pair of jeans and a short-sleeved cotton top in a raspberry color. Her skin absorbed some of its hue. With her luscious honey-blond hair worn up, she presented a prim, cool look, making him long to put his lips to the curve of her neck.

He wandered over to her, once again aware of her wildflower fragrance. "We'll be walking in that area beyond the square," he pointed out. "I know a taverna that serves flaming sausages and grilled trout to die for. But if that doesn't appeal, there are dozens of restaurants offering what you would consider traditional Greek cooking."

Purplish-blue sparks lit up her eyes. "I'm one tourist who doesn't want traditional fare."

"Then be prepared for a gastronomical adventure. Let's go."

They rode the elevator and set off for the Plaka, the oldest part of the city. The place swarmed with visitors buying everything from furniture to jewelry in the shops lining the streets.

Hunger drove them to eat before they did anything else. She ate the trout and sausage right along with him. While they sat watching people and making up outrageous stories about who they were and where they'd come from, a girl selling flowers came up to their table.

"Isn't she sweet, Nik?"

"I agree." He bought a gardenia and put it in Fran's hair. The flower gave him an excuse to touch her. He wanted to touch her and the desire was growing.

Filled with good food and wine, he ushered her through the streets so they were constantly brushing against each other. While she marveled over all the souvenir shops, he marveled over her. She didn't want to buy anything, just look.

They ended up on top of the roof at the outdoor theater. With the Acropolis lit up in the background, they watched a local film with English subtitles. "The tragic story was ridiculous, but I loved it," she confided after they left to explore another street. Nik had been so aware of her, he hadn't been able to concentrate on the story line.

"Around the next corner is a taverna famous for its ouzo. Would you like to try some?"

"I experimented the last time I was in Athens and didn't care for it, but please don't let that stop you."

He smiled. "I don't like it either."

His comment prompted laughter from her. "How unpatriotic! I promise I won't tell anyone. Let's go down this narrow little alley and see what goodies could be hiding there."

Nik guided her along, amused at the way she expressed herself.

One of the shops sold every type of cheap figurine, both religious and mythological. He thought she'd just look and keep going. Suddenly she stopped and picked up a small metal figure of Atlas holding up the world. She asked the owner how much. He named a price and she paid for it with euros.

"Shall I wrap it?"

"No. I'd like to take it just as it is."

When they'd walked a little ways further, she turned to Nik. "It's getting late and I have to go to Kellie's. Before we leave, please accept this as my gift for showing me your world today. If you dare to keep it on your office desk, it will remind you about the necessity of taking a breather once in a while."

"The table by my bed will be an even better place for it," he fired back. "Each night it will be the last thing I see before I fall asleep. What greater way to help me keep my priorities in order."

They eyed each other for a moment. "Thank you for tonight, Nik. I've never had a better time."

Neither had he. The realization had made a different man of him.

He reached for the simple gift. It meant more to him than she could imagine. Instead of her begging him to buy her something the way one of his girlfriends would have done, she'd turned the tables. Her generosity of spirit ranged from saving a baby in the after-math of a tornado, to presenting him a keepsake he'd always treasure.

"On our way back to the apartment, there's one more place you have to visit."

"Will I like it?"

"I'll let you be the judge."

Nik had been saving this stop until the end. He needed to get closer to her. The Psara taverna was housed in two old mansions with a roof garden. You could dance while you enjoyed a view of the Plaka. Getting her in his arms had been all he could think about.

He asked her to keep the figurine in her purse until later. After they'd consumed an ice cream dessert, he led her out on the floor. The band played the kind of rock whose appeal was fairly universal. At last he was able to clasp her to him while they moved to the music.

"You're a terrific dancer," he whispered against the side of her neck. "I could stay like this all night."

"I'm enjoying it, too."

"Have you dated much since your divorce?"

"There've been a few men, but if you're fishing for compliments, I can tell you now they don't dance like you."

"It's my Greek blood, but please continue. Flattery will get you everywhere, *Kyria* Myers."

Her body shook with silent laughter.

He relished the feel of her, pulling her even closer. "Don't fly back to the States tomorrow."

"I have to, Nik."

He pressed a kiss to her temple. "You do realize Kellie is running away from her husband."

The second he spoke, she stopped dancing and looked

up at him. "Did Leandros confide in you?" She sounded anxious.

"He's told me nothing, but it's clear they're having problems. I felt something was wrong from the start. Leandros isn't the same man I've known in the past."

"Neither is Kellie," she said in a tremulous voice.

Unfortunately it was Nik's fault the mood had been altered. "It's eleven-thirty. I heard her warn you not to be late. Let's go back for your cases. My driver will run us to their apartment. Are your bags packed?"

"Yes. I put them outside the bedroom door."

"Then I'll have them brought down."

As they moved through the crowds, he pulled out his phone to make the arrangements. When they reached his apartment building, the limo was waiting for them. He helped her in the back. Once he'd told his driver where to take them, he got in across from her so he could look at her. She had a glow about her he'd noticed while they were dancing.

"You're not really going to California."

She put the flat of her hands against the seat. "I don't honestly know."

"So if I flew over to the States, too, would I find you home tomorrow evening, or not?"

"Are you pursuing me?" she asked with refreshing bluntness.

"Isn't that obvious? I know you're not indifferent to me."

She stirred in place. "No woman could be indifferent to you, Nik, and you know it."

"So you're already branding me as a Romeo with no staying power."

Fran looked away. "You said it, I didn't."

"The tabloids never print the truth, but the public will consume it."

She rolled her eyes. "Give me a little credit for not believing everything I read. As long as you're still single, I guess it's your lot to be labeled. But I haven't done that."

"If this isn't about me, then it's personal where *you're* concerned."

"Not at all. But we both know you won't be making any trips to Pennsylvania."

"If you knew the real me, you wouldn't make such a careless statement."

In the silence that followed, her cell phone rang. He checked his watch. "It's five to twelve, Cinderella."

She eyed him almost guiltily before pulling it from her purse to check the caller ID. "It's Leandros—" Her voice sounded shaky before she clicked on. Once she'd said hello, the color drained out of her face. She only said a few more words before hanging up.

"What's happened?"

"It's Kellie. This evening at the apartment she became ill and fainted. They're in the E.R. at the Athens regional medical center. Will you please ask your driver to take us there?"

Nik alerted him, then moved across to sit next to her. Without conscious thought he drew her into his arms. Whispering into her hair he said, "I'm sure whatever it is, she's going to be all right."

If Nik just hadn't joined her on the seat…

If he hadn't held her like some cherished possession…

While they'd been dancing earlier, the contact had been wildly disturbing. But this comforting tenderness was too unexpected and welcome for her to move away from him. She'd been worried sick about Kellie. Now her worst fears were confirmed and he knew it.

"Do you have any idea what could have brought on her fainting spell?" His lips grazed the side of her forehead before she buried her face in her hands.

"You might as well know the truth. She's going to file for a legal separation after she's back in Philadelphia. They probably quarreled tonight. Kellie's emotions have been so fragile, I was afraid the stress might be too much."

"I didn't realize their problems had reached such a serious state. Otherwise I wouldn't have suggested the four of us take a trip together."

His sincerity reached her. "Don't feel guilty. In truth, I didn't suspect anything was wrong until she called me several weeks ago and insisted I take my two-week vacation right now. She said Leandros would be away on business and it would be the perfect time.

"They've been so happy, I couldn't believe she didn't want to travel with him the way she always does. That was my first warning all wasn't well."

"I'm sorry for them—and you." The limo pulled up near the doors of the E.R. "Let's find Leandros."

To Fran it was déjà vu as they entered the emergency room. Nik must have been having similar thoughts because his hand tightened on her arm. "Hard to believe it was only a few days ago I was rushing into the hospital to find out if the baby you'd rescued was our little Demi."

"Thank heaven it was!"

An ashen-faced Leandros came forward and put an arm around her. "Thanks for coming."

"As if I wouldn't. Do you know why she fainted?"

"The doctor couldn't find anything wrong, but he's still waiting for the blood-test results. Kellie doesn't want me in there and is asking to see you. Maybe if you talk to her, she'll settle down."

She'd never seen Leandros this frantic. "I'll go to her now. Where is she?"

"In the last cubicle."

"Try not to worry." She turned to Nik. "I'll be back out in a few minutes."

His compassion-filled eyes played over her features. "Take as long as she needs. I'll keep Leandros company."

"Thank you." She had an urge to kiss his cheek for being so understanding, but she held back. Without a minute to lose, she hurried through the E.R. and pulled the blue curtain aside.

"*Fran*—I thought you'd never get here."

"I'm so sorry, Kellie." She pulled up a chair. "How are you feeling right now?"

"Foolish. The doctor just came in and said nothing showed up on the tests. He says I fainted because I hadn't eaten all day. They gave me something to eat so I'm fine now. I'd like to get out of here and check into a hotel. The last thing I want is to go home with Leandros."

"He won't allow you to go anywhere without him. At least not tonight. Kellie? What else aren't you telling me? This is truth time. I can't do anything to help you if I don't know what's going on."

She sat up. "Not ten minutes after we arrived back, Karmela let herself in the apartment carrying a stack of work for Leandros to look over. She looked positively shocked to find me there."

Fran's eyebrows knitted together. "If she had plans to be alone with him, *she* should have been the one who fainted to realize you weren't on vacation with me yet."

"She's not the type to faint. That woman is as cool as the proverbial cucumber, treating me like I was the interloper and not his wife. No doubt she was allowed to use the security hand code to get in while her sister was alive and Leandros never deleted it.

"Leandros disappeared into the study with her for a few minutes. When she came out again, she flashed me this satisfied smile and bade me a safe flight in the morning. Fran—how could she have known my plans if Leandros hadn't discussed them with her? I don't want her knowing my business. I tell you, that was the last straw."

She groaned. "It would have been for me, too."

"When he came to find me, I was in the kitchen getting some juice and didn't say anything to him about her. He hovered around me until it drove me positively crazy, so I said goodnight and went to bed in the guest bedroom. It wasn't long before he came in and found me on the phone with Aunt Sybil. He told me to hang up because he wanted to have a serious talk with me."

"Did you?"

"Yes. I've never seen him in a rage before. He swore he didn't know Karmela would be by. The more he tried to explain his way out of it, the more I couldn't listen to him. Suddenly I felt so sick I passed out."

"I'm not surprised. Under the circumstances it's a good thing we're flying home tomorrow."

"Please forgive me, Fran. I'm ashamed to have to

confess I got you to Athens on my terms, not yours. It was horribly selfish of me when you wanted to wait until September."

"None of that matters. You need help."

"So do you," came Kellie's cryptic comment. She stared hard at Fran. "You're back late. I don't need to ask if you had a good time with Nik tonight."

"I did." It was a night she'd always remember.

"With that droopy gardenia in your hair, I can just imagine. Did he put it there before or after he kissed you?"

"There was no kiss." Except on her forehead.

"Not yet maybe, but it's coming. It's the Angelis charm working like clockwork. Just be careful you don't get completely sucked in."

"Why do you say that?"

"He already wants to go on vacation with you!"

"Kellie—he was only flirting."

"No. Nik Angelis is a compelling force in the corporate world, and he's an even more compelling sensual force when it comes to women. One of the secretaries in Leandros's office says he's had a string of them over the years. Leandros claims that when Nik wants something, he's relentless until he gets it. I can see where his persuasion tactics are leading where you're concerned."

"In what way?"

"He wouldn't think twice about asking you to quit your job at the hospital and move to Greece in order to become his niece's nanny."

Fran swallowed hard. "He already has. I turned him down. When the doctor at the hospital in Leminos mentioned he'd like to hire someone like me, Nik said something about having other plans in mind for me."

"I knew it!" Kellie muttered. "He's going to use every trick in the book to get you to take care of Demi. His plan is to make the moves on *you* to ensure victory. He's counting on a beautiful, vulnerable divorcée like you to cave. Have you told him you can't have children?"

"No, of course not."

"Then don't! That piece of information would be all he needed to get you to say yes. You can't do it, Fran, or you'll be facing even greater heartache than with Rob. He's got enough money to buy anyone he wants, but not you—" Her eyes pooled with moisture. "I say this because you're the best person I've ever known and you're *beyond* price."

"Oh, Kellie—" She gave her friend a long, hard hug.

"Promise me you won't let him get to you. If you do, it will mean you've given up on marriage altogether. You and I have talked about you falling in love again with a widower who has small children. Isn't that what you said?"

She pulled away from Kellie and wiped her eyes. "Yes, and you know it's what I'd like to happen."

"Then if you really mean that, don't get any more involved with Nik. I promise that if you do, you'll end up being stuck in the Angelis household as nothing more than a glorified servant. I don't care how strong your maternal feelings are for Demi. The years pass quickly. Think, Fran! One day she'll grow up and won't need you anymore. *Then* what will you do? You'll be too old for what you really want, and you'll live the rest of your life with a broken heart! After we're home I'll concentrate on helping you meet a terrific guy. There are hundreds of widowers looking for a wife online through a dating service."

"Ugh. That sounds horrible."

"Maybe not. You deserve to meet someone fantastic and fall in love with him. It happens to lucky couples all the time. Second marriages can be wonderful if you're not desperate, and if you take the time to meet that one person you can't live without."

"I know."

"Then remember something else. One of these days Nik's parents will bring pressure to bear and he'll have to get married, thus joining the ranks of his married brothers. They'll all have families except for you. So, what then? When Demi goes to college, will you go back to the States and get another job at another hospital, only to keep taking care of other people?"

The words stung, but she knew Kellie was saying them partly from her own pain and partly to help Fran think straight.

"You need to take charge of your life and live for *you.* I think you should have gotten out of your marriage the first time Rob said he didn't want to adopt. That was a year into your marriage. Look at the time you've wasted! I never said anything to you about it, but I wanted to."

Fran eyed her friend in surprise. "I had no idea you felt this strongly about it."

She bit her lip. "You don't know half of the things I thought about Rob and his utter selfishness where you were concerned. Your situation has made me take stock of my marriage. That's why I'm planning to separate from Leandros. I refuse to hang around another year or two while he and Karmela are involved. I don't know if they're actual pillow friends yet, but don't think she isn't lying in wait for the opportunity.

"On our drive back to Athens yesterday, it was like talking to a wall. He's in denial over her infatuation with him, but all the signs are there. After he tires of her, he'll want someone else yet expect me to look the other way. I knew it was too good to be true that he fell in love with me, but idiot that I am, I was so crazy about him, I left the blinders on."

She grabbed Fran's arms. "Don't do what I did—don't be charmed by Nik and his Greek-god looks. Don't let him get to you. Above all, don't sleep with him. He can pour it on like Leandros. It's their gift and their curse."

"*Kellie*—I've never seen you like this before."

"That's because I realize my marriage was a mistake. Karmela was in the picture from the first time I met Leandros. The warning signs were there, but I didn't pay any heed to them."

Fran was shaken because, despite her friend's bitterness, she was making sense.

"When I get back home, I'm filing for a divorce through my uncle's attorney. I'll stay with them until I figure out what I'm going to do."

"Do they know your marriage is in trouble?"

"Not yet."

Fran folded her arms against her waist. She threw her head back. "Out of all the marriages I've seen, I thought yours was the most solid. I have to tell you I'm devastated over this."

"I've been in agony since I realized Karmela was never going to go away. So don't let Nik talk you into something that will be difficult for you to get out of.

No matter how much that little girl tugs at your heart, she's not yours! She belongs to the Angelis family. They circle their own and you won't be an integral part of anything."

Fran shot to her feet, not needing to hear any more. "Do you want me to come back to the apartment tonight?"

"No. That would be the last straw for Leandros. I need to show him I'm in control and can handle life on my own. He thinks I'm a pushover. Well, no longer! He should have married Karmela. I can't imagine why he didn't."

She let out an anguished cry. "Tell Nik to drive you to the Cassandra. I've already made arrangements for you to stay there in our private suite. We'll pick you up in the morning on our way to the airport."

"I'll be ready." She leaned down to give her a hug. Her eyes misted over. "You have to know my heart's breaking for you and Leandros."

"Now you have some idea of how I felt when you told me Rob didn't want to adopt after all. But you got through that terrible ordeal. Given time, I will, too."

Fran blew her friend a kiss, then slipped past the curtain and headed for the E.R. lounge. Both men got up when they saw her. Leandros's grave countenance haunted her. "How is she?"

"She's surprisingly good and ready for us to fly home in the morning. I'll watch out for her, Leandros. I'm so sorry this has happened. Obviously she needs her space. Once back in Philadelphia, time will have a way of making her see things more clearly. One thing I do know. She loves you with every fiber of her being. Don't ever forget that." Her voice shook.

His lips tightened. "I've forgotten nothing," he rapped out. "If she still wants to fly home in the morning, I'll fly her there in my jet. We have things to discuss. As you know, we've made arrangements for you to stay at the Cassandra tonight. Tomorrow morning my driver will be there to take you to the airport. I've booked you first class on a flight leaving at eight."

CHAPTER SIX

THIS WAS LEANDROS at his most intimidating. The situation was out of Fran's hands. She gave him a last kiss on the cheek. Nik grasped her elbow and led them out to the limo where he sat next to her.

"You're staying with me tonight. It's late, and it would be absurd for you to go anywhere else when I have a perfectly good apartment going to waste. Tomorrow will be a new day. After a solid night's sleep you can make decisions. Who knows, you might even decide to finish your vacation here."

The fight seemed to have gone out of her. "You've talked me into it. Thank you," she half sighed the words. "I'm drained, as I'm sure you are. I can't tell you how much I appreciate your generosity."

He flashed her a white smile that melted her bones. "At last I can do something for you."

"How many times do I have to remind you that taking care of Demi was a joy?" All of a sudden her voice caught. "Have you had any word from your family yet?"

"Yes. My father called."

"They must miss you terribly."

"I didn't get that impression. He phoned to thank me for bringing Demi home to them. He said my mother is a different person now that she has the baby to worry about. Demi fussed and cried all day, but the girls helped her and by bedtime she'd calmed down."

"I miss her, Nik."

"She's never off my mind either. My father says having Demi there has chased away the darkness and spirits are improving. He also admitted he envies me for being able to look forward to work. I told him he retired too soon and should come back in the office for half days, or at least for several times a week."

Nik was a wonderful son. Though Kellie had spoken the truth about Nik's determined nature, there was a noble side to him she couldn't dismiss. "That must have thrilled him."

"He said he'd think about it, which tells me he wants to keep his hand in things. I told him something else."

"What was that?"

"I've gone on vacation for a week and have left all the worry to my assistants. I suggested to Father he might want to check up on things while I'm gone."

"And?" she prodded because his eyes were smiling.

"He didn't say no."

"If he's anything like you, I bet he can't wait to dig back in."

"I'm sure you're right. So you see, taking your advice is already paying dividends. If you hadn't convinced me to let go, I wouldn't have realized my father is still struggling with his retirement. I owe a great deal of what's going on at the villa to you, Fran."

Before she could think, he pressed a light kiss to her lips. It only lasted for a breathless moment, but the aftershocks traveling through her nervous system were as powerful as Kellie's warning. *Don't do what I did—*

don't be charmed by Nik and his Greek-god looks. Don't let him get to you.

He grasped her hand. "Speaking of vacations, you could use a break from worry about Kellie. Left alone with Leandros who plans to stay in Philadelphia with her for a while, she'll have time to consider everything and rethink her decision to leave him. Why don't you stay on in Greece for a few more days? If you're not there then Kellie and Leandros will be forced to confront their feelings. I know that Leandros won't want a divorce."

That sounded encouraging. Maybe Kellie had gotten through to him after all....

"To my knowledge, there's no finer man. I get the impression Kellie is his whole world."

"She worships the ground he walks on, too. I liked him the first time I met him and that has never changed. But I'm not married to him. Their personal problems are none of my business."

Except Fran knew what was tearing her friend apart. It wasn't just about Karmela. Sometimes Fran got the feeling Kellie was using Karmela as an excuse to cover her own insecurities. She'd married a powerful man whose first marriage had been happy. Kellie needed to talk to someone professional about her problems.

"In that case, let's concentrate on enjoying our vacation," Nik suggested.

Fran chuckled to cover the sudden spike of her pulse. "*Our* vacation? I didn't know we were going on one."

"Leandros wants time alone with his wife and you're still here in Greece, ostensibly to travel. Does the thought of hanging out together frighten you?"

A small tremor rocked her body.

"I'll ask you again. Are you afraid at the thought of being alone with me?"

Adrenaline spilled into her veins. "Why would I be?"

"Liar," he whispered.

His response made her laugh before she removed her hand.

"Admit you're afraid you'll like it too much."

He knew her too well. "Oh, I can admit to that already. It's what happens when the vacation is over that bothers me."

"Forget about the over part. When you're on vacation, you're not entitled to think, only to accept everything that comes as a special gift."

Her lips curved. "Your spin on the subject is without equal."

"I take it you can't wait for us to embark on our journey. Where would you like to go?"

"That's easy. How about a hike to the top of Mount Olympus?" she teased.

"The home of the gods."

"It's so famous, I want to climb it. Though I might be out of shape, Kellie and I planned to do it before a tornado swept through Greece and changed all our lives." She hated the throb in her voice.

"I can't think of anything I'd like more. We'll not only hike, we'll camp out. It's my favorite thing to do besides water sports."

"And driving," she added.

He grinned. "Your mind is a steel trap. This trip will be an experience to remember. I'll throw all my camping gear in the helicopter and we'll take off for Pironia tomorrow after breakfast. That's the start of the trailhead."

"You've climbed it, of course."

"Twice. Once with my brothers and another time with my friends."

She darted him a glance. "Is there anything you haven't done?"

"I haven't climbed all our Greek mountains yet, and I've never gone camping with a woman."

"That's probably the best idea you've ever had."

Once again he broke into the kind of deep masculine belly laughter that shook the back of the limo and warmed her insides, neutralizing Kellie's concerns for her for the moment.

Nik drew Fran to the side of the forest trail to allow a team of donkeys carrying packs to the refuge to go on ahead of them. This was a good place to stop for a drink of water. They'd been hiking for over an hour, passing and being passed by other hikers.

In another hour they would reach the refuge where everyone would spend the night. Nik had another place in mind where he would set up camp for them in total privacy. Tomorrow they'd climb to the top of Mytikas, the highest peak.

He hadn't known what to expect, but so far Fran had kept up with him, carrying her own backpack without complaint. She'd worn her hair up again to keep it out of her face. In jeans and a layered cream-colored top that her figure did amazing things for, he was hard-pressed to look at anything else.

"Are you ready to move on? We'll ascend a gorge and then you'll see the red top of the refuge."

"How high up is it?"

"Two thousand meters."

"Are we going to stay there tonight?"

"No. We'll set up our own camp above it. You don't know how lucky we are to see the mountain today. Usually it's covered with clouds. That means we'll see stars tonight."

"I can't wait!"

Neither could he.

She started off without him. He paced himself to stay alongside her as they headed for the spot he had in mind to spend the night. They'd bed down in the pines where the air would be fresh and cool.

Along the way she used his field glasses in the hope of spotting the wildlife that flourished on the mountain. After ten minutes of hiking she cried, "Oh, Nik—look at that huge bird!"

He understood her excitement. "I can see it without the binoculars. It's a bearded vulture."

"Bearded?"

"It has a mustache." She giggled like a girl. "That one probably weighs ten pounds.

"I can see why. Its wingspan is enormous."

"Three to four feet across. This is a protected eco-system with multiple climate regions. Some plants and animals here aren't found anywhere else in the world."

Her face lit up. "I'm so glad we came here. I wouldn't have missed a sight like this for the world."

As far as he was concerned, the sight staring up at him had no equal. If there weren't other hikers moving back and forth on the trail, he would have taken her in his arms and kissed the daylights out of her. "This is only the beginning," he murmured. "Come on. Let's get to our destination. I'm hungry. How about you?"

She laughed. "Do you even need to ask?" They

headed out for the tougher part of the climb, but she proved herself equal to the task. Before long they reached the refuge where the climbers could have a meal and a bed for the night.

"One more drink of water will sustain us until we reach the sacred spot."

Her lips curved upward. "Sacred?"

"It *will* be after we've christened it."

"That's an interesting choice of words," she said with a half chuckle before draining the rest of her water bottle.

Nik watched her throat work. Her natural beauty caused every male in the vicinity to take a second and third look. One of the male hikers passing by muttered in Greek to his buddy that Nik had it made for tonight with the dark blonde goddess. Nik ignored him.

For one thing, if he'd been the hiker who'd seen Fran standing there with another guy, he would have wished he'd found her first. For another, he was too happy being with her to take offense at anything.

Again he marveled that despite the tragedy that had struck their family, despite Demi's parentless state, despite the headaches of becoming the new head of the Angelis Corporation, being with Fran felt right and filled the gaping hole inside him. She brought a new sense of purpose to his life that had been missing.

Last night he'd fallen asleep holding the small Atlas in his hands, enchanted by her inimitable charisma and her extraordinary insight. He could wish he'd met her before she'd ever known her husband. But there was no use wandering down that pointless road.

The past needed to stay in the past. She was here now. That's what was important, and she was with Nik.

If she hadn't felt the connection to him growing stronger every minute they were together, she would have flown to the United States today. For now he'd shoved his deepest fear to the back of his mind.

"It's getting dark. Ten more minutes and we can call it a night. Let's go."

She followed him up the trail that had grown even steeper. "I'm surprised we're the only ones not staying there."

He smiled to himself. "They don't have your sense of adventure."

"Too bad we can't climb Mount Athos next."

Nik chuckled. "You mean the Greek mountain forbidden to women?"

"Yes, but it didn't stop the French author Maryse Choisy. Kellie and I read the paperback she wrote."

"Un mois avec les hommes?"

"That's it! *A Month with the Men*. She sneaked into one of the monasteries on the mountain undercover to see how the monks lived. In her words, she turned one of them down. Kellie and I decided she broke his heart."

"More like his pride," Nik theorized.

"To find a woman there, he must have thought he was having a vision."

Nik couldn't resist adding a comment. "She must have found him unappealing, otherwise she might have spent a much longer time there and no book would have been produced."

Suddenly the air was filled with the delightful sound of her laughter. It startled some squirrels who scrambled into the higher branches of a pine tree.

"Let's be thankful we're on Mount Olympus, where

Zeus allowed both male and female gods to romp together in the Elysian fields."

"That must have been something," she quipped. "I
always pictured those fields to be white."

"When we're up on top slipping and sliding on
the barren summit covered in rocks, you'll learn the
truth. I'm afraid mythology has a lot to answer for,"
he drawled.

"I guess I like reality better."

"Good, because we've arrived at our reality." He
headed through the trees, far enough away from the trail
so no one would spot them. Soon he came to a small
clearing surrounded by pines. Excited to be here, he
removed his pack. "In a few minutes I'll have the tent
erected and we can eat." He pulled out the big flashlight and turned it on.

"Let me help." After taking off her pack, she pitched
right in. They worked together in companionable silence.

"I can tell you've done this before. You're the perfect
person to bring on a hike like this."

"Coming from you, I'm flattered. The truth is, I used
to camp with my parents and my younger brother, Craig.
We usually took Kellie with us. She's a great camper,
too. Fearless. We'd go on lots of trips with some of our
extended families who loved the outdoors."

Nik digested everything before glancing at her. "I
didn't know you had a sibling."

"He died at fifteen of leukemia. I didn't think I'd
recover from the loss, but time took the worst of the
pain away. One day your pain over losing your sister
will fade, too."

The news sobered him. "Tell me about your parents."

"Dad works for a newspaper and has his own political column. My mother still works as an administrator at the school district. I have a lot of aunts and uncles and cousins on both sides. It makes for a big family like yours."

She'd experienced more than her lot of suffering. The death of a loved brother followed by an agonizing divorce... No wonder she had so much depth of character.

"Where have you lived since you've been on your own?"

"In a small condo."

"Not with your parents?"

"No, but it's near my parents' home where I grew up."

"You're more independent than most of the women I know. I admire you for that."

"I could have gone back home, but I need my own space. So do my parents."

They moved inside the tent to lay out their sleeping bags. He reached in another part of his pack for the picnic food they'd purchased before leaving Athens. Salad, fruit, sandwiches and a half dozen pastries.

Nik positioned the light so they could see while they sat across from each other to eat.

"Mmm, this tastes fabulous."

He flicked her a glance. "Have I told you how fabulous you've been today?"

She had to finish chewing before she could talk. "I was just thinking the same thing about you. You're so easygoing. After Rob, I—" She paused for a minute. "I'm sorry. I can't believe I bring up his name so often. Forgive me."

"What is there to forgive? You were married what, three years? It's normal."

"Maybe, but it's rude to you and disrespectful to him."

"A woman with a strong conscience. It's one of the many things I like about you." He popped some grapes in his mouth. "I'm curious about something. Did your parents name you Fran at birth?"

She reached for a morsel of baklava. "No. My legal name is Francesca, but I got kidded about it at school, so I went by Fran."

He frowned. "You were kidded because of it?"

"It sounds too pretentious. I was named for my grandmother on my mother's side."

"How would you feel if I called you Francesca?"

"Why would you do that?"

"Because it appeals to me."

"My parents only called me that when I was in trouble with them."

One eyebrow lifted. "Did that happen often?"

"More than I'd like to admit. In the seventh grade I signed up for a dance class at a local studio with Kellie without thinking about it. When my parents got the bill, they couldn't believe what I'd done. They didn't get mad exactly. Dad said it showed ingenuity, but I was still in trouble for a while."

Nik chuckled.

"And then there was the time we decided to skip our last year of high school and go to a finishing school in France. We wrote to this *pensionnat* as a lark, not thinking we'd get accepted because we applied to the school so late. Wouldn't you know my parents got another letter in the mail, this time from Paris? The directrice informed them she was happy to enroll me in the school and would they please send $2,000 to secure my place.

"Once again I got called to my parents' bedroom and they showed me the letter. I honestly couldn't believe it and told them Kellie and I had just been fooling around."

"But your parents recognized that indomitable spirit in you and they let you go," Nik divined.

"Yes. They felt the experience would be good for me."

"And was it?"

"Yes, after I got over a fierce, two-week bout of homesickness. We had the most awesome adventures of our lives and came back speaking adequate French."

Intrigued, he said, "Did you inherit your candor from your mother or your father?"

"Both my parents, actually." She wiped her fingers on the napkins they'd brought. Now that she'd finished eating, she settled back on the sleeping bag, propping up her head with her hand. "Since you've never married, tell me something. Have you ever lived with a woman?"

"No."

"That sounded final. Then tell me about the latest love interest in the life of the famous Nikolos Angelis. Don't scoff. Your legendary reputation precedes you."

He laughed instead.

"Why didn't you take her camping? I can't think of a better way to get to know someone than on a trip like this."

"Agreed." After putting the leftover food in the bag, he stretched out on his back and put his hands behind his head. "Lena would have pretended to enjoy it for my sake."

"So-o?" She strung the word out.

He turned his head to look at her. "So, I didn't feel like getting to know her better. Does that answer your question?"

Fran sat up looking shocked. "How long did you date her?"

"Twice."

"Does this happen with every woman after you've dated her twice?"

"Sometimes three, but most of the time it happens after one experience."

"You're not kidding me, are you?" she said in a quiet voice.

"No."

"If that's true, then why did you agree to bring *me* camping?"

He turned on his side and moved closer. "You're an intelligent woman. You figure it out."

"You're starting to scare me, Nik."

"Good. It's time you began to take me seriously. Surely it hasn't escaped your notice I'm attracted to you? I did everything I could to prevent you from leaving Athens. No woman has ever caused me to walk out on my family and my job to make sure she didn't get away from me. You must know how much I want you."

"You shouldn't say things like that to me. Our relationship isn't like any other."

"I'm glad you've noticed."

"Please don't come any closer. We'll both regret it if you do."

He cupped the side of her face with his free hand. "Don't pretend you don't want the same thing," he whispered against her lips. "I see it in your eyes. Right now that little pulse in your throat is beckoning me to kiss it."

"No, Nik—"

But he couldn't stop. Consumed by a desire so much greater than he'd known before, he covered her pulse with his mouth, relishing the sweet taste of her velvety skin. When it wasn't enough, his lips roamed her features, covering every centimeter of her face until he found her quivering mouth. Slowly he coaxed her lips apart until she began to respond with a hunger she couldn't hide.

Their low moans of satisfaction mingled as their kisses grew deeper and longer. Like water spilling over a dam, there was no holding back. Time lost meaning while they brought pleasure to each other. He couldn't get enough. Neither could she. When had he ever felt like this in his life? Never.

"You're so beautiful," he murmured, undoing her hair so he could run his fingers through it. "Do you have any idea how long I've been aching to do this?" Nik buried his face in her honey-blond tresses. He couldn't stop kissing her.

When he felt her hands slide into his hair, thrilling chills raced through his body. "Admit you want me, too," he said, out of breath.

"You don't need me to admit to anything," she came back.

"But I want to hear the words." He plundered her mouth once more.

"I'm afraid to get close to you."

"Because your ex-husband hurt you?"

"It's hard to build trust again."

"So I'm condemned without a trial?"

"If that were the case, I would have flown home this morning."

Nik sat up. "Don't you know I would never hurt you?"

"I want to believe that," she said in a tremulous voice.

Her husband had done a lot of damage. He could see this was going to take time. In frustration, he got to his feet. "I have to go outside, but I won't be gone long." He picked up the flashlight and unzipped the front of the tent.

"Nik—"

He swung around. "What is it?"

"Nothing. Just be careful."

Fran's heart thudded sickeningly for fear she'd offended him. She gave Nik five minutes before she left the tent to find him. Though the sky was full of stars, there was only a thumbnail moon. The darkness gave the surroundings a savage look. She walked around trying to get her bearings. "Nik? Where are you?"

"I'm right behind you," came his deep male voice.

She whirled around and almost lost her balance. His hands shot to her shoulders to steady her, but he kept their bodies apart. "Explain to me what went on in your marriage that has made you afraid to be with a man again. To be with me," his voice rasped.

"I—I lost my belief in him," she stammered. "When you give marriage your all, and it fails, the fear that another experience could turn out the same way is immobilizing. It's better not to get one started."

Fran heard his sharp intake of breath. "You're the most honest woman I've ever known, but you haven't told me everything. I want to know what he did to kill your love." His hands tightened on her shoulders. She knew he didn't realize how strong he was.

"I can't."

With a withering sound, he let her go. She had to brace her legs not to fall down. After such a beautiful day, Fran couldn't bear for there to be trouble now, but she was standing on the edge of a precipice. If she caved, she'd plunge headlong into a world where the risk of falling in love with this man would be too great.

She'd been playing with fire since agreeing to spend an evening out with him in the Plaka. Now she'd gotten burned around the edges. Better to escape him with a few scars than stay in Greece to see her whole life destroyed. This situation was no longer solely about Demi.

"Since I suggested this hike, I take full responsibility for our being here, Nik. I'd like us to enjoy the rest of the climb tomorrow. You've been so wonderful to me, I'd be a wretch if I didn't thank you for everything. Do you think it's possible for us to be friends from here on out?"

"No," his voice grated. "The situation is murkier than ever and I don't feel the least friendly toward you. But to honor my indebtedness to you for finding Demi and taking care of her, I'll be your guide until we're off the mountain. If you can't open up to me, then so be it. I'm going to bed."

"Nik—"

"Plan to be up by six. Early morning is the best time to reach the summit." He thrust the flashlight in her hands before he disappeared inside the tent.

She bit her knuckle, hating herself for bringing on this impasse. Out of a sense of self-preservation, she'd stopped things before they'd made love. He'd get over this without a problem. Fran wished she could say the same.

Tonight she'd been shaken by the most overwhelming passion she'd ever known. She'd come close to paying the price to know his possession. It didn't seem possible that after just a short time she was on the verge of giving him whatever he wanted.

After pulling herself together she entered the tent, careful not to shine the light near him. He'd climbed in his bag with his long, hard body turned away from her. Once she'd removed her hiking boots, she got inside hers.

He'd opened the screened window at the top of the tent. She could see the stars he'd promised, but they grew blurry with her tears and she knew nothing more.

"It's time to get going," Nik called to her. She let out a groan because it was still dark. "I'll have breakfast waiting for you when you come out of the tent. We'll leave everything here and pack it up after our descent."

The next two hours proved to be a grueling hike with a taciturn Nik only feeding her vital information when necessary. The trail left the sparse pines and vegetation behind. From there they followed it up a ridgeline all the way to the top. He told her this section was called the Kaki Scala. The narrow path was nothing more than scree and shale, rising straight up.

They finally stopped to drink water. She was panting, but Nik didn't seem the least out of breath. He stayed too fit to be winded by a climb like this.

The peak of Mount Mytikas was still forty-five minutes away. Fran's muscles were clearly aching so badly,

Nik declared they'd opt for Mount Scolio, the second-highest peak. It was only twenty minutes further.

When they arrived, clouds had started to form, blocking out the view of the Aegean. Maybe the elements were delivering an omen. They took some pictures with their cell phones. When she was back home, she'd have them made up so she could pore over them and feast her eyes.

"Thank you for bringing me up here, Nik."

"You're welcome."

He might be civil, but there was no softening him up. Before last night, he would have told her some fascinating tale about the gods who played here and worked their intrigues on each other. She missed that exciting man who'd brought her alive in a way she would never know again. Already she was in mourning for him.

After they signed their names in the register, he suggested they head back. Now that he'd done his duty, she sensed he was anxious to get down the mountain and fly home.

She followed him, but the descent was far from easy. Fran had to be careful where to place her feet on the slippery shale. You could twist an ankle if you weren't careful. She had a feeling that for the next few days, she'd suffer from sore knees more than anything else.

By the time they reached the tent, it looked so welcoming, she went inside and crashed on top of her bag. He paused in the entry to look down at her. She eyed him warily. "I'm worn out. Can we stay here for a half hour to rest before starting back?"

His lips thinned. "You do it at your own risk."

"Nik—please— I can't bear for us to have trouble."

He stood there and drained his water bottle, staring at her the whole time through narrowed eyes. "Has this morning's hike worn you down enough that you're ready to tell me what I want to know?"

She sat up, circling her knees with her arms. "This is so hard for me," she whispered.

"Why?"

The air crackled with tension. He hunkered down to pull some rolls and dried fruit from his pack. Being the decent man he was, he shared them with her.

"Because I want things I don't have and probably never will."

Nik squinted at her. "What kinds of things?"

"You'll mock me when I tell you."

"Try me."

"I ache for the one thing that has eluded me. Mainly, a good marriage and children. I need to put myself in a position where I can meet a man who wants the same thing. When you asked me if I'd consider becoming Demi's permanent nanny, I thought seriously about it before I told you no. Demi is precious and I already love her, but being a nanny would put me out of circulation."

"Fran—"

"I know what I'm talking about," she interrupted him. "You'd have to be a woman to understand. To be the bridesmaid for the rest of my life is too ghastly to contemplate. I still have some good years ahead of me and—"

"Just how old are you?" he broke in, sounding upset. A scowl marred his handsome features.

"Twenty-eight. I know it's not old, but having been married, I feel much older. And let's face it, I'm out of the loop. Since you've never been married, you wouldn't know about those feelings, but they're real, believe me."

He handed her some sugared almonds. "Since you're not an unmarried male, you don't have any concept of what my life is like either. Everyone sees the bachelor who can sleep with any woman he wants with no strings. My life is constantly portrayed as something it isn't and no amount of protests on my part will change it. By that blush on your cheeks, I can see you've had those same thoughts about me."

There was no point in her denying it. "After reading about you in a magazine, I might have entertained certain ideas at first, but no longer."

"Even after I came close to ravishing you last night?"

"Nik—nothing happened that we didn't both want."

"Your honesty continues to confound me."

"Why? Have most of the women you've known been deceitful?"

He put the sack of nuts back in the pack before moving closer to her. "No. The fault lies with me for never giving any of them a chance."

Fran cocked her head. "Tell me what your life has really been like, the one no one knows about."

CHAPTER SEVEN

NIK'S EYES WANDERED over her features. "Like you, I was physically adventurous and logged more than my share of visits to the E.R. for stitches and concussions from water and climbing accidents. My parents drummed it into my head that I had to get top grades or they would forbid me from doing the activities I loved.

"Since I couldn't bear the thought of that, I made deals with them. I would study hard and put in my hours at the company, then I'd be given a reward. As a result, when it came time to play, I played harder than my brothers and enjoyed my girlfriends. I went through a phase of wanting to be Greece's greatest soccer player, then that fantasy faded and I decided I wanted to be a famous race-car driver."

"You believed yourself invincible," she said with a grin.

"With top grades came other rewards. I'd been saving the money I earned, and I traveled to the States and South America. While I was climbing in the Andes I met a guy who was putting an expedition together to climb Mount Everest. When I got back from my trip, I put in for a permit to go with him. That climb changed my life."

"In what way?"

"We got caught in a blizzard and lost two of the men. When they fell, I was pulled away from the ledge. The rope saved me, but I was flung back against the rock wall and ended up with internal damage. At first everyone thought I was dead."

"Nik—"

"I was in the hospital for over two months for a series of surgeries. It took me a year to fully recover and I realized I was lucky to be alive. Like you, I did things sometimes without really thinking of the impact on the family. They'd always given me a wide berth because they knew I couldn't be stopped. It took a force of nature to bring me to my senses."

"So that's the reason you haven't climbed *all* the mountains of your country."

He winked at her. "It's one of them. When I saw the toll my accident took on my parents, I decided I'd better get serious about work. The day I joined my brothers in the upper echelons of our company's business, a lot of my playing ended.

"Despite the gossip, my experiences with women have been sporadic of necessity. I found I liked the work. The stimulating challenge of increasing profits and cutting costs appealed to me in a brand-new way. I dug in to make up for lost time. No doubt that's when I developed my Atlas complex."

"Ah. Now I'm beginning to understand."

"That was five years ago."

"How old are you now?"

"Thirty-four."

"And in that short amount of time you surpassed everyone's expectations to the point that you earned your place at the head of the company. You're young to have so much responsibility, but you've obviously earned it. I'm proud of you and so sorry you lost your sister. The pain must be excruciating."

"You've known that kind of pain, too."

"Yes. But in your case, you have that adorable little Demi who'll always bring joy to you and your family. She's so fun to play with. I'd love to see her again."

In a lightning move he grasped her hands. Slowly, he kissed her palms, sending erotic sensations through her hands to the other parts of her body. "Whenever you talk about her, I can feel this deep wound inside of you. Maybe if you talked about it, you could eventually get over it."

Oh, Nik... She lowered her head, not having counted on his exquisite tenderness.

"Tell me," he urged.

"In my later teens I developed a disease called endometriosis. A lot of women suffer from it. My case was so severe, it prevents me from ever having a child. I'd grown up hoping that one day I'd get married and have a cute little boy like my baby brother, but—"

"Francesca—"

Before she knew it, she was lying in his arms. His embrace opened the floodgates. For a few minutes she sobbed quietly against his shoulder, breathing in the wonderful male scent of him. "I'm sorry," she said at last. "Rob knew about my condition before we married. He told me he was fine with the idea of adoption. I believed him.

"Yet a year later he said he still wasn't ready. Eventually I asked him to go to counseling with me because I wanted a baby. In the first session he blurted that he wanted his own flesh and blood or no children at all. I was enough for him. His admission shattered me."

"Agape mou," Nik whispered, covering her face with featherlight kisses. Fran didn't know what the words meant, but his tone was so piercingly sweet, she nestled deeper in his arms, never wanting to move again.

Nik awakened while Fran was still asleep. Both of them were already emotionally exhausted. The fatigue after their hike had done the rest. They'd slept all afternoon. She was still curled into him with her arm flung across his chest, almost possessively, he thought.

Much as he didn't want to leave her for a second, he knew she'd be stirring before long and they needed dinner. Extricating himself carefully from her arms, he left the tent and hurried down to the refuge. The staff fixed him up with some boxed lunches and drinks.

On the way back, he phoned his helicopter pilot. Nik told him to meet them at the dropoff point at seven the next morning. After hanging up, he checked his phone messages. His father had let him know Demi was doing better.

That was a great relief. Under the circumstances, there was no reason to call him back. Nik was on vacation. Since Fran had pointed out to him that he did his work and everyone else's without thinking about it, he knew she was right.

When he entered the tent, he found Fran on her feet brushing her glorious hair. It flowed around her shoulders. Her smoky-blue eyes lit up when she saw him. "Food—" she cried. "I'm starving. Bless you."

Nik put everything down between their sleeping

bags. "Let's eat and then walk over to the stream for a bath."

Her eyes rounded. "Is it deep enough?"

"Probably not for a full submersion."

"That's just as well because I don't have a bathing suit."

They both sat down to eat. "Don't let that stop you."

She sent him an impish smile. "So you're saying you wouldn't be scandalized if I waded in without it?"

His pulse accelerated. "I would be so overjoyed, I'd probably expire on the spot of a massive heart attack."

"I love the things you say, Nik." Ditto. "Do you suppose the gods wore clothes during their picnics up on top?"

Laughter rumbled out of him. "I never thought about it. I find I'm dazzled by the sight before my eyes right here." Upon that remark, he tucked into his sandwich.

"Kellie thinks you look like a Greek god."

"Then it's a good thing she couldn't see the scars on my midsection when I was holding up the world."

Her smile warmed him in all the hidden places. "I'm sure she was talking about the whole picture. American women, and probably all the other women in existence, have a certain penchant for the authentic Greek-god look. Like I told you in the hospital, it's a good thing Demi inherited her mother's features. As for everything else, she's almost too beautiful to be real. Her black hair and olive skin are still a wonder to me."

"Just as your northern-European blond locks and violet eyes stop traffic over here."

"Just once I'd like to see that happen."

She never took him seriously. "It already did on the hike yesterday."

"What do you mean?"

"There were two guys watching you all the way to the refuge. At one point they stopped. In my hearing they commented I had it made to be with a goddess like you."

"They really called me a goddess?" She laughed in patent disbelief. "Thank you for telling me that. You've made my day." She drank her soda.

"Leandros confided that Kellie was going to find you a husband while you were here. I must say she knew what she was doing when she asked you to take this trip. My helicopter pilot Keiko wasn't able to keep his eyes off of you. As for my brothers…"

"Oh, stop—" She put down her can. "Let's get serious for a moment. Don't you think we should break up camp and head down before it gets dark?"

Without looking at her he said, "Plans have changed. Because we took such a long nap, I phoned my pilot. He'll be waiting for us at the dropoff point in the morning at seven."

He heard her take an extra breath. "In that case I'm going to the stream to take a little sponge bath."

"Do you want any help?"

"I'll call out if I need it."

Nik looked up in time to see the blood flow into her cheeks. She reached for her backpack and stepped outside like a demure maiden who sensed the hunter.

While she was gone, he cleaned up their tent. When she returned, smelling of scented soap and toothpaste and wearing a new blouse, he grabbed his pack and took off. After following the stream to a pool, he stripped and took a real bath.

Half an hour later he rejoined her in a clean T-shirt

and jeans, and found her inside her bag, reading a book with the flashlight. She'd braided her hair. It lay over her shoulder like a shiny pelt, just begging him to undo it. The woman had no idea what she did to him.

Darkness had crept over the forest, sealing them inside. All that was left to do was tuck them in for a summer's night he could wish would go on forever.

He lay down on top of his bag and turned to her. "What are you reading?"

"*The Memphremegog Massacre.* It's about a gruesome murder that takes place in a monastery. But after a day like today, I can't seem to get into it." She put the book down and turned off the light. "You were gone for a while. Any news from home?"

"Yes. My father left a message."

"Problems?" she asked a trifle anxiously

"No. Demi seems to be doing fine."

"Oh, thank goodness. Did you talk to him?"

"No. I took your advice and didn't call him back. I'm on vacation with the first woman I've ever taken on a trip and want to enjoy it."

After a silence, "Are you? Enjoying it I mean?"

"What if I told you that despite everything, I've never been happier?"

"*Nik—*"

"What about you? Are you having a good time?"

He heard her bag rustle. The next thing he knew she wrapped her arm around his neck and kissed him on the lips. "Despite everything, I'm in heaven." She kissed him again all over his face, brows, eyes and nose, as if she really meant it. "I've decided I've been in a dream all this time because no man could be as wonderful as you. Goodnight."

"Don't go to sleep yet," he begged after she let go of him and moved back to her bag. "I need to talk to you."

Something in his voice must have alerted her he was serious because she lifted her head to look at him. "What is it?"

"After you've been so open and honest with me I want you to know the truth about me. Before I was released from the hospital after my climbing accident, the doctor told me I would never be able to give a woman a child."

A minute must have passed, then, "Oh, Nik—" Tears immediately filled her eyes. "If anyone understands what that news did to you, I do. It explains so much," she cried.

He kissed her sensuous mouth. "My injuries were such that I had impaired sperm production. In a flash, any dreams I had of generating my own offspring died. Like you, I had time to come to grips with it.

"But there was a bad side effect. I found myself not getting into serious romantic relationships. If I gave myself to a woman who couldn't handle it, then I feared *I* wouldn't be able to handle it. In a sense I was emotionally crippled."

"I went through the same thing. You've been suffering all this time."

"Though it's true I hadn't found the woman I was looking for up to the point of my accident, the situation was changed after I was released to go home."

"Does anyone else know?"

"Only my doctor, and now you."

She tried to sit up, but he put his hands on her shoulders. "Let me finish. Out of the refiner's fire after losing my sister and her husband, you suddenly appeared in my life, loving my niece. Two miracles happened that day. Demi was found alive and there you were."

"Nik—"

"I don't want you to leave Greece."

"I know."

He jackknifed into a sitting position. "I'm being serious."

"Nik—I thought we were going to forget our cares and enjoy our vacation? You were the one who told me not to think about when it was over, and just take each day as a special gift."

"I can't stop thinking. The idea of you flying back to the States is ruining the trip for me."

A throaty laugh poured out of her. "You're impossible, do you know that?"

"But you still think I'm wonderful."

"Yes. That will never change."

Keep it up, Fran. "How do you know?"

She sighed. "I just do."

"You sound very sure."

"What's this all about? If I didn't know better, I'd think you were worried about something."

"I didn't know I was until you mentioned it."

"Then let's talk about it now."

"Maybe tomorrow."

"That's not fair!" she cried. "So what's going to happen tomorrow?"

"A surprise I can guarantee you'll love."

"And then you'll tell me after?"

"We'll see."

"Will this surprise be hard on the knees?"

He chuckled. "You won't have to lift a finger, let alone a foot."

"Really?"

"Trust me."

"We're going to lie on a beach all day."

"That'll come the next day."

"How about a hint?"

He inched closer to play with her hair. "It has to do with one of your obsessions."

"I don't have any."

"Yes, you do. They come with your spirit of adventure. But now I find I don't want to talk anymore. It's my turn to kiss *you* goodnight."

"I don't think I could handle that right now."

"Good. I like you best when you're a little off kilter. Give me your mouth, Francesca. With or without your capitulation, I need to taste it again."

Her back was still to him as he began kissing her neck, working his way around until he was on the other side of her. He tangled his legs with hers, crushing her to him the way he'd been longing to do. Her mouth seduced him, thrilled him beyond belief. After thirty-four years it was happening.

"I don't think you have any idea what you're doing to me," he murmured feverishly, "but I never want you to stop."

Fran's body gave a voluptuous shudder. "I don't want to stop either. I love the way you make me feel, but this is all happening way too fast and we can't always have what we want."

"Give me one good reason why."

"Because I'll be leaving Greece shortly. I don't want to be in so much pain I can't function after I get home. I don't know about other women, but I'm not able to have a romantic fling and then move on to the next one without giving it a thought.

"You and I met under the most unique of circumstances. I'll never forget you and I'll cherish every moment we've had together, but this isn't right. I take full blame for everything. Your Angelis charm worked its magic on me, but now you have to help me be strong."

Shaken by her words, Nik raised up. "Will you at least agree to see what I've planned for tomorrow before we fly back to Athens?"

"Of course."

Afraid if he kissed her again, he wouldn't be able to stop, he moved as far away as he could. Without her in his arms, the night was going to be endless.

The helicopter was waiting for them in Pironia. With Nik's assistance, Fran climbed on board, having eaten a substantial breakfast at the refuge before their final descent. The sun was already hot, portending one of the sunny days for which Greece was famous this time of year.

She felt the pilot's gaze on her as she took a seat behind him and strapped herself in. He was attractive and wore a wedding ring. Because of Nik's remarks last night she was more aware of him, of everything.

Nik handed her the field glasses. "We're going sightseeing. You'll want those." As soon as he'd fastened himself in the copilot's seat, the rotors whipped the air and they lifted off.

Her stomach lurched. She was okay in the air, but feared she could never get used to the takeoffs and landings. Then she chastised herself for thinking the thought

because she'd probably never travel in a helicopter again
once she left Athens for home.

Home. Strange how it sounded so remote. Her Grecian adventure with Kellie had turned out to be so much
more, she felt as if she'd become a part of the landscape. It seemed as though her world started and ended
with him and little Demi. What would life be like when
there was no more Nik and that sweet little girl? She
couldn't bear to think about it. Couldn't wait to see her
and hold her again.

When they'd been flying for a while she leaned forward to ask him a question. "Where are we going? Is
it still a secret?"

He turned on the speaker. "We're coming up on a
long peninsula on your left. The whole thing is called
Mount Athos."

"You're kidding! I mean, you're really taking us
there? But women aren't allowed!"

"True, but since you're dying to see it, I'll show it to
you from the air."

"Oh, Nik—this is the most exciting thing that's ever
happened to me!"

The two men smiled at her enthusiasm, but she didn't
care.

"The place is a national treasure, but you already
know that after reading about it. Still, to see it like this
will give you a greater understanding of why it's called
the Holy Mountain. I think it's one of the most beautiful places on earth."

"Have you spent time here?"

"When I turned eighteen, my father brought me and
my brothers. To me, it was like a fantasy. The various
monasteries dot the landscape. As you will see, some

of them are as enormous as castles. My favorite is the Monastery of Saint Docheiariouthe, situated right on the Aegean. The beach is pristine because the monks don't often swim."

"I'm envious of your experience."

"It was something I'll never forget. We walked everywhere, discovering caves that still house religious hermits. Do you know some of the churches have more gold than many countries keep in their vaults? The beauty of their architecture and the icons are something to behold."

"Are the monks all Greek?"

"No. They come from every country in the Orthodox world and even some from non-orthodox countries. You'll notice gardens tended with meticulous care. There's a spiritual atmosphere to the whole place."

"Mountains seem to have that essence, even without monasteries. I felt it yesterday on top of Mount Olympus. During your travels, did you ever climb Mount Sinai?"

"Not yet. Maybe one day. I hear it has monasteries, too."

Her heart ached at the thought of him going there without her.

The pilot dipped down so she could get a bird's-eye view. For the next twenty minutes she feasted her eyes on the marvels passing beneath them. She knew her oohs and aahs amused the men, but she couldn't hold back. The sights were incredible. Nik pointed out his favorite monastery.

"I can see why. The setting against the water is indescribably beautiful." He loved the water.

"If you've had enough, we'll head for Thessalonika."

"I don't think you could ever get enough of this place. Thank you so much for this privilege. Thank you for flying us here in perfect safety, Keiko. I'm in awe of your expertise."

"He's the best at what he does," Nik interjected, while the pilot just smiled.

Before long they landed at the airport's helipad where a dashing black sports car was waiting. Nik walked her over and helped her inside. "I asked my driver to bring my favorite car here so we could drive it back to Athens at our leisure. Keiko will fly our camping gear back." After stowing their packs, he got behind the wheel.

In the next moment he put a hand on her thigh, squeezing gently. It caused her to gasp. "Since the car is carrying precious cargo, I promise I'll keep the speed down."

"How fast can it go?"

"One hundred and ninety-nine miles per hour." After a pause he said, "If you'd rather I rented a car, I'll do it. The decision is yours."

She saw the heightened excitement in his dark eyes and wouldn't have deprived him of this for the world. Besides, she'd never been in a sports car. With Nik, everything was a first, but he didn't need things to add to his remarkable persona. The man himself was the most captivating male on the planet and had a stranglehold on her.

"Well now, darlin'," she drawled with an exaggerated Texas accent. "Why don't y'all show me what a famous race-car driver you really are?"

An explosion of laughter resounded in the car.

She'd said the magic words. He was in his element, and she'd given him permission to enjoy himself. That was one of the things she loved about him. Nik considered her feelings before he did anything. The fact that he always put her first put him in a special class of human beings.

He wasn't a show-off in any sense of the word, which was the reason why she wanted to see him discard his cares and have fun. A second later they wound around to the main road. After the coast was clear, they literally flew down the highway. He flashed her a smile that said he didn't have a worry in the world. It was wonderful to see him this happy after the pain he'd just lived through.

The man seemed to be in heaven, driving with the expertise of any race-car driver she'd ever watched on TV. He infected her with his excitement.

Eventually he had to come to a stop at the intersection for the next town. She turned in his direction. "I'm convinced you could have made it big in the racing world."

Nik eyed her back. "I was tempted, but some newer thrill came along."

"You're like me, always wanting to see what's around the next corner in case I missed out."

"That describes us, Fran. Since you mentioned Mount Sinai, how would you like to climb it with me?"

She blinked. "You mean before I fly home?"

"Why not? Neither of us has ever been there. It'll be a first-time adventure we can experience together."

Fran shook her head. "I couldn't take advantage of you or your generosity like that."

"I think you're afraid I'll take advantage of *you*, so I'll make you a promise. Earlier you asked if we could just be friends and finish our hike to the top of Mount Olympus. I was too frustrated at the time to reassure you. But if you'll give me a second chance, I'd like to spend more time with you. We'll travel there as two friends, nothing more."

Oh, Nik...

"Being with you has made me forget my troubles for a while. I love this feeling of freedom. You're easy to talk to, easy to be with when we don't talk. I'm enjoying your companionship. Can you honestly tell me you don't feel the same way?"

He already knew the answer to that question. How could she say no to him when she knew in her heart he was being totally sincere with her? Since coming away with him, she'd seen and felt how the years had fallen away from him. She'd been given a glimpse of the younger, responsibility-free Nik who had existed before his mountain-climbing accident. With him she felt carefree, too.

They *were* good together. Good for each other. They'd confided in each other and she felt she could trust him. After what she'd told him about trust the other night, that was saying a lot.

"Tell you what. You've convinced me to live dangerously for a little longer."

For an answer, the car shot ahead, leaving her dizzy and reeling. It took zipping along for ten minutes before she could speak. "I hate to tell you this, but you're running high on adrenaline right now."

"But you don't mind," he said with a confidence that seemed part of him.

"No." *I don't mind.* She turned her head to look out the passenger window. Her heart was palpitating so hard in her throat, she couldn't make a sound.

They drove on to the next village where he turned

off the road into the parking lot of a café. After shutting down the motor, he undid his seat belt and turned to her. "I'm going to run inside and get us some food we can eat in the car. Now that we have new plans, I can't get us back to Athens fast enough. You like lamb?"

"I adore it." Her response corresponded with the vibrating sound of his cell phone. "Are you going to answer it?"

He checked the caller ID. "It's from Sandro. That's odd."

"Maybe you'd better get it."

He flashed her another heartstopping smile. "Is that *Mrs. Atlas* talking now?" he teased.

Her soft laughter filled the car as he pulled the phone from his pocket. It was a text message. In the subject line Sandro had put *Emergency.* Nik clicked on to read the message.

Demi started a fever during the night and cries incessantly. Mother hasn't been able to get it down and called the doctor. He told her to bring her to the hospital in Mykonos. We're here now. We don't know if she's come down with a cold, or if she's still suffering from her trauma. She won't eat or drink. I promised Mother I'd keep you informed. She wants everyone here.

Nik pressed Reply.

I'm in my car approximately 160 miles from Mykonos. Should be there within two hours. Have a helicopter standing by at the dock for me. Make sure my driver is there to take care of my car. Keep me posted.

Fran stared at him after he'd pocketed his phone. "Something serious has put those frown lines on your face. Tell me what's wrong."

"Your instincts were right. Demi's back in the hospital."

"Oh, no—" Tears sprang from her eyes. "Not that little darling—"

"She's feverish and won't settle down. I'm afraid Mother's falling apart. Wait here for me. I'll be right back with the food. Sandro will keep us informed if she gets worse."

Fran watched his long, powerful legs eat up the distance and disappear inside. She feared any plans he'd had to take her to Mount Sinai would have to be put on permanent hold. Neither of them could think with little Demi in the hospital again.

Nik was back before she knew it. "I'm glad we're in this car. We ought to make it to the port under two hours. The helicopter will ferry us to the hospital."

She opened the sacks and they helped themselves to food and drink. "Your brothers told me Melina had never had other people tend Demi, so I'm not surprised she's having trouble. Of course she's comfortable around your family, but it was her parents she was bonded to. Obviously this transition is going to take more time than I thought."

"I agree. When we get to the hospital, I'm going to follow through and call a child psychiatrist for consultation. I want another opinion besides the pediatrician's. And there's another possibility. Maybe she has internal injuries like I received on my climb of Everest. Land-ing on her back like that could have damaged a vital organ and she's in pain."

"Just remember she was all right when you took her home."

"Sometimes internal injuries show up later."

"If that's true, then the doctor will find out. She's going to be all right, Nik. That child survived a tornado. She'll survive this. You're all doing everything possible for her."

He grimaced. "What if it's not enough? If our family lost her…"

She touched his arm. "Don't even think it!" But deep inside, Fran was worried about it, too. She adored that baby. This was new territory for all of them. His love for his niece had never been more evident. "I wish I could help you."

"You already have simply by being with me." He grasped her hand, twining his fingers through hers while he drove with his left. But soon he had to let her go to answer another text. They kept coming, feeding them information until they reached the helipad near the ferries.

Nik's driver jumped down and hurried around to the driver's seat while they climbed in the helicopter once more. Nik stowed their backpacks onboard. "We're flying to the hospital in Mykonos."

She sat in her usual spot and buckled up. Her emotions were so up and down, she was hardly cognizant of the takeoff. Fran found herself repeating a new mantra. *Demi can't have anything seriously wrong with her. She just can't.*

It seemed to take forever to reach the island. The pilot set them down on the pad outside the E.R. area of the hospital in the town of Mykonos. Nik helped Fran out, then gathered their backpacks before hurrying inside with her.

"Cosimo said they've got her in a bigger private room for the moment to accommodate the family. It's down this wing."

The second they opened the door, their family descended on Nik as though he was their savior. He was the force they gravitated to because he had that intangible aura that made everyone feel better.

Fran felt terrible she'd said anything to take him away from them. Yet, on the other hand, she'd seen him freed of responsibility for a few days, and he'd become a different man who'd been revitalized.

He turned to Fran. After the others greeted her, he led her over to the crib. Demi lay on her side. An IV had been inserted in her foot. She looked and felt feverish.

"Evidently she's been like this all day," Nik whispered. "Her temp is still too high."

Fran looked at his mother. She was an elegant woman with silvery wings overlaying her short black hair. "Have they done all the tests on her?"

Mrs. Angelis nodded, clutching the railing of the crib. "They can't find anything wrong. The doctor's perplexed."

"Is she asleep?"

"No, but they gave her something to help her rest in order to bring the fever down."

Nik put an arm around his mother's shoulders. "She has to be missing Melina."

His mother's eyes filled with tears. "She was the best mother in the world. It's wicked that she was taken away from us. I feel so helpless. My dearest little Demitra."

"She'll get past this, Mrs. Angelis," Fran assured her, but deep down she was weeping inside to see Demi lying there, limp. It reminded her of the way she'd found her in the bushes. "Homesickness can bring on all her symptoms, but it won't last forever," she said, if only to try and convince herself.

Nik's father, whose salt-and-pepper hair was thinning on top, had come to stand on the other side of the crib. "Of course it won't."

Unable to resist, Fran leaned down and smoothed the black curls with her fingers. "Demi, sweetheart? It's Fran. What's the matter?"

Nik slid his arm around her waist. "Sing to her. Maybe your voice will rouse her."

Fran tried several lullabies, but there was no response. She thought her heart would break and started with another one. All of a sudden Demi's eyes opened and she looked up at Fran. Then she made whimpering sounds and stretched an arm out.

There was a hushed silence in the room. All eyes were on the drastic change in the baby.

"Go ahead and pick her up," Nik murmured.

At his urging, Fran bent over and gathered the baby in her arms. "Well, hi, little sweetheart. Did you just wake up?" She had to be careful because the IV was still attached to her foot.

Demi snuggled in her arms. It was almost as if she was saying she'd missed Fran. The demonstration of affection was too much for Fran who hid her face in the baby's curls for a minute. She kissed her forehead and cheeks. "I've missed you, too. So has your uncle Nik."

She would have handed Demi to him, but he shook his head. "She wants you."

In the periphery she noticed his family. They appeared pretty well dumbstruck. "Let's see if she wants a bottle and will take it from you." He turned to his mother. "Did you bring one?"

"Oh— Yes. There are several in the diaper bag over there on the table."

Nik got one out and brought it to Fran. After pulling a chair over to the crib, he told her to sit and see if Demi wanted any milk.

Fran subsided in the chair and cradled the baby. "Are you hungry, you cute little thing? Would a bottle taste good?" She put the nipple in her mouth, not knowing what would happen.

Gasps of surprise escaped everyone when Demi stared up at Fran with those beautiful brown eyes and started drinking. Nik's exhausted-looking parents smiled at her with tears in their eyes. The relief on their faces spoke volumes. His brothers were so joyful, they squeezed Nik's shoulder.

Fran was tongue-tied and glanced up at Nik. "I honestly don't know why Demi responds to me."

His dark eyes were suspiciously bright. "You rescued her from the garden and were the first person to show her love when she came back to life. I don't think we need to look for any other answer than that. Do you?" He stared first at her, then around at his family.

His father wiped the wetness off his cheeks. "Our only problem now, *Kyria* Myers, is to convince you to stay with us a while until Demi feels comfortable again with everyone."

"She went downhill after you and Nik left the island," his mother volunteered. "Please stay." Her heart was in her voice.

Conflicted by her fear of what was happening here, Fran couldn't look at them.

"What do you say?" Nik was still leaving it up to her. She loved him for that.

CHAPTER EIGHT

"OF COURSE I'LL STAY."

As if Fran needed to be convinced...

Demi had caught at her heart the second she'd seen her lying in the bushes. She might be Nik's flesh and blood, but Fran loved her, too. "It'll be no penance to help out."

He squeezed her shoulder, filling her with a new kind of warmth. "I'll tell the doctor. As soon as he releases her, we'll all drive home together." Near her ear he whispered, "We'll do the Sinai climb later."

No. They wouldn't. But it was a beautiful thought she'd cherish forever.

Within fifteen minutes they were able to leave the hospital. It was decided Fran would be wheeled outside holding Demi so there was no chance the baby would revert back to hysterics.

The family had come in two cars. Nik helped her into the back of his parents' car before sliding in next to her. His brothers followed in one of their cars. The whole scene was so surreal, Fran had to pinch herself.

Anyone seeing her would think she was a new mother, except that Demi was too big and her coloring was the opposite of Fran's. Still, she imagined this was how a new mother felt taking her baby home for the first time. How she wished Demi were really hers! Babies were miracles, and this one happened to be the miracle baby everyone in Greece was talking about.

When they reached the villa, Nik carried their backpacks to the suite where she'd stayed before. "Let's bathe her."

"I was just going to suggest it."

They worked in harmony. He got everything out she would need to bathe the baby in the tub. Nik filled it. Together they washed her hair and played with her. Demi loved it and kicked her legs.

"That's it, Demi. Kick harder." With his encouragement, she splashed water in her face, but she didn't cry. They both burst into laughter.

"Aren't you a brave girl!"

After wrapping her up in a towel, Nik carried her into the bedroom and laid her down on the bed. Fran sprinkled some powder, then put on her diaper and a summery sleeper. Nik dried her hair and brushed the curls.

"It's time to take her temperature. I'll get the thermometer." Fran hurried over to the dresser. "Here—" She handed it to Nik.

"This isn't going to hurt, Demi." Fran held her breath while he checked it. A few more seconds and he glanced up. "Ninety-nine degrees."

"Wonderful! You're almost back to normal." She kissed the baby's tummy, producing gurgle-like laughter.

"Let's take her out to the patio. When everyone sees how happy she is, they'll all stop worrying and get a good night's sleep." Nik picked Demi up and they walked through the villa and out the doors. Twilight was upon them, the mystical time of evening that gave the island a special glow.

This time the family didn't reach for Demi. They let Nik take charge. He sat down on the swing holding the baby on his lap and patted the spot next to him for Fran. "Her temperature is down. She's had her bath and is ready for bed. You'll be glad to know Fran has agreed to stay here for a few days to help out. Hopefully it won't take long for life to get back to a new normal."

"Demitra isn't the same baby we drove to the hospital this morning," his mother remarked. She eyed Fran. "It's absolutely uncanny how she responds to you. We're thankful you didn't leave Athens yet."

Fran felt it incumbent to explain. "Before the tornado touched down, Kellie and I were on our way to hike Mount Olympus."

"Ah—you like to climb? So does our Nikolos."

"I found that out. Since Kellie wasn't well, he took me to the top. And this morning we flew in the helicopter over Mount Athos."

"An intriguing place," Nik's father interjected.

"For you men," Fran teased. Everyone chuckled.

Nik flicked her a glance with the private message that he looked forward to their climb of Sinai. She got a fluttery sensation in her chest.

"We were up early and then had a long drive back. If you'll forgive us, we're going to put Demi down and we'll see you in the morning."

His father nodded, but Fran saw the speculative gleam in his eyes as they got up to leave. Their family knew Nik never spent this much time with a woman. She could tell his brothers were equally curious about what was going on, though they made no comment. They'd be even more surprised if they learned she and Nik had been on the verge of flying to Egypt.

"Nik? I can tell your parents want to talk to you. Why don't you let me take over from here and give her a bottle?" She drew the baby out of his arms.

"Don't count on me being long."

"Take all the time you need."

Fran was glad to escape to her suite. She disappeared down the hall to the nursery and sat in the chair next to the bed to feed Demi a bottle. Once she'd sung a few songs, the baby fell asleep much faster than Fran would have thought. Maybe there was still a little of the sedative in her system. Between that and her exhaustion, she'd no doubt sleep through the night.

Fran tiptoed out of the nursery and checked her own phone. She found two text messages. One from her mom who wondered how she was doing. Fran hadn't had a chance to tell her anything yet. The other one came from Kellie.

I've been trying to reach you for two days. What's going on? Why haven't you phoned?

Fran checked her watch. It would still be early afternoon in Philadelphia. While she waited for Nik to come, she decided to phone her friend.

"Kellie?"

"Thank goodness it's you, Fran. I was beginning to worry."

"I'm sorry. So much has happened since you left Athens, I hardly know where to start. But before I talk about me, I have to know how you're doing. By now your aunt and uncle have been told everything."

"Yes, and they're being so wonderful to me." Fran heard tears in her voice.

"What about Leandros? Is he still there?"

"No. I told him to leave, but I promised to call him when I was ready to talk. He finally gave up and flew back to Athens."

Fran sank down on the side of the bed. She was sick for both of them. "Are you feeling all right physically? No more fainting spells?"

"No. My aunt says she's going to fatten me up."

"You *have* lost a few pounds since Easter."

"Enough about me. How soon are you coming home?"

Fran took a deep breath. "Not for a while."

"How come?"

Her hand tightened on the phone. "The baby was in the hospital again with a high fever."

"You're not serious."

"I wish I weren't. She's missing her parents and the family has been at their wit's end."

"Does Demi still reach out to you?"

Fran wasn't about to lie to her. "I'm afraid so. Their family is really hurt by it. None of us can figure it out. Since we brought her back to the villa, her temp is already down. It's uncanny."

"Has Nik—"

"No, Kellie," Fran broke in, reading her thoughts. "He's never mentioned the word *nanny* again. Tomorrow he's going to consult with a psychiatrist to find out what could be going on with Demi. I've promised to stay that long."

"Oh, Fran... Why didn't you come home on the flight Leandros arranged for you?"

Good question. "Because Nik volunteered to take me up on the top of Mount Olympus before I went home."

After a pregnant silence, "Did you go?"

"Yes. On the descent he got a call that Demi was back in the hospital." A little lie that could be forgiven.

"She's his number one priority. I was there before, during and after the funeral. It's clear he put Melina on a pedestal and would do anything for her. I learned he was instrumental in getting her and Stavros together. Did you know Nik was in a bad mountain-climbing accident?"

"He told me."

"Did he also tell you Melina took it upon herself to be at his bedside both in and out of the hospital? Her devotion to him was praised at the funeral."

Fran's eyes closed tightly. She didn't know that.

"If you stay any longer, you'll end up taking care of the baby. It's his way of paying back Melina."

Fran didn't believe Nik had a hidden agenda, not after the rapturous few days together when they'd both opened up their hearts. But she couldn't dismiss the nagging possibility Kellie was right in one regard. Fran was still in Greece of her own free will with no date set to go home yet. Demi's tug on her was growing stronger. *So was Nik's.*

"Are you still there? Are you listening?"

"Yes." She'd been listening to Kellie spill out her broken heart since coming to Greece. Her friend's agony went fathoms deep and colored her thoughts where Fran's relationship with Nik was concerned.

"Remember that old cliché about blood being thicker

than water? It happens to be true. Believe me, I know. After marrying Leandros, I have proof."

In Kellie's mind, Karmela had turned her marriage into a threesome. Maybe there was some truth in it, but Fran knew there had to be a lot more going on. Kellie had a hard time talking about her deepest fears. Fran doubted she'd talked to Leandros about them.

"Do you hear what I'm saying, Fran?"

"Yes." She would have said more, but she heard a noise. Nik had entered the bedroom and shut the door. Turning her back to him she said, "Forgive me, Kellie, but something has come up and I'll have to call you later. I promise."

She hung up and turned around. "I was just returning Kellie's call."

Nik stood at the end of the bed with his hands resting on his hips in a totally male stance. "Is she all right now that she's with her aunt and uncle? She was raised by them, right?"

"Yes. Physically she's fine, but emotionally, I've never seen her so completely devastated. Leandros is back in Athens."

He rubbed his chest absently. "I'm sorry to hear that, especially when it appears her pain has rubbed off on you."

Fran was gutted by her conversation with Kellie. "I have to admit I'm worried about them."

"I'm sorry. Under the circumstances I'll say goodnight and see you in the morning. After breakfast we'll take Demi out in the sailboat. She loves it. Hopefully while we're enjoying ourselves, the doctor will get back to me with some ideas, and we'll go from there."

"I'd like that. Good night, Nik."

Much to her chagrin she wanted him to grab her and kiss her senseless, but he was a man of his word and made no move toward her. Instead, he tiptoed into the nursery. She watched from the doorway as he leaned over the crib to touch Demi's hair. The sweet moment moved her to tears before he came back out.

His eyes looked like glistening black pools in the semidarkness. "*Kalinitha*, Fran."

A light breeze filled the sail. With the surface of the blue Aegean shimmering like diamonds, Fran felt she'd come close to heaven. "Where are we headed, Nik?"

He manned the rudder with the same expertise he did everything else. In bathing trunks and a T-shirt that revealed his hard-muscled body, he looked spectacular.

"Delos. It's that tiny, barren island you can see from here, only three miles away. The Ionians colonized it in 1000 BC and made it their religious capital. There's a specific reason I'm taking us there."

Fran had been holding Demi since they'd climbed onboard. They were both dressed in sun suits and hats. Fran wore her bathing suit underneath. When it got too hot, she'd take the baby below for a nap. "Is there a statue of Atlas? If so, I want to take a picture."

He grinned, dissolving her insides. "Sorry to disappoint you. He resides far away in North Africa."

"Of course. The Atlas Mountains. I'd forgotten. That explains your affinity for them."

"Maybe," he teased. "I'm afraid Delos is the birthplace of Apollo and Artemis, but that's not what's so interesting."

She kissed Demi's cheek. "We're all ears, aren't we, sweetheart?"

"At one point, the island was so sacred, no one was allowed to be born there or die there."

"You're kidding!"

"Those who were about to leave this world, or get ushered in, were rushed off to the nearby islet of Rinia."

She laughed. "Sometimes you just can't stop either one from happening."

"Somehow they managed."

"Sounds like shades of the rules on Mount Athos."

"I was waiting for you to make that connection. At least here on Delos, males and females can go ashore and walk around the ancient ruins."

"What about children? Are they permitted?"

"Yes, but Demi will have to wait until she's six or seven. This afternoon we'll just circle the island. While all the other tourists from Mykonos scramble around, we'll be able to sit back and see many of the remains from the deck."

"It's a glorious day out for sightseeing."

"With this light breeze, my favorite kind."

She felt his gaze linger on her, overheating her in a hurry. "What's the name of your boat? I can't read Greek."

"The *Phorcys*."

"A mythological creature?"

"To be sure. I was raised on the myths. When I was a boy I made up my mind that when I was old enough to buy my own boat, I'd name it for the ancient sea god who presides over the hidden dangers of the deep."

"That sounds exactly like something the protective Atlas would do."

Laughter rumbled out of his chest.

"Does he look like you?"

"Tell you what. One day I'll bring you to Delos alone." *Don't say things like that, Nik. In a few days I'll fly home and never come back here again.* "We'll walk up to the highest point on the island where I'll show you an ancient mosaic of him. He's a gray-haired, fish-tailed god with spiky crab-like skin and forelegs who carries a torch."

"Oh dear. He must have done an excellent job of keeping everyone away." They were getting closer to the island now.

"He did better than that," Nik quipped. "With his wife, Ceto, they created a host of monstrous children collectively known as the Phorcydes."

"That's terrible! How sad they never had a child as beautiful as Demi." Fran shifted the baby to her shoulder and hugged her. "If the gods did exist, they'd be jealous of Melina's daughter. Even without them, she'll need to be guarded well."

And Nik would see to that.

She lifted the binoculars he'd given her to examine the various archaeological sites studded with temples and pillars. Demi reached out to touch them, of course. The action pulled off Fran's hat, which in turn pulled her hair loose from its knot. "You little monkey." She kissed her cheeks and neck, giving up on the binoculars for the moment.

For the next hour they slowly circled the island, but most of the time Fran simply played with the baby who stood up with her help and bounced when Nik talked to her. The baby babbled a lot, causing both of them to laugh.

"She's happy and says she wants to go ashore."

"I know you do, *Demitza*, but you can't have everything you want." Fran loved the way he talked to her.

"I think it's getting too hot for her, Nik. I'd better take her below."

"Go ahead while I drop anchor in this little cove, then I'll join you and we'll have an early dinner."

Fran carried Demi down the steps to the bedroom and changed her diaper. Once she'd put her in a little stretchy suit, she walked her into the galley to feed her. Nik had brought her swing along. It worked as a high chair.

"I bet you're thirsty. I'll fix you a bottle of water first." The baby drank some eagerly. "What would my little princess like for lunch? How about lamb and peaches?"

She grabbed some bottled water for herself and sat down to feed Demi. After a minute Nik appeared. With his olive skin, it didn't take much exposure from the sun to turn him into a bronzed god.

"There's nothing wrong with her appetite," he observed, reaching for a water, too. He sat down next to the baby and watched the two of them. In such close quarters, Fran could hardly breathe because of his nearness. She felt his warmth and smelled the soap he'd used in the shower earlier.

"If you want to finish feeding her, I'll get the food out of the fridge." Anything to keep busy so she wouldn't concentrate on him to the exclusion of all else.

Demi obviously adored Nik and thrived on his attention. Between his smiles and laughter, she couldn't help but be charmed by her uncle. Nik would make a wonderful father one day. Demi was lucky to have him in her life. Just how lucky, she had no idea.

Fran put their meal on the table—salad and rolls, fresh fruit, pastries and juice. A feast.

"This is delicious." She smiled at him. "I see there's nothing wrong with your appetite either." He'd eaten everything in sight.

"That's because you're with Demi and me. We thrive under the right conditions."

"If you'll notice, I ate all my food, too," she admitted.

He flashed her a penetrating glance. "I noticed." After wiping the corner of his mouth with a napkin, he got up from the table. "Come on, little one. It's time to sleep." He picked up the swing with her in it and carried it into the bedroom.

Fran followed with a bottle of formula. Once he'd turned on the mechanism that started it swinging, she handed her the bottle. Demi looked up at them and smiled the sweetest smile Fran had ever seen before she started drinking.

Nik moved Fran over to the bed a few feet away. "We'll have to stay here until she goes to sleep, so we might as well make ourselves comfortable."

She lay down on her side, facing the baby. Nik moved behind her and put his arm around her waist. His sigh filtered through her hair splayed over the pillow. "This is what I call heaven."

They stayed that way without moving. Fran was so content in his arms, and the sound of the swing had a hypnotizing effect on her. When she looked at Demi, the little darling had fallen asleep.

Fran suspected the gentle rocking of the boat had put Nik to sleep, too. But in that regard she was mistaken. In an unexpected motion he rolled her over so she was half lying on him. "Sh-h," he said against her lips before his hungry mouth covered them in a long, languid kiss that went on and on, setting her on fire.

Her need of him was so all-consuming, she couldn't hold back her desire. For a time she felt transported.

"I know I promised I'd treat you like a friend," he whispered in a husky voice, "but it won't work. I can't stop what I'm feeling." He was actually trembling. "I've never wanted any woman in my life the way I want you." His fingers tightened in her hair. "Before I forget all my good intentions, you'd better hurry up on deck while you can. I'm giving you this one chance before all bets are off for good."

Something in his ragged tone told her he meant what he said. If she stayed here a second longer, there'd be no going back and it would be her fault, not his. It shocked her that he had more control than she did.

But when she finally found the strength to move off the bed and get to her feet, she heard him groan. It almost sent her back into his arms until she saw Demi lying there in the swing. Fran's gaze took in both of them.

Neither of them will ever be yours. Go upstairs now, Fran.

She didn't remember her feet touching the ground. When she reached the deck, she threw off her sundress and dove into the water. It was late afternoon now, when the sun was its warmest near the shore. Delightful. But the wonder of it was wasted on Fran who swam around while she struggled with the war going on inside of her.

Should she engage in one mad moment of passion at the age of twenty-eight, then have to live out the rest of her life tortured by the memory? Or should she do the smart thing and avoid the fire? It meant she'd never know joy. Either option was untenable. Thank goodness for the water that hid her tears.

When she finally started back to the boat, she discovered Nik on deck holding Demi. She swam over to the side. "Demi?" she called out and waved her arm. "Can you see me?"

"She's squirming to jump in with you."

A different man had emerged from the bedroom. This one was calm and collected, her urbane host until she left Greece. She died inside, knowing the other one wouldn't make a second appearance. As he'd said, he'd give her one chance. Fran hadn't taken it in order to avoid sabotaging her own happiness. Now she had to pay the consequences.

"The water's wonderful. I'll come onboard so you can cool off."

Nik would never cool off. He'd come down with a fever when he'd first met Fran. With each passing day it had climbed higher until he was burning up. He'd already taken a big swim that morning in cooler water before anyone was up. It had done nothing to bring down his temperature. There was only one antidote, but the thought of it not working terrified him.

Afraid to touch her, he let her climb onboard by herself. She put on her sundress over her yellow bikini. Her movements were quick, but not quick enough. At the sight of her beautiful body, he practically had a heart attack. With Demi in her swing, he could unfurl the sail and raise the anchor.

She hunkered down next to the baby and kissed her, then looked in his direction. "Don't you want to swim?"

"Maybe tonight. I'd prefer to take advantage of the

evening breeze on the way back. Mother will be missing Demi by now."

"Of course. How long did she sleep?"

"Until five minutes ago."

"She doesn't act like she's hungry yet. I think I'll hold her for a while."

Fran couldn't keep her hands off the baby. She walked her over to the bench and sat down with her, giving her kisses on her tummy that made Demi laugh. While she was preoccupied, Nik set sail for Mykonos and guided them toward the villa. By seven-thirty, he brought the boat around and it glided gently to the dock.

In a few minutes he helped her out of the boat with Demi and followed with the swing. No one was on the patio yet. That was good. At the top of the steps he put the swing down and they entered the villa without passing any family members who might pick up on the tension between them.

"I'll start Demi's bath," Fran called over her shoulder. "When she's dressed, you can take her to your mother."

"Good. I'll pick out an outfit." He opened the cupboard and reached for a sundress. In the drawer he found some white stockings and little matching shoes. He put everything on the bed. When he peered in the bathroom, Fran had just finished washing the baby's hair.

She looked up. "Demi's such an easy baby, she's a joy."

"She has Melina's nature."

When Fran lifted the baby from the water, he grabbed a towel and wrapped her in it before carrying her into the bedroom. For just a moment it hit him that his sister really was gone. Tears stung his eyelids. He hugged the baby to him while he fought to regain his composure.

"It's all right to cry, Nik," Fran murmured gently. "Even Atlas has do it once in a while. The problem is, emotion catches up with you when you least expect it. I know what that's like. Even if it's a horrible adage, the pain will ease with time."

He lifted his head. "I'll keep that in mind." Nik lay the baby on the bed and dried her hair.

"Oh—what a darling outfit!"

"I bought it for her several months ago, but it was too big at the time."

"Now it's the perfect size! With her skin she'd look beautiful in any color, but I dare say peppermint pink trumps them all." She held it up in front of Demi. "Don't you love it, sweetheart? Your uncle picked this one out especially for you."

The baby got all excited and touched the hem. Warmed by Demi's reaction, Nik's crushing sense of loss faded. He got busy powdering and diapering her. Fran's eyes shimmered a violet blue as she handed the dress to him. "You do the honors."

"When I bought this, I never dreamed I'd be the one putting it on her." His fingers fumbled with the two buttons in the back. Fran helped the baby to sit up so he could fasten it. Then she put the stockings and shoes on her tiny feet.

"One more minute while we comb her hair." Fran dashed over to the dresser for it. "She has a head of natural curl. What a lucky girl." Nik watched her style it to perfection. "There you go." She kissed her on both cheeks. "Now you're all ready to go see your *yiayia* and *papou*."

"How did you know those words?" She continually surprised him in wonderful ways.

"I've been listening to the children talk. In France I used to walk through the park near our school and practice my French with them. They make terrific teachers, *Kyrie* Angelis."

To hear her speak any Greek excited him no end. "I'm impressed."

"Why don't you take Demi to find your folks? I'll hurry and shower so I'll be available if you need me. But I'm hoping she had such a good time with us, she'll be able to enjoy her grandparents without me before she has to go to bed."

Nik left the room carrying Demi and found his parents in the living room talking with Stavros's parents. He'd been so focused on his own pain, he'd forgotten they mourned their son and needed Demi's love, too. Four pairs of eyes lit up when they saw their granddaughter decked out like a little princess. For the next few minutes he sat with them while the baby was passed around. Dinner was about to be served. They gravitated to the patio where the rest of the family had congregated.

He put Demi in her swing with a fresh bottle of formula and told them he'd be back. On the way to his apartment he swung by Fran's. There was something he had to say to her, and he couldn't put it off any longer.

"Fran?" He knocked on her door.

His breath caught when she opened it wearing a pair of pleated tan pants and a white blouse. Fresh from the shower, she'd fastened her damp hair at the back of her head with a clip. She'd picked up some sun and wore no makeup, except a frosted pink lipstick, because she didn't need any.

"I take it Demi's all right so far."

"I left her on the patio with the family. We'll see how she does. Before I shower and change, I need to talk to you. It's important. May I come in?"

"Of course."

He shut the door with his back and lounged against it. "What happened on the boat made me realize I can't go on this way any longer."

Fran stood a few feet away from him, rubbing her hips with her palms in a nervous gesture. "Neither can I. While I was showering I came to the decision that I have to leave in the morning, no matter what."

"I have another solution."

"There's isn't another one."

"There is, but I've hesitated to mention it because we've only known each other a week. I want you to marry me."

"Marry?"

The world spun. She turned clumsily and sank down on the side of the bed before she fell. Kellie's warning rang in her ears. *He'll do anything to get you to take care of Demi.*

"You don't want to marry me," she whispered.

"You're terrified again."

She looked away from him. The nerve palpitating at the base of her throat almost choked her. "You know the thrill will wear off."

"I've never been married, but you have. That's your bad experience talking."

"Be serious, Nik."

"I don't know how to get any more serious. I just asked you to be my wife and am waiting for an answer."

She kneaded her hands. "You're not thinking clearly. For one thing, I can't give you children."

"That goes for both of us. We'll adopt."

"That's what Rob said."

"Don't you dare compare me to your ex-husband," he ground out. "To prove it to you, we'll get the adoption papers ready in my attorney's office before the wedding ceremony. The second it's over, he'll get the process moving with the quickest speed possible."

She shook her head. "You don't know what you're saying."

"But I do because I've found the right woman for me." He cupped her face in his hands. "I'm in love with you, Francesca Myers. I can't honestly tell you when it happened, but the point is, it's finally happened to me. I believe it's happened to you, too, but you're too frightened to admit it yet."

Before she could take a breath, he lowered his head and closed his mouth over hers, giving her a kiss that was hot with desire. *A husband's kiss with the intent to possess.* When he finally let her up for air, he pressed his head to her forehead while he tangled his fingers in her hair. "I can't let you leave Greece. We belong together. You know it, and I know it."

Tears ran down her cheeks. "You say this now, but you might not always feel this way."

"I'm not Rob," he bit out. "Your ex-husband did a lot of damage to you, but he's not representative of most males I know, and certainly not of me."

She wiped away the moisture with her fingers. "You've overwhelmed me, Nik."

"Sorry, but it's the way I'm made. Up on Mount Olympus, you told me I was wonderful and you'd never change your mind about me. Was that a lie?"

A ring of white circled his lips, revealing his vulnerability. It was a revelation to her. "You know it wasn't."

"Then prove it and tell me what I want to hear."

She bit her lip. "I need to think about it, Nik."

His jaw hardened. "You still don't trust me?"

"It's not that. I can hardly trust the situation. As I told you in the tent, this is all happening too fast."

"How long did it take your father before he knew he wanted to marry your mother?"

She half laughed through her tears. "Mother rear-ended him in a parking lot at the college. When he got out of the car, pretty furious about it, she ran up to him full of apologies. He said one look in her eyes and he was a goner."

Nik kissed her lips. "My parents had a similar experience when they first met. It happens to lots of couples. Why not us?"

"But our circumstances are different. I've been married, and you haven't. You deserve to start out with a single woman who has no past. I'm a has-been."

"So am I. Don't forget my legion of women I've left in the dust."

"How could I possibly forget them?" she croaked.

He hugged her to him. "I'm madly in love with *you* and everything that formed you into who you are. That includes warts, Rob and Kellie, who won't want me for her best friend's husband."

"I'm afraid she won't while her marriage is in trouble. Oh, Nik—" She flung her arms around his neck and sobbed.

"Am I getting my answer yet?" he whispered into her hair.

She eventually lifted her head and stared at him without flinching. While she had the courage, she needed to ask him something. Her whole life's happiness depended on his answer.

"Nik— Try to be baldly honest with me because I'm going to ask you a hypothetical question."

"Go on."

"If we'd met under different circumstances and there'd been no Demi, do you think you would have asked me to marry you?"

An eerie silence crept into the room. He didn't move a muscle, but she sensed his body go rigid. Instead of the look of desire she'd always seen in his eyes when he was around her, he scrutinized her as though she were an unknown species of insect under a microscope. The longer he didn't say anything, the more fractured she felt.

"What kind of a hold does Kellie have on you that she could turn you into someone I don't know?"

"This has nothing to do with Kellie."

"The hell it doesn't." His wintry voice hit her like an arctic blast, prompting her to fold her arms to her waist. "Tell me what she said to you."

"She's been worried you'd do anything to get me to take care of Demi."

His face morphed into an expressionless mask. "I guess we'll never know if she spoke the truth or not, will we?"

Following his delivery to its ultimate conclusion, a gasp escaped her lips.

"Your advice to let my family come up with solutions has produced fruit. Ever since the funeral they've been in the process of looking for a nanny and expect to interview some candidates as early as tomorrow. For that, I thank you.

"However, you won't be among the prospects because you'll be on a plane flying out of Mykonos airport in the morning to join your best friend in the States where you came from. I hope you'll both be very happy together. Since I don't expect to see you again, I'll say goodbye now."

He was out the door so fast, she was incredulous.

What have I done?

Absolutely panicked, Fran wanted to run after him, but she didn't know where to go to find him. Doing the only thing she could do under the circumstances, she picked up the house phone. Nik had told her the housekeeper would answer.

When she did, Fran asked her if she could find either Sandro or Cosimo and tell them to come to the phone. In a few minutes, Cosimo came on the line.

Without preamble she said, "I hate to disturb you, but I—I'm afraid Nik and I just had words," she stammered. "I *have* to find him."

"I just saw him leave the villa."

Her heart plunged to her feet. "Do you know where he was going? I have to talk to him, Cosimo. It's a matter of life and death to me."

After a distinct pause he said, "He was headed for the marina. When he's stressed, he spends the night on his sailboat away from everyone, but don't tell him I told you that."

"I swear I won't. Bless you."

CHAPTER NINE

NIK RAN TO THE BEACH. After tossing his T-shirt on the sand, he plunged into the water and swam out to his boat moored on the other side of the dock. It was a good distance away, but it was the workout he needed.

He'd never been one to turn to alcohol, but he'd never been this gutted. When he reached the boat, he'd drink until he passed into forgetfulness. If the gods were kind, he wouldn't wake up.

The same stars that had lighted the sky above their tent on Mount Olympus now mocked him as he torpedoed through the water to his destination. When he rounded the pier, he heaved himself over the side of his boat.

A moonlight sail in calm seas sounded perfect. When he was far away from shore, he'd drop anchor and stretch out on the banquette with a bottle of Scotch. With the canopy of the heavens to keep him company, he'd drink himself into oblivion. Always one for adventure, who knew if it wouldn't be his last…

He went down the steps to the galley and rummaged in the cupboard till he found the bottle he was looking for. No glass was needed. Back up on top, he undid the ropes, then walked toward the outboard motor. It would take the boat beyond the buoy. If the wind didn't pick up, it didn't matter.

As he leaned over to turn it on, he thought he heard a voice call out, but the sound coincided with the noise from the motor. It was probably a gull. He put the throttle at a wakeless speed. The boat inched away from the dock. When he was young, he used to pretend he was a thief on the boat, sneaking away into the night.

That's what he felt like right now. Sneaking to a place where he could get away from the pain.

There went that cry again, stronger this time. That wasn't a bird. It was human! He cut the motor.

"Nik—"

It sounded like Fran. Was he hallucinating when he hadn't tasted a drop of Scotch yet? His head shot around behind him. He saw a form doing the breast stroke, trying to catch up.

"Wait for me!" she cried.

Galvanized into action, he slipped over the boat and swam to her. She practically collapsed in his arms while he trod water with her. "Put your head back and take deep breaths."

Her arms tightened around his neck. "I'm all right." Her lips grazed his cheek. "I was afraid you'd l-leave. I couldn't let that happen before t-talking to you first."

"Come on. Let's get you onboard and into some dry clothes. Your teeth are chattering. Let me do the work."

In no time he'd helped her up over the side. She'd plunged in the water wearing the same pants and blouse she'd had on earlier. With her hair streaming down, she looked like a shipwreck victim plucked out of the sea, albeit one more beautiful than he could begin to describe.

He gritted his teeth. "You could have broken your neck."

"But I didn't."

Nik helped her down to the galley and pushed her into the shower. "Take off everything. I'll leave a towel and robe hanging close by."

"Th-thank you."

After he'd found the desired articles for her, he went back up to weigh anchor, then he headed down to his bedroom. Luckily he kept a pair of sweats and a T-shirt onboard. He removed his swimsuit and got dressed.

While he waited for her, he made coffee for both of them. Having a sweet tooth, he added an extra amount of sugar to both mugs. She'd need it after her workout.

Right now he chose not to think about why she'd come. The fact that she'd put herself in jeopardy to catch up to him would do for starters. The rest could come after she was fully revived.

A few minutes later she appeared in the tiny kitchen in his blue toweling bathrobe. Her freshly shampooed hair had been formed into a braid. She smelled delicious. He handed her the coffee which she drank with obvious pleasure.

"Oh, that tastes good."

He lounged against the counter sipping his. "How did you know I was out here?"

"I ran after you. Cosimo saw me and volunteered to stay by Demi. I raced as fast as I could, but you move like the wind. Kind of like the way you drive your car. That was a thrill of a lifetime for me."

"I was in a hurry," he muttered.

"I know. It was all my fault. Every bit of it. Forgive me. Kellie never used to be like this, but the problems in her marriage have made her so unhappy, she doesn't see anything working out for herself, or me."

"Their situation isn't ours."

"You think I don't know that?" She put the mug down and grasped both his arms. "She jumped to all the wrong conclusions from an outsider's perspective, but she lost sight of one thing. I love you, Nik. You have no idea how much." She slid her arms around his neck. "Help me, darling. I can't reach your mouth and I need it more than I need life."

Not immune to her pleading, he picked her up and carried her to his bedroom. But after laying her down, he sat beside her. She tried to pull him down. "Nik—you have to forgive me," she implored him.

His eyes smarted. "I'm the one who needs forgiveness. I fell in love with you the moment we met, then panicked because you were leaving on a trip with Kellie. I had to think of a way to keep you in Greece so we could get to know each other. I used Demi shamefully as my excuse."

"I can't believe it!" she cried for happiness.

"On our camping trip, I was building up the courage to tell you about my medical problem when you told me about yours. After that I couldn't hold back. On our drive home, I would have asked you to marry me, but then we got that call about Demi."

"But I almost ruined everything with that awful question." She broke down in tears. "Please forgive me, Nik."

"I think I like this ending better. To watch you swim toward my boat as if your life depended on it told me I hadn't been wrong about you. I couldn't swim out to you fast enough."

Her face glistened with moisture. "Are we through talking now?"

He chuckled. "Not yet, but soon. Let's get back to the house and relieve Cosimo. He deserves a break if Demi has fallen apart again. They all do."

A half hour later, Nik grasped her hand and they tip-toed into the nursery. Cosimo had dealt with a miserable Demi until they got there. Now they were finally alone with the baby, who'd fallen asleep.

He pulled Fran close. "Since the hospital in Leminos, I've had this dream we'd get married and adopt her. I honestly believe Melina made sure she was dropped literally at your feet so you'd become her new mother. That's why Demi reached out to you."

Fran hugged him with all the strength in her. "It felt like heaven had delivered her expressly to me."

"Then let's adopt her as our own miracle daughter and give her all the love we can. Later on we'll adopt another baby and another after that."

"You're making me too happy, Nik." She sobbed against his shoulder.

"We need to get married soon so she'll become bilingual in a hurry."

"I've got to learn Greek fast! Oh—I'll have to resign from my job at the hospital."

"We'll tell my parents in the morning." He rocked her in his arms for a long time. "I'm going to enjoy seeing the look in their eyes. They're not going to believe their youngest upstart son is finally going to settle down."

"They've had to wait a long time." She laughed through the tears. "Mine won't believe it either. They're going to adore you."

"You've already got my family wrapped around your little finger."

"It's you I'm worried about. Let's go in the bedroom so we won't wake up Demi."

He pulled her into the other room before cupping her face. "I want to spend the rest of the night with you, but I'm old-fashioned and would like your father's permission to marry you before I work my wicked ways with you. My bachelor days have come to an end. You're going to be my precious wife and I want to do everything right."

"You *do* do everything right. So right, I don't know how I was ever lucky enough to have found you. Just be with me for a little while. We'll stay dressed on top of the covers," she begged.

His lips twitched. "Once I start touching you, I'll never stop. I want you to be able to tell Kellie that I didn't coerce you into marrying me."

Her eyes filled again. "I wish I'd never told you anything about our conversation."

"Hush. I'm glad you did. Now we don't have any secrets. That's the way it should be. When you think Kellie's ready, you can tell her about our mutual problem."

"She'll be mortified when she learns what happened to you on that climb."

He smoothed the hair off her forehead. "But you'll know how to comfort her. She needs a lot of that right now while her marriage is suffering. That's one of your special gifts. Now kiss me like you mean it, then let me go for tonight. Tomorrow, and all the tomorrows after that, will be a different story."

"Nik—"

CHAPTER TEN

Three weeks later...

"TIME FOR YOUR NAP, sweetheart." Demi had finished her lunch. Fran took her from the high chair and carried her through the penthouse to the bedroom they'd turned into a nursery filled with adorable baby furniture and curtains.

After changing her diaper, Fran put her down in the crib. She sang her one song. "Now be a good girl for Mommy and go to sleep. I've got a lot to do before your daddy gets home tonight."

Her watch said one-thirty. There was still the table to set in the dining area and the kitchen to clean up, not to mention making the bed and getting herself ready later. She'd bought a new black dress with spaghetti straps in the hope of wowing her new husband.

Today marked their first-week anniversary as man and wife. She was making some of Nik's favorite foods for a special dinner she wanted to be perfect. Fran had gotten the recipes from his mother and had already been on the phone with her twice to make sure she was doing the moussaka right.

The traditional recipe called for eggplant and meat

filling. "But the trick," his mother said, "is to layer in potatoes and zucchini to make it even richer before you top it with the bechamel sauce. Use heavy cream. My Nikki will love it."

Fran loved her new mother-in-law and smiled as she hurried back through the rooms to the kitchen. She hardly recognized Nik's elegant bachelor domicile anymore. The penthouse was still filled with light and open, but a family lived here now, complete with a baby. It contained the kind of clutter that turned a house into a home. She was so happy it was scary.

Today Nik had gone to the office for the first time. She'd missed him horribly.

Because of the baby, they hadn't taken an official honeymoon yet. In another month they hoped Demi would be able to handle a few days away from them, but none of it mattered. Once they'd said their vows at the chapel in Mykonos with their families looking on, they'd become insatiable lovers.

The only thing to mar the event was Kellie's absence. After she'd learned there was going to be a wedding, and had been told the true facts, she was desolate for all the things she'd said. But Nik had gotten on the phone and put her mind at ease. Just when Fran thought she couldn't love the man more, he did something to win her heart all over again.

Unfortunately, Kellie hadn't been feeling well and decided not to make the flight over.

Fran believed her, but she also knew she was afraid to come to Greece. Leandros kept an eye on her even when they were apart. He would know if she returned to attend the wedding. Fran promised to stay in close touch with her.

Nik had taken another week off in order to be home. When they weren't playing with the baby or eating, they found joy in each other's arms. Fran was existing on an entirely different level of happiness. It transcended what she'd known before.

The thought of tonight after they'd put the baby down and could concentrate on each other sent heat surging through her body. It was embarrassing how eager she was, but she loved her husband so much, she couldn't hide it if she tried.

She hurried into their bedroom barefooted to get busy and was just smoothing the duvet when she was grasped at the waist from behind and spun around.

"Nik!" she squealed in shock and joy. No one looked more gorgeous than he did, especially in his tan suit and tie. "You're not supposed to be home until tonight! You've caught me looking terrible."

His dark eyes devoured her. "Every husband should be so lucky to come home and find his wife in a pair of shorts like yours. I have to admit my T-shirt adds an allure, but I think we'll dispense with it."

"Darling," she half giggled the words as he put actions to his words and followed her down on top of the bed she'd just made.

"There's no help for you now," he growled the words into her neck. "I peeked in on Demi and she's out for the count."

"But today's your first day back."

"It was." He plundered her mouth until she was breathless. "Sandro told me I was worthless and sent me home."

"He didn't—"

Nik rolled her over so she was lying on top of him.

"No, he didn't. Actually, I sat at my desk and didn't hear a word my assistant said to me. My bros came in to eat lunch with me. When I couldn't carry on a coherent conversation with them, I knew what I had to do."

He turned her on her back once more. "Something smelled good when I walked in."

"It's my surprise dinner for you."

That heartbreaking smile broke out on his handsome face before he pulled a necklace out of his pocket. "This is a choker of gemstones the color of your eyes. It's for seven days of bliss," he murmured as he fastened it around her neck. "Happy anniversary, you beautiful creature. If a man could die from too much happiness, I'd have expired a week ago."

"I love you, Nik. I love you," she cried as rapture took over. She forgot everything until they heard Demi start to fuss much later.

Nik groaned and slowly relinquished her mouth with a smile. "We're going to have to do something about this. While I was in my office, the thought came to me that you could work with me. We'd bring in a playpen for Demi."

Laughter bubbled out of Fran. "That would be a novelty for about ten minutes before it turned into a disaster, but I love the idea of it. Maybe if your father put in two days a week, you and I would have more time together and could sail around the Aegean with our little girl. What do you think?"

He planted a long, hard kiss on her mouth. "I love the way you think. I'll call him later."

"Go ahead and do it right now. Think how happy it will make him."

Nik frowned. "What's the matter? Are you tired of me already?"

"Darling—" She leaned over him, kissing every centimeter of his face. "You know better than that. I just thought if you do this now, my Atlas will stop worrying about him. I'm afraid I'm very selfish and want all your thoughts centered on me."

"Don't you know they are?" he asked in a husky voice. "Why do you think I came home early today?"

She pressed a kiss to his lips. "Then humor me."

He groaned again. "Hand me your phone. Mine is on the floor with my clothes."

"Where they *should* be."

Laughter escaped his throat. "Whoever dreamed I'd be married to such a 'wicked' wife?"

"There's still a lot you don't know about me." With a chuckle, she took her phone from the bedside table.

As he pressed the digits, she whispered in his ear. "Tell him we need him to start work as soon as possible. I want you all to myself for as long as you can stand me. When the tornado brought Demi to me, it also brought her uncle. *It was written in the whirlwind.*"

* * * * *

HER BABY WISH

PATRICIA THAYER

To all the couples who know
the struggles and pain of infertility.
I pray you all will be blessed some day.
And a special congratulations to Michelle and Rod.

CHAPTER ONE

"I NEED you to come back home."

Trace McKane's grip tightened on the pitchfork as he spread fresh straw around Black Thunder's stall. He'd waited two long months to hear his wife say those words. The only problem was she didn't exactly sound sincere, and too many harsh words had passed between them to repair the damage so casually.

"I can't see how that's going to change anything." He continued to cover the floor as if Kira's presence hadn't affected him at all. But it had. He'd give up the family's Colorado ranch to have things back like they were before their problems started. And from the look of things lately, that might not be too far from the truth.

"Trace, please, just hear me out," she said.

He stopped his chores and finally looked at her. "Why, Kira? Haven't we said enough?" He straightened and tipped his hat back off his forehead. This was the first time he'd chanced a close up look at his wife since he'd moved out. She'd kept her distance, and so had he.

She placed her hands on her hips. "Oh, you made

your feelings perfectly clear. Things got rough so you walked out, without even trying to work things out."

"We were getting nowhere."

Kira Hyatt McKane was a natural beauty with curly wheat-blond hair that hung to her shoulders. She had an oval face, with a scattering of freckles across a straight nose and full, pouty lips. Her large brown eyes locked with his, causing his pulse to shoot into overdrive.

He wasn't going to take the bait and fight with her. "It's better I moved into the bunkhouse," he told her. He hated that they couldn't make their marriage work.

Yeah, he'd been running away. He'd spent a lot of time moving the herd to a higher pasture for the approaching summer. Many of those nights he'd slept under the stars, anything to keep from facing his lonely bunk. To keep from thinking about how he couldn't—no matter how much he loved Kira—make his marriage work.

"We both needed a breather."

God knew he'd missed her. The torture went on as his gaze moved over her navy T-shirt and the faded jeans that hugged her curves. Shapely hips and legs that he'd touched and caressed so often that he knew where every freckle was hidden. He also knew exactly where to touch to bring her pleasure.

He glanced away. Don't go there. That was past history. Their future together was bleak. He never thought he was a greedy man. He'd only wanted a traditional marriage; a wife to come home to and children to carry on the legacy of the ranch.

That had been when the trouble started, when their

marriage began to crumble and he couldn't do anything to stop it.

"Spring is a busy time," he told her. Especially this year since he had that payment due to his half brother, Jarrett. And it didn't look like there was much chance he could come up with the money.

Kira shook her head. "I know, Trace." She sighed. "And turning away from our problems doesn't help."

He cursed. "Yes, Kira, we have problems, but face it, lately we've been unable to come to terms with things. And I'm tired of beating my head against a wall." When he saw tears form in her eyes, he wanted to kick himself.

"I never meant for it to be this way."

He shrugged. The last thing he wanted was to argue. In the months before their separation that was all they'd done. Then they'd stopped talking altogether. What broke his heart was knowing he hadn't been able to give her what she needed.

"I just wanted us to be a real family," she added in a whispered voice.

"You had a funny way of showing it." He'd needed her to stand by him, and help him with his struggles with the ranch, but she was obsessed with her own problems.

Her eyes filled with tears. "There might have been a solution to help us both."

How many times had they tried? Even counseling, with some stranger listening to every way he'd failed his wife. He'd done about everything he could think of to make their marriage work. "How? More counseling?"

Kira shook her head. "I never should have asked you to go to counseling. I'm the one who's got the problem," she said, her voice husky with emotion. "I'm the one who needs to deal with things."

"As long as you feel that way, then you don't need me around."

Kira stepped closer and began to speak, but stopped. With a swallow, she tried again. "But, Trace, I do need you. I need you to stay with me another six months so I can have a baby, then you can have your divorce."

Trace glared at her. "What the hell?"

So finally she'd gotten his attention.

The first moment she'd seen Trace McKane, Kira knew for sure that he was the perfect man for her. That hadn't changed. Tall and lean, the handsome cowboy had gained his muscular build from years of working the McKane's Cattle Ranch. He had brown hair that always hung too long, brushing his shirt collar. His green-gray eyes were deep-set and when he looked at her she felt he could see into her soul. At first that had intrigued her, now it frightened her. The past months apart told her she didn't want to face a future without Trace. He was the one person she'd allowed to get close when she'd come to Winchester Ridge, Colorado, to take a guidance counselor job at the high school.

But there were some secrets she could never share…with anyone.

Now it was too late to do anything to save their marriage. "We received a letter today," she said, pulling the folded envelope out of her pocket. "It's from the adoption agency." Her voice trembled. "We've passed another screening for a baby."

Trace's eyes narrowed, then he threw his head back and laughed. "It's a joke, right?"

She didn't expect this reaction. "No."

"So for months we've been giving everyone the impression that we're the perfect couple and acceptable parents. Then we break up and we get the okay."

Kira squared her shoulders and looked him in the eye.

"No one knows you moved out, and I don't want anyone to. Not yet. Not until we receive a baby."

He froze, his jaw clenched. "If you want the divorce so bad, then adopt as a single parent." He tossed the pitchfork against the railing and marched out of the stall.

Kira hurried after him. "Trace, wait. Just hear me out." His fast pace had her nearly running to keep up. "We'll both get what we want. I'll have a baby, and you'll be free to marry someone who can give you what you want…children."

He stopped abruptly. "You have everything figured out, don't you?"

She shrugged, trying to hide her pain, wishing he'd say he'd stay with her and together they'd raise the baby. "No, but I know you want your own children. I can't give you that."

His eyes flashed his pain. "Yeah, I wanted a child— with you. But it didn't happen, and I wasn't enough for you." Without waiting for another word, he started out of the barn, leaving her in shock.

"It wouldn't be enough for you, Trace," Rushing after him, she caught up to him again on the small porch of the bunkhouse. "I loved you and our life together." She meant it. Her life on the ranch with Trace had been perfect. For a while. Then her dream had slowly unraveled. It seemed as if God were punishing her for her past. She didn't want Trace to be punished because of her. That's the reason she had to put an end to this.

She forced away the thought. "Trace, I have a chance for a child…maybe my only chance. You can remarry and have a dozen children. So if you could be happier without me, I'm willing to let you go."

Trace closed his eyes and gripped the wooden post. He didn't know if he could handle this again. Their marriage had gone through so much turmoil while they'd tried several procedures to be able to conceive a baby. Toward the end, he couldn't take the look on her face every time they failed, until finally, the pressure drove her from him. He might have been the one who'd moved out of the house, but emotionally Kira had left him long before that.

Now, after long weeks of separation, he'd become reconciled to losing her. Then her sudden appearance today made him ache with want and need. But she was here only because of her need for a child, and to end their marriage.

"Do you honestly think we can pull this off? The last words we spoke to each other weren't exactly loving."

"The pressure is off now," she said. "We just have to go through the motions of being a couple. I've accepted that I may never conceive a baby, but I can still have a child." She held out the letter. "The agency says we've met their requirements and we can move on to the next step."

How could he forget the classes, the long inter-views, the background checks. They'd even been fin-gerprinted. He glanced from the paper in her hand to the hopeful look on her face. He felt the familiar tug in his chest.

"They'll send someone out for a home study. To visit with us and see our home."

"So what do you want me to do? Play the loving husband?"

She rested her hand on his arm, her dark eyes pleading. "Would that be so hard?"

Damn, she didn't play fair and he had trouble denying her anything. "I don't think we can pull it off, Kira. Not where we are right now."

She paused. "It's only for about six months. That's how long it takes for the adoption to be final." She looked sad. "Is it that hard to pretend you love me?"

The next evening, seated at the kitchen table at the house, Kira tried to finish the end-of-the-year paper-work, but her mind kept wandering back to Trace.

"What else is new?" she grumbled as she got up and went to the coffeemaker. After refilling her mug, she walked to the window and stared out at the breathtak-ing view of the Roan Plateau. She'd come to love this place. So different from the busy streets of Denver.

Five years ago she'd come to Winchester Ridge to start a new life. With her new college degree in hand, she'd come to interview for a teaching position at the high school. She'd gotten the job and needed a place to live.

The town's real estate broker, Jarrett McKane, had shown her an apartment, then taken her to lunch. At the local café, they'd run into his younger brother, Trace.

It had been an instant attraction. After that she'd accepted a few more dates from Jarrett in the hope of running into Trace.

Finally two weeks later, the rugged rancher showed up at school and asked her out. It seemed like forever before he kissed her, but it had been well worth the wait. She closed her eyes, remembering his slow hands skimming over her, softly caressing her skin.

Trace's kisses were lethal. She remembered each touch of his lips against her heated flesh. How hungry he'd made her, stirring her desire. Suddenly warmth ran down her spine settling low in her stomach. Her eyes shot open as she groaned in frustration.

"Oh God," she whispered as she sank against the counter, her body aching. Never in her life had anyone made her feel the way Trace McKane had. After her parents' automobile accident and death, she'd been alone for a lot of years. She'd thought she'd finally found a home, a place where she could belong.

Yesterday, she'd wanted to beg Trace to come home, but her own pain and hurt prevented it. She knew the past few months she'd been horrible to live with. But how could any man understand the anguish she'd gone through, not just with the pain of her disease, but knowing she hadn't been able to conceive a baby?

She glanced back through the window, seeing the light on in the bunkhouse. "Oh, Trace, would you have loved me if you knew the truth about me?"

The past flooded back. She tried to push it away, but it always hovered close enough to force her to remember, taking the brightness away from any happiness she tried to grasp. Maybe the guilt had been what drove her, caused her to keep pushing Trace away.

The familiar sadness blanketed her. With each passing month her fertility problems had loomed ever darker. With the endometriosis, her chances diminished daily until the day would come when she'd probably need more surgery to relieve her of the recurring scar tissue.

But with the passing of time, her dreams seemed to be fading anyway, along with her marriage.

The sound of the back door opening caught Kira's attention. Living this far out in the country, she knew it could only be Jonah Calhoun, the ranch foreman. Or Trace. Her heart raced as she waited, and her hopes were rewarded when her husband walked into the kitchen.

She tried to breathe but it was difficult. Trace McKane still affected her in the same way he had when she'd first met him. It was obvious he had just showered and put on a fresh shirt and jeans. Hope spread through her as she realized he might have done it for her.

"Hi," she managed. "Would you like a cup of coffee?"

He nodded. "I could use one." He walked to the counter and took the steaming mug she offered. Then Kira picked up her cup and started for the table.

"I thought caffeine was bad for your condition," he said.

She was touched that he remembered. "I usually don't drink it, but tonight I have work to finish. I need all the help I can get to stay alert."

"I guess school is getting out soon. So it looks like it's going to be a busy time for both of us." He drank from his cup, then studied her. She felt the heat of his silver gaze spread over her, warming her. She hated they were talking so politely, when she desperately wanted him to take her into his arms and tell her he wanted to move back permanently to be her husband and father to her baby.

He glanced away. "Cal wants to know if you're still planning the senior roundup to be here this year."

She nodded. "I hope to. The kids have been talking about it for weeks. That is, if it's okay with you?"

He shrugged. "Not a problem. Cal just wants a head count so we'll know how many hands we need to hire."

Trace leaned against the counter, trying to relax. Impossible. Since his dad's death three years ago, he'd had to run the cattle operation mostly on his own.

"Do you have a date set for the roundup?" she asked.

"In two weeks."

She nodded. "That's perfect. Graduation will be over, so we don't have to worry about interrupting study time."

Trace hated the silence lingering between them. What he hated most of all was feeling like a stranger in his own house, a stranger to his wife.

"Have you given any thought to what we talked about?" she finally asked him.

"It's kind of hard not to." He shifted his weight trying to ease the tightness in his chest. "You tell a man you want to adopt a child, and in the same breath give him his walking papers."

"I'm sorry, Trace. I never wanted it to turn out this way. But in the end it might be best for both of us."

He heard the tears in her voice. "Is it really that easy, Kira? Well, it's not for me. If I agree I also sign papers for this child. I'm responsible for him or her, too."

"Trace, I know I'm asking a lot."

"No, you don't," he interrupted her. "You're asking me to move back into the house and take responsibility for a child, then just to walk away."

She wanted more, so much more from him. But she couldn't ask for another chance. "I don't expect to have things be like they once were. Yes, we have to live in the same house, but if we're lucky enough to get a baby, I'll handle all the child's needs. I won't ask for any help."

He was silent for a long time. "And after the six months, I sign away all rights to the child."

He made it sound so calculating. She managed a nod.

He cursed and turned away.

"Please, Trace, I'm afraid if we tell the agency we're not together now, then later, I'll have to start from the beginning as a single parent."

He drove his fingers through his hair. "I'm not sure I can do this, Kira."

She bit down on her lower lip. "Please, I want this opportunity, Trace. It might be my last chance."

Trace fought to control his anger. It had always been about a baby. What about them? Why couldn't she offer to work out their problems? Instead of wanting to push him aside when he wasn't needed any more.

"Trace, I don't magically expect us to return to our roles of husband and wife. I'll move into the guest room and you can have your bedroom back."

This was all so crazy. Trace wasn't sure if he could resist Kira, living under the same roof. If he moved back into the house now, it'd be damn difficult to resist going to her bed.

He placed his coffee mug in the sink, then went to her, bracing his hands on either side of her. He stared into those honey-brown eyes, knowing there were secrets hidden in their depths. Secrets she wouldn't share with anyone, not even with him. "You talk about this situation like it's a business transaction. I have my doubts about us being able to pull this off."

She swallowed hard, but didn't speak.

His attention went to her mouth, tempting him like no woman ever had. His heart raced and his gut tightened. He ached to taste her, to stir up those feelings that made him crazy with need. It had been so long.

"Trace." Her voice was a throaty whisper as her hand came up to his face. "Can't we try?"

Her sultry voice swept over him like a caress. He closed his eyes, picturing her in their bed, willing and wanton, welcoming his kisses, his touches as he moved over her heated body.

"Damn you, Kira." His mouth closed over hers in a hungry kiss. She wrapped her arms around his neck as he jerked her against his body already hard with desire. Her mouth opened on a sigh, and he dove inside to taste her. He moved against her, hungry for the contact. It wasn't enough, he needed all of her.

But Kira couldn't give it to him. Would they ever be able to be what the other needed?

He broke off the kiss and stepped back. "I've got to go." He headed to the door only to have her call to him.

He didn't turn around, knowing he'd weaken to her request. "Kira, I need more time."

"Please, Trace." She hesitated. "Just keep up the pretense that we're married until you decide what to do."

In his heart Trace would always be married to Kira. He'd loved her since the moment he laid eyes on her. That hadn't changed. But could he hang around and watch their marriage die a slow agonizing death?

He faced her. "So you expect me live in limbo until the adoption goes through?" The words stuck in his throat.

She blinked, looking surprised. "No. I'm asking if you would give it six months until they give us permanent custody. After that I won't try to hold you, or make you responsible for the child. I'll move into town and not ask anything more of you. As soon as I get another counseling job, I'll move away."

Damn, there it was. She couldn't say it any plainer. The chant rang repeatedly in his head. *She only wants a child.* "You're asking a lot, Kira."

"I know," was all she said in her defense.

"What do I get out of this deal? What are you willing to give me?"

She blinked at his question, but soon recovered. Her arms tightened around his neck. "What do you want, Trace? If it was me, all you had to do any time was walk through that door. I've been here the whole time, wanting you."

His body stirred at the feel of her length pressed against him. The easy way would be to give them what they both wanted. He wasn't sure he could, knowing in the end he could lose everything anyway. Everything. Not only would he give up Kira, but a child.

"Like I said, I'll have to think about it." He removed her hands, and walked out before he changed his mind. Before he did something crazy like agreeing to her request.

CHAPTER TWO

OF ALL mornings to oversleep.

Kira pulled her leather satchel from the back seat, slammed the car door and rushed off across the parking lot toward the large brick building, Winchester Ridge High School. And the nine o'clock meeting.

After Trace had left the house, she hadn't been able to finish her work until well after midnight. Then she lay awake a long time, reliving her husband's visit, their kiss.

Trace's familiar taste. The way he held her, reminding her how well their bodies meshed together. She delighted in the fact she could still make his control slip, just as hers had. She had to stop herself from trying to convince him to stay and make love to her.

Oh God, it had been a long time since Trace had touched her.

"Mrs. McKane, are you all right?"

Kira shook away the fantasy and glanced at her student, Jody Campbell. "Oh, Jody. Yes, I'm fine. Just a lot of things on my mind." She picked up her pace toward the counselors' office, realizing the student was staying right with her. "What are you doing out of class?"

"Mr. Douglas let me leave early because I needed to see you." The pretty girl hesitated. "It's about volunteer time at the retirement home. All the kids voted it as our class project, but some don't have enough hours to come to the senior roundup."

"Give me the list and I'll talk to them," Kira said as she stopped at the counseling department's door and took the paper.

Seeing Jody reminded her that she'd gotten a notice from her English teacher. The promising student's work had been suffering the past month. Kira hated that her own personal distractions had caused her to neglect one of the best students in the senior class.

"Why don't you come back at three o'clock? We should talk."

Jody hesitated again. "I work at four so I need to catch the three-thirty bus."

She couldn't let this slip any longer, not with finals next week. "Well, I could give you a lift if you like and we can have a quick chat."

Her once-enthusiastic student kept her eyes cast down. "Okay."

Kira signed Jody's pass and sent her off to class just as the bell rang. She walked inside the guidance office and into the first glass cubicle. She hated being distracted from her work. And these last few weeks, it had been especially difficult for her to keep focused on a job she was crazy about. She loved doing extra things to stay involved with the teenagers.

Kira was the sponsor for this year's senior class, including all activities. Doing service hours and giving back to the community was an important part of their curriculum. It helped to develop their social skills, and it looked good on their college applications. She rewarded those students with senior roundup at McKane Ranch.

Winchester Ridge was a small ranching town, but the teenagers loved to spend the day helping with the roundup and branding. Followed by a barbecue and barn dance that closed out their senior year with wonderful memories.

Kira sank into her desk chair. Not all kids were that lucky. Suddenly the last fifteen years faded away as her thoughts went back to her own high school days. Shy and naive, she'd been passed around to so many different foster homes it had been difficult to make friends. So when someone gave her attention, she'd been eager for it, and easy to be taken advantage of. Those lonely years had been a big motivator for her career choice.

At the sound of the knock on her door, Kira looked up to see her fellow counselor and friend, Michelle Turner, peer in.

"Michele," she greeted. "Are you coming for the meeting?"

"It's been postponed until one o'clock," her friend said as she walked inside the small enclosure and closed the door. "Kira, are you all right?"

She gave her friend a bright smile. "I'm fine."

The young teacher sat down in the only other chair. "No, you're not."

Kira shook her head. Michele had been the one person she'd confided in about her inability to conceive. The fellow teacher had been her first friend when she'd come to the western Colorado town. "No, really. We've gotten word from the adoption agency."

Michele's pretty blue eyes lit up. "Oh, that's great news." She frowned. "Why so sad?"

Kira shrugged. "Hormones, probably. And Trace. He's a little hesitant about the idea."

Michele leaned forward. "You two have been through a lot over this and now that you're so close to having a baby, he's probably a little scared."

And he wants his own child, Kira added silently. "It's more." She looked her friend in the eye, knowing she'd never betray her confidence. "It hasn't been easy living with me this last year."

"You've gone through a lot, trying to have a baby."

Kira released a shuttering breath. "Trace moved out to the bunkhouse two months ago."

"Oh, Kira." Michele shook her head. "Isn't that just like a man? When they can't deal with things, they up and leave. Well, I know Trace loves you."

And Kira wasn't so sure of that anymore. "I might have pushed him too far this time. We both said things that can't be taken back." She recalled the hurtful words she'd thrown at him. And yesterday she mentioned the "D" word. It was all or nothing now.

"Then march out to that bunkhouse and convince him to come back home."

"I'm not sure that will work."

"How do you know if you don't try? So go and

seduce your husband." Michele glanced at her watch. "I've got to get back. Can we do lunch later in the week?"

"Sure. Are you going to help chaperone at the roundup?"

Michele grinned. "I wouldn't miss it. Is your good-looking brother-in-law going to be there?"

Kira was surprised by her friend's interest in Jarrett. "I'm not sure."

Michelle waved off the question then hugged her. "I'll see you later." She walked out.

Kira leaned back in her chair. Could she get Trace to come back home, and get him to change his mind about the divorce? Could they work together to repair their mess of a marriage?

She thought back to the last time Trace had wanted to be close to her. In the weeks before he'd moved out, her once-loving husband hadn't wanted to touch her, or even be in the same house with her. And she couldn't blame him. The sad part was she'd driven him out. Out of his own home.

Trace loved the McKane Ranch, one of the oldest in the area. He was a cattleman like his father and grandfather before him. There had been times when she was a little jealous of his dedication, maybe if he'd talk about the operation with her it would help. Even when he'd bought out part of his brother's land, she hadn't been asked anything about it until it came time to sign the loan papers. She just wanted to feel like a part of his dreams.

Kira felt her chest tighten with the familiar ache. The

same feeling she'd had when she'd lost her parents in the accident and her grandmother wouldn't take her into her home. *Rejection.* When she had to go into foster care, then from home to home. *Rejection.* When she fell in love with the first boy who gave her the time of day, he'd abandoned her, too. *Rejection.* Now, her marriage…

Kira sat up straighter. Why was she thinking so much about the past? She'd worked so hard to put those years behind her. A glance at the calendar gave her the answer. It was approaching the seventh of June. Fifteen years had passed and it still hurt like a fresh wound.

No! This baby was going to change things. She was going to have her family, even if it was only part of one.

"Kira…"

She turned around to see Trace at the door. He was dressed in his usual jeans and Western shirt, his cowboy hat in his hand. With her heart pounding, she stood.

"Trace." He never came to her school. "Is something wrong?"

"Do you have some time to talk?"

"Sure." She stepped aside. "Come in."

He glanced around the busy office. "I'd rather go somewhere else. Can you leave for a while?"

She checked her watch. "I'm free for the next hour."

"Let's go for some coffee."

"Sure." Kira grabbed her purse, stepped out into the hall and together they walked out of the building. When Trace placed his hand against the small of her back, she shivered.

"Are you okay?" he asked.

"Yes," she lied. "I'm fine. I just need some coffee."

He gave her a sideways glance. "You should switch to decaf."

She studied his profile. Trace McKane had always been serious by nature. He didn't smile easily, but when he did he was irresistible.

They were quiet as he helped her to his truck, then drove past all the recently built, chain restaurants to the older section of Winchester Ridge to Bonnie's Diner. Still a favorite with the locals.

They took a booth by the picture window. The red vinyl seats were worn and cracked, repaired by tape over the years. The place was clean and the food good. Right now, there weren't any customers, only the sound of a country ballad coming from the old fifties-style jukebox.

Trace signaled the waitress for two coffees and sat down across from Kira. He wondered if he should have waited until she got home to talk with her.

After what happened between them last night, he should be staying away from her, completely. But here he was, sitting across from her. Just looking at her had him working to breathe normally. Nothing had changed. Kira Hyatt had gotten to him from the moment he laid eyes on her, right here in this diner. It had been the only time he'd ever won out against his older sibling. For once Jarrett hadn't gotten the girl. Younger brother, Trace had.

But Trace had nothing now. Not a wife. Not a marriage. It helped to remember the bad times. That kept him from storming back into the house they'd shared for five years. To a life he'd thought was perfect, but reality hit and he'd learned nothing was perfect.

That it hit home again as he recalled that Kira only wanted a six-month marriage.

The waitress placed their mugs on the table. The older woman, Alice Burns, gave them a warm smile. She'd worked here for as long as he could remember. "Well, how are Mr. and Mrs. McKane doin' today?"

"Just fine, Alice," Trace answered.

"How's your granddaughter?" Kira asked.

The fifty-something woman grinned. "Best not get me started on little Emily. But she's gonna have to share me soon because Carol's pregnant again. A boy this time."

Kira's smile froze. "That's wonderful. Congratulations."

Alice eyed the couple. "You two should think about having a few yourselves." Before they could answer, the waitress walked away.

Trace watched Kira fight her emotions as she took a drink.

"Alice didn't know, Kira," Trace said.

"I know that." Kira wrapped a strand of golden-blond hair behind her ear, leaving the wispy bangs along her forehead. "Why did you need to see me?"

Okay this was all business. "A woman from the adoption agency called after you left."

Her brown eyes widened. "So soon. What did she say?"

"I didn't get to talk to her. Just a message on the machine. It just said that she'd call back again."

"Darn, I wonder if she'll call the office." She glanced at him. "Did she leave a number where I could reach her?"

It hurt when she used the word "I" and not "we". He pulled the paper from his pocket and slid it across the table. "I don't think you should call her just yet."

She looked hurt. "But I have to."

"What are you going to tell her, Kira?"

She blinked at him. "We're just talking to her, Trace. I don't want to delay the process, it takes a long time. We're probably just going to be put on a waiting list."

"I still have to pretend we're married."

"You are married—to me." She lost her attitude. "But as I told you the baby will be my responsibility."

So she hadn't changed her mind. He was to do nothing concerning the child. "We aren't even living under the same roof."

"I never asked you to move out in the first place."

"You know why I did, Kira. We were headed for disaster." He'd hated leaving, and if she'd asked him to stay just once, he would have in a heartbeat. Now, it was too late.

She sighed. "Please, just listen to what Mrs. Fletcher has to say, that's all I ask."

"Okay, I'll talk with the woman. See what she has to say."

"Really?" Tears flooded her eyes. "Oh, Trace, thank you."

He raised a hand. "Don't thank me, yet. I'll agree to another home visit. Afterward we'll see where we go from there. I can't commit to anything more."

She nodded. "Does that mean you're moving back to the house?"

Before Trace could come up with an answer they were interrupted.

"Well, look who's wandered in off the range."

They both glanced up to see Jarrett McKane standing at their table. He was tall, athletic and good-looking. He knew it, too. Jarrett knew a lot of things, all you had to do was ask him.

Trace straightened. He didn't want his half brother here. Not now. "Hello, Jarrett."

"Trace." His brother turned to Kira. "Hello, pretty sister-in-law."

Kira smiled. "Hi, Jarrett."

Grabbing a chair, he turned it around and straddled it. He glanced between the two of them. "You two look serious. There wouldn't be trouble in paradise, would there? Kira, you just let me know if this guy isn't treating you right and I'll knock some sense into him."

Kira shifted in her seat as she continued to smile at her brother-in-law. "Everything is fine, Jarrett, but thanks for asking."

At their first meeting when Kira arrived in town, Jarrett had laid on his easy chair but it hadn't taken her long to realize that Jarrett McKane was out for himself. He was attentive to his women though, but that was another problem, there were a lot of women.

Both brothers were handsome, but Jarrett had been the school sports hero and a college graduate. Meanwhile Trace had stayed and worked on the ranch with his father, going to college locally.

"Anytime." He looked at Trace. "I need to talk to you about our arrangement. Could you come to my office?"

"Later. Kira and I are talking right now."

"Seems like you could do that at home. Hell, you sleep in the same bed." There was a wicked look in Jarrett's eyes. "That's right. It's branding time so you sleep out with your calves." He winked at Kira. "Makes for a lonely wife left at home."

"And sometimes I sleep out with the calves, too," Kira said, worried things might come to blows.

The brothers had never been close. Jarrett had been six years old when his mother died, and his father, John, remarried Claire, and a year later she had given birth to Trace. The distance had grown when their parents retired and moved to a warmer climate in Arizona. Now, both parents had passed away.

"My brother's a lucky man to have you. Although I tried my best, he won you fair and square." He winked at Kira. "But it's still a long way to go before the score is even, bro."

Later that afternoon, Trace rode toward the barn. After returning from town, he'd saddled up Thunder and went out to check the herd. He'd wasted the morning already when he needed to finish things before the roundup.

He rotated his tired shoulders, felt his eyes burn, a sure sign that lack of sleep had taken a toll on him. And confronting his brother hadn't exactly made his day. He'd wanted to spend more time with Kira, but they hadn't managed that, either. So far, they'd talked very little of what was most important to him: their marriage.

Trace climbed off his horse and walked him into the

barn. The immaculately clean structure had been the result of too much time on his hands. Since moving to the bunkhouse, he'd tried to stay busy, and his already organized barn had gotten a complete sweep, with every piece of tack on the property being cleaned or polished.

It had been his sleep time that suffered. Even his fatigue hadn't helped him on those long nights. He walked his stallion into the stall, removed the saddle and carried it to the tack room. On his way out, he ran into his foreman, Cal.

"Hey, Trace. What's up?"

"You tell me, Cal," he said. "How many men have you got for the roundup?"

The forty-one-year-old foreman, Jonah Calhoun, took off his hat and scratched his gray-streaked brown hair. A single man, he'd worked for the McKane Ranch for years, and was also Trace's friend. "Besides our two part-time hands, another half a dozen like you asked. I also ran into Joel and Hal Lewis at the feed store. They're willing to come and help out, too, as long as we can give them a hand next month."

Trace nodded. "Can do. I'll give them a call."

Together, they walked back to Thunder's stall. Trace removed the horse's bridle and blanket, then took the brush and began grooming him.

Cal snapped his fingers. "Oh, I forgot, your brother stopped by earlier, looking for you."

Trace didn't like Jarrett dogging him. "He found me at the diner."

Cal frowned. "I thought you went to see Kira."

Trace nodded. "We went for coffee."

The foreman smiled. "Good idea, take her to the place where you two met."

"I just wanted to talk to her. Alone."

The smile grew bigger. "Get anything settled?" Then he raised his hand. "Sorry, Trace, that's none of my business. I'm just glad you two got together."

Trace continued to stroke the animal. "We were talking until Jarrett showed up."

The foreman's eyes narrowed. "He seemed bent on seeing you. What's he up to?"

Cal knew as well as Trace that Jarrett never did anything unless it benefited him. "He probably wants to know when that last payment I owe him is coming."

The foreman frowned. He knew the conditions of the loan. "Are you late?"

Trace shook his head. "No, but I'm not sure I can make the full amount on the final payment." He could lose it all.

"Would your brother give you more time? I mean, with the market the way it is."

"I doubt it. When has he ever done me a favor?"

Five years ago, Jarrett couldn't wait to sell off most of his share of the ranch, and offered Trace the first opportunity to buy it. Trace hadn't hesitated, but things had been tight this past year, and the payment was due to Jarrett in thirty days.

"I might have to sell the breeding bulls."

"No way. You need another year or two to build the herd. There's some serious money in those guys. Rocky will sire some good stock."

Trace put down the brush. "But I can get ready cash

for them. Joel Lewis is interested. And I can't lose everything now." His thoughts turned to Kira. He could lose more than the ranch.

"You know Lewis is mostly talk. Look, Trace, I have some money saved I could loan you."

Trace was touched by the offer. "Thanks, Cal, I'm grateful for the offer, but it's not a good idea to borrow from friends."

"Maybe I want to invest if Jarrett is threatening you. Not a full partnership, but just a percentage of the place." Kind light-blue eyes studied Trace. "Well, maybe you can talk it over with Kira before you nix the idea."

Trace walked out of the stall. "She's never shown much interest in the running of the ranch."

"Maybe she would this time."

Trace pushed his hat back and sighed. He didn't want to add to their troubles. "She has enough on her mind."

Cal nodded. "If you say so. Well, I guess I better go put away the feed that was delivered."

Trace stopped him. "Has Kira said something to you?"

"No. She just always asks about things, and seems genuinely interested when I tell her." The foreman shrugged. "But I can't tell you how to talk to your wife, Trace."

He hadn't been talking to Kira at all until she'd come to see him yesterday. And she wasn't going to be his wife much longer. "Hell, I've been living in the bunkhouse for the past two months. I haven't been doing such a great job of it myself."

"And you don't need a lecture from me. But I think if there are problems with the missus, living out here and keeping things from her isn't the best way for fixin' things between you."

Cal was probably the only one who knew about their problems. "The adoption agency notified us. Kira wants me to move back to the house and pretend we're a happy couple."

A smile appeared on his friend's face. "You don't look very happy about it."

"All she wants is six months. After the adoption becomes final she's going to leave."

Cal raised an eyebrow then he said, "I know it's been rough. Kira's gone through a lot and she wants a baby."

"So do I. And how can I just walk away from a child?"

"Who says you have to? You can still be the kid's father, Kira's husband. Who's to say you can't get an extension on the six months?"

So much had already passed between them, so much hurt. He didn't know if they could go back to how it was before. "I don't know if I can."

"If you're not ready, then take it slow."

Trace never had been one who shared things, but Cal was as close as they came. He valued his opinion, and advice. "She wants me to stay in the house but not in the same room."

His friend smiled slowly. "Hey, it's a start."

"Trace?"

At the sound of Kira's voice, he turned to find her standing in the barn entrance, holding a bag of groceries.

"Kira." He walked toward her and took the sack from her. "Is there a problem?" Great, is that all he could come up with?

She glanced away shyly. "I had an easy afternoon at school and decided to cook supper." She looked at Cal and smiled. "Hello, Jonah."

"Kira, it's nice to see you."

"It's nice to see you, too. I hope you're ready for about thirty teenagers coming out."

"Are we ever ready?"

Kira laughed. "I guess not, but it's fun."

Trace found he was jealous of their easy banter. "Is there a reason you came to see me?"

Kira looked at him. "I wanted to ask if you'd come to supper." She turned back to Cal. "You're welcome, too, Jonah."

The foreman blushed. "Thank you for the invitation, Kira, but it's my bowling night." He tipped his hat. "I should finish up my chores." He leaned toward his friend and whispered, "Slow and easy." Cal turned and walked out.

"What did he say?" Kira asked.

He shrugged. "Just something I need to remember."

An hour later when Trace stepped inside the house, the scent of apples and cinnamon teased his nose. Ordinarily he didn't take time to look around; he'd grown up in this house, but today he was mindful of it all.

A wide staircase led to a second floor where there were four large bedrooms. The living room was painted gray-green to offset the dark woodwork and floors. An overstuffed green sofa faced the used-brick fireplace.

That was when he noticed them, Kira's touches. An easy chair she'd bought for him right after they were married, saying he needed a place to relax. The large coffee table where the photo album of his childhood rested. More family pictures hung on the brightly painted walls. His family, not hers. He remembered her saying she lost her parents' pictures while moving around in foster care. He'd never thought much about her being alone in her life. She'd always seemed so outgoing and everyone liked her.

Trace moved quickly down the hall through the dining room, which was a sunny-gold color trimmed in oak wainscoting. The scent of lemon oil rose from the long, drop-leaf oak table and eight high-back chairs that had also belonged to his parents. He entered the kitchen, the one room that he and Kira had changed. And it had needed it. Everything had been out-of-date, from the appliances to the cupboards. Just a few months after their small wedding, the room had been gutted and everything was replaced.

A bowl of red apples sat on the round maple table. Everything looked the same, but it wasn't. He wanted desperately to push time back to when everything was perfect in his marriage.

He found Kira at the counter, taking pieces of chicken from the skillet. She glanced over her shoulder and smiled. "Hi."

He had trouble finding the words. "Hi. Am I too early?"

"No. Just in time."

His gaze combed over her. He was starved for her. Denying himself the pleasure she could give him had been punishing. Today she had on one of her prim schoolteacher blouses, his favorite, a rose-pink one that brought out the color of her skin.

He swallowed back the dryness in his throat. "How did school go today?"

"Fine," she said. "Everyone is complaining about finals."

He leaned against the counter. He'd missed talking with her. "I remember that age, it seemed to take an eternity to get to the end of school."

She smiled and started setting out the food. "The seniors are anxious to graduate, and get me out of their hair."

He knew that wasn't true. They all loved her. The girls considered her a friend, and the boys were half in love with her. She was young, barely thirty-one, and attractive. They all gravitated to her. "And a lot are going to be heartbroken at saying goodbye to you."

"What does that mean?"

"You've always given your students a lot of attention."

"And that's a bad thing?"

"No, it just means you're dedicated, and very good at what you do. Not to mention pretty."

Kira couldn't believe she was blushing at her husband's compliment. Trace had told her she was attractive before, but not for a long time. He hadn't talked to her at all.

"Thank you," she said.

He shrugged. "I'm not saying anything that isn't true."

"It's still nice to hear," she said. They looked at each other for a long time. Kira tried not to react, but it was impossible. Trace McKane was a handsome man. She'd thought that the first time she'd seen him. She'd been in town less than twenty-four hours before falling hopelessly in love. Something she'd never thought would happen, but the quiet rancher somehow convinced her to trust again. His slow hands and eager mouth coaxed her into giving herself to him, and they married within two months. From that first night of loving to now, she'd never regretted that decision.

She turned and opened the refrigerator to get the milk. The cool air felt good against her heated face. She couldn't believe how nervous she was acting. He was her husband, for God's sake. No, Trace hadn't been her husband for weeks. And sadly that wasn't going to change.

CHAPTER THREE

AN HOUR later, Kira sat at the kitchen table and watched as Trace finished the last of his meal.

He leaned back in the chair. "That was delicious, Kira."

She let out a breath, not realizing she'd been holding it. "I'm glad you liked it."

He gave a half smile. "Can't deny I've always loved your fried chicken."

And she loved his praise. "I shouldn't fix it. It isn't exactly healthy, especially the gravy."

"Once in a while won't hurt me."

It definitely hadn't hurt his waistline, she thought, visualizing the six-pack abs hidden under his shirt. She nodded and started to get up. "Coffee?"

He touched her hand to stop her and she felt a sudden jolt. "I'll get it," he said.

Kira relented, but her hungry gaze followed Trace to the coffeemaker. He stood nearly six-feet-two-inches tall, and since she was nearly five-nine, she loved his height. Her attention moved over a Western shirt that outlined his broad shoulders and narrow waist. She loved that long, lean look, especially when he wore Wrangler jeans.

And nothing else.

Heat suddenly swarmed her body just as Trace turned around. He gave her a curious look, but remained silent as he walked back to the table. He set down the mugs and she noticed his hands. Memories flooded her head, as she recalled his firm, but gentle touches, how he stroked her, bringing her pleasure.

He took a seat across from her. "I'm glad to see you've taken my advice and are on the decaf."

She sat up straighter. "I realized I need more sleep."

"We could all use a little more of that." His gaze locked with hers. "Though I doubt I can blame my problem on the caffeine."

Kira swallowed hard. She wanted to explore his comment further, but couldn't. They had another topic that needed attention. "I called Mrs. Fletcher at the agency," she said in a rush.

Trace didn't look surprised. "I figured you would." He set down his mug. "What did she have to say?"

"She wants to come for another home visit the first of next week."

Trace took a sip of coffee, then asked, "What did you tell her?"

"That I'd check with you, but Monday seemed okay for us." Kira held her breath, waiting, praying that Trace would agree to this.

"What are we going to say to her when she gets here?"

She hesitated, feeling her heart pounding. "That we want a baby."

Trace met Kira's anxious gaze. He could see how much she wanted this. There had been a lot of disappointment in the past two years for both of them. She'd gone through so much, both physically and emotionally, trying to get pregnant.

His own excitement began to build. A family with Kira. Was it still possible?

He wanted to make their marriage work, but her need for a child had become an obsession, leaving no room for them. By the time he moved out, she seemed relieved he was gone. Once she got her child would she turn her attention back to them? Either way he couldn't deny her.

"I'll be around Monday."

Those big brown eyes widened. "Really? Oh, Trace."

She jumped out of her chair, threw her arms around his neck and hugged him. Trace reached for her, gripping her by the waist so they both wouldn't topple over.

Kira ended up on his lap and when she pulled back there were tears in her eyes. "Thank you," she whispered.

He couldn't resist, and brushed away a tear off her cheek. Seeing her rich brown eyes staring back at his caused his blood to stir. It always had, but he couldn't let it happen, not after all the pain they'd caused each other.

He stood her on her feet. He got up, too, then backed away but ran into the counter. "You don't have to thank me. We'd always planned on children. I haven't agree to everything."

She refused to look away. "Under the circumstances…and reasons you've agreed to do this, I still thank you."

The hard ache in his body told him he was crazy to be this close to Kira. "Like you said it's a long waiting list." He drew a breath and inhaled that soft, womanly scent that was only her.

"Well, you've made me very happy." She leaned forward and placed a tender kiss on his mouth. He sucked in a breath as another jolt of desire shot through him. "And I promise I'll give you what you want."

"That'd be a first time in a long time," he murmured, trying to guard against his weakness for her.

"You know what I mean," she added. "You're doing this for me, I promise when it's over, I won't contest anything."

What had happened to them? At one time, he'd wanted to give her everything. They'd planned a lifetime together. Now, she wanted nothing from him, especially not his love.

"I should go," he told her, not wanting the conversation to go sour if they brought up any more of the past hurt. "I need to go check on that bad section of fence. I don't want Rocky to wander off," he rambled on. He stole another look at her and his pulse accelerated, weighing down each step he took.

"We still have things to talk about," Kira called to him. "Maybe after I'm home from school tomorrow."

Trace nodded, then headed for the back door, praying she wouldn't stop him. He worked to remember the misery they'd caused each other during their last months together. He hurried out into the cool night, and it felt good against his heated skin, but even jumping into a pool of ice water wouldn't cool off his need for Kira. He doubted anything would, ever. That still didn't give him any hope that they were meant to be together.

The next morning, Kira had renewed hope that things were going to work out. She knew she needed to take things slow with Trace. He never rushed into anything.

She walked into her office to find Jody waiting for her. When Kira had driven the girl to her job yesterday, there wasn't much time to talk about anything except plans for the senior roundup. That was why Kira had set up this morning's meeting.

Jody stood. "Hello, Mrs. McKane."

"Good morning, Jody." Kira unlocked her office, went inside and set her things on her desk. After putting her purse in the bottom drawer, she motioned to Jody to take a seat, then she did the same.

"Okay, Jody, there are no distractions now." She worked up a smile. "It's just you and me." She took the file from her in-box and opened it. "I've talked with your teachers, Mr. Franklin and Miss Meehan, who informed me your grades have dropped considerably as of late. Jody, is there something going on, has something happened?"

The young girl looked pale, almost sickly. Her blond hair was long, but it looked unkempt today. She wasn't wearing any makeup, not even lip gloss. So different from the impeccably groomed girl Kira had known. Jody looked tired, no exhausted. Then it started adding up, the bad grades, and the sudden breakup with her boyfriend. Could Jody be pregnant?

Kira's heart sank as she worked hard not to look down at the girl's waistline. "I know I'm your guidance counselor, but I hope after our four years together, I'm your friend, too."

The student glanced away and shrugged. "I know you've helped me so much." She hesitated. "It's just…it's hard to talk about."

Jody Campbell lived with her single mother, and money was always tight. With Jody's high grade point average, Kira had been working tirelessly to help her get scholarships and financial aid for college.

"Jody, two months ago you were excited about going away to college. Has something changed that?"

She drew an unsteady breath and nodded. "Ben and I broke up." Tears filled her eyes. "He signed up to go into the Army."

"I'm sorry, Jody." Ben Kerrigan was another senior. The two had been dating for the past few months. She could see the girl's heartbreak. "When does he have to leave?"

A tear rolled down the girl's cheek. "The end of June. He said he won't have time for me, and doesn't even want to write me, or anything. He said it's better this way." The girl broke down and sobbed.

Kira reached for Jody and hugged her close. "I'm so sorry."

She knew too well how much teenage romance hurt. And in some cases you never lost the scars. Her thoughts went back nearly sixteen years earlier to her first love, Mike Purcell. Mike had broken more than her heart—he'd nearly destroyed her when he hadn't stood by her. That painful time still lingered in her memory. She had never shared it with anyone, not even Trace.

She blinked away her own tears and pulled back. "Jody. Listen to me. If you need me, for anything, I'm here."

The girl nodded, taking the tissue from Kira. "It's too late," she whispered.

"No, it's not. Unless you're changing your mind about college?"

The girl glanced away. "It would be hard for my mom if I go away. She depends on me."

Mrs. Campbell had depended on her daughter, and wasn't eager to see her go off to college. "Yes, but having a degree would make it so you could make more money. And what of your dream to be a nurse?"

"Maybe some dreams never come true."

Kira took the girl's hand and felt her tremble. "I know it seems hard right now, but you can do it. You are so talented."

She didn't look convinced.

"Okay, I won't push for now. Just don't blow off your finals."

"It's too late, I can't catch up."

"No, it's not too late. I've talked with both teachers. They'll give you makeup work, and if you do well on the final, you'll be okay. So you've got three days."

"But, I can't—"

"You can, because I'm going to help you," Kira insisted. "I want you back here after lunch."

Jody looked surprised. "Why? Why are you doing this?"

"Because I care about you, Jody. Right now you need to know that someone has faith in you. Someone cares."

Something Kira never had, until Trace. She just hadn't realized it soon enough. Now it was too late.

Trace paced the main room of the four room bunkhouse, but stopped to glance out the window. Kira was well-past due being home and there was a storm brewing. A big one. He checked his watch—it was after five o'clock.

"Why don't you just call her?" Cal said.

It was silly to act as if he didn't know who the foreman meant. "She's probably busy with graduation stuff. It's just she never pays attention to the weather."

"Then warn her." The wind picked up and lightning flashed in the dark sky.

Trace pulled out his phone and punched in Kira's number. When she didn't answer, he cursed his stubborn, independent wife and headed outside. The rain began falling in big drops and just as he reached his truck, her Jeep Cherokee pulled up next to the house. Anger mixed with relief as he ran toward her. Seeing her frightened look, he remained silent. He took her by the arm, rushed her up the steps and through the back door.

"Where the hell have you been?" he demanded as he forced the door shut against the strong wind.

Inside the mudroom, she put her briefcase down on

the washing machine, then wiped the rain from her face. "I was helping a student, Jody Campbell, then I took her home."

"There's a severe storm warning. Didn't you hear it?"

"Not until I got into the car." She glanced out the window. "It's bad, isn't it?"

Another flash of lightning and the electricity went out. "I guess that answers your question."

He went to the pantry and pulled out the flashlight and a box of candles. No matter how brave Kira acted, he knew she hated storms. He hurried back into the kitchen and shined the light toward her. "You okay?"

"Ask me after this storm passes."

"I don't think there's any chance of that for a while. There's a series of them across the area. It could go on all night." He called Cal on his cell. "How are things down there?"

"I'm heading over to the barn to check the horses. If there's any problems, I'll let you know."

He turned back to see Kira, lighting the half-used candles. The threatening clouds make it darker than normal at this time of day. They had a generator, but he didn't feel it was necessary right now.

The rain pelted against the roof, and Kira jumped at another flash of lightning, followed by the booming sound of thunder. "I should buy some new ones."

"Do you want to start up the generator?"

Kira sat down in the kitchen chair. "Not unless we have to go down to the basement."

Trace glanced out the window, but couldn't see

anything with the blowing rain. "I'll check the forecast." He walked into the den they'd used as an office, and she followed. He had a battery-powered radio and flipped it on to the local weather channel.

"No tornados sighted in the area, so far. But the warnings won't be lifted for the area until after midnight."

She sighed. "I was afraid of that."

Even in the shadows, he could see her hand pressed against her stomach. Something he'd seen her doing many times during their marriage. It helped ease the cramps that came with her monthly period. It also gave them the sad news that once again they'd failed, failed to conceive a child.

He released a breath. There had been far too many of those times. And it had only gotten worse after the fertility treatments. In the end he could hardly bear to continue to try for a baby, or watch her heartbreak when the same result had been repeated with no pregnancy.

Trace swallowed his own pain. "Come on, I'll fix you a cup of tea." He waited for her to stand, then led her back into the kitchen. He turned on the gas stove, then went to the cupboard and took out a mug and tea bags.

Waiting for the water to heat, Trace leaned against the counter and studied Kira. She was dressed for summer, in her bright blue T-shirt and a long, flowered skirt, covered mostly by a bulky sweater.

It wouldn't be sexy to anyone else, but he knew what lay underneath. Long smooth legs, and a cute bottom and curves that drove a man wild.

She looked up at him, and her sweater opened. He didn't stop his open examination of her breasts. Her nipples quickly hardened under the thin material. He felt his own body respond and he looked up at her dark eyes. He didn't have to ask her if she wanted him, he could see it in her heated gaze. God, she was easy to read. It was one of the many things he loved about her. She didn't play games when it came to sex. If she wanted him, she let him know. And she was definitely letting him know now.

Suddenly the teapot whistled and he shook away any thoughts about carrying this any further. He removed the kettle, poured the water into the cup and placed it in front of her.

"You hungry?"

She shook her head. "My stomach is a little unsettled."

Seeing the stress in her face, he asked, "Cramps?"

She nodded as if embarrassed.

"You should be in bed."

The rain pelted against the windows. "I'm not going upstairs in this storm."

"Did you at least take your medication?" He knew she hated to resort to the painkillers, but sometimes she didn't have a choice.

She didn't respond.

"Where is it?"

"The bathroom, upstairs."

Trace grabbed the flashlight and headed out toward the stairs. He went into the room they'd shared for the past five years. He felt like the intruder now. Lightning suddenly illuminated the space, showing the neatly made bed. Kira never would go off and forget to make it. Something he knew she'd learned early on in foster care.

He liked it messy. He liked her messy after making love in the early mornings. When the sun wasn't up just yet, and all was fresh and new, the problems were pushed aside and they were lost only in each other. He shook away the thought as a crash of thunder rumbled through the house.

He went into the medicine cabinet and grabbed her pills, then went to the closet and took out a pair of sweatpants and a sweatshirt, along with a pair of tennis shoes. He hurried back downstairs and handed her the bundle. "I thought you might be more comfortable in these."

She looked surprised and pleased. "Thank you."

He went to the sink and got her a glass of water. On his return she was already removing her skirt. He went to the refrigerator, making himself busy, trying to think about food, and not his wife stripping off her clothes.

She stopped and took the medicine with a drink of water.

"Lie down and try to relax."

He walked back to the refrigerator and took out some bread, lettuce and sliced ham. Then he grabbed a plate from the cupboard and prepared the tray, wishing that a pill could make the problems between them disappear.

Ever since the moment he'd fallen in love with Kira, he'd known there was something she'd kept back. A tiny part of her that she'd never shared with him. He figured it had something to do with her parents' death and her years in foster care.

Her one living relative was a grandmother, Beth

Hyatt, but as far as he knew, Kira hadn't been in touch with her since their marriage. Whenever he asked about her family, Kira clammed up, only saying her parents had died when she was young.

Sometimes her eyes showed such sadness and no matter how much he'd reassured her, he couldn't make it go away. Could a child do what he never could?

Trace walked to the sofa and found Kira lying on her side, her legs pulled up, indicating she was still in pain.

He placed the tray on the coffee table and sat down at one end. Without a word, he placed Kira's head on his lap. He reached under her sweatshirt and touched her warm skin. He began a slow, circular motion over her back and down her spine. In the past, this helped relax her and ease her suffering.

Kira shifted a little and released a soft moan. He continued to stroke her skin, feeling his own need surfacing, but he didn't have to touch Kira to want her. He could stand across a room and she'd just have to glance at him and he wanted her. Hell, he'd been sleeping in the bunkhouse these past weeks and it hadn't changed anything.

She groaned again, then started to roll over.

"Stay still," he said.

"I can't. My stomach hurts." She managed to turn over on her back. Without hesitation, he placed his hand on her abdomen and continued the gentle motion.

"Is this helping any?"

"Oh, yeah," she murmured. "You can stop in about an hour."

It killed him to see her in pain. With the progressive

disease, her periods seemed to have gotten more and more painful. And no one could do much to help her.

"I expected you to be asleep before this." He ached to stretch out beside her, to hold her close.

She smiled sleepily. "The pills are doing a good job. Just don't tell my students I'm a druggie."

"Your secret is safe with me."

For a few moments, it seemed like old times. But it wasn't and he had better remember that. Playful words didn't make a marriage work.

But he sure as hell would like to know what did.

Kira was in heaven. She didn't know if it was the pain medication or the fact that Trace was there holding her. She liked this dream. She fought the drugging sleep because she didn't want to wake up and find him gone again.

She felt him get up, then before she could protest, he lifted her into his arms. "Trace?" She couldn't even open her eyes.

"Shh, darlin', the worst of the storm is over and I'm taking you up to bed."

She smiled and curled in closer to his warmth. "Oh, I like the sound of that." But suddenly she felt the soft mattress as he laid her down and pulled away.

"Don't go," she whispered as she reached for him. "Please, Trace, don't leave me."

She felt his weight on the mattress, then his reassuring words. "I won't, Kira. I'm here."

With his comforting words, she let herself drift off

to sleep. She felt his kiss against her hair. For the first time in weeks she allowed herself to think that maybe everything would be all right.

Kira's comfort was gone by morning when she woke up and found herself alone. There was no sign of Trace, or that he'd been there during the night. Even though she wanted to stay in bed, she got up, into the shower, then dressed for work.

Downstairs, she found coffee already made and poured herself a cup. She went to the window and glanced at the sunny morning and a deserted bunk-house. Trace's truck was gone, too.

Disappointed, she knew he and Cal were probably out checking the herd. She wondered if there was any damage to the outer buildings. Would Trace even tell her if there were? He'd always been pretty closemouthed about the running of the ranch.

She'd shown more interest in the first couple of years after they were married. Once they'd started concentrating on a baby, she'd stopped horseback riding.

Looking back, she realized how much she'd pulled away from him with her self-absorbed guilt about not being able to conceive a baby. Trace had only been loving and supportive, never saying anything about the cost of medical procedures their insurance didn't pay for. That had been thousand of dollars.

That only added to her guilt. And when Trace suggested they take a break from trying, she blew up. Didn't talk to him for a week, then they fought some more, saying things that hurt. Things they couldn't take back. She drove him away, first emotionally, then finally, physically he packed his clothes up and moved to the bunkhouse.

Kira went to the sink and poured her coffee out. Not her proudest moment. She loved Trace more than anything, but she had to push and push to see if once again someone she loved left her. And he had.

Kira brushed a tear from her cheek.

Trace didn't have a clue about what was going on inside her. But it wasn't his fault. In the past, she'd only let him see what she wanted him to see.

She'd been unfair to him, but most importantly right now, she hadn't been honest, either. That had to change if they were going to survive. He deserved to know the truth. But, after all this time, could she take the chance that he might not forgive her?

Did it even matter? In six months, she'd lose Trace forever.

CHAPTER FOUR

BY NOON the next day, the heat was pounding against Trace's back. It was nearly unbearable to work, but he kept going. They had to get the storm-damaged roof replaced on the feed barn.

"Man, you'd think the rain would cool things off," Cal said, as he took off his hat and wiped his forehead on his sleeve.

Trace moved another shingle into place, knowing he had no extra money to replace it. "We're in for more rain tonight. So we better get this done, or we'll lose all the hay and feed."

"It was one heck of a storm, but at least they got the electricity back on this morning." Cal reached for a nail and hammer. "I bet Kira was frightened. I wasn't surprised when you didn't come back to the bunkhouse last night."

Trace continued to work. "She wasn't feeling well. Once she took some medication, she finally fell asleep. I guess I did, too."

"Looks like I'll be losing a roommate soon."

"It doesn't look like that to me," Trace argued. "Nothing is settled."

Cal grinned. "If you say so."

"Damn, straight, I say so." Trace pounded in a nail for emphasis. "Can you get more work done and do less talking?"

"Sure, boss." Cal glanced toward the road. "But I doubt you will." He nodded to the black, luxury sedan. "Seems Jarrett has found you again."

Trace turned around to see his brother climb out of the car. This was not what he needed today. "I better go get this over with."

Trace made his way down the ladder and caught up with his brother at the corral gate. Jarrett was dressed in tailored navy slacks, a fitted white dress shirt and Italian loafers that probably cost more than Trace's entire wardrobe.

"Hey, I thought I told you to come by the office."

"I've been busy," Trace said. That was the only excuse he was giving him.

"We're all busy, but this is business. Didn't want to say anything the other day with Kira there but the loan payment is due."

"Not until the end of June," Trace corrected. "Don't worry you'll get your money." He started to walk away, but Jarrett stopped him.

"Hey, I'm not here to hound you. I'm here to make you an offer."

Trace frowned. His brother never did anything unless it benefited him. "Not interested."

"Come on, Trace. You haven't even given me a chance."

"Okay, what is it?"

"How about I buy back that southwest section of land? Then your loan will be paid in full."

Trace remained silent for a moment, knowing without a doubt his brother was up to something. "Are you going to develop that section?"

Jarrett shrugged. "Eventually, when the market recovers. Westchester Ridge is growing with new businesses and housing will be needed." He glanced toward the mountains. "There's a lot of pretty scenery around here."

"And I plan to keep it that way. We've talked about this, Jarrett, I'm not crazy about running cattle up to a tract of homes." He started to walk away.

"What if I put in writing that I won't develop that section of land for ten years? Would you be willing to listen then?"

"What is it with you? When Dad and Mom died you couldn't wait to unload your share of the ranch. I bought you out, now you want some back." He shook his head. "What are you up to?"

Jarrett's gaze darted away. "I'm not at liberty to talk about it now."

"Well, then I'm not talking, either."

"I guess I'll just wait until you lose it all," his brother called to him.

"I haven't lost anything. You'll get your money."

"Sure you can afford it?" He cocked an eyebrow. "Adoption can get pretty expensive."

Trace's chest tightened. Of course Jarrett would have been contacted by the agency. "I'm handling it. Now, I need to get back to work." He marched off, refusing to argue any longer with his brother.

Mostly Trace hated that he didn't have all the money. He was going to have to come up with some other way to pay off the loan. Worse, how was he going to be able to give Kira what she wanted, too?

After getting Mrs. Fletcher's phone call that morning, Kira finished her appointments at school and hurried home. The counselor had asked if she could move up the interview time for today instead of Monday. Kira would have liked the rest of the week to prepare, but she couldn't say no.

Except she couldn't get ahold of Trace. She'd been calling him for hours, but kept getting his voice mail. It was nearly one o'clock when Kira pulled into the driveway. She rushed into the house and put on a pot of coffee, then straightened up the kitchen. She called down to the bunkhouse and left a message for Trace. Then tried his cell phone again, before noticing it on the table. He must have left it last night.

A shiver went through her as she recalled the feel of his arms around her. The way she felt pressed against his strong body during the storm. Kira wanted that again. If only she could convince Trace to come back home, and back into their marriage.

Kira's thoughts turned to the possibility of a baby. Is that what Mrs. Fletcher would tell them today? There was also the intense scrutiny for an adoption. They could dig up a lot of things from her past. They knew about her time in foster care. All those years she hadn't shared with Trace.

He deserved to know the truth.

There was a knock on the back door. Kira took a calming breath, put on a smile and opened the door to find a middle-aged woman with a big smile and warm blue eyes.

"Kira McKane?" she began, "I'm Lucy Fletcher from Places in the Heart Agency."

"Welcome, Mrs. Fletcher. Please, come in."

Kira stepped back and allowed the woman to walk inside the big farm kitchen.

"Oh, this is lovely." She glanced around the newly remodeled room. There were maple cabinets and natural stone countertops and the walls were painted a spring green.

"Thank you. My husband and I remodeled right after we were married. I just wish I could spend more time at home." Kira directed her to the round table. And they sat down.

Mrs. Fletcher opened her briefcase and took out a file. "I know you've worked with Jessica Long for the past several months, but I'm taking over some of her cases while she's recovering from surgery. I hope that's not a problem."

"Not at all."

"Good. When opportunities arise, there's no time to wait." She glanced over the paper. "You're a high school guidance counselor. So are you planning to stay home if you have a child?"

Kira hesitated. She wanted to, if they could afford it.

"There's no wrong answer, Kira. It's hard these days to make it without two incomes."

"I'd like to stay home, of course, but adoption is expensive."

Mrs. Fletcher nodded. "It's true you have to help absorb the expenses of the biological mother. One good thing about working in the school system, you have holidays and the summers off." She glanced around. "Is your husband going to be here today?"

"I hope so. I just realized that he left his cell phone here on the table this morning. And after the storm he needed to check for damage. He usually comes in for lunch."

"Good, I'm anxious to meet him." She smiled. "Why don't you show me your lovely home?"

"Sure." Kira took a breath and stood. "Would you like to see the nursery?"

"Eventually. Maybe we can start downstairs."

Kira relaxed some as they made their way through the rooms until the tour finally ended upstairs in the master bedroom. The walls were painted a soft blue, to offset the large, dark furniture.

She had made the bed this morning, but she couldn't help but recall last night with Trace. How he held her so tenderly. She quickly shook away the memory.

"The antique furniture belonged to my husband's grandparents. I discovered it in the attic after we were married. I don't think Trace was crazy about bringing it down."

"It's beautiful."

The next room across the hall was the nursery. Kira hesitated, then opened the door. It had been a while since she'd come in here. The walls were a buttery-yellow, with an old rocker she'd sanded and painted white. And there was a hand-carved cradle that had been in Trace's family for generations.

"Oh, this is lovely." Mrs. Fletcher walked to the row of windows that overlooked the pasture. "I see you are prepared." She went to the cradle. "Is this another treasure from the attic?"

Kira nodded. "I know we'll need a proper baby bed, but it's hard to get too excited, yet. I don't want to be disappointed."

"I hope that isn't the case, too." Mrs. Fletcher gave her a soft smile. "You and your husband have been very cooperative, releasing all your records to us." She glanced down at her notes. "We've just received your medical file states that you have advanced endometriosis. No miscarriages, but a live birth."

Kira hesitated, then knew she couldn't risk a lie and cause her to lose this chance. "Yes."

Mrs. Fetcher blinked in surprise. "You have a child?"

Kira's heart drummed against her chest, she paused, then rushed on to tell the social worker what she'd never told anyone. "Yes, I had a child fifteen years ago. I…I gave him up for adoption."

"I see." Lucy Fletcher studied her, then said, "I appreciate you telling me, Kira."

"Do you think this will hurt our chances for a baby?"

"Of course not." The woman touched her hand. "I believe you did what was best for everyone, especially the child."

Just then Kira glanced up and caught sight of her freshly showered husband standing in the doorway. Panic froze her, seeing the intense look from him.

Mrs. Fletcher turned around. "Oh, you must be Trace. I'll Lucy Fletcher from Places in the Heart. I've looked forward to meeting you."

Trace accepted her hand and shook it. "It's nice to meet you, too. Sorry, I'm late, I needed to shower off the mud."

"We did get quite the storm last night, didn't we."

"And I needed to do some repairs first thing this morning."

Kira couldn't help but wonder how much of the conversation Trace had overheard. "I explained to Mrs. Fletcher you forgot to take your cell phone with you. So I couldn't get hold of you."

Mrs. Fletcher stepped in. "I've enjoyed spending time talking with your wife while she showed me around your beautiful home."

"Kira has done most of the decorating." Trace stood beside her, but he didn't touch her.

"Well, if you have a few minutes, Trace, I'd like to talk with you both."

"Let's go downstairs," Kira suggested, praying there wouldn't be any more talk about her past. She led them into the dining room, then went to get the coffee.

In the kitchen, Kira willed herself to stop shaking. If Trace overheard she'd deal with it. If he hadn't she needed to tell him. Everything. With a calming breath, she returned to the dining room table with coffee and cookies. She sat down next to Trace. He continued to answer questions she knew he'd been asked before by the other counselor.

Finally Lucy Fletcher sat back and eyed the two of

them. "Would you both be available again on Monday afternoon?"

Kira immediately nodded. "Of course."

Trace hesitated. "You have more questions?"

Mrs. Fletcher shook her head. "I'm in agreement with Jessie Long that you two would make wonderful parents. It's a birthmother who wants to speak with you."

"Birthmother?" Kira said, barely capable of breathing.

"Yes. I gave her your file and she's asked for a home visit." Mrs. Fletcher smiled. "She has chosen you two as possible parents for her baby."

Heart pounding, Kira glanced at Trace, unable to read his thoughts. She turned back to Mrs. Fletcher. "She wants to meet us?"

"You said you don't have a problem with an open adoption. Have you changed your mind?"

"No! It's just I didn't expect it would happen so fast."

"Sometimes that's how it works. So is Monday afternoon okay?"

Kira didn't know how to answer, but Trace took it out of her hands. "Monday will be fine."

Mrs. Fletcher stood. "Good. We'll see you here then."

Kira walked the woman out and stood on the porch until she got in her car and drove off. Hugging herself, she tried to control her trembling as a hundred thoughts raced through her head. A baby. Were they really going to get a baby?

Her excitement died knowing she had to face Trace.

Had he heard their conversation? And how was she going to try to explain why she'd kept her past a secret? What if Mrs. Fletcher brought it up again? She turned to go back into the house, praying Trace still cared for her enough to listen to her reasons.

Inside, she found Trace carrying the cups to the sink. He didn't look at her. Instead he busied himself with the cleanup.

She couldn't let him shut her out again. "Do you have time to talk before you go back to work?"

He grabbed the towel and wiped his hands off, then looked at her. "Don't you think it's a little late for that now?"

Trace had gotten Kira's voice message on the bunkhouse phone. Filthy, he'd jumped into the shower and dressed before he'd headed to the house to meet with Mrs. Fletcher. He'd known how important this was to Kira, and to him, too. He was willing to go through another round of invasive questions. Anything to help Kira. So she could have the child she'd always dreamed of.

He heard Kira's voice from the nursery, but by the time he went into the room, she'd stopped talking. She'd looked surprised to see him there. But wasn't he supposed to play a part in this?

"What do you mean there's nothing to talk about?" Kira asked.

"It seems already settled and Monday we're going to be talking to a woman about raising her child. It's what you want, Kira."

She looked hurt. "You agreed for her to come here. Please tell me now if you've changed your mind."

Trace's mind was reeling. He didn't realize it would be this hard. He'd be lying if he said he didn't want a child with Kira, but like this? He began to think about the next six months, living in the same house. Just walking by her and inhaling her heavenly scent. He would never feel her warmth, her softness against him. When he raised his head, those big brown eyes stared up at him, mesmerizing him.

All the things he would lose forever. This short time was all they had together. Was this the only way he could be a part of her life?

"It's happening so fast," he said.

"Isn't it better this way?" she asked.

Trace studied Kira. He could see the strain on her face, knew how anxious she was. She wanted a baby, even at the cost of their marriage.

He walked toward her. "This is life changing, Kira. You're taking on a lot by yourself, trying to raise a baby."

"I don't have a choice."

"There's always a choice." He stared down at her. He wanted her. If only to taste her mouth, bury himself into her body. But that would be a temporary fix for their problems.

He sighed. He had some thinking to do.

"I've got to get back to work." He practically ran out, more frightened than he'd ever been in his life that he could lose everything. And he wasn't talking about the ranch.

* * *

Later that afternoon, Kira stood in the Winchester Ridge High School auditorium, trying to concentrate on the graduation rehearsal that was going on. But it wasn't working. Between her lack of sleep, and the earlier visit from Mrs. Fletcher, her head was all over the place.

Especially Trace's disappearance. She'd planned to try to talk to him some more, but he conveniently couldn't be found. Worse, her plan had backfired. She'd hoped for some enthusiasm about the possibility of getting a baby, instead Trace was off brooding.

The last thing she wanted was to end their marriage. She loved Trace. When the letter arrived from the agency, she'd hoped her husband wanted to work on saving it, too.

Now with the graduation ceremony tomorrow, she had no choice but to be at school. Then she had to get through the class roundup Saturday before the seniors would go off for the summer. After that she would have Trace alone. They couldn't go on avoiding each other. She knew she'd pushed him away over the past year with her mood swings, her needy attitude. That wasn't going to happen again.

She sighed. In the beginning of their marriage it was simple. He'd loved her, and she'd loved him. Then with her difficulties to conceive a baby, things had turned sour. Instead of turning to each other, they'd turned away. So how could she ask him to just forget everything and convince him to be her husband again? So instead she offered him a divorce with no strings. She just prayed he wouldn't take it.

Tears burned behind her eyes. What she wanted more

than anything else was the chance to make another go of their marriage. Maybe if she'd been honest with him from the start things would be different, but she couldn't even tell him about the child she'd given away. The child who claimed a big piece of her heart.

Hearing her name called brought her back to the present. Kira looked up in time to see the last of the students march across the stage as the principal handed them a substitute diploma. Then they all returned to their seats, the recessional march played and the students filed out. Kira followed them. Once outside she gathered the group for last minute instructions.

"Another thing, class," she began, then looked up feeling her throat tighten. She'd known most of these kids since they were freshmen. Now, some were going off to college, some to the military and others into the work force. She only prayed that she'd given them enough help to survive. More than she ever got at their age.

"This is the last time I'm going to be able to say that." She looked up at Jason Rush, Steve Matthews and Michael Begay. All of them were well over six feet tall. "It's been a delight to have you all this past year," she said, fighting the emotions. "I'd like to continue our friendships, so please…please, when you celebrate be smart. Please don't drink and drive."

She reached up and tapped Steve on the side of the head playfully. "I worked too hard for any of you to end up as roadkill on the highway."

The group released a groan.

"No, I don't want to hear any excuses. I just want your promise."

There were disgruntled murmurs of response, then the group dispersed. All except Jody Campbell. She seemed to be hanging back. Maybe she wanted to talk again. Kira walked toward the young woman.

"Do you need a ride home, Jody?"

"I can walk," the girl said as she hugged her slim body. She looked too thin in her baggy jeans and T-shirt.

Kira glanced up at the threatening clouds as the wind began to pick up. "Come on, Jody. If I don't give you a ride you'll get drenched."

The girl reluctantly followed Kira to the car. Once they were inside the Jeep Cherokee, the sky opened up. Hearing the rain pelt the top of the car, Kira decided to wait out the downpour. She looked across the seat at her sullen passenger.

"You know, Jody, I'm proud of you. You managed to ace your finals and save some of your grade-point average."

"I lost out on first honors, though." She shrugged. "Oh, well, I'm not going to college anyway."

Kira hated it when any of her students gave up. "Jody, there are other ways to go to school than going away. You can attend community college."

Jody brushed her blond hair from her shoulders and stared out the rain streaked window. "I told you my mom can't afford for me to go to college."

"You could apply for a student loan," Kira suggested. "I'll help you fill out the paperwork."

Jody turned to her. Tears clouded her eyes. "I don't

want your help." She began to sob. "You're wasting your time on me."

"Don't say that, Jody, you're worth every bit of my time."

The girl glanced away. "It doesn't matter anymore, nothing matters." She started to climb out, but Kira reached for her.

"It matters, Jody. Please, don't be so hard on yourself. I promise I won't talk about college. Just tell me you're coming to the roundup."

"I have to work that day."

"That's a shame since you've worked so hard on organizing the party. You've got to come, Jody."

The girl hesitated.

"I promise it'll be the last thing I'll ever ask of you. Come on, you need to celebrate."

"I'll try," the girl said, then jumped out of the car, and ran off in the rain.

Kira didn't go after her. She knew from her own experience that she couldn't make Jody confide in her if she didn't want to. But Kira was going to be darn sure that she was there for her. And she had a strange feeling the girl was going to need her.

Trace was angry with himself for riding Thunder so hard. And had it accomplished? Nothing. He climbed down and immediately removed the saddle and blanket, then began walking the lathered horse around to cool him down.

"Sorry, fella. You're the one who had to put up with my bad mood today."

Twenty minutes later, Trace led him into the barn and stall, then started brushing him.

"Did the ride help your mood?"

Trace looked over the stall gate to see Cal.

"Probably not." He stopped brushing. "I've got a lot on my mind. You have a problem with that?"

He shook his head. "You're the boss. I'll just stay out of your way." Cal started to leave, then stopped. "Is the senior roundup still on? Are the kids still coming?"

"As far as I know it is, but maybe you should ask Kira."

Cal looked past him toward the doorway and smiled. "I think I will. Hi, Kira, we were just talking about you."

Trace glanced over his shoulder and saw her. She was dressed in jeans and a red and blue print blouse. Her hair was pulled back, showing off the delicate line of her jaw, the softness of her skin.

"Hi, Jonas." She nodded. "Trace."

He didn't have much to say back. "Cal wants to know about the roundup."

"That's why I'm here." She directed her attention to Trace. "I need to double-check on things."

"As long as I have bodies to bring in the herd, you can do whatever you want." The last thing Trace wanted to do was pretend that everything was perfect between them all day, but why disappoint the kids.

"You sure?" she asked. "With the day of activities, the music and dancing afterward? It's a long day."

"Why would it be any different than in the past four years?" Senior roundup had been Trace's idea after they'd first gotten married.

"Because it is different this year," she told him.

"I've got things to take care of," Cal said and disappeared from the barn.

"That's separate," he said, continuing to brush Thunder. "The roundup has nothing to do with us."

"Trace, it all has everything to do with us." She came to the railing. "I guess we can put off the personal stuff until the roundup is over. But we can't ignore the fact that there is a counselor and birthmother coming Monday."

He closed his eyes a second and took a breath. "Surely we can get through a day together. Call it practice for our interview to see if we qualify as the perfect parents."

When he opened the gate and stepped out, she touched his arm to stop him. "I know the past few months have been hard, but is it that difficult to act as if you care about me? My feelings for you haven't changed, Trace, I love you." She rose up on her toes. Her hand slid up his chest, burning a path of need that threatened to destroy his resolve.

With a groan, Trace captured her mouth in an eager kiss, hating his weakness for her. Yet, it didn't stop his wanting her, needing her. He drew her against his body, hoping to ease some of the ache. It didn't. He released her with a jerk, his breathing labored. Seeing the desire in her rich brown eyes, he had to glance away.

"You can't deny you still care about me," she argued.

"A few heated kisses doesn't make a marriage, Kira." His gaze moved over her pretty face, unable to ignore the hurt his words caused her. He cupped her face. "I couldn't give you what you wanted then, Kira. I'm not sure I can now."

So why in the hell did he want to try so badly?

CHAPTER FIVE

I couldn't give you what you wanted, and I'm not sure I can now.

Trace's words still echoed in her head as Kira walked out to the back porch at dawn on Saturday. Over the last forty-eight hours she tried to stay hopeful. Hopeful that he would say yes to staying with her during the adoption process. It was a perfect opportunity to work on their marriage. That was if he still wanted to be a part of her life, and their baby's life.

All those answers had to be put off until the roundup was over. Once alone Sunday night, they could discuss things and make a decision before the biological mother's visit on Monday.

Trace had stayed away from the house as he prepared for the roundup. And even though she'd had the graduation to help supervise, Kira still found time to think about the future.

Would it include Trace, and a baby?

Now she just had to get through this day, the senior roundup. Kira stepped off the back porch and walked toward the rows of tables that had been set up the night before by the graduates' parents, grateful their kids would have a safe place to celebrate. To protect the guests and the food from the hot sun, several canopies shaded the area. A big banner hung across the barn that read, Winchester Ridge High School Senior Roundup, Class Of 2009.

Kira smiled. She loved doing the party. Both Trace and she had enjoyed it the past. And as far as she could tell, he was okay with it this year, too.

Some of the senior boys had showed up ready to ride in the roundup. They were gathering in the corral with their mounts. Then she saw Trace lead Thunder out of the barn and head to the group. She watched him give directions to the men, then grabbed hold of the saddle horn and easily swung onto his mount.

Panic rose in Kira when she realized that he was ready to leave without saying goodbye. Then he looked in her direction, giving her a sliver of hope that he wanted her to send him off like she had in the past. Trace shouted something to Cal, then walked his horse in the opposite direction, toward her.

Kira caught up to him about halfway. "You're leaving already?"

He nodded and watched the group of men walking their horses through the gate toward the range. "I want to have the herd back by ten. Barring any problems, we should be."

Nodding, she stepped closer to stroke Thunder, but the animal was anxious to take off, too. "The rest of the kids should be here by then to help with the branding."

He tugged on the reins to get the stallion back under

control. "I'll send one of the hands back ahead of us." He hesitated. "Just to make sure none of the kids get in the way. I don't want anyone to get hurt."

"We have some of the dads assigned to help out."

She couldn't take her eyes off Trace, and the way he handled the horse. In jeans and a chambray shirt, he wore his usual belt with the large buckle with the McK brand. It had belonged to his grandfather.

"Be careful," she said, placing her hand on his knee. If the contact bothered him, he didn't let on. Darn. "And tell the men there'll be plenty of good food waiting for them."

He cocked an eyebrow. "Will there be some of your potato salad?"

The request surprised her. "I might be persuaded to whip up a batch." She already had it made and chilling in the refrigerator.

She'd been encouraged after he'd kissed her last night, knowing he was fighting his feelings toward her. She wasn't going to make it easy for him, either. She stared at him, catching his incredible gray eyes.

"Be careful today."

"I'm not foolish, especially with green kids to look out for."

Her fingers flexed against his knee. "Just make sure you look out for you, too."

Trace started to speak, but someone whistled to him. He glanced at the riders off in the distance. "I've got to go."

"Stay safe." She stepped back as he tugged his hat lower, kicked Thunder's sides and they shot off. She trembled as she watched until he disappeared over the horizon.

"Now, I'd say that man wants to stay married."

Kira gasped as she swung around. She found her friend smiling at her. "Michele. I didn't expect you so soon."

Her fellow counselor smiled. "You weren't exactly paying attention. So I take it things are okay with you two?"

Kira released a breath. "It isn't that simple." She knew she had to tell Trace everything. "There's a lot we need to deal with."

Her friend frowned. "Maybe you should skip the talking and go straight to…other things."

That had never been the problem. "I can't rush Trace." Kira had never lived in one place long enough to make any close friends. Not before Michele.

"Well, if it were me, I'd hang onto that cowboy any way I could." Michele looked around. "Um, do you think Jarrett is going to show up today?"

Kira frowned, surprised at her friend's question. "Why would Jarrett come today? He's never helped out before, well, not since I've been here."

"I ran into him at the diner yesterday." Michele shrugged. "I told him about today, and he said he might drop by."

Kira studied her. Michele was interested in her brother-in-law? "Well, if he does it's because he wants something."

Michele grinned. "Yeah, and I'm hoping it's me. You're not the only one who wants a good-looking McKane man."

* * *

Three hours later, Trace was riding drag behind the herd. Thanks to the recent rain, there wasn't much dust kicked up. Just the steady sound of mamas calling to their calves.

He relaxed in the saddle, letting Thunder do the work as he glanced at the incredible scenery. North was the Roan Plateau and thick rows of tall pines of the White River National Forest. He had grown up in this area, hunted and fished here all his life. He never wanted to live anywhere else. He wanted to continue on the family tradition, to raise a family here on McKane land and hand it down to his kids.

Sadness took him by surprise. Now his marriage was possibly coming to an end. What was he supposed to do, just walk away and find someone else? Trouble was, there wasn't anyone else for him. He'd known that the second he'd laid eyes on Kira Hyatt. He fell in love. Now, she wanted to end it all.

Suddenly a few calves ran by and caught up with their mamas, then Cal rode up beside him.

"Did you get them all?"

The foreman nodded. "Yeah. Jerry's hanging back to make sure."

Trace glanced over nearly three hundred heads. "That's about a hundred and fifty calves to brand. It looks like we'll be busy today. If we get them separated fast, break for lunch, then we can work four teams on the branding irons and castrating. We should finish up by afternoon."

Cal grinned. "That's if those senior boys are willing to work. Remember there will be teenage girls hanging on the fence watching them."

"Then you'll have to keep them in line."

Trace could still remember Kira's first roundup, and how distracted she'd made him. It was long before there had been a senior roundup. They had only been dating a few weeks. He shifted in the saddle, recalling that had been the first night he'd made love to her. He released a long breath. That seemed like another lifetime ago.

"Sure, boss," Cal said. "Are there any other miracles you want today?"

Trace remained quiet, but there was one. All he'd ever wanted was Kira, but it might take a miracle to save their marriage.

"They're coming," one of the kids yelled.

Kira climbed up on the stock pen fence, and excitement raced through her as she looked for Trace. It was hard not to be swept up in it. She could imagine a hundred years ago the ranchers' wives doing the same thing, cheering for their men as they brought in the herd.

About a dozen teenage girls were all decked out in their best Western clothes. Kira smiled. Some things never change. It was all about the boy getting the girl. She glanced down at her own dark denim jeans, and new teal Western-style blouse. Since she wasn't planning to do any branding, she could dress up, too.

Would Trace care, or would he be too busy with his work? In the past, he'd always noticed her. Maybe he didn't say a lot, but he couldn't hide his reaction.

When Cal rode in, he assigned jobs to the boys who were to help separate the calves from the cows. Mooing sounds filled the air as the first of the herd arrived.

Things got busy as riders did their jobs to corral the herd.

Trace arrived and was busy shouting orders when suddenly a calf bolted away. He shot off after the wayward bovine. Kira was mesmerized watching the two, man and horse working in unison, cutting off the animal and forcing him back.

"Well, that was impressive," Michele said.

"Thunder is a great cutting horse."

"The cowboy isn't bad, either."

Kira finally smiled. "No, he's not." She glanced past her friend to see Jody arrive.

She started toward the girl who was dressed in faded jeans and a white blouse. She didn't have any fancy boots, just athletic shoes. The girl reminded Kira so much of herself at that age.

"Jody, I'm so glad you could make it."

"I can't stay too late. My mom can't pick me up."

"Then I'll take you home," Kira offered. "You're not missing all the fun."

"But I didn't bring anything to wear to the dance tonight."

Kira smiled. "I have something you can wear," she whispered. "I'm sure we can find something you like."

Jody looked surprised. "Really?"

Kira nodded as another classmate, Laura Carson, came up to them. "Please stay, Jody. This is our last time the class will be together."

Jody glanced around, sadness etched on her face. "But Ben's here."

"So what?" Laura said. "He's a jerk anyway. We'll hang out together."

"How about I put you two in charge of the food tables?"

The two friends exchanged smiles. "Okay."

"Then let's get the other girls together and haul the food out. The guys will finish soon and be hungry."

Jody and Laura gathered up some classmates and they headed off to the kitchen.

"Oh, to be that young and carefree again," Michele said.

Kira nodded, but realized she hadn't felt carefree since the day her parents died and she was left alone.

Trace had been busy most of the day, and so had Kira. Their paths had only crossed once when he'd gotten in line for the noon meal. She served him a plate of fried chicken, a big helping of potato salad and a smile.

He liked the smile the best.

Now, one hundred and forty-one calves had been branded, and eighty-seven castrated into steers which he'd once planned to run in a summer herd. But with the loan payment coming due, he needed to sell them off now, along with some of his heifers. If he got enough money, he could hang on to his breeding bulls a while longer. They were a big part of their future and keeping the ranch going.

A dark sedan car pulled into the driveway, catching Trace's attention. The tall, athletic, Jarrett McKane climbed out and walked toward him with that cocky attitude that demanded people's attention. And he got it.

Trace was surprised, but more suspicious of his brother's casual appearance in faded jeans and a dark Western shirt. What reason would Jarrett have to show up at the roundup?

Trace's thoughts turned to his older brother's business proposition. It would be easy to hand back the land, but he knew Jarrett had never felt the same way he did about the ranch. If someone wanted it, for the right price, his brother would sell. Somebody had to want that section of land—and badly—for Jarrett to work so hard to get it back.

"Hey, bro, I hear you could use some help," Jarrett said.

"I'd say you were a little late. We finished the branding a while ago. But if you really want to help out, Cal can use your help separating the yearlings." He raised an eyebrow. "That is, if you still remember how to ride a horse."

His brother's eyes narrowed. "As I recall, I've beaten you in a few rodeos."

Jarrett had beaten him in a lot of things. "Then prove it."

"I will, but first, I need to say hello to a few people."

Trace took hold of his arm. "I won't have you wheeling and dealing at Kira's school function."

"You're pretty protective of the little mother-to-be."

Trace stiffened as he glanced around. "I'd appreciate it if you'd keep that to yourself. Nothing is definite yet."

Jarrett relented. "Sure."

"I mean it, Jarrett."

"Okay. Okay." He pulled away and walked off, but

slowed his gait when Michele Turner came toward him. Then together the two went toward the branding pens.

"Trace."

He turned around to see Kira. He put on a smile. "How's it going?"

"Good, so far. We're just about to start the contests. Are you able to help with the cutting competition? Mark Petersen is going to handle steer wrestling, and Cal will do the roping."

Trace shook his head. "Where do these kids get so much energy?" They started walking toward the branding pen. "I could use a nap."

She smiled. "I wouldn't mind one, either."

His gaze locked with hers. "You think they'd notice if we disappeared?"

Kira swallowed hard, and turned away. "Yeah, I think so."

Trace's body tensed. He tried not to remember those past lazy afternoons when they'd go up to the bedroom and make love for hours. Where had those carefree days gone?

"I better get going," he murmured, then turned and walked away. He quickened his steps. He didn't need to be thinking about Kira right now, especially since they hadn't been intimate in months.

He groaned and kept walking. Today was about the kids. He needed to keep his desire for Kira out of it.

A nearly impossible task.

Kira stood at the corral fence along with the other kids and parents, watching Trace work Thunder. She'd always been in awe of her husband's skill with horses. He looked so at ease on the powerful stallion, but there was no doubt who was in charge. Trace.

She glanced down at his gloved hands. She knew that along with that power came gentleness. A shiver raced through her, recalling the nights he'd stroked her, caressed her body, bringing her endless pleasure.

"He's pretty good."

Kira fought a blush as she turned to find Jarrett next to her at the railing. "Yes, he is."

A mischievous grin appeared on his face. "That's because I taught him everything he knows."

Cheers broke out from the crowd. "Really?" She hadn't known her brother-in-law as a young man. And just barely got to know him better over the past few years because Trace and he weren't close. A few holidays here and there when their folks were alive. "Since I've never seen you on a horse, I can't judge."

"And you're loyal to your husband."

"Always."

"Lucky guy."

She'd known Jarrett was attracted to her when she first came to town. But the minute she saw Trace, she couldn't think of anyone else. "Okay, what do you want, Jarrett?"

"Can't I give my sister-in-law a compliment?" He looked toward the corral. "I know things have been rough for you both lately." He glanced around, then lowered his voice. "Well, what I mean is the adoption."

Of course Trace's brother would be interviewed by the agency. She stepped down from the railing and Jarrett followed her away from the other people. "We're still in the beginning stages. I'd appreciate it if you kept it quiet for now."

"Of course." He paused. "I never realized that things…I mean I know you two wanted kids, but I never dreamed it was like this."

She managed a smile and touched his arm. "It's okay, Jarrett. I've accepted it," she lied, not wanting to go over this now, or with him.

He nodded. "Well, if there's anything I can do. There's a doctor I knew in college. He's made a name for himself in the fertility field."

It was nice that he wanted to help, but they'd already been to two specialists. "Thank you, Jarrett. We've been to doctors, and it hasn't helped." She blinked back tears. "Hopefully adoption will give us the family we want." She told him about the appointment on Monday.

"That's great news." He hugged her. "Is there anything I can do to help? I know it's expensive."

Kira started to answer, when she heard, "We can handle it."

They both turned to see Trace.

She stepped back from Jarrett, seeing the look on her husband's face. Jealousy? "Trace. I thought you were working with the kids."

He moved up beside her and stood close. "Cal and some of the other hands are handling the competition." He looked at her, but his gray eyes were unreadable. "Thought you might need some help."

She managed to pull her gaze away from his. "I've just been waiting for the DJ to set up for the dance. Jody Campbell organized everything, she's assigned all the kids with a job." She glanced around the area. "Maybe I should go find her. If you men will excuse me."

Trace watched Kira walk off. He wanted to go after her, and he would, just as soon as he figured out why his brother was here.

"Okay, what's going on, Jarrett?"

"I told you, I just came by to help out. You should have called me about the roundup."

"I've called you for help over the years. You've always been busy. Why is the ranch suddenly important to you?"

"Just because I don't want to run the place doesn't mean I don't care about the ranch."

"Then prove it. Don't call in my loan in thirty days. Give me more time."

Jarrett hesitated. "If you really don't have the money, do you think you can keep the ranch going?"

"Yes, the ranch is making money. I just have other expenses." He hated telling his brother the details. "Like you said, adopting a baby is expensive. If I need to, I'll sell off my breeding bulls."

Jarrett looked distracted, and Trace caught Michele walking toward them. "Come by my office next week, we'll talk." Jarrett rushed off before Trace could say anything.

Trace had wanted to look up to his older brother, but years of watching him take from people and receive all the benefits of the favored son had changed that.

The one time Trace came in first had been with Kira, when she'd chosen him over his brother. Now, he could lose her, too. If that happened, it didn't matter if he kept the ranch, or not.

CHAPTER SIX

THE afternoon was in full swing as Trace kept busy sharing his expertise with the kids. He had Jake Petersen on Thunder, instructing him on the art of cutting.

Kira noticed that the teenage girls were watching intently. Most of the females were eyeing the boys, but a few of the mothers had their attention square on her husband.

Had Trace noticed it, too? Did he notice the other women? Desire other women? A woman who could give him a child?

Suddenly cheers broke out in the arena as Jake completed his task. The boy pumped his fist in the air in celebration. Kira smiled, refusing to let anything interfere with this great day. It was for the kids. Next, Ben Kerrigan climbed on the horse and began his turn. Although he wasn't as successful, the crowd cheered him on. All except for Jody.

Kira noticed the teenage girl stayed back from the group, but when Ben got down from his ride, she was waiting for him at the corral gate. After talking a moment, Ben shook his head and stormed off.

Not good. Kira threw up a prayer, hoping it was nothing more serious than a silly fight, that she'd been wrong about a possible pregnancy. Something she knew about firsthand and could change your life, forever.

Kira heard her name called and turned around and saw Trace walking in her direction. "Want to try a turn at cutting?"

"You're kidding. You want me to make a fool of myself in front of the kids?"

"You're a good rider, Kira. I doubt you could ever look foolish." He tugged on her arm. "Come on, I dare you."

Just then a chant started amongst the kids. "Mrs. McKane. Mrs. McKane." That and Trace's sexy grin, she couldn't resist. The kids began to cheer as Trace led her to the horse. "Just remember it's been a long time since I've been on a horse."

"It's okay, Kira. I'll be close by," he assured her.

"Promise?" That had been something they used to say to each other.

He nodded. "Promise."

Kira tore her gaze away to concentrate on her task. She placed her foot in the stirrup and found Trace's hands on her waist, boosting her up. Once in the saddle, she pulled her cowboy hat down on her head to shield her eyes from the bright sunlight, then looked at her husband. "Refresh me on what to do."

"First of all, relax." He reached up and placed her hands on the horn, letting the reins go slack. "Let Thunder do the work."

"Yes, sir."

With a wink, he strolled to the side of the corral and

called out instructions. When one of the boys released a young steer, the cutting horse took off, twisting and turning, trying to maneuver the cow back toward the fence. Kira kept her legs pressed firmly against the horse and her hands on the saddle horn. It took a while but she relaxed as Thunder did his job, then the bell rang to signal time was up.

The kids broke into cheers as Trace came out to help her off. "You were great," he said, then surprised her with a quick kiss on the lips. The crowd roared with approval. A sudden heat rose to her face as Kira made her way back to the fence. *Don't make anything out of his attention,* she told herself. *It's only for show.*

Two classmates, Amy and Marcy, rushed to her. "Oh, Mrs. McKane, that was so cool," Amy gushed. "And Mr. McKane is so good-looking." Then the girls ran off giggling, quickly distracted by another boy riding Thunder.

Back to work. Kira turned her attention to the barn and the truck unloading the audio equipment for the dance in a few hours. At the patio area she saw the volunteer fathers starting up the barbecues for the hamburgers. She checked her watch to see that everything was on schedule.

"Mrs. McKane."

Kira turned around to see Jody and Laura hurrying toward her.

"Jody, Laura, are you having fun?"

They answered with smiles. "Oh, yes," Laura said. "We're going to eat soon. By then the DJ will be ready to start the music. Some of the girls want to change their clothes. I've put the Girls Only sign on the bunkhouse door."

Kira thought about the room that Trace had been staying in and wondered if he'd locked it. "Do you know what rooms to use?"

"Mr. McKane gave us permission to use three rooms and a bathroom. He said he locked the rooms we can't use. And Cal will make sure the boys stay away."

"Good. Laura, would you ask your mother to help supervise?"

"Sure. Come on, Jody."

Kira placed a hand on Jody. "I need her to help me with something first." Kira wanted Jody to stay for the evening, and if that meant finding her something to wear, then that's what she'd do. "She'll meet up with you later."

At the girl's nod, Kira took Jody to the house.

"You don't have to do this, Mrs. McKane."

"I know. But I want you to stay and enjoy the party. You're a graduate, this is supposed to be a wonderful time for you. Enjoy it."

They passed several mothers in the kitchen, setting out the leftovers for supper. With a promise to be back soon to help out, she took Jody through the house and up the stairs.

"Your house is so beautiful, Mrs. McKane."

"Thank you. It's my husband's family home." The first home she'd had in a very long time, since her parents' death. She wondered how much longer she would call it home.

Kira walked down the hall into the master bedroom,

but when she turned around she'd lost her companion. Then she saw Jody across the hall in the nursery.

"Jody."

The girl jumped. "I'm sorry." She pointed to the cradle. "Are you going to have a baby?"

"Sadly, no." Kira forced a smile. "Trace and I would love to have a child, but so far, it hasn't happened."

"Oh. Sorry, I didn't mean to be nosy."

"It's okay." Kira nodded and together they walked into the master bedroom. She went to the closet and began the search. She pulled out a couple of gauzy skirts and a peasant blouse. Kira glanced at Jody. "What size are you, about a four?"

The girl hesitated, then nodded.

Kira stopped. "Don't worry, Jody. I've never worn these clothes to school. No one will know that they aren't yours. Besides, don't girls borrow clothes from friends?"

She nodded. "But you're my guidance counselor."

Kira smiled. "Not anymore."

Jody finally smiled, too. "I guess not."

"Okay, I think this multicolored skirt will work. It has kind of a Western look." She went to the dresser and took out a bright-pink, cotton top and a wide belt. Then she went to the closet again and found a denim jacket. "It'll get cool tonight." She glanced at the girl's white canvas shoes. "I think your shoes will work with the outfit, but if not, I have boots."

The teenager eyed the clothes draped on the bed. "These are so beautiful. What if something happens to them?"

"They're only clothes, Jody." Kira headed out. "When you leave, go out the front door and no one will see you. Now, you better get dressed. I'm depending on you to help supervise the party."

"Thank you, Mrs. McKane."

"You're welcome." Kira shut the door and was surprised to see Trace waiting for her in the hall. "Trace. Is there a problem?"

"No, but since the girls have taken over the bunkhouse, I was going to shower and change here. Then I heard you in there with Jody."

He was coming to their bedroom to change. "Can you wait a few minutes?"

"I could shower in the guest bath, but my good jeans and boots are in the closet," he suggested.

"You go and I'll bring you your clothes." She nudged him toward the bathroom.

He hesitated. "Have I told you what a great job you're doing today?" He jerked a nod toward their bedroom. "And getting Jody something to wear was awfully nice of you."

She shrugged. "She doesn't have the money to dress like the other kids." Kira glanced away. "I know what it's like to be different. To feel left out."

He only nodded, then went to the bath, and closed the door. Soon, she heard the sound of the water running in the shower.

The bedroom door opened and Jody stepped out. "Oh, Jody, you look so cute," Kira told her.

"You think so?"

"Yes, just let me put a little makeup on you," She

guided her into the bathroom. Ten minutes later, she'd fixed her hair and added color to the girl's cheeks. Pleased with her work, Kira sent Jody off to her friends.

Trace felt foolish sneaking down the hall in his own house, practically naked. And he wasn't about to put on his dirty clothes. Not hearing a sound, he peered into the bedroom. His heart shot off pounding when he found Kira standing in front of the full-length mirror. She had on a bright pink and green sundress, and a matching sweater. Her hair was pulled back from her pretty face, hoop earrings hung from each delicate lobe.

She turned and suddenly gasped when she saw him. "Trace. Oh, I'm sorry, I forgot your clothes."

"It's okay. Is the coast clear?" He glanced around, then stepped inside, closing the door behind him.

He couldn't help but notice how her gaze roamed over him. It was so intense it felt like a caress. His breath grew labored, his body definitely aware. "I need to shave. Are you finished in the bath."

"Oh, yes, of course."

In the past, he'd play this little game and they'd end up in bed. Now, they both seemed awkward, unable to speak. He walked across the room into the bathroom they'd once shared. It smelled of Kira, her shampoo, her body spray.

He drew a breath like a suffocated man.

She came to the doorway. "I should get back to the party."

He opened the cabinet and was surprised to find all his things still there. He took out his shaving cream. "It should only take me ten minutes and I'll be down." He found he liked her standing there, watching. It was like so many times they'd shared and taken for granted. He caught her reflection in the mirror as he applied the cream to his jaw. She still hadn't left.

"You did a nice thing for Jody."

She shrugged. "It's important she feel good about herself."

He took a swipe across his jaw with the razor. "I'd say you helped her with that tonight."

"Kids can be cruel."

Trace knew that Kira was talking about herself. Although she never talked much about her life in foster care, he knew it had been a bad time. He'd never gone without in his childhood, not for the basic things anyway. So he couldn't share that experience with her.

He paused. "I never want you to feel that way, Kira. Ever again."

She swallowed. "Oh, Trace, I don't. You've always made me feel special. You've given me a great home and life here."

Then why did he feel like he'd let her down?

Two hours later, the barbecue was finished and the music had started just outside the barn on a portable dance floor that had been set up for the nighttime festivities.

Several kids were already dancing, including Jody. She looked adorable. For the next hour, the music switched back and forth between country and rock. When the country came on a lot of the parents made their way to the floor, showing up the kids with their two-stepping.

Cal and some of the ranch hands hung around playing chaperones, making sure the teenagers didn't go off by themselves. There had been strict rules for tonight's party, but that didn't mean some weren't going to try to break them.

She glanced around to see Trace talking with some of the fathers. So far he'd kept his distance since their meeting in the bathroom. Her breathing grew labored, recalling his near-naked body. All at once Trace looked her way. Their gazes locked momentarily, then someone called to her.

"Mrs. McKane."

Kira turned around to see Laura Carson hurrying toward her. "Have you seen Jody?"

"No, I thought she was with you."

The girl's eyes narrowed. "She was until Ben started bugging her. I left them alone because I was hoping they would talk and work things out." She pointed toward a group of trees. "The last time I saw them, they were over there, talking. Later, I saw Ben back with his friends but I can't find Jody anywhere."

"Did you ask Ben?"

She nodded. "He said he didn't know or care where she was."

Well, he was going to care. "Don't panic yet, I'll go look for her."

Kira was worried this would happen. She searched the area and ended up near Ben Kerrigan. She motioned for him to come to her.

"What's up, Mrs. M?"

"I'm concerned about Jody. I can't seem to find her. Would you know where she is?"

He shrugged. His gaze refused to meet hers. "Maybe she left."

"No, I was going to take her home later. I heard you two talked earlier. Was she upset about something?"

He glanced around nervously. "Maybe. We broke up a few weeks ago. She wants to get back together. I told her no way."

"Is that all you told her?"

He didn't say anything.

"At least tell me what direction she went."

"I don't know, maybe that way." He pointed past the corral.

Kira didn't say anything. She took off, knowing there was an upset girl out there, alone. Panic raced through her. She knew what that felt like.

Stopping to grab a flashlight from the barn, Kira headed through the empty corral toward the grove of trees. If Jody wasn't there she'd go back for help, but the last thing the girl needed was an audience for her humiliation.

She approached the trees and heard something. The soft sound of crying. Kira pointed the light toward the ground and kept walking. On a downed tree log, she found Jody. Her legs were drawn up and her head was on her knees, sobbing.

"Jody," Kira whispered as she approached.

The girl suddenly straightened and looked at her. "Who is it?"

"It's me, Kira McKane." She walked to her. "Are you okay?"

"Yeah, I'm fine." She stood and moved away. "Please, just leave me alone."

"I can't, Jody. And you're not okay. Let me help you."

She shook her head. "No! No one can help me. Everybody will hate me when they find out…" She started to walk away.

"No, Jody, they won't. I won't, I promise. I want to help, no matter what it is." Kira hesitated, trying to choose just the right words. "Let me help you."

"Why?"

"I understand what you're going through."

"No, you don't. Nobody does. And Ben doesn't care. He said he never cared about me. And now, he'll hate me."

"That's not true. He's just scared. So are you."

"What do you know about it?"

Kira took a breath and released it, catching movement by a tree. She tensed even more when she recognized the familiar silhouette. Trace. He stepped out so she could see his face in the moonlight. Luckily Jody couldn't.

"I know what it's like to feel alone," She continued to talk. "You think you have nowhere to turn, no one to trust enough to tell them you're pregnant."

She gasped. "How did you find out?"

This wasn't how she wanted Trace to learn about her past. Tears filled her eyes, praying he would understand. "Because I've been there, Jody. I was fifteen. And pregnant."

* * *

Trace froze, fighting to draw air into his lungs as he stared at his wife. Kira? Kira had a baby? In five years of marriage, she'd never told him.

"You're just saying that," Jody countered.

He tried to make out Kira's face in the moonlight. He heard the pain in her voice as her arms hugged herself.

"No, Jody, I'm not," she went on to say as she went to the girl. "And I felt exactly like you do right now. Alone. Like there's nowhere or no one to turn to. But there is, Jody."

The girl began to sob again. "No. My mother can't handle this. I…I let her down. Oh, what am I going to do?"

She took the girl's hands. "Jody, listen to me. You're not alone. There's help out there, and a lot of options for you."

Jody was quiet for a long time, then asked, "What happened to your baby?"

There was a long pause. "I gave him up." Kira's voice was raw with emotion. "I had no family to help me, and I was too young to keep him."

Jody looked up and started to speak—that was when she spotted him in the shadows. "Oh, Mr. McKane." She stumbled to stand.

Kira turned around, too. "Trace."

"Sorry to interrupt." He stepped further into the lit area. "I just wanted to make sure you were all right."

Kira went to him. "We're fine."

"That's good. Then I'll leave."

"No, we'll go back with you." She squeezed Jody's

hand. "We'll talk more later. We'll deal with this together, Jody."

The girl nodded. "Thank you."

This time Kira had no doubt that Trace overheard her admission. Maybe it was better it happened this way. She wouldn't have to figure out a way to explain why she gave away her son. The guilt she'd felt every day since. And no matter what kind of absolution she got from him, it wouldn't make up for the loss she'd felt every day for almost fifteen years.

The night had finally come to an end as Trace watched the last of the graduates and their parents drive off.

Everyone had been exhausted from the day's events, but the roundup was completed successfully and the students had a great time at the party, not realizing what had gone on behind the scenes.

Trace looked at the house. He needed to talk to Kira. With everything going on at the party, there hadn't been time. He fought the anger building inside him. Though could anyone blame him? She'd kept a secret from him, a big secret.

He released a breath and walked up the back steps to the house. No matter how it ended up, it was time she told him everything about her past.

After sending Jake Peterson's dad off with the last of the tables and chairs, he walked into the kitchen and found Kira wiping off the counter. There wasn't much evidence left of the party. She finally turned around and met his gaze. "Oh, Trace. Is everyone gone?"

He nodded. "Yeah, it's just you and me. What about

Jody?" The last he'd seen of the girl had been after they'd brought her back. She sneaked her upstairs until the party ended.

"Laura's parents took her home. I'm going by tomorrow to help her explain things to her mother."

Trace nodded, but he was barely holding it together. Why were they discussing mundane things when their marriage was hanging by a thread? And it was weakening quickly with the weight of the secret she'd kept from him. Just another thing she couldn't share with him

"Were you ever going to tell me, Kira?" When she started to speak, he raised his hand. "And no more excuses, you owe me the truth. In two days we have another visit from the adoption agency, and a birth mother."

She hesitated, then said, "I know you won't believe me, but I was planning to tell you tomorrow."

"Is that what you were talking about with Mrs. Fletcher when I walked in the nursery that day?"

She nodded. "She was going over my medical records, asking about miscarriages and live births. I didn't want to lie."

That did it for Trace. "But it's okay to lie to your husband."

"I didn't exactly lie, Trace."

"No, you just omitted something very important in your past."

"It was a painful past. I never shared that time with anyone. Can't you understand I wanted to forget, to start over," she pleaded. "I wanted a life with you."

He cursed and looked away.

Kira felt the familiar rejection shoot through her body, nearly crippling her. But somehow she found the strength not to let it show.

"Okay, Trace," she began. "What do you want to know? How I could give up my own baby? How could I let a boy talk me into sex at barely fifteen?" She glared at him. "Don't you know all foster kids are wild? We'll do anything." More tears flooded her eyes, blinding her. "I was no better than trash."

"Stop it," he ordered.

"Oh, but you want to hear the truth, don't you? Do you have any idea what it feels like to be an outcast, to have no friends?" She paced along the island counter, glad it was separating them. "It wasn't so bad in grade school, but by the time I was in high school, kids wanted nothing to do with me. Then Michael came along and gave me a little attention, and I grabbed it. Gullible me, I believed him when he said he loved me." A laugh escaped as she swiped at the tears on her cheeks. "Oh God, it had been so long since I'd heard those words. Then when I told him I was pregnant, he acted as if he didn't know me.

"I was devastated," she said in a hoarse whisper. "Worse, the father of my baby was my foster family's nephew. I was packed up so fast and shoved out the door, I didn't know what was happening."

"Where did you go?"

"Girls like me go into a group home. There were several of us who were pregnant. I stayed there until I delivered my baby. My little boy. But I couldn't keep him."

She tried to hold it together, but failed, covering her

eyes she began to sob. Then she felt Trace's arms around her, holding her.

"I'm sorry, Trace. I know I should have told you. But I was afraid that you wouldn't want me either."

"Shh, Kira. Don't talk."

Trace couldn't stand to hear any more of her pain. What she had to go through alone. He was hurt by her lack of trust, but he understood why she'd kept the secret.

Why she desperately wanted another baby.

Kira lifted her head, pain etched on her face. "It's better now that it's out in the open. I was wrong to push you for a baby, Trace. I'm sorry for everything." She turned and hurried out of the room.

He was left dazed. She truly thought that he would leave her because of her past. Why not, everyone else had in her life. He wanted to go to her, but knew if he did he had to make the commitment he was staying, if not as her husband, at least as the father to a baby. He knew he wanted to be both he just didn't know how to make it happen.

A chill rushed through him at the thought of never having Kira in his life. He wouldn't have much of a life without her. The past few months had proven that. He made his way through the house, and when he reached the stairs, took them two at a time and nearly ran down the hall to their bedroom. The door was open and he looked inside to find Kira on the bed.

His chest tightened painfully. "Kira," he breathed.

She wiped her eyes and sat up. "Do you need some clothes?"

"No. I don't need any clothes. I came to see you."

Her blond hair was mussed, her brown eyes were searching for any encouragement from him.

His eyes watered and his throat tightened. "I wish I could have been there for you." He thought about the agony she must have gone through trying to fill that void in her life. "I understand why you want a baby so desperately." She had no family, except for a grandmother who hadn't wanted her and a child she hadn't been able to keep.

A son Kira had never been able to see grow up.

He came further into the room. Now, he understood so many things. And he loved her more for her strength to survive the cards life had dealt her.

"So you're going to leave me, too."

He swallowed. "It would be easier to forget to breathe. Do you have any idea how many nights I've lain awake in that damn bunk, thinking about you? Thinking about the talking, the sharing, and about how we used to turn to each other in the night and how sweet it was to hold you in my arms. How loving you was heaven. How badly I wanted you."

Kira sucked in a breath, eager to hear every word, praying she wasn't dreaming.

He reached the bed, his gray gaze locked with hers, his voice husky with emotion as he continued, "It's been hell."

Kira's eyes searched his. "For me, too. I know I turned away from you and that hurt you."

He placed his finger against her lips. "No more talking, Kira. Not now." He leaned forward and brushed a kiss over her mouth. She froze as his lips slowly moved over hers, drawing feelings out that she hadn't acknowledged in so long.

She wanted Trace, and she knew he still wanted her. He broke off the kiss and studied her. "I want you, Kira. Don't push me away, not tonight."

"Oh, Trace, I won't." She wrapped her arms around his neck and kissed him, letting him know her desire. It wasn't long before they had stripped off their clothes.

Under the covers, Trace pulled her against his body and his hands moved over her. Soon he made her forget everything.

At least for a little while, everything was perfect between them.

CHAPTER SEVEN

AT DAWN the next morning, Kira opened her eyes to see the familiar surroundings of the master bedroom. And to the once familiar feel of Trace's body as she lay pressed against him. She shifted her gaze to his face relaxed in sleep.

She stared up at the ceiling and recalled every precious moment they'd shared. The few hours they'd stolen together. It had been like their first year of marriage before her obsession for a baby. Before Trace learned of her past. And it didn't solve anything.

Her eyes filled. After last night it was going to be harder to stay away from Trace, but she had to. If she wanted to survive giving him up, she had to find a way.

Trace stirred and instinctively drew Kira tighter against him. She forced herself not to react. She fell back into a doze waking again only when, she felt him move away and get out of bed. Slipping on his jeans, he pulled his T-shirt over his head as he walked out of the room.

Kira opened her eyes as her husband walked out of the bedroom, relieved that they skipped the-morning-after-talk. He'd probably gone off to do chores. She collapsed back on the pillow, trying not to think about their perfect night together. No matter how good they'd been together, it still hadn't changed anything. They had problems. And in the end, she still couldn't give Trace a biological child.

Trace stood in the kitchen trying to hold onto his common sense. A perfect night in bed with his wife didn't mean their marriage was back on track, but it was the closest they'd been in months. And he wanted this to be a new beginning for them. Although words weren't spoken, he knew she still loved him. He felt the same way.

He poured some coffee. But he couldn't help but have hope, hope that they could make it work between them.

He went to the refrigerator and took out the orange juice. After filling two glasses, he carried them to the table. There were two place settings already set out for their breakfast.

Kira walked into the room, wearing a floral satin robe. He immediately paused, registering she didn't have a damn thing on underneath. Great. Had she suddenly run out of clothes? He sucked in a long breath and released it.

"I thought we could use some coffee and a little sustenance," he informed her.

Kira went to the table and picked up a mug. She brushed her blond curls back from her face and took a sip. The fabric clung to every curve of her luscious body.

"Thank you," she told him.

He also savored the hot brew, letting the caffeine kick-start him. Then he watched as she sipped from her mug, her big brown eyes locked on him. He could feel the tension.

"You want a sweet roll?"

"Maybe later," she said. "I think we should talk?"

He turned a chair around and straddled it. He didn't have much choice. "Okay, tell me what's on your mind?"

Kira joined him, sitting down across from him. "What happened last night wasn't planned." She held up her hand. "And I want you to know that I don't expect anything from you."

He tensed. "So we just used each other for comfort."

Her eyes widened. "Stop putting words into my mouth. A lot happened yesterday, and I turned to you because I trust you…and I care about you."

"And I care about you. Dammit, Kira. Do you think I can just turn off feelings after all these years."

"Right now, we're both too vulnerable to jump back into this." Kira knew she had to protect herself. "I think we should back up a little while."

"You mean for six months, until you get a baby."

She tried not to flinch. "I want to use the six months to see how we get along."

"And then you walk away."

She sighed. "No, so we can both rebuild our lives. I thought you agreed to this?"

"I agreed to meeting with the counselor. We're well past that."

"Okay, here's your chance. Tomorrow, we're possibly going to meet a birth mother who may choose us." She took a breath and released it. "That's hard to comprehend."

He remained silent and let her talk.

"I know it's happening quickly, Trace, but we need to make a decision." She set down her mug and looked at him. "I know you were blindsided yesterday when you learned about my baby, but it's something I can't change. So now, we have to decide if we move ahead."

He could hear the trembling in her voice. He wasn't too steady, either. He'd made a lot of mistakes in the past.

"There's nothing to forgive, Kira." He wished he could have been there for her. "And I know how much adopting a baby means to you."

Kira tried not to get too excited over Trace's words. "So you want to go along with it for…six months? To see how things work out."

She watched his eyes flare. "Your idea isn't foolproof, Kira. What happens if we don't get picked tomorrow?"

She'd be heartbroken. "I have to stay positive. I didn't want you to feel trapped, either."

"Trapped into what? We agreed to adopt a long time ago."

"We need to act as if we have a real marriage for the full time, Trace." She blinked back tears. "I don't want a man who walks out if things get tough."

"Isn't that what you're going to do, eventually?"

She ignored his sarcasm. "So are you moving back home?"

He paused. "I can't just jump back into it as if we never had problems."

"I know. That's why I'll be moving into the guest room."

"Like hell!"

She suddenly got hopeful.

"I'll sleep there."

She worked hard to hide her hurt. "If it's what you want?"

"Hell, no, it's not what I want." He shot up and marched to the window. "This isn't easy for me, Kira. And last night with you didn't help. I hate to fail. But if we're lucky enough to get a baby and that's no sure thing," he warned before shrugging. "Who knows, we might just get along."

Barely containing her excitement, Kira boldly walked over to Trace, raised herself up on her bare toes and brushed her mouth across his. Hearing his groan, she deepened the kiss and he quickly joined in. By the time she pulled back she could see the desire in his eyes. "That was to officially welcome you home." She turned and strolled off. Her husband needed something to think about on those lonely nights in the guest room.

A few hours later, heading into town, Trace was still wondering if he'd done the right thing by moving back into the house. Kira had gone to see Jody, and he needed to talk to his brother.

Since it was Sunday, Jarrett was at home. Trace drove

to the custom-built home on the land that his brother had kept when he sold him the half of the ranch their parents had left him.

The two-story, modern structure sat on a hill with rolling green lawn in front, and the back overlooked a picturesque view of the mountain range. Trees lined most of the property, adding privacy to the large deck and hot tub.

Trace made his way along the blue stone walk and rang the bell. His brother quickly answered, dressed in jeans and a blue collared shirt.

"Hey, Trace, you made it. Come in."

"I said I'd be here." Trace stepped into the slate tiled entry, then into a huge great room with a stone fireplace that took up most of one wall. Oversize brown leather furniture made up a cozy seating area around the hearth. He followed his brother across the hardwood floors to the dining room, off a kitchen with black cabinets and marble countertops.

"Nice place."

Jarrett frowned. "You haven't been here before?"

"No. I guess my invitation got lost in the mail."

His brother ignored the comment. "You and Kira are always welcome anytime."

"I'll pass that along to my wife." He didn't care if he was added to Jarrett's social list or not. "Okay. So what do you want to talk to me about?"

"I have everything laid out here."

Trace turned and looked at the table. "What are you talking about?"

"The property deal."

He had contracts drawn up? "I never said I would sell, just that I'd talk to you."

Jarrett studied him. "Come on, bro, you know you can't come up with the payment."

Was his brother just waiting for him to fail? "You know nothing, *bro*. I have the money."

His brother motioned for Trace to take a seat, then he sat across from him. "We both know that the adoption costs could run to a sizable amount."

Trace didn't want to talk to Jarrett about this. "I'll take care of it."

"What if you can't? You could lose the ranch and the baby."

And Kira, he thought. "Okay, what's your plan?"

"Simple." Jarrett slid a paper across the table. "I want to buy back the section of the land that borders my property."

Trace didn't believe this was out of the kindness of his brother's heart. "We talked about this before, Jarrett. I don't want that land developed with homes."

"And I won't, not for ten years."

That made Trace suspicious, too. His brother didn't do anything that didn't benefit himself. Yet, did Trace have any other options? The past few years, they'd had a lot of expensive medical procedures for Kira, costs that the insurance hadn't covered, combined with two lean years of cattle profits. The money he'd held back for emergencies was nearly gone.

He glanced down at the property agreement. The balloon payment was due the end of June. Three weeks. He looked at his brother. Something told him not to trust him. There had been too many times his older brother had used him.

"Can you give me a week to think about it?" Trace asked.

Jarrett hesitated, then nodded. "That's about all I can give you."

Why was that important if his brother wasn't going to do anything with the land? He needed to think about this.

Jarrett nodded. "Also, I wanted to give you this card for Kira."

Trace took it. "Dr. Thomas Faulkner, Fertility Specialist."

"We knew each other in college and kept in touch. I told Kira about him."

Why the hell was Jarrett discussing anything with his wife?

"I thought she'd mention it to you."

Trace thought they'd exhausted every avenue on fertility. Besides, they were ending their marriage. He suddenly thought about the parting kiss she'd given him earlier. Between last night and this morning, it didn't feel like things were ending to him. "Did she say she wanted to get in touch with this doctor?"

Jarrett shrugged. "I don't think you should give up, Trace. That's another reason you should sell me back the land."

Trace didn't want to listen anymore. "I need to go. I'm meeting Kira for lunch," he lied.

Jarrett watched Trace. "Okay, but think it over…this is a good deal for you."

Trace knew from experience that wasn't true. His brother was up to something, and he was going to find out what it was.

Two hours later, Kira tried to hold on to the afterglow as she drove into town. Not just from Trace making love to her last night, but because he was moving back into the house, and agreed to the adoption. Okay, it was only to the guest room, and he wouldn't be around to be a daddy to her baby, but it was a start. A big one. Although he seemed angry about her dismissing their love making, at least they were talking again.

Kira sobered as she turned down Elm Street toward Jody's house. It wasn't the best neighborhood, bringing back memories of her own childhood. When she was a little girl, she remembered her parents had lived paycheck to paycheck, so when they'd died, there wasn't any extra money to help raise their only child. Just the little that her grandmother got, but the ailing woman decided not to take her granddaughter in.

Kira pushed away the bad memories and parked at the curb of the small rental house. The lawn needed to be mowed, and the house could use a fresh coat of paint. It amazed her that Jody could deal with all this and still make the grades in school. Kira was going to do everything she could to help her now.

She climbed out and went up the walk. Soon, the door opened and Jody greeted her. The teenager looked tired and worried.

"Hi, Mrs. McKane."

"Hello, Jody." She hugged the girl. "How are you feeling today?"

"Better now that you're here." Jody nodded toward the door. "My mom just got up. It's her day off so she sleeps in."

Kira knew she was making excuses for Marge Campbell. She'd bet that it was Jody who took care of things around the house, along with going to school and working a part-time job.

"We're going to deal with this together, Jody."

Tears flooded Jody's eyes.

Kira hugged her again.

"Jody, who are you talking to?" Mrs. Campbell came to the door. "Oh, Mrs. McKane. What brings you here today?" Dressed in an old chenille robe, the forty-plus woman pushed back her wild, bleached-blond hair. Years of hard living showed in her lined face.

"Hello, Mrs. Campbell. Sorry to bother you, but Jody and I want to talk with you."

Marge Campbell glanced back and forth between the two, then slowly opened the squeaky screen door. Inside, the living room was furnished with a faded print sofa and two mismatched chairs. Although the ashtrays had been emptied the place still reeked of cigarette smoke.

Jody directed her to the sofa. Once they were all seated, Kira exchanged a glance with Jody.

"If this is about Jody going away to college," the mother began, "it just isn't possible. I need my daughter here to help out."

"No, Mom. It's not about college. I'm pregnant," the girl blurted out.

"What?" Marge gasped. "You promised you wouldn't do anything. That you'd stay away from those boys." She jumped up from her seat. "Now, what are we going to do raising some kid's brat? I warned you this would happen." She wheeled around on her daughter. "Who did this to you?"

Kira stood. "Mrs. Campbell, please can't we sit down and talk calmly about what to do?"

"She's going to get rid of it that's what she's going to do. I'm not going to be saddled with another kid. I've been through that once. Never again."

Kira could see the hurt on Jody's face. "Your daughter isn't saddling you with anything. This is her decision to make. She can get financial help if she decides to keep the child."

"Well, she's not bringing the baby here. So she can just get out right now."

After his visit to Jarrett's place, Trace returned to the ranch, packed up his things from the bunkhouse and carried them up to the house.

Things were far from perfect, but he would deal with it. He only had to stay out of his wife's bed. Sure. He couldn't even stop himself remembering how willing she'd been in his arms last night. In the dark they didn't need words, just their bodies to express their need for one another. He'd never shared that level of intimacy with anyone but Kira. How could he live without her now?

That was the reason he was going to use this time to try to make things work. He might go crazy wanting his wife, but he had to think beyond his own needs; there could be a baby added to the mix. Maybe if he'd worked harder, instead of moving out, he'd have a wife, a lover. He couldn't leave her now, especially with the possibility of a baby. Not without a fight, anyway.

He'd finished putting his shaving kit in the bathroom when he heard the back door open. She was home. Good. Cal could handle the chores today, and he could spend the day with his wife. Just maybe he could convince her to change some of the rules. He hurried down the steps and went into the kitchen to greet her. He quickly stopped when he saw she wasn't alone, Jody Campbell was with her.

Kira saw him. "Oh, hi, Trace."

"Kira. Hi, Jody."

She shyly looked away. "Hello, Mr. McKane."

He turned back to a nervous Kira.

"Jody is going to be staying with us for a few days. Her mother was upset about the…news. So I brought her home to discuss options."

So they weren't going to be alone. Hiding his disappointment, he turned to his houseguest. "Welcome, Jody. You stay as long as you need."

"Thank you, Mr. McKane."

Kira turned to their guest. "Why don't you go upstairs and rest? The guest room is the door just past the nursery. We'll bring your suitcase up later."

The girl nodded and left the kitchen. Once alone, Kira released a breath and turned to her husband. "I guess I should have called, but Jody was literally out on the street." She frowned. "You sure you don't mind her staying here?"

He shook his head. "A few days won't be bad."

Kira grimaced, hoping Trace would understand. "It might be longer. Her mother didn't take the news of the baby well. I want to make sure Jody has some kind of support."

"What about the baby's father? Shouldn't he be here for her?"

"Jody said she tried to tell him, but he wouldn't listen."

"Maybe he'll listen to me," Trace said. "He's got to take responsibility."

"Ben leaves for the Army in a few weeks. He's not a bad guy, but he's a kid, and Jody will be eighteen next month." She shook her head. "Neither one of them are ready for this. I'm sorry, but when her mother threw her out, I just couldn't let Jody go through this alone."

He stepped closer, taking her hand. "She's lucky to have you, Kira. I just had some plans for us today. I thought we could go riding."

"You wanted to take me riding?"

"You sound surprised. I thought we should practice getting along—since Mrs. Fletcher will be watching us."

Kira was thrilled Trace wanted to spend time with her. It had been so long since they'd done anything carefree. "Could I get a rain check?"

He nodded. "Seems we have another problem. I just moved my things into the guestroom." He raised an eyebrow. "Have any idea where I put them now?"

* * *

When Kira woke the next morning, smiling, she stretched her arms out. She reached across the big bed but Trace wasn't there. Not that she should expect him to be. Although he'd come to their room to give the appearance all was normal, after Jody retired for the night, he had gone to the bunkhouse. Since Trace was up before the sun, their houseguest wouldn't even suspect he wasn't sleeping next to his wife.

That hadn't stopped Kira from missing him. She better get used to it, though, because his absence was going to be a permanent feature soon enough. Trace was only playing the part of attentive husband.

Kira got up and headed for the shower to help her focus on her day. This afternoon Mrs. Fletcher was coming with a special visitor. And it could mean they'd have a baby by summer's end. Kira tried to hold in her excitement, but couldn't as she began singing in the shower.

Thirty minutes later, she went downstairs and found Jody doing the dishes.

"Good morning, Jody," she greeted her. "I hope you slept okay."

"Good morning, Mrs. McKane. I slept fine. The bedroom you let me use is so pretty."

"It is pretty, isn't it?" Kira smiled and went to the coffeepot and poured a cup. "I especially love the old iron bed. I found it in the attic." She sipped from her mug. "I'm sure glad that my husband's family didn't throw anything out."

"Your house is beautiful. I hope you don't mind, I

dusted the living room. I can fix you breakfast if you want."

"Jody, I didn't bring you here expecting you to work."

"I just want to help out."

"I know you do," Kira said. "But I think it's more important that you see a doctor. Have you been to one?"

"I went to the clinic on Main Street just to confirm my pregnancy."

"How far along are you?"

"Fourteen weeks."

Kira sat down at the table and motioned Jody to do the same. "Have you thought about what you want to do?"

Jody shook her head. "Only that I can't end this pregnancy."

"What I told you, Jody, about me giving my baby up. It was the right decision for me, and the best for my baby. That doesn't mean it's what's right for you."

"I know that." Jody's gaze met hers. "I'm never going to tell anyone about what you told me."

"It's okay, Jody," Kira assured her. "I'm not ashamed of what I did. My baby was given a life I never could have offered. Two parents for one thing."

The girl looked thoughtful. "I don't know what I want to do."

"Well, we'll go to the doctor first. I'll set up an appointment for tomorrow. What time are you working today?"

Jody gasped. "I have the dinner shift."

There was no way Kira was going to miss Mrs. Fletcher. "I have an appointment here this afternoon, so you can take my car."

"I can't drive your car."

"Why not? You have a driver's license don't you? I trust you."

Tears filled the girl's eyes. "You've been so nice to me. I don't know what I'd do…if you hadn't took me in."

Kira hated to see the girl's lack of confidence, but she understood it. "You're easy to be nice to, Jody. Don't let anyone tell you anything different. And I'm going to stand by you for as long as you need me."

She knew too well what it was like to be alone, and pregnant. Maybe she could make a difference in Jody's life.

"They're here," Kira gasped.

Trace went to the kitchen window in time to see two women get out of the car. He recognized Mrs. Fletcher, but his attention went to the young girl with her. She was tall and slender, her stomach protruding with the late stage of pregnancy.

"Do I look okay?" Kira turned to look at Trace, brushing at her blue print sundress. Her wheat-colored hair was pulled away from her pretty face.

"You look perfect," he said truthfully. "Please, Kira, take a breath. She's going to like you. Remember, though, this is an interview. We might not even find out anything today."

He needed to stay calm, too. Mainly because he didn't want Kira disappointed if things didn't work out.

Her hand rested on his arm. "What about you, Trace? Are you sure this is what you want?"

He wanted whatever Kira wanted and a baby would be nice. "Yes, Kira, this is what I want. Now, we better go answer the door before they leave."

Together they walked to the back door and opened it as the two women came up the steps. "Hello, Mrs. Fletcher," Kira called.

The counselor smiled. "Trace, Kira, it's nice to see you again." She stopped on the porch to make the introductions. "This is Darcy Heaton. Darcy, this is Trace and Kira McKane."

"It's so nice to meet you, Darcy," Kira said and took her hand. The greeting was repeated by Trace to the girl in her late teens or early twenties.

"Hello," the girl said shyly. "You have a beautiful place here. I always wanted to live in the country."

"I could show you around if you want," Trace said. "We just finished the roundup this past weekend, and this morning shipped off the steers to the feedlot. But we have several horses."

Darcy's eyes lit up. "I love horses."

"Then let's go to the barn and I'll introduce you to Thunder."

Trace walked off with the young mother-to-be, followed by Mrs. Fletcher and Kira. Once inside the barn, he took Darcy along with him to see each animal. Thunder was willing to show off a little. Cal arrived with his mount, and Darcy was intrigued even more. They explained about the ranch operation, then Kira suggested they come into the house.

For the next hour, Kira found it easy to talk to Darcy as she and Trace showed her around the house. They sat down and had iced tea and cake while Darcy asked questions about the ranch. Then finally they ended up in the baby nursery. After a few moments Kira noticed that Trace and Mrs. Fletcher had wandered off, leaving her alone with the girl.

"This is a pretty room," Darcy said as she touched the cradle. "I like the yellow."

"Since I don't know the sex of the baby, I think it's a safe bet. But it's a good color to add pink or blue to."

Darcy nodded, eyeing the walls. "Do you want a boy or a girl?"

Kira couldn't help but wonder if this was a test. "Honestly, Darcy, it doesn't matter to us. We've tried everything for the last few years. We just want a baby to love."

Darcy nodded, then suddenly she looked sad. "I want to keep my baby, but I can't. My boyfriend, Wade, was in college." She hesitated. "He was so happy when he got the news about the baby. We were going to be married, but then, he was killed three months ago in a car accident coming to see me."

"Oh, Darcy." Kira fought to keep from going to her. "I'm so sorry."

A tear found its way down Darcy's cheek. "I can't raise my baby by myself. I have no family and it's important to me to know my baby will be loved and in a good home."

Kira felt a little shaky. "Your baby will be loved here. This home has seen several generations of McKanes. If you decide to let us raise your baby, he or she will be a McKane, too."

Darcy looked thoughtful. "I never had much of a home growing up, so it's important my little girl does."

Kira's heart tripped. "Your baby is a girl?"

"Is that all right?"

Tears filled Kira's eyes this time. "A little girl is perfect."

Just then Trace and Mrs. Fletcher walked into the room. He went to his wife's side. "Is everything okay?"

She nodded. "Darcy's baby is a girl."

Darcy went to Mrs. Fletcher. "I've decided."

The counselor sobered. "Are you sure, Darcy?"

"I'm sure." The pregnant girl placed her hand protectively on her stomach. "Trace and Kira, I want you to be the parents of my baby."

CHAPTER EIGHT

IN LESS than five weeks they were going to be parents.

The next evening, Trace glanced at Kira across the truck's bench seat as they rode into town. She hadn't stopped smiling since the announcement from Darcy. He wanted this for her, but it was all happening a little fast.

Just a few hours ago they'd all sat down at the kitchen table, Mrs. Fletcher laid out what Darcy would need. Top of the list was paying for the birth mother's medical bills. When the counselor gave him the approximate amount it nearly staggered him. Where was he going to get that kind of money? Thoughts of his brother's offer came to mind, but he quickly pushed them aside and turned his attention back to Kira.

Last week they were barely talking, now they were going to be parents. He let out a breath. No matter what she said about doing this on her own, he couldn't just walk away from her or this child. Somehow he had to figure out a way to keep her.

"Trace?" Kira's voice interrupted his thoughts. "Are you having second thoughts?"

"No, just a little overwhelmed."

He looked at his wife who was all dressed up for their night of celebration in town. Jody's idea and treat. Kira looked beautiful dressed in a silky blouse that outlined her full breasts, and a flowing skirt that hit the middle of her shapely calves. Even her feet looked sexy in a pair of high heeled sandals. She was distracting as hell. How was he supposed to live with her for the next six months, and not touch her, or kiss her?

"If it's the money, I planned to use the savings in the teachers' credit union."

Trace knew Kira had the account since before they'd married. He'd insisted it was hers. "I think you should hang onto it for now. I'll talk to Jarrett. He wants the southern section back. He'll pay well for it."

Kira turned toward her husband. "No, Trace. You wanted to keep that land, if just so he wouldn't develop it. Besides, I'm the one who asked you to do this."

He worked to control his anger. "We both wanted this adoption, Kira."

Tears welled in Kira's eyes. "Oh, Trace. You don't owe me this."

He pulled into the restaurant parking lot and shut off the engine. "Look, Kira, you already refuse to take anything from me, I sure as hell can at least help with this." And he was going to do a lot more whether she liked it or not. There was a child involved now.

Kira sat there staring out the windshield. She had hoped they could work this out, but Trace hadn't said much during the discussion with Lucy Fletcher. He hadn't expressed to her that he really wanted to be a family. Okay, she'd pushed him into this. And she hadn't a choice but to offer him a six-month deal.

If they couldn't make their marriage work, there would be a child involved then. At least this way, Trace could move on and have a family of his own.

She turned to him. "Thank you, Trace, for today. I promise I won't ask anything else from you."

"Ah, Kira." He reached for her and drew her against him. "You can ask me for anything."

She closed her eyes, reveling in their closeness, letting herself dream. The same dream she'd carried around since childhood. To have someone love her enough to always be there. She'd thought it was Trace, but in the end he would leave her like everyone else.

"We're going to make this work, Kira," he whispered in the darkness as he drew her closer. "You're going to have a baby."

Her heart gave a jolt as she raised her head. The truck was dark enough she couldn't see his eyes, but she felt them on her. "I wish I could be what you needed, too, Trace. I wish—"

Suddenly her words were cut off when he cupped her face and his mouth came down on hers. She only moaned as his lips coaxed hers until she gave in and opened so he could deepen the kiss.

He finally pulled back, his breathing labored and her hand felt the pounding of his heart. "Don't ever say that, Kira. You're everything a man could want."

"I couldn't give you a child," she managed to whisper.

He started to speak, but headlights from another car drew them apart. "We better go in," he said.

Trace climbed out of the truck and took the time to cool off as he walked around to the passenger side and helped her out. Their eyes locked in the dim parking lot. The mountain air hadn't helped—he wanted to kiss her again, then turn around and take her back home. Show her how much she meant to him.

Instead he escorted her toward the restaurant. Once inside the high-end steak house, Kira excused herself to go to the ladies' room.

"I'll check on our reservation," Trace said and went to the desk to speak to the young girl. "McKane."

"Oh, Mr. McKane. Your table should be ready shortly, Mr. Rhodes from EnRockies is waiting in the bar."

Trace quickly realized the girl's mistake; it wasn't the first time he'd been mistaken for his brother. Jarrett must be having a business meeting. "There must be a mistake. My wife and I have a reservation tonight. We're Jody Campbell's guests."

The young girl look flustered. "Oh, you're the other Mr. McKane."

Great. Now, he had the distinction of being the *other* brother. "I'm Trace McKane," he said as Kira returned to his side.

"Yes, here it is." The hostess smiled, embarrassed. "Your table is ready now, Mr. McKane." She called for a waiter, and he escorted them to a circular booth. Kira slid into the seat, and Trace was close behind her. After ordering cocktails, they were left alone.

Kira looked at him. "Is everything okay?"

He nodded. "Just a mix-up with the reservations. Seems Jarrett is here for a meeting."

"Wonder who Jarrett's wining and dining tonight."

Trace wondered, too. "Have you ever heard of a company called EnRockies?"

She frowned. "That's the name of the energy company drilling for natural gas in the area.

"Why would Jarrett be having a meeting with them?"

Kira shrugged. "Probably trying to lease them office space in town."

"Maybe." But an odd feeling gnawed at Trace. If the real estate business was so bad why would his brother want the land back? Something wasn't right.

"I can't believe he's looking to buy part of the ranch back."

"I don't want you to worry about it, Kira."

"How can I not? You could possibly lose part of the ranch."

"McKane Ranch is a big place. Dad meant for it to be divided between Jarrett and me, anyway."

Kira didn't look convinced. "That's great if he wanted to ranch, but we both know he'll develop the land if the price is right." Sighing, she leaned back. "I'm sorry, I shouldn't have said that. I don't know your brother that well."

"He's my *half* brother. And don't be sorry, Kira. It's true. I'm surprised Jarrett has stayed in Winchester Ridge. Of course he's made a good living being the hometown hero." A title he was all too familiar with having grown up in his older brother's shadow, the best quarterback to ever play at Winchester Ridge High School. "Who wouldn't trust him?"

Kira couldn't believe Trace could still be jealous of

Jarrett. "He's a little too smooth for my tastes." She looked down at her husband's hands. His palm was rough from hard work, but could be so gentle, remembering his touch against her skin. "I prefer the rugged type," she continued, unable to stop herself. "A certain cowboy got my attention from the first day I arrived in town."

Trace's intense gaze locked with hers. "I guess I owe my brother for taking you to lunch." He leaned in closer to her. "That day I walked into the diner and saw you, you took my breath away." His voice turned husky. I don't have all the smooth words and moves, Kira. I'm just an ordinary guy who works hard to make a living."

It had always amazed her that he never knew the effect he had on people, on women. "Nothing about you is ordinary, Trace McKane."

He looked embarrassed.

She nodded. "I've made a lot of mistakes, Trace. You deserved to know about my past."

Her keeping that secret had hurt him, but he understood why she found it difficult to open up about it. He also knew how hard her life had been. The toughest part was knowing she had a child out there that she couldn't see. The only child she would ever give birth to. "I hated that you couldn't come to me."

The waiter dropped off their drinks, and asked for their order. Kira decided on the salmon, and Trace a steak. The waiter picked up their menus and left them alone.

Kira lowered her voice. "I know I should have trusted you, Trace. But at the time, I was made to feel ashamed about what happened, and the only way I could put it behind me was to bury it. I never planned on meeting you. When we started dating everything was so perfect. I was afraid I would lose you if you learned I gave up my baby."

Trace shook his head. "Like I said, Kira, that wouldn't have happened."

Kira still couldn't believe it—they were finally talking. Maybe if they'd managed it sooner, he'd be moving back into their bedroom, and not the guest-room.

She suddenly heard someone say her name.

Kira looked up to see Jody arrive at the table. "I'm glad you made it." The girl smiled, dressed in her uniform. A white Western blouse and black jeans.

"You didn't need to do this, Jody," she said.

"I know, but I wanted to thank you for letting me stay with you."

"You should be saving your money."

"I am. And I make good tips here. So order what you want—we get a discount on the food." She glanced over her shoulder, then back at them. "I better get back to my tables. Have fun." She hurried off.

"She looks so much better now."

Trace stared after Jody. "You've given her hope."

Kira turned her velvet-brown eyes to him. "So you don't mind her staying with us?"

"She's not around much to be a bother." Although he'd like to have more privacy with Kira. "Besides, she needs us."

She smiled. "Thank you."

He hated her acting like a stranger. "Hell, Kira, it's

your home, too. It has been since the day I carried you over the threshold nearly five years ago."

She glanced away. "Things are different now."

He hated this time frame she'd concocted. "I don't want to be different, Kira. I can't walk away from the child, or from you. And I'll be damned if I'm letting you. Not if there's a baby involved."

The rest of their meal was eaten in silence as was their drive home. Kira wanted to talk about what Trace had said, but he'd clammed up.

Men.

They pulled up at the back door and she climbed out of the truck, not waiting for him. Well, she wasn't about to let him make a statement like that and refuse to explain.

They walked into the kitchen. "If you've changed your mind about the adoption, Trace McKane, you better tell me now."

"What makes you think that?"

"Maybe because you said you weren't going to walk away if there's a baby involved."

He glared at her. "That's true. You seem to think that I can sign papers, then turn around and walk out the door."

"No, *I'm* walking out the door," she corrected. "The baby is the only thing I'm taking." She never let herself feel the ranch belonged to her. "This is your place, your land."

"Dammit, Kira. That's what I mean. Why can't you believe me? I don't want you or the baby to leave."

Her breath stopped as she replayed his words. But before she could speak the sound of a car distracted her.

Soon Jody walked into the dimly lit kitchen. "Hi. You guys home long?" She smiled.

"No, not long," Kira said. "Thank you again for dinner."

"Yeah, thanks, Jody. Now, we all need sleep," Trace said as he locked the back door, then came back and took Kira's arm, leading her through the house to the stairs. Jody followed.

Kira's heart raced as they made their way down the hall and Trace opened the master bedroom door. "Good night, Jody," he called to her.

"Good night," the girl called as she went to her room.

Once Jody was out of sight, Trace pulled Kira across the threshold and closed the door behind them. He pushed her back against the raised wood panels. The room was dark, but she could feel his rapid breathing on her face.

"Let me turn on a light," she said, wanting to move away.

"No, Kira. It's better like this." He sighed. "I have something to say to you."

She shut her eyes tightly and began to pray. "Please don't say you're not going through with the adoption."

"No, I wouldn't do that. It's just not going to be your way. I want to negotiate a new deal. I want to be a father to this baby girl...and I want to be a husband to you." There was a long pause. "With no time limit."

Kira's chest tightened. "What if it doesn't work?"

"Then it won't be because we didn't try hard enough." He leaned forward and brushed his lips across hers.

She gasped. "Our track record isn't good, Trace."

She slipped her arms around his neck, knowing she couldn't let him go.

"At least we'd have tried," He kissed the side of her neck as his arms wrapped around her waist. "And I want to try with you, Kira. And for this baby."

His mouth found hers in the dark as if a magnet drew them together. The kiss grew intense along with their need, a need that hadn't diminished in their long months apart.

"Oh, Trace," she breathed as he broke off the kiss. She tried to come up with more resistance, but she was weak.

"Trust me, Kira." He tugged on her arm and together they walked to the bed. Slowly he began taking off her clothes, but she soon grew impatient and helped the process along, then did the same for him.

As she lay down on the mattress Trace leaned over her, his hands working their magic on her body, stealing her breath away, along with any doubts.

"We'll make this work, Kira."

Hope sprang inside Kira. Was this really going to happen? Was she finally getting her wish? A family.

A blissful three days and nights had passed, and Kira woke every morning, smiling. Trace had been a wonderful, attentive, considerate lover since the night they…renegotiated their marriage. Of course they had to steal their time together around their houseguest. But that was good practice for when their own child was here.

She walked into the kitchen to find Jody at the stove, cooking bacon. She glanced at the clock to see it was only seven o'clock. She told Jody repeatedly she didn't need to fix breakfast, but the girl kept doing it anyway.

"Jody, you should sleep in since you worked late last night."

The girl turned around. "Oh, Mrs. McKane. It's okay, I usually get up early."

Kira went to the coffeepot and poured a cup. "But you need your sleep, too."

The teenager's coloring had looked better this past week. "I'll rest later. I want to help out." The girl studied her for a while. "I don't want you to worry that I'll still be around when your baby comes. Cal is helping me figure some things out."

Jonas had been helping her? "Have you heard from your mother?"

Jody shook her head. "I don't expect to."

It was sad that her mother couldn't be there for her. But the baby's father needed to take responsibility, too. "Jody, have you told Ben you're pregnant?"

The girl took the bacon out of the skillet. "No. I tried at the party, and I've called, but he won't talk to me."

"He needs to know about the baby."

Jody turned around, tears in her eyes. "That's what Jonas says. But Ben will hate me."

Kira understood that feeling; she'd been there herself. "Ben has no cause to hate you. He helped make this baby."

"And he needs to take responsibility."

They both turned to see Trace and Cal standing at the doorway. They walked in and Trace came to Kira and kissed her, then turned to Jody. "If Ben won't listen to you, I think I should talk to him."

The girl blinked in surprise. "You don't have to do that, Mr. McKane."

"Someone has to. It's time for him to man up," Cal spoke up. "When does he go off to the Army?"

"In a few weeks."

"Then there's time," Trace said. "We'll drive you into town today." He rubbed his hands together. "Now, how about some breakfast? I'm starved."

"Me, too," Cal added.

Jody beamed. "I just need to cook the eggs. Is scrambled okay?"

The two men nodded. "That's our very favorite," Cal answered.

The teenager went to work, Cal went to get coffee, and Trace sat down at the table. He winked at Kira as she joined him.

She smiled in return. "Thank you for standing up for Jody. I don't think many people have."

"I'm just practicing for when we have our daughter."

It had been getting easier for Kira to believe. That she and Trace were going to be parents. A child together. "So you don't mind that the baby's a girl?"

"Mind having two beautiful women in my life? I don't think so."

She gripped his hand. Things were getting better every day. "I think we're pretty lucky, too."

After chores Trace and Kira drove Jody into town to see Ben. He glanced in the rearview mirror of the SUV and saw the nervous teenager in the back seat. A strange protectiveness came over him.

"Jody, it's going to be all right. Ben just may surprise you."

Jody nodded. "I think he suspects already. I think that's why he's been avoiding me."

Trace looked at Kira, then turned onto Ben's street. After finding the right house, he parked in front. "Well, that's going to end now."

"Do you want us to go with you?" Kira asked.

Jody shook her head. "No. I need to tell him by myself." She climbed out of the car and walked to the door.

"Are you sure we should let her go on her own?" Trace said, watching Jody.

"I think she wants to hear what he has to say." Kira sighed. "I hope she doesn't have any delusions that they're going to get married and raise this baby."

Trace glanced at Kira. "This has to bring back bad memories for you."

She shrugged. "Teenage girls at that age want love."

"And teenage boys are only after sex."

Kira kept her gaze on the house as she swallowed. "In the end everyone gets hurt."

Just then Jody came running out the front door. She climbed into the back seat and wiped at the tears streaming down her face. "Please, just go."

"What happened?"

"Ben doesn't want anything to do with the baby. He said it wasn't even his, and just to get rid of it." She sobbed. "It is his, Mrs. McKane. I loved Ben. There's never been anyone else."

Trace fought his anger as he climbed out of the car and marched up to the house. He rang the bell, but got no answer. So he began pounding until finally Ben came to the door.

The teenager stood eye to eye with Trace in height, but was about twenty pounds lighter. He looked shocked and a little frightened to see who was on the porch. "Mr. McKane."

"That's right, Ben. Let's see how you handle what I have to say."

His gaze went to the car, then back at Trace. "If it's about Jody—"

"You're damn right it's about Jody. And your child. The girl didn't get pregnant on her own. She came to ask you to help, and you humiliated her by saying the baby wasn't yours."

"Well, how would I know, she could have been with someone else."

"Do you honestly believe Jody would lie to you?"

The boy glanced away as he shook his head. "No. But I can't have a kid. I'm going into the Army."

"What about Jody? She applied to college. Instead she's going to be raising a baby."

The boy didn't say anything.

"As least think about what Jody is going through. Help her decide what to do. If she does decide to keep it, are you going to be a part of the baby's life? I guess what I'm trying to say is act like a man. If you're man enough to join the Army, you should be man enough to accept your responsibilities." He turned, stormed off the porch and back to the car, knowing he'd taken on the job of Jody's protector for the long haul.

All he could think about was no one had been there for Kira.

Two days later, Trace rode out to the land that was soon—if he couldn't find any money—going to be Jarrett's. He pulled up on the rein, and just sat back in the saddle. He'd always loved this area covered in rows of birch trees. It was prime property that Jarrett had initially wanted for himself. But at the time, his brother had wanted the money for another project and the home he wanted to build. That had been when they'd struck the deal.

Trace had agreed to a five-year plan to pay Jarrett for the property. The land he'd thought to use for raising a herd of free-range beef. He needed a few years to prepare the grazing land, and to put up fencing to keep the cattle in the allotted area. There would be a lot of up-front expenses, but in the long run the payoff would be worth it.

Ranchers these days had to have numerous business ventures to keep afloat. He'd thought about following his neighbors and opening some land to hunters, maybe building some cabins to rent. That, too, took capital. And he didn't have any right now.

So maybe what he had to do now was make sure that the McKane Ranch would be around for future generations. That meant selling this prime section back to his brother.

There were other priorities now. Kira, and the baby

that would arrive in just weeks. Oh, boy. He sucked in a long breath. Getting used to the idea took some doing.

A girl. Would she like to ranch? Maybe not. It was a hard life. But who was to say they couldn't adopt more children? Whoa! Slow down, man. She wasn't even born yet.

His thoughts turned to Kira. They'd come a long way in the last few weeks. He'd been welcomed back into their marriage bed. More importantly, he'd managed to convince her he wanted to be a part of her and the baby's future.

He smiled, thinking about Kira back at the house already adding pink paint to the walls in the nursery. And maybe he should help her.

Trace pulled on Thunder's reins to turn and started back to the house when through the trees he spotted a vehicle. He rode toward the property line that separated his and Jarrett's land and saw what looked like a survey crew marking off areas.

They stopped when he rode up. "Excuse me, is there something I can help you with?"

"Hello, Mr. McKane, I presume. Trace McKane?"

"That's me.

The man walked closer. "It's nice to finally meet you, Mr. McKane. I'm Frank Rhodes and this is John Thompson. We're from EnRockies and we're doing a survey."

There was that name again. What was Jarrett up to? It was still his property. "You do know that this is my land. I never agreed to any survey."

Frank Rhodes frowned as he exchanged a glance

with John Thompson. "Mr. McKane, I was assured that you'd already okayed us having access to this section."

"By who? I hold the deed to this land." At least he did until he couldn't make the balloon payment.

"Jarrett McKane. He said he'd talked to you."

Trace felt the anger building. "About what?"

"About leasing the mineral rights under your land."

"What the hell?"

Rhodes hurried on to say, "It's directional drilling, Mr. McKane. There won't be a drilling tower on your land at all. EnRockies has always followed the strict guidelines of the Bureau of Land Management to protect the environment. If there are any more concerns, I assure you we will answer any questions."

"I have one big one. My brother. He never told me about any lease." Trace thought back to Jarrett's eagerness to buy back this land. That wasn't going to happen now. "Do you think you could come by the house in a few hours? I'd like to discuss this at length."

"We would be happy to. I'll give Jarrett a call, too. I want to get this settled."

Thunder shifted away. "Believe me, it's going to be settled once and for all."

CHAPTER NINE

Two hours later, Kira stood in the nursery and eyed her handiwork. The light pink vertical stripes below the white wainscoting looked great. This was definitely a little girl's room.

She also had her eye on a white Daisy Garden crib she'd spotted in the shops. The bedding had pink and yellow colors with a floral design. It was an extravagant purchase, but Trace was fine with her using the money in the credit union, so she didn't mind borrowing a little from it.

Excitement raced through her. She was going to be a mother. All these years of dreaming, praying for a baby and now it was going to happen.

As much as she wanted the experience again of a baby growing inside her, she was already in love with this little baby. She planned to do everything possible to bond with this child, to welcome Jenna Margaret into the McKane family.

The door slammed downstairs, bringing Kira out of her reverie. So Trace had come home to help her with the painting. She smiled and headed down to the kitchen, thinking how nice it would be to have her husband around once again. She reached the kitchen, but no Trace. She tracked him down in the office, bent over the desk going through files.

"Trace, is something wrong?"

He didn't even look up at her. "There's plenty wrong. I found a survey crew in the south section. The land I was going to sell back to Jarrett."

"Who was doing the survey?"

"EnRockies," he said, then filled her in on the rest of the story.

"No, Jarrett wouldn't do that to you." She'd always believed there was good in her bother-in-law.

"You're defending him?"

"I'm not, but why would he do this behind your back?"

"Money. It's not enough he's leasing them his own land, he wants more. Mine." He slammed a drawer. "Forget that, he has no regard for my feelings about drilling on McKane land."

Kira had only known what she'd heard in town, from students who had parents employed by this company. There seemed to be more positive than negative about EnRockies.

"I think you should listen to what they have to say."

Trace stared at Kira. She didn't understand, this was a bond he'd shared with his dad. Their love of the land. "Dad trusted us to protect the ranch. And by the looks of it with Jarrett, I'm going to have to do it on my own."

"Trace, I want to help you, too. All I ask is that you calm down and find out more information."

How could he stay calm when he could lose everything? "Why? It's not going to change my mind, Kira." He frowned. "And since when have you cared about the ranch? You've been wrapped up in other things."

His words hurt her. "I've always cared, you just chose to exclude me."

An hour later, Mr. Rhodes arrived at the house. Kira came into the room and introduced herself. She refused to be shut out of the meeting. If they were going to make their marriage work, she needed to be a part of everything, and that included the ranch operation. She listened to the lease offer and bit back a gasp when Mr. Rhodes quoted the amount of money that would be paid out monthly.

She tried to read the map of the area, telling them where they had drilling towers located. How the Bureau of Land Management and the state of Colorado had approved the project.

"Like I stated earlier, Mr. McKane," Rhodes began, "there won't be any tower on your property."

"But close," Trace challenged. "Close enough to the Roan Plateau."

"It's no secret you and your brother's properties are prime locations, but the drilling can be done by one tower, which Jarrett has already agreed to place on his property."

Kira watched her husband struggle to remain calm. So she came up with a question. "How long is your company's lease for, Mr. Rhodes?"

"It varies, Mrs. McKane, but when we leave, the

land is left just like it was before we began drilling. We plan to do everything possible to protect the environment and that includes the wildlife. So that means we have to proceed slowly and cautiously in selecting locations around the plateau's base."

Suddenly there was a knock on the back door and Jarrett walked into the kitchen. He glanced around the table. "Looks like you started without me."

"You got that wrong, brother. You started a long time ago and left me out altogether."

Mr. Rhodes stood. "I'll leave you all to hash this over. We'll talk again. Here's my card. You can reach me anytime." He nodded to Kira. "Mrs. McKane."

Kira let their guest walk out on his own. She wasn't about to leave the brothers alone.

Trace spoke first. "Were you ever going to tell me?"

"Why? You'd just reject the idea."

"So instead you tried to take away my land and go ahead when you know how Dad would have felt about this?"

"The ranch will still be here, Trace. Besides, Dad gave us the ranch."

"But you never wanted to work it."

"Is it so hard to believe that I don't want to work eighteen hour days and never know if you'll make enough to live on?"

Kira was steamed by her brother-in-law's arrogance. She wouldn't blame Trace if he threw Jarrett out of the house.

"I do just fine," Trace argued. "Making money isn't all that makes a person happy."

"That may be all right for you. I want a better life and the lease will guarantee that."

"It also doesn't mean I have to go along with it."

"Fine. But you're going to lose the land anyway. Word is you don't have the money to pay off the loan, Trace. That means it comes back to me. I'd say I win either way." He grinned. "Once again I'll come out on top, little brother."

Kira could only watch the scene unfold like a bad movie. She wanted to help her husband, but knew he wouldn't appreciate it. Trace had to handle this his own way.

"I have other ways to get my hands on the money."

Jarrett smiled. "It's just a matter of time before you can't keep up the ranch. You'll be borrowing until there's nothing left."

"Get out of my house, Jarrett. And don't come back."

Jarrett looked at Kira. "Call if you need anything."

She couldn't believe the nerve of the man. "You'd be the last person I'd call." She moved closer to her husband. Jarrett finally turned and left.

"I'm sorry, Trace."

Trace stiffened when Kira touched him. He pulled away and walked to the back door. "I need to get out of here."

"Trace, wait," she called to him. "Let me help."

He glared at her. "You can't, Kira. I'm about to lose everything."

Kira felt a pain deep in her chest, making it hard to breathe. He said "I" not "We." Like so many times before when it came to the ranch, she'd been excluded from his life.

* * *

Trace couldn't think clearly so he stalked out to the barn. A long, hard ride on Thunder was safer than getting behind the wheel of his truck.

Inside, he went into the tack room where he found Cal. With a nod, he grabbed a bridle and his saddle.

"I'm going for a ride." He walked out into the barn.

Cal followed him. "What's going on, Trace?"

"Nothing, I just need to get away."

"I saw the EnRockies' truck and Jarrett's car. I take it the meeting didn't go well."

Trace lifted the saddle onto the stall railing, opened the gate and went inside. "Yeah. My brother's trying to pull a fast one." He went on to explain the situation to his foreman.

"I have to admit, the man doesn't let anyone get in his way. What are you going to do about it?"

He slipped the bridal on Thunder. "No way is Jarrett getting the land back."

"Good. So you're talking a deal with EnRockies?"

Trace blew out a long breath. "It goes against everything Dad wanted."

Cal hung his arms over the railing and watched Trace saddle the horse. "Your daddy isn't here. He didn't have the problems you're facing, either. If you want to run a cattle operation, plus stop Jarrett, you'll need capital."

Trace looked at his friend. He'd earmarked most of his savings for the adoption. "What do you expect me to do?"

Cal raised a hand. "You have options, Trace. You can borrow the money from me. Or you can sell off your breeding bulls, or look over EnRockies' proposal. It might not be that bad."

Trace began running some of the things Rhodes had said through his head. "They want to do directional drilling onto my land." He tightened the cinch and dropped the stirrup in place. "The drilling tower and roads go on Jarrett's side of the property. I can't stop that."

"I think a lot of the reason this bothers you so much is because your brother's involved. Right there it seems shady." Cal was quiet for a moment, then said, "What does Kira think?"

Trace shrugged. "It doesn't involve her."

"It sure as hell does. She's your wife."

He didn't want a lecture. "I know that." He led his horse out of the stall. It was all a mess.

Cal went after him. "Come on, Trace, don't get all stubborn about this and close up."

Trace turned and glared at his friend.

The foreman backed off. "Okay, one thing at a time. At least ride over to Joe Lewis's place. They drilled on his ranch last year. It seems to me it would be nice to have extra money coming in every month to ease your worries, even help start up those projects you've always wanted."

Kira had suggested the same thing. Trace stopped outside the corral. "What, are you moonlighting for the energy company?"

"No, I'm just a friend who doesn't want you to lose everything. I know what this place means to you, but even if you lose it all, don't lose Kira. You two love each other."

* * *

Three hours later, Trace still wasn't back and Kira wasn't sure what to do. Kira was both angry and worried. How dare Trace just walk out. What did she expect? He'd done it before.

She marched into the office. This had always been Trace's domain, but no more. She began to go through the financial files and found the ranch account. It had a pretty hefty balance after the selling of the calves. Yet, she also knew that the land payment was coming due. She went to the accounts payable and scanning the pages discovered the last payment was due to Jarrett at the end of June.

Kira gasped, seeing the considerable amount. This would pretty much wipe them out. How would they survive if she wasn't going back to work in the fall? And there were the adoption costs and Darcy's medical bills.

"What are you doing?"

Kira jumped and looked toward the doorway to see Trace. Why did she feel so guilty? "Since you wouldn't share the facts with me, I was seeing how much we owe Jarrett." She stood. "I had no idea it was so much."

He walked to the desk. "The payments over the years were reasonable, but the balloon is due."

"You should have told me, Trace."

His gaze held hers. "I was handling it."

Kira felt the tightness in her chest as he continued to push her away.

"Besides, we haven't exactly been on speaking terms in the past few months."

Another dig that hit hard. "There's money in the credit union. You can use that."

Trace shook his head stubbornly. "At this point it wouldn't do any good. That's your money anyway."

"No, it's ours."

There was a long silence, then Kira spoke up, "Trace, maybe we should sit down and talk with Mr. Rhodes. You didn't get the chance to listen to the stipulations about the mineral lease."

Trace didn't hide his tension. "This is a cattle ranch, Kira. It has been for three generations."

She started to speak, but he stopped her. "I need to handle this."

Trace's dismissal hurt her. If she hadn't known before, she knew now, he didn't want her to be a part of his life.

Over the next few days, Kira wasn't encouraged about her relationship with her husband. Trace spent his evenings in the office. He hadn't even made an effort to come to bed until late. Their magical nights together, their promises of a future together seemed like a fleeting memory.

She had hoped that their bedroom would be a place where they reached out for each other, to share things, to work on renewing their commitment to each other.

But Trace had turned away from her.

Breakfast time hadn't been much better. Even Jody was uncomfortable around them. So when the teenager needed a ride to work, Kira offered eagerly to get out of the house.

Kira drove the car up to the highway toward town.

"Mrs. McKane..." Jody began.

"It's time you called me Kira."

The girl smiled. "Kira. Ben asked me to marry him."

This was a shock to Kira. "Oh, my. So you two have been talking, a lot." There had been nights she'd heard Jody crying. She'd comforted her, but knew she had to work through things herself. "Have you decided on what to do?"

"Not marry Ben for one thing. We're too young." Her voice lowered. "And he doesn't love me. Besides, Ben wouldn't be around. He'd be in the Army, and I'd be here alone."

"So you've decided to raise the baby yourself?"

The girl sighed. "I don't know yet. But I know I need a place to live."

"You're welcome to stay with us for as long as you like." Crazy since Kira was beginning to wonder where her home would be, but she would take Jody with her.

The girl shook her head. "No, that's not fair to you or Mr. McKane. So Cal is helping me find a place. My boss at the steak house has been wonderful. He says I can stay on as long as I'm able to work."

"That's good. It's still going to be hard, though. So please stay at the ranch, at least until the baby is born."

"I'm hoping not too long. Cal's got an idea where I can live cheap. The place will need some repairs, but he's offered to do them."

Seemed Cal had taken Jody under his wing.

"I can help paint and Cal said there's some furniture there," the girl said excitedly. "And I can get my bed from my mom's house. I paid for it anyway."

Kira glanced away from the road to Jody. "Sounds like you've thought about this."

"You and Mr. McKane have been wonderful to let me

stay with you, but I can't anymore. I should be paying you rent. And I still need to get a car, but I have some money saved. Because I'm a single mom, I can get some help with my medical bills. And Ben's going to help out."

Kira smiled. Jody had always been an organized student. This shouldn't surprise her. She drove into the restaurant parking lot. "What about your mother?"

"I'll be eighteen soon, so I don't have to ask her anything. Besides, she's moving away." The girl lowered her head. "Seems I've embarrassed her."

Kira parked the car. "If you were my daughter, I'd be so proud of you. You have a lot to handle for someone so young."

"You were young, too, Kira, when you had your baby," Jody said and hesitated. "Do you think you made the right decision? I mean giving your baby up?"

Kira still felt the emptiness; she always would. "I'll always feel the loss. But yes, I gave him a chance at a better life, better than I could give him. It wasn't easy, but it was the only way for me."

Jody smiled. "I'm glad you're getting a baby now."

"So am I."

"Thanks for bringing me to work. I'm going to spend the night with Laura, and she'll bring me back to the ranch tomorrow."

"Good. I'm glad you're hanging out with your friends. Have fun and I'll see you tomorrow."

Jody grabbed her overnight bag and got out of the car. Kira watched her go inside, then she pulled out of the parking lot. She headed across town to the teacher's credit union. Her stubborn husband refused her help, so she was taking matters into her own hands.

An hour later, she'd finished filling out the loan application and was told she'd get an answer in a few days. With renewed resolve, she headed back to the ranch. She knew Trace would probably be upset, but she couldn't let his pride take everything from him.

When she pulled into the driveway she was surprised to find Mrs. Fletcher waiting for her. She climbed out of the car and walked over to the counselor.

The sad smile on Lucy Fletcher's face caused Kira alarm. "Hello, Kira."

"Mrs. Fletcher. Is something wrong?" Oh God, please, no. Her anxiety grew. "Is Darcy okay?"

"Darcy is fine and so is the baby." She glanced around. "Is your husband here?"

"I'm not sure. Do you need to speak to him?"

Mrs. Fletcher hesitated. "Could we go inside?"

Okay, this wasn't good. They walked up the steps together and went into the kitchen. "Please, tell me why you came all this way."

"I have some news." She sighed. "Darcy got a call from her boyfriend's mother. It seems that she never knew about Darcy until she went through her son's things." A long pause. "She's offered to help Darcy raise the baby."

Kira's heart stopped as she sank into a kitchen chair. "Is she serious?"

"Yes, I checked it out." Mrs. Fletcher sat, too. "When Marion Clark learned about the baby she contacted Darcy and begged her to come live with her. Darcy agreed. Together they're going to raise the baby. With her son's death, Marion wants a part of him."

A tear found its way down Kira's cheek. She hated this, but deep down she understood. If there had been someone to support her, she would have kept her son, too. "I'm glad Darcy has someone to help her."

"I'm so sorry, Kira." Mrs. Fletcher took hold of her hands. "Darcy was adamant about finding a home for her child. She wanted you and Trace to raise her baby." She paused. "There was always a chance the mother could change her mind."

"I know." She was numb.

"I assure you, you and your husband are back on the list."

Another list. Her time had run out on her having a family with Trace. Kira stood. She couldn't talk anymore. "Thank you for everything, Mrs. Fetcher."

"You're welcome, Kira. I'll be in touch." She walked to the door. "Goodbye."

Kira didn't speak, she just walked upstairs to the nursery. She ran her fingers along the new crib and the dresser that had arrived just yesterday. She looked at the wall where the name JENNA was spelled out in large ceramic letters.

There was no baby girl.

She'd never felt so alone. So lost.

CHAPTER TEN

TRACE had taken Kira's advice and that afternoon drove over to see his neighbor, Joel Lewis. Together, they saddled two mounts and rode out to the EnRockies' drilling tower. The energy company had built an access road across the Lewis's pasture, but that was the most noticeable change. The high tower was partly hidden by the tall pines.

"It's not bad," Joel said as he leaned forward against the saddle horn. "I mean I had concerns at first, but in this day and age, farmers and ranchers need all the help they can get." The longtime neighbor looked at him. "I'm sure my daddy and yours would have raised a stink, but it's a different world now."

Trace couldn't help but think of all the money he owed, and how much easier it would be to have some extra income. "So you're okay with this arrangement?"

He nodded. "The extra money comes in handy when you have two college-aged kids, or when the wife needs a new car. We even took a vacation last year and started a retirement fund."

Trace thought about his parents and their struggles

running the cattle operation. He looked ahead to his own future. Would it be with Kira and the baby?

The sound of Joel's voice broke into his thoughts. "You've got it easy with your lease offer," he began. "It's Jarrett's property that's going to house the tower and handle the truck route. They're only going to do directional drilling onto your property. What's to think about?"

Trace sighed. "I guess I was just wondering what my dad would do."

Joel nodded. "It's your place now and you're the one fighting to keep it." He glanced around. "Where else could we live and enjoy this incredible backyard? Besides, I wouldn't survive in the city, nor would have wanted to raise my sons there. Have a couple of your own kids, Trace, and you'll change your mind quick."

It suddenly hit Trace. He had to think about his responsibilities to Kira, and the child. No matter what the original arrangement, he was definitely committed to the roles of husband and father.

This energy lease could help secure their financial future so he could continue to ranch. And so much more. Kira wouldn't have to work. He thought back to the past few days and his avoiding her. He needed to let her know how much he wanted her to be a part of his life, to include her in this decision.

Suddenly he couldn't wait to get home to talk to her about this.

"Thanks, Joel. You've helped a lot."

"Good. And if need be, I'll take Rocky off your hands."

They turned their horses back toward the barn. "Afraid

not, Joel, that bull is going to be too busy, but I'd be happy to sell you one of his calves."

"Sounds like you're in the ranching business for a long time."

"What can I say? It's in my blood." He thought about the baby coming soon. "I plan to stay here to see another generation take over." And he was going to do everything he could to convince Kira to stay by his side for a lifetime.

Thirty minutes later, he pulled his truck up beside the barn and headed toward the house to talk with Kira. If they were going to make their marriage work, he needed to listen to her. He'd made it to the back porch when he heard Cal saluting him.

The foreman caught up to him. "I was wondering if you have any plans for the old foreman's cottage?"

Trace frowned as he looked past the new bunkhouse to the small house that had been abandoned for years. "It's just storage for my parents' stuff." He looked at his friend. "Why, did you want to move into it?"

Cal shook his head. "No, Jody needs a place to live."

Trace hadn't figured their houseguest was staying much longer. "Isn't she going home to her mother?"

Cal shook his head. "Her mother's leaving town. Jody hasn't any other place to go."

"She's leaving her daughter?"

"Jody will be eighteen next week. Her mother doesn't want to be saddled with a teenager with a kid. She's moving on with her new boyfriend."

Trace couldn't help but think of Kira at that age.

There hadn't been anyone for her, either. "The cottage must be in bad shape."

"Not so bad. There's some water damage in the bathroom, but I can fix that. And a good cleaning would help a lot."

"I don't want Jody living out there until it's fixed up," Trace said. "And I'm sure there's plenty of furniture in the attic to furnish the place."

"Thanks," Cal said. "Now, the biggest job will be to convince her to stay."

"I'm sure Kira can manage that." Trace started backing away. "Speaking of Kira, is she in the house?"

Cal nodded. "She came back about an hour ago. That Mrs. Fletcher was here, too. She didn't stay long, though."

Trace tried to remember if the counselor was scheduled to come by. Had he missed a visit? If so, why hadn't Kira called him? He hurried into the house.

"Kira," he called. The only sound was the refrigerator clicking on.

He walked through the house to the staircase. Taking the steps two at a time, he felt his pulse drumming in his ears as he reached the second floor, then down the hall. She wasn't in the bedroom, then he heard a noise in the nursery. He pushed open the door and found Kira on the floor. With a screwdriver in hand, she was taking apart the crib he'd put together just a day before.

His heart beat erratically as he moved to his wife's side. "Kira, what's going on?"

Refusing to look at him, she continued her task. "We're not getting the baby."

His throat threatened to close up. No baby. "Why?"

She gave a shaky sigh and closed her eyes. "Darcy changed her mind." A tear rolled down Kira's cheek. "She wants to keep her baby."

It felt as if a huge weight landed on his chest, making it hard to breathe. No. He was just getting used to the idea of becoming a father.

"Oh, Kira." He reached for her but she avoided his touch.

"Don't." Kira climbed to her feet and moved away. "Don't tell me it's going to be okay because we both know it's not. It's never going to be okay, Trace. Not ever again." She swiped at the flood of tears.

Trace stood and went after her, but she continued to back away, his heart clutched in pain. Losing the baby was hard, but losing Kira was harder. Suddenly he felt his world being ripped apart.

"God, Kira, I know this hurts. We were warned this could happen." The words were so feeble. "We're still on the list. We can still have a baby."

"Another list!" she cried. "Then what? We wait some more and maybe have another baby jerked away again?"

Kira shook her head. She couldn't keep doing this to herself. Every time she began to hope, it was ripped away. And Trace. This had been their last chance.

"No, I'm not doing it anymore. I can't, Trace."

"Okay, we stop for now."

"No, I've stopped for good." Kira raised her gaze to his. There was pain in his beautiful gray eyes. It hurt her to know she couldn't be what he needed. It was time to stop it. "Your dream doesn't have to end, Trace. You can still have children."

He frowned. "What are you trying to say?"

She couldn't lose her nerve now. It was killing her to send him away, but better now than later when they ended up hating each other. She had to do what was best for Trace and the legacy he wanted to leave.

She straightened and wiped away her tears. "You can have the family you want, just not with me."

"I don't want a family unless it's with you."

She shook her head. "I can't keep doing this." She glanced away from his confused look. "And I can't keep putting you through this, either."

"You're not putting me through anything I don't want to do. I agreed to the adoption."

She straightened, fighting tears. "Well, I'm through." She stared at him. "Our original deal was for six months. We didn't get a baby, so you're off the hook."

"Off the hook?" He looked as if she'd struck him. "That's all you think of our marriage? That I came back because of the baby?"

She managed a nod, praying to stay strong. This was for the best.

Trace turned and walked out.

It was over.

With no desire to sleep, Trace took out his frustration by working through the night. By morning he had worked up a good anger as he continued his labor, mucking out stalls, repairing fence. He headed over to the foreman's cottage to see what needed to be done.

Anything to keep him from thinking. Thinking about what he was about to lose. Everything.

He heard the sound of pounding in the foreman's cottage and wandered over to find Cal busy at work on repairs.

Trace maneuvered through the boxes stacked in the small living room to find his foreman in the kitchen putting down new subflooring. He was surprised how much Cal had gotten done since yesterday.

"You're not wasting any time."

"Jody needs a place." Cal stood and pushed his hat back. "Since you've pulled an all-nighter, I take it things aren't good between you and Kira."

"We're not going to get the baby," Trace said.

He frowned. "So you left?"

"Sometimes we're not given a choice."

"And you're just going to give up?"

He hated to keep beating his head against the wall. "She's not fighting for me, either."

Cal sighed. "Marriage isn't a contest, Trace. It's hard work. Kira is hurting. She probably said things she didn't really mean."

"What are you, a marriage counselor?"

"No, but I've been there, dammit. I messed up big time. I walked away without fighting. It cost me my wife and my daughter."

"You have a daughter?" Trace asked.

"She's not mine anymore. I gave her up and I let my ex-wife's new husband adopt her. She'd be about Jody's age."

Trace watched Cal swallow hard.

"I regret it every day. Hell, Trace, I'd crawl back if I could have my family again, but I was too damn bull-headed to see anything beyond my pride."

Suddenly Cal glanced toward the doorway and saw Jody standing there in her jeans and T-shirt.

The teenager smiled shyly. "I'm sorry to bother you." She looked at Trace. "There was a phone call and I heard the voice on the recorder. It sounded important, and Kira isn't around. Here's the man's name and number." She handed him a piece of paper, then looked back at Cal. "I hate to ask, but do you think you could take me to work?"

"Sure. What time?"

"In two hours."

He nodded. "Just come and get me when you're ready."

After Jody left, Trace looked at the note paper to see the name of Greg Carlson from the Teacher's Credit Union. Trace pulled out his phone and punched in the number.

It rang twice then was answered, "This is Greg Carlson."

"Hello, Mr. Carlson, this is Trace McKane. You left me a message."

"Yes, Mr. McKane. We wanted to let you and Mrs. McKane know that your loan has been approved. Since this is a joint loan, I need you to come in and sign some papers before we cut a check for Jarrett McKane."

Trace wasn't sure how to react. Kira had applied for a loan? To pay Jarrett? "Could you just put a hold on the paperwork until I talk to my wife?"

There was a pause. "That's not a problem. We can hold it for forty-eight hours."

"Thank you, Mr. Carlson." He flipped his phone closed. "Dammit, why did she do that?"

"Do what?" Cal asked.

"Kira got a loan to pay off Jarrett."

Cal raised an eyebrow and folded his arms over his chest. "Okay, now, tell me she doesn't care about the ranch. And you."

CHAPTER ELEVEN

THE next morning, Trace went to his brother's office downtown. There weren't any pleasantries or announcements as he bypassed the blond secretary and walked through the door. He found Jarrett on the phone.

The young woman ran after him. "Sir, you can't go in there."

His brother hung up the phone and stood. "It's okay, Sarah. I've been expecting him."

The blonde backed out and shut the door. "Well, it's about time you showed up," Jarrett said.

"I wanted the satisfaction of telling you, you're not taking my land. I was just with Frank Rhodes and signed a contract with EnRockies. You'll have your check for the land in plenty of time before the due date."

Jarrett shrugged. "You can't blame a guy for trying."

"Why, Jarrett? Do you hate me so much that you want to destroy me?"

"Hell, I don't hate you. I saw an opportunity and took it." Then his shoulders sagged as he leaned a hip on the desk. "The real estate market is a mess. I had to do something to save my business."

"If you'd let me know about EnRockies' offer from the first, maybe we could have worked together."

In his younger years, Trace had always looked up to his big brother. He was popular and a talented athlete in school. Trace had been shy and uncomfortable around girls. But Jarrett never had time for him. As adults, it had become a competition.

"Honestly, I didn't think you'd go for it."

"But you never asked. We're supposed to be family, Jarrett."

His brother didn't say anything as he studied him. "Did Kira talk you into signing on for this deal?"

The question hit a nerve. He'd never gotten the chance to talk to her. "She's with me on this. We're adamant about keeping the land. EnRockies' lease seems to be the best way to assure it. Now that section of land is mine free and clear."

Jarrett smiled. "You're married, bro, nothing is completely all yours, and since you're having a kid, you're going to need all the extra money you can get."

Sadness shook Trace. That dream was long gone. "There isn't going to be a baby."

His brother's smile faded. "Sorry to hear that. What happened?"

Trace found he was angry. "The biological mother is going to keep it." *And Kira doesn't have any need for me any longer,* he added silently.

"Okay. What's your next move?"

Trace didn't want to share his private business. "I don't have any." He suddenly felt defeated. "Kira's pretty upset."

"Which is understandable," Jarrett told him. "But there are other options out there."

It was strange talking to his brother about this. "Not when this baby was the main reason we've been together. Now that's gone."

Jarrett shook his head. "Nothing is gone until you let Kira leave. Come on, Trace, I know you're brighter than that." He smiled. "You managed to steal her away from me."

"Hell, I can't make her stay."

"Then give her a good reason not to leave," he began as he folded his arms over his chest. "Have you told her how much you love her, and that you can't live without her?"

Trace straightened. "What is this, Romance 101? I've tried."

"Seems to me a woman who goes out on a limb to get help so her husband can keep his ranch isn't a woman who doesn't care."

"Have you been talking to Kira?"

"No, but the credit union called about the balance on the loan. Like I said, a woman doesn't risk her future if she's leaving."

"That was before we lost the baby."

"So she just turns off her feelings for you?" He shook his head. "I don't think so."

Trace felt sad. "What about the baby? I can't fix that."

"No one expects you to, but hold on to her until you get another shot at it. You're going to have the financial means to pursue other avenues, too." He walked around the desk, sorted through his Rolodex and pulled out a business card. "When you're ready, give this fertility specialist a call."

Trace shook his head. "No, Jarrett. I can't handle this again."

Jarrett paused with a frown. "You can't handle it? What about Kira? Think what she's going through right now. And she doesn't have any family to turn to."

Trace started to speak, but knew it was true. Even he'd walked out on Kira. It had been her who'd come to him, begging him to move back to give her a chance at a baby. To give them a chance.

Even after he learned about the child she'd given up years ago, he felt hurt she hadn't shared it with him earlier. A revelation hit him. All along, he'd been the one who never gave her a reason to trust him. Maybe she felt she couldn't count on him to stand by her. And when she needed him the most, he'd run out on her. Again.

He glanced at his brother. "I need to get home."

Jarrett smiled. "Give Kira my love."

Trace headed for the door, praying it wasn't too late to do just that.

"You're not leaving town, or Trace," Michelle said.

That same morning, Kira paced her friend's apartment. "It's the only way. People won't understand why we broke up and I can't answer all the questions. It's the only chance for Trace to start over." She brushed a tear off her cheek. "He can find someone. Someone who can give him a family."

"What about you?" Michelle asked. "You deserve a

life, too, Kira. A man who loves you. And don't try to say that man isn't Trace."

She recalled yesterday when she was so upset about losing the baby. He'd left her. "He walked out."

"Maybe because you didn't give him a chance."

Kira swung around to deny it and suddenly a wave of dizziness hit her. She reached for the back of the chair to steady herself.

Michelle rushed to her side. "You okay?"

Kira sank into the chair feeling a wave of nausea. "It's probably because I haven't eaten today."

"Great. Like you can stand to lose any more weight." Her friend walked into the small kitchen and took out some yogurt. "Eat."

Kira caught the aroma of the fruit flavor and her stomach roiled in rebellion. She barely made it across the room and into the bathroom before she lost what little food was in her.

With a groan, Kira leaned against the counter. Michelle handed her a cool washcloth. "Could this be more than lack of food?"

"Stomach flu. I haven't felt good for a few days."

Michelle gave her some mouthwash, then helped her to the sofa. "How many days?"

"Two or three, I guess."

"What are your other symptoms?"

"I haven't had any energy. Upset stomach, but a lot has been going on…with the baby and all."

Michelle's eyes widened. "And Trace has been staying in the guestroom since moving back?"

Kira felt herself blush. "Mostly."

"Okay, you better give me some more symptoms."

It suddenly dawned on Kira what she was asking. "No, it's not that, could never be that. The doctor said it would be close to a miracle."

"I'm Catholic. We believe in miracles. My mother and I have had you on our novena list for the past year." She shrugged. "So why not? Are your breasts tender? When was your last period?"

Kira refused to answer, because she refused to hope. "It's too crazy to think about."

"It's not crazy."

She shook her head. She couldn't even hope.

"There's only one way to find out." Michelle grabbed her purse off the entry table. "I'm going to the drugstore." Before she could stop her, her friend was gone out the door.

Kira didn't want to take a pregnancy test. She'd taken dozens over the past few years and they'd all come back negative. She didn't need that today.

Ten minutes later there was a knock on the door. Thinking Michelle forgot her key, Kira got up and opened the door to find Trace.

"What are you doing here?"

Trace hadn't expected Kira to greet him with open arms, but he'd hoped for a warmer greeting. "I've been trying to find you." He walked in. "We need to talk."

"We've said everything, Trace. I'll be out of the house in a few days."

"I don't want you to move out. I want us to stay together."

She walked across the room. "For how long, Trace?"

Tears flooded her eyes. "Until the next time I try to get involved in your life?"

"Can't we go back to the house and talk this out?"

She shook her head, fighting tears. "No, it's better this way. I'll come back another day when you're not around and move the rest of my things. And I don't want any part of the ranch. It was never mine."

"Yes, it is. The ranch is yours, too. You're my wife, Kira. I was wrong not to include you in all decisions concerning the operation."

He could only watch as she fought her emotions. "No, I don't want any part of the McKane Ranch. So just please go, Trace." She pointed toward the door and, as if by magic, it opened and Michelle walked in.

"I got you the last test at the drugstore." Kira's friend pulled a box from the bag. She froze when she glanced up to see they weren't alone. "Oh, Trace."

"Michelle." His gaze went to the box. He'd seen the same pregnancy test in their bathroom cabinet back when they'd been trying for a baby. He swallowed the sudden dryness in his throat as he glanced at Kira. Pregnant? Could she be pregnant?

"It's the stomach flu," she assured him unconvincingly.

"But you don't know for sure."

She didn't answer.

He went to her and took her by the arm. "We're going home." As they headed for the door, he grabbed the pregnancy test from Michelle.

"Good luck," she called to them.

Trace knew if he was going to have a chance to repair

things between them, it was going to take a lot more than luck. He had to convince Kira that he wasn't going to give up on them. No matter what the test said.

CHAPTER TWELVE

THIRTY minutes later they arrived back at the ranch. Silently Trace led Kira through the house and upstairs to their bedroom, and into the connecting bath. Before she could argue, he set the test on the sink, then walked out, shutting the door behind him.

Kira relented and after the deed was done, she came out ready to give Trace a piece of her mind. "I don't appreciate you railroading me into doing this. The test will only show what we both already know." Her voice softened. "That I'm not pregnant...once again."

He got off the bed, but didn't apologize. "How long for the results?"

"Five minutes."

Kira released a breath and watched as he paced the room they'd shared over their five-year marriage. The memory of the night he'd learned her secret flashed into her head. The one night they'd made love and the times after that. Could they have made a baby? Could those nights in Trace's arms have created a miracle? She shook away the thought, refusing to let herself hope.

She straightened. "You go look, I can't go through the disappointment again."

He studied her. "It could be different this time."

"I don't want you to get your hopes up."

"Why not? After your last procedure six months ago, the doctor said removing the scar tissue could possibly help you conceive."

She sank against the dresser, trying to ignore the glimmer of hope. "Please, Trace, don't. I can't take seeing your disappointment again."

He walked to her. "Is that what you think? That I brought you back here just to find out if there is a baby?"

She was unable to look him in the eye.

"I brought you here because I wanted us to talk in private. So I could apologize to you."

"Why?"

"For walking out on you, especially yesterday." He paced as if agitated. "You needed me, Kira, and I felt helpless to do or say the right thing. When you pushed me away I was hurt. And maybe you won't believe this but I wanted the baby, too."

He sighed. "I wanted her for us. All I thought about was that little girl, how she was going to be the start to our family…the next generation." He forced a laugh. "I was looking forward to teaching her to ride, to rope and herd cows." When he glanced back at Kira, there were tears in his eyes, too. "How selfish is that?"

"Oh, Trace, that's not selfish. We all have dreams for our children."

He nodded. "Of course, she might have wanted to be

a ballerina," he went on. "But none of that mattered, only that this baby would be ours."

"I'm sorry, Trace," she breathed. "At the beginning I pushed you into this adoption. Neither one of us was close to being ready for a family."

"That was my fault, too, Kira," he admitted. "I excluded you. You had a full-time job. I didn't think you wanted to be involved with the ranch, too."

She knew how hard it was for him to admit that. "I only wanted to share your life, Trace. Your love for the ranch."

"I wanted to share your past, too," he answered, his hurt surfacing. "No matter how bad it was for you. I wanted to share your pain." He went to her, gripping her arms. "I was never angry that you had a child. God, Kira, you were so young. What you did was so unselfish. You gave your son the best chance at life. No matter what it cost you. I guess my problem was I wished you could have shared it with me."

"I was wrong not to trust you. But I thought if you knew my secret, I would lose you."

He reached for her and cupped her face in his hands. "God, Kira. You could never lose me." He kissed her hard and long, and when he broke away, they were both breathless.

He moved back a fraction, but she could feel his breath on her face. "From the moment I laid eyes on you, I couldn't think of anything else. You had me spooked as a green colt. You have no idea how many times I drove to the school to see you, then stopped short of going inside. I'd turn around, drive back to the ranch and convince myself that someone as beautiful as you wouldn't want to go out with me."

His admission thrilled her. "It took you thirteen days to ask me out, Trace McKane. Thirteen long days."

He blinked at her statement, then he sobered and said, "I'm not good at saying all the fancy words, Kira. But you need to know that you're my life. You're all I ever wanted. The only woman I've ever loved."

With her heart racing, she couldn't speak.

"I was wrong to exclude you from ranch business," he went on. "My mother didn't get involved, so I took it for granted you weren't interested, either. And when things got tight, I didn't want you to worry."

"I wanted to help," she said. "I'm working, making a salary, too. Besides, you were spending ranch money on all my medical procedures."

"I'm your husband. It was important to me that I take care of my wife. But I admit, with the adoption costs and the balance due on the loan to Jarrett, it was going to be hard." He moved closer. "Then Mr. Carlson called from the credit union, saying your loan came through."

She shrugged. "I knew you'd be upset, but I only did it so you wouldn't lose everything."

Trace sighed. He'd never loved Kira as much as he did in that moment. He leaned down and brushed his mouth across hers again. "You're what's precious to me, Kira." Her brown eyes were luminous. "When I came back here this morning and found you gone, I thought you'd left for good. I've never been so scared. This ranch doesn't mean anything to me without you."

"But you can't let Jarrett take your land. Please, Trace, don't be too stubborn to take the money."

He smiled. "We don't need it now, as soon as you sign the papers, EnRockies will drill on the land."

Her brown eyes widened. "Really?"

He nodded. "It's time we had a little security for our future."

"Our future?"

"Yes, yours and mine." He slipped his arms around her. "Like I was saying earlier, I came looking for you because I wanted to convince you to give me another chance. Give us another chance. I promise never to walk out on you again." His gaze locked with hers. "We'll have rough times, but we'll work on them together. When you cry, I'll hold you. When you're hurt, I'll share your pain." He cupped her face in his hands. "We'll deal with the joys and disappointments together."

"Oh, Trace."

"I love you, Kira. Never forget that."

"I love you, too, but, children—"

"I told you before, Kira, kids would be a bonus. I married you to share my life." He sighed. "I guess I'm just going to have to prove it to you."

His mouth captured hers in a kiss he hoped would convince her just how he felt about her.

Kira was weakening, but Trace always had that power over her. His hands moved over her body; soon she ached with need. She needed him now as never before. She wrapped her arms around his neck and deepened the kiss. He groaned and yanked her top from her jeans and ran his hand over her stomach.

He broke off the kiss and whispered, "Tell me I haven't lost you, Kira. That you'll give us another chance."

"Oh, yes, Trace."

He lifted her in his arms as her mouth came down on his. He carried her to the bed, set her down and finished undressing her as his mouth worked over hers, teasing her lips with his tongue. His fingers released the clasp on her bra and let her breasts spill out.

Kira arched her back as his hands cupped her, then his mouth captured the sensitive nipple. She gasped at the pleasure, but his tenderness caught her by surprise.

Trace raised his head. "Did I hurt you?"

She blinked. "Sorry, they're just a little sensitive."

He froze. "How sensitive?"

Kira knew what he was asking. She covered his hand and brought it back to her breasts. "Just a little."

"Damn. The test." He started to get up, but Kira wouldn't let go of him.

"Don't, Trace. Don't spoil this." Love and desire for this special man consumed her. "Stay and make love to me."

His brown hair was mussed, his beautiful gray eyes searched hers. He finally nodded and leaned down. "I promise you, Kira, someday we'll have a baby. It might take a little longer, but it'll happen. And together we'll raise our family. Here. At our home."

She suddenly felt pretty lucky. That's what she'd been looking for all her life. "That's all I need, Trace. Like you said, everything else is a bonus."

EPILOGUE

It was late afternoon as Kira stood on the porch and watched volunteers set up the tables and portable barbecues for tomorrow's senior roundup. Although she'd taken off work the past year, she wasn't about to disappoint this year's class by canceling their party at the McKane Ranch. So tomorrow there would be about fifty kids and hopefully a lot of parents here.

Michelle had taken over the job of organizer, and she'd even roped Jarrett into helping out. The two seemed to be getting pretty close. So had the two brothers. Jarrett was even going on the roundup with Trace tomorrow.

She shifted little Nathan on her hip. The seven-month-old was getting big. She smiled at the cute little boy. It was hard to believe he'd grown so fast. He was thriving around his extended family.

"Here, I can take him for you."

She turned to see Cal coming up the steps. "I thought you were helping with setup for tomorrow."

Nathan reached out for his uncle Cal. "What can I say, I'm organized." He raised the boy high in his arms, causing him to giggle. "Besides, I promised Jody I'd bring Nathan to the house."

Kira was proud of Jody. She was working and going to college, plus raising her son. "She's supposed to be studying for finals."

"I know, but she wants to give him a bath and spend some time with him before he goes to bed."

Kira looked toward the foreman's cottage. The outside had been painted cream with burgundy shutters, and bright flowers lined the porch. Inside was nearly perfect, too. Cal had made sure of that. He'd taken both Jody and little Nathan under his care, playing uncle to the boy. It had been good for both of them.

"I'm worried that Jody isn't getting enough sleep."

"I'm getting plenty of sleep."

They turned as Jody joined them. She'd filled out since the birth of her son. The pretty girl was more sure of herself these days. Why shouldn't she be with all she'd accomplished this past year?

She was immediately drawn to her son. "How's my big boy?"

Nathan grinned showing off his two tiny teeth. She took him from Cal. After a series of kisses, she cuddled him close to her, and said, "I guess I needed a Nathan fix."

Kira's chest tightened. She understood the feeling. There was nothing like holding your child close.

"Then I guess…you can have a break," Kira said.

The girl started down the steps, then paused. "Have I told you lately how much I love you all, you, Cal and Trace? I wouldn't be able to bathe my baby every night if you all hadn't been there for me."

Okay, that made the tears fall as they thought back to the roundup a year ago. "And you're thanking us by paying it forward." After Jody graduated, she was going into social work to help troubled teens.

"I'm a long way off before I can do that."

Cal spoke up. "But the good thing is you're working toward it. And making us all proud."

Jody swallowed hard but didn't speak. Kira saw the emotions play across the girl's face. All her life Jody hadn't had many people behind her. Now she had a lot.

Kira waved to Nathan as mother and son left to go home. Their home for as long as they needed it.

Suddenly Kira's attention was drawn to the corral and to a lone rider. Her stomach got a funny feeling as she watched Trace sit atop Thunder. Her cowboy, husband and lover. Man of her dreams. All of the above.

When Trace spotted her, he tipped his hat and climbed down off the horse. He handed his reins to one of the two ranch hands they'd hired a few months ago. The extra money from the lease helped Trace expand the operation.

He started toward the house in his usual fitted Western shirt and faded jeans covered by rust-brown chaps. She knew he'd been checking the herd that was to be rounded up and branded tomorrow.

By the time Trace climbed the back steps, she felt breathless. Nothing had changed since they'd met. He still had that effect on her.

"Howdy, ma'am," he said.

She glanced over his dusty clothes. "Looks like you've been busy."

"I do have to work occasionally. I sure could use a shower." He stepped closer. "Care to join me?"

She smiled. "I might be talked into it."

His mouth closed over hers nearly before the words were out. The kiss grew deep and thorough, pulling her against him.

Suddenly there was a sound of a cry from the monitor on the railing.

He broke off her kiss with a groan. "Sounds like someone is hungry."

She nodded. "Okay, you go shower and I'll feed our daughter."

He started for the door, but paused. "Oh, I forgot to tell you that a John Kelsey and his son are coming by later to look at the bay mare, Sadie."

She paused. Trace had gotten into breeding horses this past year. He'd bought the bay mare with the idea of breeding her.

"This could be too good to turn down. Like you." He bent to kiss her again and the baby let out another hard cry.

"You better get her."

Kira raced up the steps and into the nursery. In the crib was four-month-old Jenna. "Hey, sweetheart, are you hungry?"

Her daughter whimpered as she waved her tiny arms and legs. Kira picked her up and cradled her precious baby in her arms. She was their miracle. After a quick diaper change, Kira sat in the rocker and unbuttoned her blouse. Once the child was rooted on her breast, Kira began to rock, looking down at the infant who resembled her daddy, but had her own brown eyes.

Kira closed her eyes, recalling the day she nearly lost it all until she let Trace talk her into giving their marriage another chance. They'd promised to love one another and to face whatever happened together.

The pregnancy test had been forgotten until much later when Trace came out of the bathroom holding the colored stick in his hand. That and wearing a big grin.

It showed positive. Kira had gotten pregnant.

After all the trying and praying and testing, she'd finally gotten pregnant. Little Jenna had been conceived the night Trace had learned about her past.

It hadn't been an easy time. She was high risk from the start, and the last few months had been spent in bed, but she carried their daughter thirty-seven weeks. Born three weeks early at a little over six pounds, the baby was thriving now.

Trace stood in the doorway, amazed at the sight. He blinked, hoping he wasn't dreaming as he watched his wife feeding their child. He'd never thought this day would come.

There was never a picture so beautiful, and so humbling. Kira had gone through a lot to get here, to have this baby. It took him a long time to understand. Then the day of Jenna's birth as the doctor put her in his arms, it all became clear. He never thought he could love so completely. Both his girls.

He walked in. "Mind if I join you?"

Kira smiled as she burped their daughter. "Sure." She switched breasts and soothed Jenna with a calming hand. She turned to him. "You look and smell a lot better."

He kissed her. "Glad you approve." He placed a kiss on his daughter's head, too. "I have plans once Jenna's had her fill."

Kira raised an eyebrow. "I thought you had someone coming by."

"We have time." He brushed a kiss across her lips, leaving them both wanting more. "I'll always have time for you and our daughter. You two will always come first."

"I know. A baby reestablishes your priorities."

"She makes me realize what's important in life."

Kira lifted the baby to her shoulder, patting her gently. It wasn't long before Jenna fell asleep and Kira carried her back to the crib.

Once the nursery door closed, Trace pulled his wife into his arms and kissed her. Their lips met as he removed her already open blouse. By the time they reached their room, she was half naked.

Kira couldn't have been happier or more turned on. "This is crazy in the middle of the day."

"We have to steal the time now wherever possible," he told her. "It's nearly five o'clock." He laid her on the bed and stared down at her. His eyes were filled with need and love.

"Have I told you lately how beautiful you are?"

"Yes, but feel free to elaborate." Kira helped him undress, her hands aggressively removing his clothes. His chest was broad and muscular, his waist narrow and hips taut and lean. His desire for her was evident.

Kira drew him down on her, loving the feel of him against her, also loving the precious words he whispered as he loved her slowly and completely. She clung to him, laughing and crying at the same time when the release came to them.

Trace pulled her to his side, not releasing his hold. "I love you," he said breathlessly.

"And I love you, too."

She sighed contently. "Our life is perfect."

"Just about," he said and kissed her forehead. He sat up on the bed. "But I'm hoping it's about to be."

Kira didn't know what her husband was talking about. He'd been showering her with gifts since they'd gotten back together.

"What did you do, Trace?"

"I guess you'll just have to wait about thirty minutes. Go take a shower and relax." He stood and began to pull on his jeans. "I'll listen for Jenna."

She didn't wait to be asked twice. She went into the bathroom, showered and shampooed her hair. After she dressed, Kira came downstairs to find Trace holding their daughter in his arms. He was talking to her, and she was making those cute sounds at him.

Trace saw her and his eyes brightened as he gave her the once-over. "Oh, darlin', you look good."

She glanced down at her black jeans and bright blouse, then glanced back at him. "You're not so bad yourself, cowboy."

He grinned. "Maybe we should go back upstairs."

"I thought you had a horse buyer coming soon."

He glanced out the kitchen window. "That would be John Kelsey." He took a breath and released it, then looked back at her. "That's not exactly the truth."

She stood next to him to see a car pull up in the driveway. "What's not exactly the truth?"

"John Kelsey and his son, Jack, aren't coming to look at a horse. They coming to see you, Kira."

Her eyes narrowed. Trace opened the door and guided her out to the porch. She caught sight of a tall man about forty-five. He smiled at her, then turned to the teenage boy.

Kira's breath caught when she saw the tall boy with curly blond hair and dark eyes. Her heart began to pound. It couldn't be. Not after all this time. She'd never hoped, never dreamed.

Tears flooded her eyes. She looked at Trace. "How? Why?"

Trace reached for her with his free hand. "You deserve this, Kira. It's time you met your son. Besides, Jack wanted to meet you, too."

She took a needed breath. "Really?" She couldn't move, but looked down at the boy waiting at the base of the porch.

Kira looked back at her husband. He had given her everything she'd been looking for all her life. He'd held out his hand to prove his support, his promise to share her pain and her joy.

"I'm here, Kira. I'll always be here."

It had taken a while, but she finally believe that he truly loved her. This was her home. "I know," she whispered, then took his hand and they walked down together.

As a family.

DOCTOR, MUMMY... WIFE?

DIANNE DRAKE

CHAPTER ONE

Dr. Del Carson stumbled out of bed and groggily dragged herself into the nursery. A blue ceiling with white clouds, yellow walls with blue and white ducks and puppies greeted her as she turned on the overhead light and sighed.

"What now, sweetie?" she asked in a typically sleep-deprived thick voice as she trudged over to the crib and looked in at the six-month-old, who looked up at her and laughed at her with glee, as if he was eager to get his day started in the middle of the night. "Is it a diaper, or is this just your way of making sure your mommy doesn't get to sleep more than an hour at a time?"

Or maybe he just had her wrapped around his little finger; since it was just the two of them, she'd spent the first six months of his life catering to his every need.

It didn't matter, really. This was what she'd signed on for when she'd decided to become a mom, and any chance to make her baby's life better was welcome.

Tonight Charlie was particularly restless, all bright-eyed and ready to play, but, personally, she was played out. Even though the diaper seemed clean and dry, she changed it anyway out of habit, then sat down in the Victorian rocker, the one her mother had rocked her in, rocked little Charles Edward Carson until he was ready to go back to sleep for another hour. Two if Del was lucky.

Single motherhood was difficult, and she got all the support she could want from her family and friends. Being an only child, though, she missed the camaraderie of a sister or brother to take part in Charlie's life. He had no aunts or uncles, no cousins. Not on her side, and the father's side didn't matter since he was just a matchup on paper. A statistic that had struck her fancy.

It made her wonder sometimes if she should have another baby so Charlie wouldn't be raised in an isolated situation the way he was now. Del was a firm believer that children did better with siblings, and that was a thought she had tucked away in the back of her mind to visit in another year or two. "We'll get it worked out, Charlie," she said to the baby in her arms. "One way or another this will all have a happy ending."

The issue of single motherhood to deal with took an awful lot of hours when it was just the two of them—her and Charlie. She was continually amazed how much time someone so young could take up in the span of a single day. It was as if he'd hatched a plan to run away with every free second she had. But she loved it, loved her choice to become a mother on her own. No father involved, except Donor 3045, and she was grateful for his good genes because he'd given her such a healthy, beautiful child. The perfect child, as far as she was concerned.

She loved being a mother, even with the inconveniences. Loved spending time with her son. "My one and only true love," she would tell him. "For now it's just the two of us against the world."

Her parents lived in Costa Rica. They were supportive but not close by, which was one of the reasons she'd chosen to do this now. Her parents would have spoiled little Charlie rotten, and that was fine up to a point, but not to the extent she feared they might have gone. After all, five years in a horrible relationship had made them spoil her rotten when she'd finally found the courage to end it. That was just who they were, but she didn't want to raise a spoiled-rotten or privileged child. So they'd made their plans and, accordingly, she'd made hers. And she didn't regret it one little bit.

"Well, Charlie," she said as she put the baby back into his crib. "Are you going to let your momma sleep the rest of the night?" She was so tired she gave some thought to simply curling up in the rocker and pulling up a comforter. But little Charlie was fast asleep, so she held out some hope for three hours of sleep before he woke up and wanted to be fed, changed or just cuddled some more.

The life of a single mom. It wasn't easy, but she was taking advantage of it because in another two weeks' time she was trading in her maternity leave and returning to her medical practice with some on call and nighttime exclusions. Charlie was going to the hospital day care so she'd have easy access to him whenever she needed her baby fix. Sure, she was going to miss him. But she missed her old life, too, and she happened to be a staunch advocate of women who wanted it all. She certainly did. Every last speck of it except the part where there was a man included, and she wasn't ready to go there again. Not for a very long time to come. If ever again. And if she ever did that again he was going to have to be awfully special. Someone who'd love Charlie as much as she did.

Del, short for Delphine, sighed. She loved her work as a pediatrician in a private practice attached to Chicago Lakeside Hospital. In fact she had a passion for her work that couldn't be quelled by anything but work. Yet somehow, now that she was a mom, she knew her sensibilities had changed. To a doctor who now had a child, those little coughs and colds meant so much more. And when a mother's instinct dictated something wasn't right, the mother's instinct won. Being a mother-pediatrician rather than a plain old pediatrician was going to be a big advantage and, as much as she hated thinking about leaving Charlie behind for her work hours, she was looking forward to getting back to her normal life and trying to make all things fit together. It wasn't going to be easy, but if there was one thing Del was, it was determined, and she was determined to make sure all things worked together in her life.

"Good night again, love," she said quietly as she tiptoed from the room, turned on the night-light and lumbered down the hall back into her own bed. Unfortunately, sleep didn't happen as quickly as she'd hoped, and she lay awake staring off into the dark for about half an hour before her eyelids finally drooped. "I'm a lucky woman," she whispered into the dark as she was drifting. "I have everything." A beautiful child, a strong, supportive family, a good job. Best of all, no man to interfere.

She'd given away five *long* years to a man, always holding out the hope that he was the one who would complete her life. Problem was, he was completing the lives of several other women while she and Eric were going nowhere. So when she finally opened her eyes at the five-year point and took a good, hard look at the situation, she kicked him to the curb and decided she was in charge of creating and fulfilling her own dreams. No one else except one anonymous sperm donor needed.

It was a good choice, and as she drifted off to sleep, she did so with a smile on her lips.

Dr. Simon Michaels took a look out over the receptionist's shoulder at all the mothers and fathers waiting with sick children. It was cold and flu season, and if he didn't pick up the bug from one of these kids it would be a miracle. "How many more do I have to see?" he asked Rochelle, the girl at the desk. Rochelle was a tiny little thing who looked like one of the patients, and by comparison Simon felt he overshadowed her by a good foot. He, with his broad shoulders and longish brown hair, had to make sure he didn't treat Rochelle as a kid because, after all, she was well over twenty-one, and very efficient in her job.

She looked over the top of her glasses then laughed. "That's just what's left of the morning appointment block. You're going to have at least that many this afternoon, and tonight's your night for on call, so look out. Around here we look at Halloween as scary but not for the same reason most people do. We'd much rather see a goblin than a flu bug."

"Any word on when the mysterious Del Carson will be back?" He'd been hired to replace Del during her leave, then asked to stay on as a permanent member of the pediatrics clinic team. He'd heard of Del, but never met her. In fact, what he'd been told was that she was an excellent doctor, if not an overprotective mother who didn't want to come in for fear that she might contract some disease and take it home to her baby. He didn't know if that was true or not, but the only truth he knew was that she was merely a name in passing. Someone who would be his boss when she returned.

"Be patient," Rochelle warned. "She'll get here when she's ready. That new baby of hers is taking up a fierce amount of her time right now, but I expect she'll be back in a couple weeks or so, if she doesn't change her mind and stay home another half year." Rochelle smiled. "She loves being a mother."

"And there's no father?"

Rochelle shook her head. "Her choice. And she's proud of it, not shy in the least to talk about it."

"Well, that's something you've got to admire—a woman who knows what she wants and goes out and gets it." It couldn't be easy, and it would get a whole lot more difficult once she was back at work. He wondered if she fully realized what she was letting herself in for. "Can't wait to meet her. It will be nice having more help," he said, even though it wasn't his intention to complain. And he wouldn't. After all, he had a job in the location of his dreams. He was finally back home in Chicago after all those years in Boston and, as they said, "There's no place like home."

In fact, he lived only a few blocks from where he was raised. All within sight of the Navy Pier and the lakeshore. It was good. Pediatrics was such a full field here, though, that when he'd got the call to come and interview, he couldn't believe his good luck. No place at County Hospital, no place at Lakeside. Just no place. Then this spot came open—the pediatric clinic attached to Lakeside—and it was a godsend at a time that couldn't have suited him any better. Divorced from Yvette, who hadn't turned out to be the woman he'd thought she was, working in a practice where he was clearly never going to advance, cynical about life in general, feeling as if the whole world were closing in around his bad choices... Coming home was better, even if his workload was crazy big right now.

What the hell did that matter, though? It wasn't as if he had anything else going on in his life other than his work—a situation that suited him just fine. In fact, to avoid some of the long lonely nights he even took call for his colleagues just to give him something to do. Some might call it crazy, but he called it picking up the pieces of his broken life.

"So the plan is for her to be back in two weeks?" He grimaced. There were two weeks of work waiting to see him right now, and he was the only general pediatrician in the house today. The other two had succumbed to the virus that was being spread like wildfire. Leaving him to roll up his sleeves and just pitch in, keeping his fingers crossed that he stayed healthy so he could handle the workload.

Pulling up his surgical mask and snapping on a fresh pair of gloves, he sighed. "Send in the next one."

Rochelle chuckled. "Wouldn't it just be quicker to go out there, sit them in a circle and look at them as a group?"

"What would be easier would be flu shots. But people don't think about getting vaccinated until they're already sick with the flu."

She pointed to her upper arm. "Got mine. Hope you got yours."

"I've been a pediatrician too long not to." But that didn't mean he wasn't susceptible. Because vaccinations weren't foolproof, as his colleagues had discovered.

Two more weeks and Del Carson might reappear. Admittedly, after six months of hearing glowing reports about her, he was anxious to meet her. "You don't suppose we could convince Dr. Carson to come back early, do you?" he asked as he grabbed up the next patient chart. Five years old, fever, runny nose, cough, generally out of sorts.

"She values her baby time. She'll be back when she's back."

Of all the bad timing to be on leave... He signaled for his nurse, Ellie Blanchard, and off they went, back to work. Vaccinating children and parents alike, dispensing antinausea medicine, and generally just trying to make it through the day. "Next," he said as he stepped into Exam Four. "And get me two more ready to go. We've got a lot of patients to see in the next hour."

Glancing up at the clock on the wall, he shook his head. Not enough time. Not nearly enough time even if he worked through his lunch hour.

No trying to hide it, she had tears streaming down her cheeks as she handed Charlie to the day-care director then headed down the winding walkway to the clinic. It wasn't as if she didn't trust the center to take good care of him. They had an excellent reputation and the staff in general spoke very highly of them—but this was her baby she was handing over and being only a building away didn't make any difference. She hated doing it. Considered at the very last minute whether or not she was ready to go back to work or if another six months' maternity leave might be called for.

But one look at the swamped clinic told her she was doing the right thing. Other children needed her, too. And admittedly, she did feel that tingle of excitement the moment she stepped through the front door—a tingle that told her she was back where she belonged.

There were lots of single moms just like her who left their children and went to work every day. She didn't have someone to support the two of them. It was up to her. Besides, she loved her work. Still, she was sniffling as she approached her office door and went inside. Leaving Charlie behind made her feel so empty, so alone. "Suck it up," she told herself as she pulled on her lab coat, the one with her name embroidered onto the pocket. "You knew this was how it was going to be when you did this."

Still, she hadn't counted on it being so difficult. "But

you're lucky," she said as she looked in the bathroom mirror and touched up her streaky eyes. "You've got excellent day care and you're only a few steps away." A few steps that seemed like miles. Damn it! She wanted to be home with her baby even though she knew she was needed here. Torn in half—that was how she felt. Completely ripped down the center.

Taking in a deep breath, she exited her office and stepped almost directly into the path of a doctor she didn't recognize. The new hire? "Sorry," she said, trying to find a smile for him even though it simply wasn't in her to be found.

"You must be Dr. Carson," he said, extending his hand to her.

She gripped it weakly. "And you are... Was that Dr. Michaels?"

"Call me Simon."

"And I'm Del," she said, appraising the hunk of man standing right in front of her. OK, so she'd vowed off involvement, but she could still look, and what caught her attention first, outside his very soft hands, were his stunning green eyes. They were serious, but she could almost picture them smiling and sexy.

"Well, Del, I'm glad you're finally back. We've been too busy to make much sense of our patient load for a while, and we've needed you."

"My baby needed me more than the clinic did."

"I imagine he did," Simon said, "but you haven't been here and the pace has been crazy."

She looked over his shoulder to a normal waiting room. "Looks like things are under control to me."

"Want to know how long it's been since I've been able to take a lunch break?"

She laughed. "No guesses from me. We all have to make sacrifices, Dr. Michaels. Some bigger than others."

"You're referring to leaving your baby in day care?"

"That, and other things." But mostly that.

"Well, at least it's a good day care and nearby. That's an advantage for you."

"But I don't have to like it."

"All I said was I'm glad you're finally back. You were needed."

"And I appreciate that, but I was also needed at home." Where she wished she could have stayed. "But it's nice to be missed. I take it you don't have any children?"

He paused for a moment, then winced. "No children. Divorced. No future plans for anything except working."

"And yet you complain about too much work."

"Not complain so much as remark. We're busy here. We needed you. Simple as that." He chuckled. "Almost as much as you need me."

"Well, you've got me there. We do need you, especially right now."

Simon nodded. "During the flu outbreak the average wait time was an hour per patient. Which is too long for a sick kid to have to sit there and wait."

"See, you could have told me that right off."

"Pent-up frustrations," he said. "I've been working hard."

"I can see that." She smiled at him. "Well, you're

right. An hour is too long. We like to guarantee no more than twenty minutes. Shorter if we can get away with it."

"Sorry about my attitude, but all I could picture in my mind was you sitting at home playing with your baby when we had patients lined up in the hallways."

"Trust me, it wasn't all play. Babies require a lot of work."

"I know, I know. I'm think I'm just tired…I know it must have been hard work, especially on your own," he said.

"So how about we get off to a fresh start? Hello, I'm Del Carson and you're…"

"Simon Michaels." He held out his hand to shake hers and they both smiled. "So how was your maternity leave?"

"Great. I hated for it to be over with but all good things must end. So, how many patients do we have to see this morning?"

"About twenty, barring emergencies."

She nodded. "I'll grab some charts and get started."

"And after I get my foot out of my mouth, I'll do the same."

Del laughed. "You were right up to a point. I was entitled to my maternity leave and I don't regret taking it. But things shouldn't have gotten so out of control here at the clinic. Someone should have called me and I might have been able to get a couple of our specialists out here to help with the overflow."

"I tried," Simon confessed, "but I'll admit my attitude might have been better."

"I didn't read anything about a bad attitude in your

application or your letters of recommendation. And even though I never met you until just a few minutes ago, I called your superiors in Boston and they gave you glowing reviews."

"Probably anxious to get me out of there. I'm a pretty fair doctor but I do let things get to me too easily, I suppose. You know, take it all too personally."

"We all do at times. And I suppose especially the newcomer who's being the logical target." For a moment, a softness flashed through his eyes.

"Six months *is* a long time to be away."

"Not long enough," she replied. "I was actually thinking about another six, but I love my work as much as you seem to love yours. So I came back."

"Straight into the arms of a disgruntled employee."

"Nice, sturdy arms, though. And I'm willing to bet they hold no grudges."

"Me? Hold a grudge?" He laughed outright. "Grudge is my middle name. Ask my ex-wife."

"Think I'll stay out of the family problems."

"So, I understand you're raising your baby all on your own."

"Yes, it's just Charlie and me but that's the way I planned it."

"Well, I suppose that's the way to do it if you want to keep your autonomy."

"More like my sanity." They meandered down the hall to the clinic's nursing hub and she picked up the first chart off the stack. "And contrary to popular belief, I *am* sane."

"Reasonable, too, dealing with me as diplomatically

as you have this morning. I must confess that when I heard you were coming back I put together some mighty well-chosen words for you."

"So I noticed," she said as she opened the chart and looked at the info contained inside. "But they could have been worse." The first patient was a child named Sam with some sort of rash. Her first fear was a communicable rash and her next fear was that she might transfer something to Charlie. Truth was, if she didn't get over her irrational fears, she wasn't going to be any good as a pediatrician anymore. Most kids that came in were communicable and if she worried about carrying something home to her baby every time she came into contact with a sick kid, she'd drive herself crazy. Plus there was also the possibility that she might be too cautious to make a proper diagnosis. Obsession. That was what it was called. She had an obsession, and she wondered for a moment if she should seek professional help for it. But the instant she stepped in Sam's exam room and saw the rash she knew the poor kid was miserable. He was obviously allergic to something with which he was coming into contact.

"Does it hurt or itch?" she asked him.

"He scratches it like crazy," Sam's mother answered as Sam's eyes filled with big, fat tears.

"When did it start?"

"Three days ago?"

"What happened three days ago that changed his routine?"

"Nothing except...we went picking pumpkins in

the pumpkin patch for Halloween. He's not allergic to pumpkins, is he?"

"You've had pumpkins in your house before?"

"Every year," the mother replied.

"And what about the pumpkin patch?"

"This was our first year to go."

"I'm betting the rash is connected to the pumpkin plant."

"He's allergic to the plant?"

"Has there been anything else new introduced in his life since the rash popped up?"

"Not that I can think of," the mother answered, a frown on her face indicating she was thinking. "No new food, no new clothes, my laundry detergent hasn't changed."

"Then for now, let's go on the assumption that he has an allergy to the actual pumpkin plant and if the rash doesn't clear up in a few days or it comes back we'll investigate other possibilities and take some tests. For now, I'd rather save him the trouble, though. So, any of the over-the-counter hydrocortisone creams will help with the rash, and I'm going to give him a shot today that should speed things along."

She looked down at Sam, who looked back at her with big, sad eyes. "Will it hurt?" he asked.

"A little bit, but you're a big boy and you can take it." In reality Sam was only five and at an age where needles really scared kids. Some people never outgrew the phobia and she didn't want to make this too traumatic on this poor child. "Anyway, let me go get you some ointment samples, and have the shot prepared, and I'll be back in a couple of minutes."

True to her word, Del appeared back in Sam's room a few minutes later with a syringe full of antihistamine and a bag full of samples. Once she'd convinced Sam the needle wouldn't hurt that much, she gave him the injection, and wrote down instructions for his mother to follow, including the antihistamine to be taken three times a day in small doses. "This should clear up in about three days," she told Sam's mother on the way out. "If it doesn't, call me. In fact, call me either way because I'm curious if he is allergic to pumpkin vines. That's kind of an odd allergy…"

Actually, nothing in the allergy world was odd. People had reactions to everything—to the expected as well as the unexpected, as in Sam's case.

Her first day back dragged. She couldn't get herself into the rhythm to save her soul. And between her hourly calls to check on Charlie and her work she was ready to go home by noon. But she'd just have to understand that this was the way it was. She loved her baby and she worried. Although, by the time her fourth call rolled around, she was sure the child center over at Lakeside was probably sick of her calling. So she vowed to not call after she took her lunch hour with Charlie. Which turned out to be around one o'clock.

"Momma missed you," she said, picking him up and kissing him, then walking around the room with him.

"Am I being a nuisance?" she asked Mrs. Rogers, the director.

"Pretty much, yes," she answered, smiling. "But the first few weeks aren't easy. So we're pretty forgiving."

"I miss him, and it's all I can do to keep from coming over here, getting him and taking him home."

"You're not the first, and you won't be the last," Mrs. Rogers replied. She was an older woman, short gray hair, and a registered nurse, retired.

No one could have better credentials or more experience with children, and Del considered herself lucky that they'd had an opening for Charlie, as the child center was usually booked months in advance. As it turned out, she'd reserved a spot even before he was born in the anticipation of returning to work and the timeline had worked out perfectly.

Del sighed heavily as Charlie snuggled into her and dozed off. "It's amazing the way they can change a life so drastically, isn't it?"

Mrs. Rogers laughed. "Too bad we can't keep them all young and innocent, the way he is now. But if we did we wouldn't get grandbabies, and I've got to tell you there's a certain sense of satisfaction in being a grandmother."

"How many grandkids do you have?" Del asked her as she laid Charlie back down in the crib.

"Five, so far. One on the way."

"That's awesome," Del replied.

"What about your parents?"

"Grandparents in absentia. They live in Costa Rica and travel back every couple of months to spoil Charlie."

"No husband?"

Del shook her head. "By design it's just the two of us."

"I admire a woman who knows what she wants and goes out and gets it."

"And I admire you for taking such good care of all these children."

"My assistants and I love children, and, since we're all retired pediatric nurses, it's a good way to still stay involved."

Del smiled as she kissed her sleeping Prince Charming goodbye and returned to her clinic, feeling much more relieved than she had only an hour ago. In fact, this was the first time she thought it might actually work out, working full-time instead of part-time as well as being a full-time mom. At least, there was room for optimism in the scenario now. For which she was glad because she loved her work with a passion.

"Little Tommy Whitsett is here," Rochelle said to Simon as he left an exam room where the child had a blueberry stuck up his nose. "I think it's another case of nurse-maid's elbow." Where a quick tug of a toddler's arm oftentimes resulted in partial dislocation of an elbow ligament. In Tommy's case it was a chronic condition, one caused when his older brother tugged a little too hard on Tommy's arm, causing the ligament to snap out like a rubber band and not reset properly. It was typical of toddlers and Tommy would most likely outgrow the tendency in another year or two, but until then there was nothing really fixable as it wasn't a serious injury. And the fix was easy. One gentle pop usually set the ligament right back where it belonged. Tommy got his lollipop and went home to have other wrestling matches with his brother.

"Have him shown to Room Three," Simon said, and joined Tommy there a moment later. This was the third time he'd seen the child for the same injury in the past couple of months.

"I'm sorry this keeps happening, Doctor," his poor, red-faced mother said. "But when they get to playing…" She shrugged.

"No big deal. He'll outgrow this eventually, and that will be that."

"But I feel so foolish coming in here so often. I'm afraid it might look to some like I'm an abusive parent."

Admittedly, at one time Simon had wondered if Tommy's handling at home was too rough, but he had a different attitude now that he'd met the cause face-to-face—a much bigger, sturdier brother—and witnessed the worry in Tommy's mother's face. "Boys will be boys. You just happen to have one who's a little more elastic than the other one ever was. No big deal. Maybe have a word with his big brother to try and per-suade him pulling his brother's arm isn't such a great idea."

"I have tried, Doctor. It always scares me."

"A lot of mothers get petrified if their child coughs or sneezes. That's the proof of parenthood, I guess."

"You're not a parent, are you, Doctor?" she asked him.

He hesitated for a minute, then shook his head. "Haven't had that opportunity yet." If ever again.

"Well, it's not easy."

He thought back to Del and recalled the strain on her face at simply leaving her baby behind in a safe environment. Maybe he should have more empathy for her, going through separation anxiety as she was. But he found that difficult as he didn't know how to show it for someone who'd made deliberate choices. Like Yvette, who'd pulled Amy out of his life altogether. He'd been the only father the child had known, albeit he was the stepfather. Then when his ex-wife met someone else, his feelings for Amy didn't matter. So he was understandably still bitter and some of his personal reactions still reflected that. "You're right. It's not easy," he said to Tommy's mother.

"I guess," Tommy's mother said. "But I wish it was sometimes."

"Parenting is never easy. It makes us realize just how powerless we are in so many situations. And I know you hate that vulnerability, but in your case you've got two fine, healthy sons and at the end of the day that's quite an accomplishment."

"Let me tell you a secret, Doctor. There's never an end to the day. Parenting is so hard, and it never stops."

"And you love it, don't you?"

"Except for when I have to bring Tommy in for another case of nursemaid's elbow." She smiled. "But I wouldn't change a thing."

"Challenging case, Dr. Carson?" Simon asked after he walked Tommy and his mother back to the waiting room.

"If I thought you were interested because you were

really interested, I might answer that question, but somehow I think you'll snipe at me for taking the easy cases today since you're so distracted, so all I'll tell you is that we divide them as they come in and leave it at that."

"That's right. I'm not a partner. Just a lowly employee. I'm not privy to the inner workings of what goes on around here."

"You're causing a scene over a case of pinkeye?"

"You're treating pinkeye, I'm treating a kid with possible asthma. Are you going to tell me it all evens out?"

"I'm sorry for your diagnosis," she said sympathetically. "And if you'd rather not…"

"It's not that I'd rather not. But what I was wondering is if we get to pick and choose our cases or if we just get them according to what's up next, and who our established patients are."

"If you're trying to insult me, I have thick skin, Doctor."

"Not trying to insult you, Doctor. Just trying to figure things out now that you're back."

"Well, figure this out. It's a fair system. I don't take all the easy cases and assign the tougher cases to my colleagues. You were treating an easy case of nursemaid's elbow when I was treating a little girl with Erb's palsy. Unless a patient requests a specific doctor we take whoever's up next, regardless of the easiness or severity of their condition." She bit her tongue to hold the rest in but didn't do a very good job of it because the rest slipped out. She knew this had to be tough on

Simon, working in basically a new situation, especially with his credentials. "Trust me—it's fair."

"It's always good to know my standing."

"Sure it is. You got stuck in a jammed-up clinic when I was gone and you're blaming me for it. So now you want some answers. Can't say that I blame you. Reverse the situation and I'd be asking the same questions."

Simon kicked off his shoes and set his mug of coffee next to the sofa. Sighing, he popped an old classic movie into his DVD player then dropped down on the couch with his bowl of cold cereal, contented to spend the evening vegetating.

He'd gotten off to a rough start with Del and, to be honest, was surprised she hadn't fired him on the spot. There really was no excuse for his questions, especially when he knew the answers. But he'd been in the mood to antagonize someone and Del had seemed to be it.

The thing was, he'd called to talk to Amy this morning and was told by her latest stepfather that he had no rights to the girl any longer, to please not call back or he'd be served with a restraining order. Damn! He missed her. Red hair and freckles, with a little gap between her front teeth—sometimes he swore he'd stayed married to her mother just because Amy was so endearing. But that was obviously over and now he wasn't even allowed to talk to her any more. It hurt. It stung to the bone because he missed Amy with all his heart. Didn't know how he was going to get along without her. And Del, well…she'd just caught some of his fallout. Wrong place, wrong time and with a child who was making her so happy—happy the way he'd used to be.

Well, one thing was for sure. He'd never, ever get involved with a woman who already had a child. It just opened him up to getting hurt again.

In the meantime, he owed Del a big apology for being so confrontational over everything today. She didn't deserve it just because she'd had a child.

He owed her an apology and it wouldn't keep until tomorrow. He opened his clinic information packet and found her cell-phone number. On impulse, he dialed.

"Hello," she answered, almost in a whisper.

"Del, this is Simon Michaels."

"And?"

"I may have been a little harsh with you today."

"Not so I noticed," she lied. "It was a tough day for everybody."

"Still, I wasn't myself and I'm calling to apologize."

"No need. I wasn't at my best, either, this being my first day back and all. Look, you woke up my baby. I've got to go. Can I call you back?"

"No need for that. I just wanted to apologize."

"Thanks, Simon," she said, and with that she hung up on him. And he actually chuckled. She was interesting, to say the least. Definitely her own woman marching to her own beat.

CHAPTER TWO

"HE'S NOT VERY pleasant at times," Del said to Charlie as she gave him his nightly bath. "On the verge of rude and insulting. Then he calls and apologizes. Like what's that all about?" Although he did exude a general sexiness about him, which was nothing she was going to admit out loud. Even when brooding he was sexy and she wondered, for a moment, what kind of social life he had going for himself. "It's none of my business," she told Charlie. "And I want you to point that out to me every time I have a straying thought about the man. OK? He's handsome and has the ability to be charming, but that's as much as I want to notice."

The baby's response was to splash around in the water and giggle.

"I'm not sure why my partners would have chosen him, except for the fact that he's a good doctor, but that was their decision, not mine. And his credentials are good. At least he's licensed here in Chicago, which saved a little bit of hassle. But that attitude…I've got to tell you, Charlie, you're not going to grow up to be a man like he is, who goes back and forth. I'll swear by all that I know as a doctor and what I'm learning as a mother that you're going to have manners and respect." Yeah, until he was an adult; then he could do anything he wanted, which scared her because somewhere there was probably a mother who'd said the same thing to her baby Simon. And look at the way he'd turned out. "I suppose a mother can only do so much," she said as she pulled Charlie out of the baby bath and wrapped him in a towel. "But I'm going to teach you anyway and keep my fingers crossed I don't go wrong somewhere." Not to imply that Simon's mother had gone wrong. Because Simon did have manners and just a touch of arrogance to offset them.

"Now, let's get you dressed and I'll read you a story. How about the one with the giraffe, tonight?" Sure, it was all in her mind but she thought that was Charlie's favorite story. Of course, any story might have been his favorite, as he seemed delighted by everything she read him, including pages from a medical journal she'd read aloud to him one evening when she was trying to catch up on her own reading. It was the mother-child bond that mattered, the one she'd missed all day today while she'd been at work.

But on the other hand, work had had its number of fulfilling moments, too, and it was good getting back. She was still plagued with guilty feelings, though. Those weren't going to go away, and she could foresee the time when the conflicts would become even greater, such as when Charlie learned to walk, or started talking. She didn't want to miss those things, but it was conceivable he might say his first word to Mrs. Rogers or take his first step when she wasn't around to see it. Sacrifices. Yes, there were definite sacrifices to be made, and she could feel them tugging at her heart. But she was still drawn to being a pediatrician, and while she felt guilty about working she felt no guilt at all about the work she did. It would have been nice, though, to have that proverbial cake and eat it, too.

Well, that wasn't going to happen. She had a child to support now and her savings, while sufficient, weren't enough to carry her through until he went to college. So off to work, get over the guilt. She supposed in time it would lessen, but her preference would always be to be there for her son.

"Once upon a time, there was a giraffe named George, who was shorter than all the other giraffes in the jungle. 'Why can't I be tall like my mother?' he asked." This is where Del tickled Charlie's tummy with a stuffed giraffe. "'Why can't I be tall like my daddy?'" She tickled Charlie's tummy again and took such delight in watching him laugh and reach out to hold his giraffe. "'Why can't I be tall like my brother...?'" And so the story went, until Charlie usually wore himself out and went to sleep. Which was the case tonight. He dozed off before the end of the story, clinging to his stuffed giraffe, and she tucked him into his crib, crept out and made sure the night-light was on for when he woke up later as she hated the idea of her child waking up in total darkness and being afraid.

Afterward, Del fixed herself a cup of hot tea and settled down on the couch to catch up on some reading, but she was distracted by her cellphone, which she'd set to vibrate now that Charlie was down. She'd been awfully rude to Simon and for no reason other than Charlie couldn't wait a minute or two—which he could have since he hadn't been crying for her. She'd set a bad example for Charlie even if he was too young to understand that. But there would come a time when he would and she dreaded that day. So in the end, she picked up her phone and made that call.

"Simon," she said when he answered. "This is Del."

"Let me guess. You want me to go in tonight."

"You caught me at a bad time earlier," she said.

"Apparently."

"Look, I had just got my baby to calm down and go to sleep after his first day away from me, and you disturbed him. You're not a parent, so you wouldn't understand," she said.

"No, I'm not a parent," he answered, then sighed so loud into the phone she heard it.

"Well, you couldn't understand what I'm talking about, but I like my evenings undisturbed."

"Which is why you've begged off call for the next six months."

"It was a compromise. Originally I was going to take off a whole year to stay home with Charlie, but that didn't work out so I decided to come back during the days so long as I have my evenings and nights to myself."

"Not that it's any of my business."

"Look, Simon. I called to apologize for being so rude. We got off to a bad start and when you called to apologize I wasn't in the frame of mind to deal with it."

"Guilty-mother syndrome?"

"Something like that."

"I understand children, Del, but I don't even pretend to understand their parents."

"You would if you were a parent."

"Well, thank God I'm not. My marriage was hell and it makes me queasy thinking we could have easily brought a child into it."

"So you're divorced."

"Blessedly so."

"Sorry it didn't work out. Is that why you hate women?"

"Who says I hate women?"

"Your scowl, every time I looked at you today."

"Well, I don't hate women. I'm just...wary."

"Sorry you feel that way. Anyway, I just wanted to let you know I'm sorry I was abrupt with you on the phone earlier. Normally I silence my phone so I won't be disturbed, and people who know me know when to call and when not to call."

"I didn't get the memo," he said.

"Then I'll make it simple. Evenings are my time unless it's an emergency. That's the memo." He was impossible and she was already dreading working with him. But what was done was done. He was hired, the partners were happy with him and he was a hard worker. Everyone in the office shouted his praises, so it had to be her. He rubbed her the wrong way, or the other way around. Anyway, her feelings for the man were no reason to give him grief, so before she hung up the phone she made a silent vow to tolerate him in the office. If he did his job and she did hers there'd hardly be any time to socialize anyway.

"So, as I was saying, I'm sorry for being so abrupt and it won't happen again."

"Let's call it a professional standoff and leave it at that."

"Professional, yes, of course. But that's all. And just so you'll know, you don't even have to acknowledge me in passing if you don't want to."

"Wouldn't that look unfriendly?" he asked.

"Maybe. But who's going to notice."

"Everybody." He laughed. "Are you afraid of me?"

"No, not really. I'm just not in the mood to have a man in my life—especially one I'll be working closely with."

"You formed that opinion of me after one day?"

"I form fast opinions."

"You must. But just so you know, I don't hate you and I don't even dislike you. I got off to a bad start this morning because of some personal matters and it carried over. But it has nothing to do with you." He smiled gently. "In fact, I've felt bad all day for the way we got started."

"You did?" she asked.

"I'm not usually quite so abrupt."

"Neither am I."

They both laughed.

"So tomorrow maybe we get off on a better foot?" she asked.

"Well, now that that's settled, let me be the one to hang up this time." With that he clicked off.

* * *

Her second and third days at work went a little better than her first, but she still missed Charlie so badly. Her situation with Simon didn't improve, though. She tried being friendlier, and he reciprocated, not in an out-and-out way but at least in a friendlier manner. Still, to Del their relationship felt distanced. Cordial but not particularly friendly. And somehow she had the impression it didn't have anything to do with her. At least she hoped it didn't because she wanted them to be just a touch more than cordial.

It was the fifth day when he actually greeted her with some hospitality. "Would you mind taking over a case for me?"

"Symptoms?"

"First, he's four years and his mother admitted to some pretty heavy drinking during pregnancy."

"So let me list some symptoms for you. Poor impulse control, poor personal boundaries, poor anger management, stubbornness, intrusive behavior, too friendly with strangers, poor daily living skills, developmental delays—attention deficit/hyperactivity disorder, confusion under pressure, poor abstract skills, difficulty distinguishing between fantasy and reality, slower cognitive processing. Stop me when I hit five of these."

"You hit five of the symptoms a long time ago."

"So you know what it is?"

He nodded. "But you're the expert in treatment for FAS."

"I'll be glad to take a look and get started with a plan,

but you do realize that most treatments respond best to behavioral therapy. Poor thing's going to be saddled with a disability for his entire life."

"Well, you're the best one for the job," he admitted.

That took her by surprise. "Thank you. I appreciate the compliment," she said, almost stumbling over her words.

"Look, is there any chance we could start over... again?"

"Maybe," she said, hiding a smile. She liked this side of him and she was glad she was finally going to coax it out of him, if for no other reason than a better working relationship. "Is the mother or father more responsive now?"

"Child's under protective service. He has a foster family who really cares."

"That's a step in the right direction."

"Anyway, I told them we have an expert on staff so I'm leaving it up to you to schedule them in. I slid the note with his file reference under your office door."

"I appreciate the vote of confidence," she said.

"When you've got the best on staff you'd be crazy not to."

She didn't know whether to take that as a compliment or a disparaging remark in disguise. For a moment or two she'd been flattered, but now...she didn't know. It seemed more like a professional request and not something that spoke to his opinion of her abilities. Oh, well, she decided. It was what it was, whatever that might be. "I'll read the file and call the foster parents to see what we'll be addressing."

"I appreciate it," he said as he walked away.

"Do you really?" she whispered. "I wonder."

It was hard getting a beat on the good Dr. Del. One minute she seemed friendly enough and the next she was glacial. So, what was her game? Simon wondered as he watched her stride through the hall without so much as a glance in his direction. Did she hate men? Or did she feel that he jeopardized her position at the clinic? Whatever the case, they were barely any further along than they'd been two weeks ago when she'd first come back to work, and now it was becoming frustrating. While he didn't expect a friendship out of the deal, he did expect a civil work environment, which she barely gave him but only because it was required. And, it was getting to him. Maybe it was the whole social conquest of the deal but he did have to admit the more she stayed away, the more he wanted to get close. With her long, nearly black hair and her dark brown eyes, she had a drop-dead-gorgeous body that begged to be looked at and he enjoyed the looking.

Was she becoming a habit or an obsession? Maybe a little of both. But he wasn't the only man doing the looking. He was, though, the only one she treated with woeful disregard. Except in the professional capacity and there she was cordial.

Well, never let it be said he was the one who gave up the fight. "How's little Curtis doing?" he asked.

"It's like you thought. Fetal alcohol syndrome. He's got a tough life ahead of him but I got him in a program that has some luck treating kids with his disorder. I'll be following him medically. He's a cute little boy."

"I'd be interested in learning more," he said, out of the blue. "Maybe we could get together sometime and you could give me some pointers."

She looked almost taken aback. "Um…sure. Why not?"

"You name the time and place," he said, "and I'll be there."

"Friday night, if I can get a sitter? Or do you have plans?"

He chuckled. "Plans? Me have plans? Not for a long, long time."

"Good, then, Friday it is…" She paused. Frowned.

"Anxiety over leaving the baby behind?"

"Other than my work days it's the first time I'll have left him."

"Well, you need a night away from the kiddies—all of them. Some good old-fashioned adult company. So how about we grab a pizza and you can give me the basic crash course on FAS? I understand you've done some writing on it and presented some lectures."

She shrugged. "I used to, but I'm not inclined to take up my time that way, now. Oh, and we'll have to make it an early evening because I don't want to disrupt Charlie's schedule. In fact, instead of going out for pizza, how about we order in? Then I won't have to get a sitter or disrupt anything."

"A night in with you and…?"

"Charlie. Named after my dad."

"A night in with you and Charlie. Sounds doable."

"Great, come over early, around six. He's usually tired out from day care and ready to go down for a nap for an hour or so. We can have the pizza then. Then after bedtime we'll talk about FAS, if that's OK with your schedule."

She almost sounded excited. It was as if she was starved of adult interaction. She must have been to invite *him* over. Of course, she still wasn't going to get too far away from her baby. There'd been a time when he was like that with Amy. He'd been married to Yvette for six months before knowing of her existence. When Amy's dad had dropped a small child at their door, Simon had immediately stepped into the role of protective father. He'd been the one to feed her, and put her to bed and spend evenings at home with her while Yvette was out running around. He'd been the one to take care of her when she was sick, and take her off to her first day of school. He'd gone to "meet the teachers" night and to the play her first-grade class had put on. Never Yvette. And with that kind of relationship he'd never expected Yvette to simply yank Amy out of his life the way she had. But it was done now, and there was nothing he could say or do to change that. His parenting days were over and, yes, he could understand Del's overprotectiveness because he'd been much the same way.

She reminded him of him, back in happier days. Which was why he resented her. She had what he wanted. But he didn't want it from another one like Yvette, who came equipped with a child already. He wanted his own child next time, one that couldn't be ripped away from him the way Amy had been. "It sounds fine since I don't have anything else to do."

She jotted down her address and gave it to him. "Good. I'll see you then."

"Do you drink wine, or are you...?"

"Nursing? No, I'm not. You can't put your child in the day-care center if he or she's still nursing. So it's strictly the bottle and baby food all the way. And yes, I drink wine. Not much, though, since I work with FAS and I've seen what alcohol can do to a child."

"Then you wouldn't be offended if I bring over a bottle?"

"If you're not offended that I'll have only one glass."

He nodded. "One glass it is." It sounded more like a business transaction than arranging a date, even if it was a working date. So maybe in Del's mind it was a business transaction. Who knew? Admittedly, he was a little disappointed by her attitude, but what had he expected? A real date? They were hardly friends, barely cordial colleagues, and all of a sudden he'd asked her out. Of course, she had a child, which made her safe and he supposed that was part of it. He felt safe with Del because of his personal resolution. So, it wasn't such a bad situation at all. And it would save him from spending another long, dreary night at home alone, looking at pictures of Amy or mulling over how much he missed her.

"Well, he's down for a nap, and the pizza's hot so what say we dig in?" Simon said, pouring himself a glass of wine and leaving the bottle on the table so Del wouldn't feel pressured into drinking if she didn't want to. As it turned out, she poured half a glass and sipped it almost cautiously as they ate their pizza and talked about the clinic. "He's a cute kid," Simon said. "Your Charlie."

"Thank you. I think so, but then I'm a little partial."

"Better that than some of what we see come into the clinic."

"Why did you choose pediatrics?" she asked.

"Liked it when I rotated through when I was an intern. Liked the kids, like the way they're braver than many adults. And they show so much heart and trust. I think it's the vulnerability and trust that got to me. Most adults don't have that. They're cynical, or mistrustful. I remember one patient who told me right off the bat he had the right to sue me if he didn't like the way I treated him and the hell of it was, he had his choices but as an intern I didn't have those same choices, as in not treating him. Luckily his diagnosis turned out to be something simple, but you know the guy never even said thank you. He simply accused me of overcharging his insurance company. Which is one of the reasons I went with children. They're not so vindictive."

"Most adults aren't, either. You just happened to have a bad one at a time in your early career where you were open to influence."

"I gave some thought to going into a straight family practice but I just didn't like treating adults the way I enjoyed taking care of the kids."

"Which is a good reason to go into pediatrics. Family practice's loss."

"Not really a loss so much as I never gave it a fair trial. I'd already decided I wanted to treat children."

"Because you like kids that well?"

"Generally, yes. Says the man who isn't a father."

"You don't have to be a father to be a good pediatrician. All it takes is a passion for what you're doing."

He looked away for a minute, turned deadly serious. "I had this one little guy who was born with cerebral palsy. He wasn't too severe but he had some limitations in walking and coordination, and the way he took to his physical therapy just made me so proud of him. He worked hard, never complained, never questioned. Just did what he was supposed to do when he was supposed to do it and I suppose he was my turning point. I'd always thought I'd be a surgeon, or something a little more showy, but with the kids I found that I liked the courage I saw every day. So I stuck with children and I have no regrets. Now you tell me yours."

"There was never a choice for me. I never had any grand delusions of going into one of the higher profile types of medicine. I liked children, liked working with them, and I think a lot of that stems from my childhood pediatrician, Dr. Dassett. He was a kind man and I was never afraid of going to see him. So even when I was a kid myself I always told my parents I was going to grow up and be just like Dr. Dassett. And here I am."

"But FAS? How did you get interested in that?"

She shrugged. "One of my earliest patients was born with FAS and it interested me that a mother could do that to her child. So, I studied it, and eventually specialized in it." She took a bite of pizza and washed it down with a sip of wine. "I still can't explain the mind that thinks it's OK to do that to your child, but my job is to coordinate care when I get the opportunity. Admittedly, we don't see a lot of that at Lakeside, but I do get called out on referrals to other local hospitals from time to time."

"Isn't it discouraging?" he asked her as he grabbed up his second piece of pizza.

"Very. But somebody has to do it, so why not me? I see all the expectant mothers who drink—it's all just selfishness, or that 'bury your head in the sand' attitude where you think it can't happen to you. And odds are it won't. But occasionally…" She shrugged. "It's one of the ugly sides of medicine, but I can do it and make a difference, which makes me glad I've chosen FAS as my specialty because when you see one of these kids succeed…" She smiled. "If you want pretty you become a beautician. If you want to make a difference you become a doctor. And personally, I've always wondered what's up with someone who wants to practice proctology. Now to me, that's a field of medicine I'd rather not think about."

Simon laughed. "When you put it in those terms, I can kind of agree with you. But for me it's radiology where you don't get much patient contact. I like patients. Like working with them, like curing them or making them feel better, and viewing film and images just isn't what I care to do. Although the world certainly does have need of great radiologists, especially in so many of the specific treatments and tests that get referred to them. Most everything starts with an X-ray of some sort, I suppose, but I can't see myself in that role."

"So do you like Chicago?" she asked. "Is that why

you applied here? Or were you just looking to get away from Boston and Chicago is where you were accepted?"

"I'm from Chicago originally and I wanted to get back here. Had that little hiccup called marriage back in Boston when I was finishing my residency, which didn't make moving home too practical since my wife was born and raised in Boston and wouldn't leave there for me, even though I begged her. So I had to be the flexible one. And then she moved to Chicago anyway, so I did, too. It's nice to come home to the big city. Not that Boston is small, but I love the lakeshore here, which is where I grew up, love the Navy Pier and all the park along the river." He smiled. "It's nice to be back where I belong. So are you from here?"

"South side. Some people call it Indiana, but once you get past Merrillville, which is where I'm from, it all turns into Chicago whether or not it really is. I love a happening city. Love the restaurants, the theater, the museums. And like you I'm hooked on the lakeshore. I can't wait until Charlie's old enough to go to the Museum of Science and Industry, or take a ride on the Navy Pier Ferris wheel. I've got big plans for him. Already have him enrolled in a private school for when he's old enough."

"Well, the coincidence is, we live only a block apart. And I was raised three blocks from here. So who says you can never go home? Because I have and I'm glad to be here."

"Are your parents here?"

"Same condo building I was raised in. They love

it, too, although now that they're older they winter in Florida."

"My parents vacationed in Costa Rica and loved it so much they stayed. Now with Charlie, though, they come back every couple of months, which is good because he's really the only family they have."

"No brothers or sisters?"

She shook her head. "Just me. And you?"

"One brother, who's also a doctor, and a sister, who's a military surgeon."

"Your parents wouldn't happen to be doctors, would they?"

"My dad was a surgeon, my mom was a teacher."

"And they both worked and raised you kids at the same time?"

He nodded. "It worked out."

"My parents were both practicing physicians. My mother has had fits with me now that I've chosen to have a baby and work at the same time, which is what she did. She wants me to stay home with Charlie, and they'll help me out financially if I need it. First grandchild and all."

"Doesn't sound like a bad deal," he said, taking his third slice of pizza.

"But it's not my deal. I want it all, and that includes my job. Speaking of wanting it all, I hear someone stirring in his crib. Sounds like it's bath and snack time for Charlie."

"Does he like it?" Simon teased.

"Give him time." She hopped up and went to get

Charlie, then brought him out to see Simon. "Want to hold him while I get his snack ready?" she asked.

"Sure," he said, but reluctantly. He stretched out his arms to take the bundle from Del as she got a jar of smooshed bananas ready for Charlie. Then when she took him back the baby giggled in anticipation of what he knew was coming.

"He loves his bananas," she said, putting him in his high chair. "Everything but vegetables. He spits out anything that's green."

"Smart kid. Vegetables..." He turned up his nose. "Not a big fan myself unless they're on my pizza."

Snack time was finished, then came bath time, play time and bedtime story, and Charlie was ready to crash for the night. Or at least part of the night. So she put him down and came back out to the living room only to find that Simon was cleaning up the kitchen mess Charlie had made. "You don't have to do that. He hasn't got the finesse of fine dining down yet so half of everything goes on the floor."

"What's a few spilt bananas among the boys?" he asked, laughing. "Besides you look tired and I thought some help might be welcomed."

"Help is always welcomed, but I thought you wanted to talk FAS."

"Not tonight, Del. I've had a nice evening so why ruin it with something so serious?"

"In that case I might be up to another half glass of wine before you leave, if you don't mind."

"Want to keep the bottle?"

She shook her head. "Drinking alone is sad. Even if it is wine."

"Which is why I never drink alone," he replied. "It doesn't go with cold cereal anyway."

"Cold cereal?" she asked as he wrung out the washrag and placed it on a drying rack inside the sink cabinet door.

"My usual evening fare. Unless I stop and take something home with me like Chinese or Thai. Trust me, eating is not high on my priority list."

"But you don't look emaciated."

He laughed. "I'm not emaciated. I just have bad eating habits. Besides, I usually have a pretty good lunch at the hospital. The doctors' cafeteria is fairly respectable."

"What about a home-cooked meal?"

"What's that?" he asked.

"What I'm going to cook for you Sunday night if you don't have other plans. I'm not a gourmet chef by a long shot but I do love to cook, and I've been practicing for the time when Charlie starts to eat real food. So, dinner?"

"You sure you want to do this?"

She nodded. "I'm working tomorrow, but I'm off Sunday, so I think I can whip up something you'll like and maybe we can talk FAS then."

"What time?"

"How about eight o'clock, after Charlie's down for the first part of the night?"

"He doesn't sleep through the night yet?"

"He's rambunctious. And eager to get up and play. What can I say? He's all boy."

"And you indulge that?"

"I embrace it." She smiled. "Love it, too, even if the clinic staff has to suffer my grumpiness the next day."

"So now I'll know why to stay away from you on the days you look frazzled."

She shrugged. "I've enjoyed our evening, Simon. You're very considerate, actually. Better than what I expected."

"You were expecting an ogre?"

"Not so much as a grouch."

"Well deserved."

"But you're not really a grouch, either. Just someone who's preoccupied."

"Not so preoccupied as grumpy."

"Why?"

"I had a daughter, Amy. Stepdaughter, actually. Raised her from being tiny and when her mother and I divorced, I lost the battle. She had a restraining order taken out on me. I can't see her, or talk to her. When I'm grumpy that's usually what it's about."

"Simon, I'm so sorry. I didn't… Can't even imagine…"

"Most of the time I still can't imagine it, either. But it is what it is and so far there's been nothing I can do about it."

"You've gone to court?"

"Several times without any luck. Yvette says no, that my presence wrecks her little family and she doesn't want me around. So I'm excluded."

"I wish I knew what to say or do."

"So do I, but the battle is over and I lost." He shrugged. "And Amy's the one left to suffer."

"I can't even imagine what I'd do if someone took Charlie from me."

"You'd let it tear you up. You wouldn't sleep, or eat. You'd walk around in a blur."

She corked the wine bottle and handed it to him. "So you would consider coming over Sunday night for dinner?"

"Looking forward to it," he said, taking the bottle of wine from her. "My days off get lonely."

The brush of his smooth hand across hers gave her goose bumps. Luckily, she was in long sleeves and he couldn't see them, but she could surely feel them skipping up and down her arms. "Good night, Simon."

"Good night, Del," he replied, then headed to the front door of her condo. It was on the twenty-first floor overlooking the lake, and she wondered since he lived only a block away if it also overlooked his condo. But she didn't ask. Didn't want to be tempted. Didn't want to catch herself going to the window and gazing out wondering if he was gazing back.

It was physical attraction, that was all. But she did like him better than she had before this evening. In fact, she liked him a lot. If only Eric had been this nice to be with she might not have left him, but he'd been a bully. Never lifted a finger to help, always criticized, and most of all he always cheated and lied afterward. Somehow, she didn't see those ugly traits in Simon. In fact, now that she knew him a little better personally, she had an idea he was full of good traits. Except for his grumpy days, but now she knew what that was about and felt bad for him.

Del frowned as she put Charlie to bed. Life was good to her. Very good. She was glad for what she had.

CHAPTER THREE

SATURDAY WAS BUSY and complicated after her first non-date date with Simon. They had time to catch a quick lunch in the doctors' cafeteria but she missed out on Charlie's lunch altogether. She felt guilty about that but there was nothing she could do because work came first.

"You OK?" Simon asked her that afternoon.

"I miss Charlie. I hate not being there for his lunch."

"I'm sure he won't notice."

"I think he will. It's part of his routine now. And I'm sure he misses it."

"Babies are forgiving at that age. Take him to the park or something on his way home. I know it's getting chilly out so his outside days to play are numbered until spring. In fact, take off work now and I'll cover for you."

"Do you mean that?" she asked excitedly.

"Of course I mean it. Take Charlie out and go have some fun."

She was taken aback by Simon's generosity. And to think her first impressions were that he was grumpy. Yet he was the furthest thing from ill-tempered she could think of. "You're sure?"

"It's a beautiful day. We're not busy for once. Go take advantage."

Stirred by the moment, Del reached up and kissed him on the cheek. "Thank you. You don't know how much this means to me."

"Yes, I do," he whispered in return as she sped to her office to grab her jacket. "I really do."

The afternoon couldn't have gone more perfectly. They played in the park, stopped at the pier for dinner and ice cream and went home exhausted. By the time the doorman buzzed them in, Charlie was sound asleep, his face covered with chocolate.

"Looks like you two had a big afternoon," he said. Del smiled.

"We did. Sort of a gift from a friend."

"He must be a good friend."

"Getting to be." More than she'd ever anticipated.

"Well, have a pleasant evening. And tell Charlie he looks good in a chocolate moustache."

Laughing, she caught the elevator and rode all the way up thinking of Simon for most of the ride. She was looking forward to fixing dinner for him tomorrow night, which made her wonder what these growing feelings for him were all about…

CHAPTER FOUR

"I WASN'T SURE what the proper etiquette was so I brought flowers." Simon handed Del a spray of white and red carnations at the door before he entered her condo. "Hope nobody here's allergic to them." Truth was, they were a last-minute detail. He knew it was appropriate to bring a hostess gift like a bottle of wine, but she'd take months to drink the whole thing and it would turn to vinegar in the meantime, so flowers were second on his go-to list, not that he'd ever bought flowers for anyone before. But for Del, and all her feminine ways, they seemed appropriate.

"They're lovely," she said, taking the flowers from him and stepping back to let him in. "You really didn't have to, Simon, but I'm glad you did."

He wondered for a moment if the gesture was too romantic, as he clearly didn't want to shoot that intention out there. Sure, Del was drop-dead gorgeous, and she was actually very nice when they were getting along. But now he worried if the flowers signaled something more than a thank-you for the dinner tonight. "Well, my mother taught me it was customary to take a hostess gift and…"

"And you had a very conscientious mother."

"She insisted on all things done properly and I can almost hear her berating me for skipping a hostess gift."

"Well, flowers are perfect. They brighten up the place." She dug out a vase from under the sink, filled it with water and put the flowers in it, then set the flowers on the kitchen table. "Sorry, but I don't have a formal dining room here. When I bought the place I never anticipated having someone else living here with me, so I sort of low-balled my expectations of what I wanted in my living space. But I'm going to have to upgrade to something larger pretty soon to make room for the both of us, especially when Charlie gets a little older."

"I have too much space. Don't know what I was thinking when I bought it but I've got enough space to host an army. Bought the condo back in the days when I'd anticipated having some visitation privileges with Amy. Unfortunately, that never happened. So I've thought about downsizing but what's the point? I'm settled here and it's as good a place to stay as any."

"Well, if you ever decide to sell, keep me in mind. I figure I've got about two more years here, if that long. Oh, and I want to stay in the neighborhood. I love the lakeshore." She showed him to the kitchen table, where he took a seat and she poured him a glass of wine.

"You bought that for me?"

"It goes with dinner…lasagna and salad."

He smelled the delicious meal cooking. "How did you know Italian is my favorite?"

"Because Italian's everybody's favorite, isn't it?" she said, laughing as she pulled lasagna from the oven and popped in a loaf of garlic bread.

"Did you ever think about moving away from here... from Chicago?" he asked as he poured a glass of wine about one-third full.

"I had offers. Still get them because of my specialty. But I like it fine just where I am and don't feel inclined to uproot myself and Charlie just to take another job. And you? Now that you're back home, is it for good, or can other bright lights tempt you away?"

"You know what they say about Chicago. Once you were born and raised there it will eventually call you back home. I'm home this time. Nowhere to go. And nothing else particularly interests me. Came back when Yvette moved Amy here and I don't feel inclined to move away."

"We're just a couple of old fuddy-duddies stuck in our ways, aren't we?" she asked.

If only she knew how stuck he was. Simon raised his glass and clinked it to hers. "Here's to a couple of old fuddy-duddies."

"Fuddy-duddies," she repeated, then laughed. "Although I wouldn't say thirty-five is old."

"Your wisdom is, though."

"Why, Doctor, I think you just paid me a compliment whether or not you intended to."

Oh, he'd intended to. Del was wise beyond her years. And so settled into her life. He envied her that, in a way. Of course, there'd been a time when he'd thought he'd been settled into his own ways and look how that had turned out! Disastrous, pure and simple. That was his one and only mistake, though. Next time he'd know better.

"I meant to," he said. "You've accomplished so much in so few years, and now you're a successful mom. That's an amazing life no matter how you look at it, Del."

"Well, you're not so shabby yourself. I read where you were the head of your clinic and you gave it all up to come back home and take a lesser position just so you could be back in Chicago."

"I'll advance again. I'm not worried about that. And even if I don't, I like where I am."

"Are you sure, Simon? It seems to me that you prefer bigger challenges than we can give you."

"I'll admit I miss the challenge, but this is fine. It gets me exactly where I want to be." Closer to Amy.

"But you're not committed to staying with us if something better comes along?"

"We'll talk about that if and when we need to. Until then, how about we eat? I'm starved for that lasagna."

Dinner turned out to be a pleasant affair, from the salad course right down to the tiramisu she'd fixed for dessert. They talked about their childhoods and compared neighborhoods and schools, discussed families and friends. Avoided work and life goals pretty much altogether. And before he knew it dinner was over and he was stuck in the odd place on whether to extend the evening by staying on a little longer or going right home. Charlie took care of that problem, though, as he awoke and started crying.

"Look, you take care of the baby and I'll see myself out," he said.

"You don't have to leave," Del replied. "It'll only take me half an hour or so to get him to go back to sleep."

"He's the priority, Del, and I don't want you rushing him through a routine he needs just because you feel guilty neglecting me. So, I'll go, and see you at work tomorrow."

"I'll bring leftovers for lunch," she said.

Was that an invitation to lunch? "Sounds good to me," he said, not at all sure what her intention was. Maybe she'd just hand him a bowl of lasagna and go on her merry way, or there was the possibility they'd sit together and enjoy a leisurely lunch. Whatever the case, he wasn't comfortable asking, so instead he walked over to Del, gave her a tender kiss on the cheek and thanked her for the evening. "It's nice to get out for a change."

"You don't date?" Del asked Simon as he headed toward the front door.

"Nope. Too soon. The wound hasn't healed enough and I'm generally not that trusting of relationships right now." If ever again.

"Too bad because I think you'd make a terrific date for someone. Maybe you'll meet someone in the clinic or the hospital."

Except he wasn't looking, as most of the women who fell into his age category had children and he wasn't going to do that to himself again. He'd been hurt badly the first time and he wasn't going to do that again. "Thanks again for the evening," he said, then disappeared out the front door.

* * *

"He's different, Charlie," she said as she laid her baby back down in his crib. "He seems like he'd be a great candidate for someone to date, yet he won't date. Maybe his divorce hit him harder than I assumed it did. But the thing is, I don't think he's even looking for companionship. He seems happy being single."

Charlie looked up at her and giggled.

"Well, I'm glad you think it's funny. But mark my words, one of these days you're going to be out there looking and it's not going to be easy finding the right one. Just look at the mess your mommy made of her life for five years. That should teach you something."

Five years of bullying and verbal abuse and she hadn't gotten out of it quickly enough. But she'd lived in the hope that Eric would change at some point, not that he ever had. It had forced her to change, though. Forced her out on her own into the world, where she'd had no choice but to make it all by herself. Surprisingly, she'd discovered she liked it that way. Liked everything about it including her notion to get inseminated and have a baby on her own, owing to her biological clock ticking and all that. Her doctor had told her time was running out for her. Her ovaries were beginning to fizzle out. No, she wasn't too old to have a baby yet, and that was still a ways off, but she hadn't wanted to put it off any longer since she really intended on having a brother or sister for Charlie somewhere down the road.

So one year from her breakup date she'd embarked on a new adventure and she'd loved every minute of it from the pregnancy to the birth. Having Charlie was the single best thing she'd ever done and she didn't regret even a moment of it.

Charlie reached his hands up for her to hold him and, while she normally didn't give in to his little stall tactics, tonight she wanted to feel him in her arms. "OK, so you win just this once but don't think your mommy's going to be a pushover all the time, because it's not going to happen." Although it was happening more and more now that she was working and leaving him behind. "He's a nice man, though, Charlie. Just like yesterday when he covered so we could have time in the park together. I'll admit that Simon and I got off on the wrong foot but that seems to be behind us now."

She hoped so, anyway. Because she really liked him and could even fancy herself dating him sometime. Not that she intended for *that* to happen. But it was caught up in her daydreams. So she pushed it aside and sang Charlie one of his favorite little songs. *Down in the meadow by the itty, bitty pool…* as she glanced at the bouquet of flowers and smiled. Honest to goodness, this was the first time anybody had ever given her flowers and it made her feel special.

"Room Three has an advanced case of bronchitis," she said in greeting to Simon the next morning. "Room Two has a broken arm—just a greenstick fracture, I think. We're waiting for X-rays. And Room One has a little girl who's just started having periods and she has the cramps. So take your pick."

"Good morning to you," he said, looking up on the sign-in board. There were six other cases signed in to various other doctors. "Looks like today's going to be a busy one."

"It happens," she said, giving him a big smile.

"Then I'll start with the bronchitis and work my way down. How's that sound?"

"I'll take the cramps," Del volunteered. "At age eleven I think she'll be more at ease with a female doctor."

They parted ways and Simon went to have a look at his bronchitis patient, a little boy named Bart. He was eight. "How long have you been sick?" he asked Bart.

"Three days," his mother answered. "At first we thought it was a cold."

"Well, we'll get that fixed right up for you. Give you some medicine and send you home to rest. And you'll be up and around inside five or six days."

"Thank you," his mother said. "I was so afraid it would be something worse." She brushed a tear off her cheek. "I don't know what I'd do if he got really sick."

"You'd bring him here and we fix him up."

"It not easy being a single mother...no one there to help me through it."

"I can imagine how hard that is." Simon gave Bart a shot and a prescription and sent them on their way. Thinking about Amy in the intermittent seconds.

"Cute kid," Del said in passing.

"Mom's single. Having a rough time of it. No support." He sighed. "I told her I knew how hard that could be."

"You've got great empathy, Simon. Being a single

mom without having support's got to be the hardest thing in the world. I'm lucky I've got all kinds of support."

"I learned to be empathetic and not to judge after I became a pediatrician."

"It's good that you care so deeply. I mean, word eventually got around when I was pregnant and I lived some pretty rocky months where I heard things like, *'She's a doctor, she should have known better.'* And, *'She's a doctor, how could she be a good example to our older patients?'*

"It hurt, Simon, and I'd be lying if I said it didn't. But it was my choice not to tell anybody the circumstances at the time because that would have only brought on more speculation and rumors. So I gritted my teeth and worked through it."

He admired her for her convictions and knew she was right. But he still thought of Amy and Yvette and wondered what kind of support Amy got from her mother.

He'd always been the better parent to that child, and it hurt him thinking what situation Amy might be living in now. But there was nothing he could do about it, just as there was nothing he could do to convince Yvette to allow him to have more time with Amy.

Yvette certainly wasn't abusive, more like negligent, but she'd be the type who put off an illness for too long, or sign away permission to a virtual stranger. She certainly wouldn't have been worried the way Del would be, or Bart's mother. Maybe those thoughts were where all his angst was coming from. Then to look at Del and see what kind of a super mother she was...that just made him angrier thinking how Amy deserved something like that.

"You're one in a million, Del," he said. "A lady with strong convictions who puts up with the ridicule simply to get what she wants. I admire that in you."

"Thanks," she said.

"Anyway, I'm going to run over to the hospital to check on some patients. Got a couple I'm worried about." And getting his mind back on work would take it off Yvette.

"That's nice of you, Simon. I like it when a doctor goes above and beyond the call of duty."

The more she got to know him, the more she liked him. He was certainly unique to their staff in the way he cared. And she didn't even mind that gruffness in him. Most of it was justified considering the situation with his stepdaughter.

She wondered how long someone with his talent would stay around, though. Amy might move somewhere else. Or he'd have other offers. Offers better than any they could do for him. In fact, she could see him in charge of a hospital pediatrics department, he was so authoritative. That was what worried her. She liked having him here, liked his skill, and as far as she was concerned he was on the open market for something better. Well, it was one of those bridges she'd have to cross when she got to it, she supposed.

"Well, all my patients are doing fine," Simon said, strolling down the hall. "And everyone is happy. So what's next on the board?"

"Twins. Both with runny noses and fevers. Aged two. And a mother who definitely frets to the point of obsession."

"Good," he said, grabbing the chart off the stack, then heading down to Exam Five, where he found two-year-old twins, both with simple colds, and a mother who was worried to death. With all the worrying he'd been doing over Amy lately, it was nice seeing a good mother. It restored his faith in humanity.

"The lasagna is in the fridge with your name on it. Eat as much as you'd like. In the meantime I'm going to run next door and see Charlie. He's expecting me."

Admittedly, Simon was a little disappointed, but not surprised that she preferred to spend her lunch hour with her son. In fact, he would have been surprised if she hadn't. "Have a nice lunch hour," he said.

"Any time I'm with Charlie is nice," she replied as she trotted toward the front door of the clinic. Unfortunately, one of her patients walked in at the same time she was leaving and she had no recourse but to see the child. So she had the girl checked in and spent the next thirty minutes with her, only to send her over to the hospital for an appendectomy. By then it was too late to go see her son but Simon was on his way over there to check on a couple of patients so she stepped into the men's locker room to ask him to check on Charlie for her.

"Simon," she called out to him, admiring the lines of his body in the transparent curtain.

"Care to join me?" he teased.

She liked the contours of his lean body. And yes, even doctors could admire. Which she did. Immensely.

"Since I didn't go over there at lunch and he'll be going down for his afternoon nap any time, I was wondering if you might check in on Charlie for a minute to make sure he's OK."

"Sure," he called, then stepped out of the shower with nothing but a towel wrapped around him. "Now, you can either stay and watch me dress, which I wouldn't mind because I'm not really shy, or you can leave. Your choice." He grinned. "Want to think about it for a couple minutes? I'll be glad to wait." He adjusted his towel a little tighter around his mid-section so it wouldn't accidentally fall.

"Sorry," she mumbled, then backed out the door, leaving him laughing as she exited.

"I am a doctor," she said, as he left the locker room a few minutes later all scrubbed and fresh and ready to go. "It's not like I haven't seen a naked man before."

"But you haven't seen *this* naked man, not that he cares. But people might talk, especially if someone walked in on us while I was still naked," Simon said, coming up behind her.

Del blushed. "I wasn't thinking."

"I was," he said, grinning. "And it's been a while since I caused a lady to blush the way you are right now."

"But I didn't mean to…well, you know. Come gawking. All I wanted to do was ask you to look in on Charlie for me."

"Which I'll be glad to do." These were the words to

which he departed and surprisingly, ten minutes later, Del got a short movie texted to her phone. It was Charlie, who was fast asleep, looking all innocent only the way a baby could. She texted Simon back to thank him, and saved the movie in case, well, she wasn't sure why since she'd see her baby in another few hours. But she was so touched by the gesture she didn't have the heart to get rid of it. And over the next hour, while Simon was at Lakeside checking in on various kids, she couldn't count the number of times she replayed that ten seconds' worth of video, thinking not only of Charlie but of Simon when she did.

"I've almost worn out the video," Del said as Simon walked through the clinic's front door. "Thank you so much for doing that for me."

"No big deal," he said. "I was there and it didn't disturb Charlie, so what the hell? I decided one video was worth a thousand words."

"Or more," she said, standing up on her tiptoes and giving him a kiss on the cheek.

He blushed and backed away. No way was he going to become that involved with Del, so he wasn't going to let it start even in the simple gestures. "What's up next?" he asked uncomfortably.

"A couple cases of the croup, an advanced case of diaper rash and a general physical. Take your pick."

"I'll start with the diaper rash," he said and grabbed up the chart and headed down to Exam Four. "Good afternoon," he said on his way in the door. "I'm Dr.

Michaels, and I understand someone here has a persistent case of diaper rash."

"I've tried everything," the mother said. She looked worn out. "And nothing works."

"Well, take off Angela's diaper and I'll have a look."

Outside in the hall, Del stood and watched the door behind which Simon was treating a baby. She sighed. No, she wasn't in the mood to get involved with anyone, but another time, another place, and it might have been him. Except he seemed as uninterested as she did. So it was a no go all the way around. But he surely would have been a great dad for Charlie, if she'd been in the daddy-hunting business.

Except she wasn't.

"Too bad," she whispered as she walked away. Yep, too, too bad.

CHAPTER FIVE

IT WASN'T THAT she needed the company; wasn't even so much that she wanted it. But when Simon asked her and Charlie out for dinner she found it hard to turn him down. He understood the restrictions, too. Home by seven thirty so she could go through her evening routine with her son. Bath time, bedtime story, a little song, then sit with him until he was fast asleep. It was a routine that really didn't give her much time for a normal social life for herself, but that was fine and dandy with her. This was all she needed in her after-work hours. "I need to stop and pick up some diapers," she told Simon, before he followed her home in his car so he could drive them on their date for three. "And some baby food, if you don't mind waiting."

"I'll be glad to go with you—that way you won't have so much to carry."

"Would you?" she asked. "I'd appreciate that." Suddenly, she found herself looking forward to their abbreviated evening together. It had been a long time since she'd had a real date and while this was not so traditional, it was real enough that she was excited to get out for a little while. Life with Charlie was fulfilling, but she did miss adult companionship outside of work sometimes. So they made a quick stop at the grocery store, then she took her car home and changed clothes, changed Charlie and was back out and ready to go in a matter of minutes. In the meantime, Simon had fixed the baby's car seat in the backseat of his car just as if he knew what he was doing.

"Tell me about Boston," she said as they entered the restaurant. "Did you like it?"

"I loved it. It's such a historic town, so picturesque. And so expensive. I had to rent a parking space outside my town house that cost me fifty thousand a year. And I had to walk a block to get to it. By most standards that's obscene but that was part of the charm living in a Boston town house."

"That's why I like Chicago. It may be large but it's not inconvenient. And I love all the services and sights here. And the fact that in most areas you get parking to go along with your condo. It's all included in the price of the unit."

"I like that, too, and that's one of the reasons why I came back. Home is where the heart is, and this is home to me." The heart, and Amy.

"Do you ever miss Boston?"

"Some, but I miss Amy more." He sighed. "And you?"

"I was in Indianapolis with Eric for a while before he was in medical school. During our last year of medical school I'd already decided I wanted my own life, no outside interference from anybody. Eric and I were actually estranged the last year we were together, only it

was just easier to ignore it. But I'd started making plans
for when he was gone, and having a baby was part of
it. Charlie wasn't an afterthought, but more like a sign
of my independence." She smiled wistfully as she gave
him a bite of food. "He's part of my liberation...the
best part because I really did want him so badly, and
my lack of relationship had nothing to do with it. And
of course, the clock was also ticking.

"You're not that old."

"I didn't want to be that old when I had him, either.
So I made the decision and stuck by it.

"Good for you," he said, picking up the baby spoon
and giving Charlie another bite to eat.

It came so naturally to him, she thought. Just like the
baby seat. It must have been looking after Amy. It was
as if he was meant to have a child of his own. Of course
maybe it was the pediatrician coming out in him, too.

"Well, it's nice being on my own. I was a mess at
first, right after the breakup, and I almost gave in a
couple times when he begged me to take him back. He
promised to change. But he had habits that don't change
so easily, like those other women in his life. And after
all those years I found out he didn't even want children.
He knew I did. I'd talked about it, told him I couldn't
wait until we started to have our family, and he always
said one day we would. Then I caught him cheating,
and who wants to bring a child into that situation?"

"You knew he was cheating?"

"I suspected for a while, but I was afraid to confront
him because I didn't want to know. That was me with

my 'head buried in the sand' phase. Once I pulled it out, though, I discovered just how much was out there that I'd missed, and how much I was going to miss if I continued to hold on to him. My baby being the biggest thing. I wanted one so badly..." She brushed a tear from her eye. "So, did your ex cheat on you?" she asked him.

He shook his head. "She was faithful as far as I know. Just bored because she didn't bargain on a doctor keeping a doctor's hours. And back in Boston I worked pediatrics in the ER, which kept me pretty busy most of the time. So when she started complaining, I took a job in a clinic, but I still had long hours as I was the director and I didn't get the eight-to-five job she thought I'd get. Then there were my on call hours, hospital rounds...it was a busy job and she simply got tired of sitting around waiting for me to come home. So one day I came home to divorce papers and that's all there was."

"Did you love her?"

"I loved the idea of her, but I fell out of love with her because of all her nagging. I had a job to do and she never could understand that I was busy. So, after the divorce, she remarried someone who could give her all the attention she needed."

"You sound bitter."

"Maybe I am. She certainly surprised me without any kind of warning. Married one day and on my way to a divorce the next. It was a shock, to say the least."

"I'll bet it was," Del said, noticing that Charlie was nodding off. "And on that note, I think we need to call it a night." Too bad, too, as she was enjoying herself with

Simon. It was good getting to know a little more about him, and telling him about her. Although there was still something she couldn't put her finger on. Something deeper in Simon that he wasn't talking about. About Amy? About the deep pain he went through when he lost her? She could see it in his eyes, hear it in his voice. Sense it in the way he wrung his hands as he looked as if he were a million miles away.

Still, in spite of it all, she liked him. He was a good doctor, which was where it started, and good with Charlie, too, which, for her, was where it all ended. Right now she was simply too frightened to get involved again. It didn't mean she never would, but not now. Not until she worked it around her head that she had it in her to trust completely another man. Not just for her sake now, but for Charlie's, too. He counted in all this. In fact, he counted in a big way.

"Why don't you bring Charlie and come to my place tonight?" he asked on their next day off together. "I'm a fair to good cook and I can make something Charlie will like."

"You really don't mind me bringing Charlie?" She wasn't sure why she was on the verge of accepting, but she was. Maybe it was because she enjoyed his company, or just needed an adult social situation. But she was tipped toward accepting.

"Not at all. He's a cute kid. Good manners for six months."

"We'd love to come." Well, there she'd done it. Gone and accepted.

Which left her in the same spot as she'd been in before. Getting involved where she didn't belong.

Simon smiled, but he also sighed. Maybe it wasn't what he really needed, either, wasn't where he needed to be. But they were growing closer and she liked him. So what did a little dinner again among friends matter anyway? It wasn't as if this were a date, and she wasn't going to let this turn into anything but two friends having dinner together. That much was for sure. Nothing but dinner. End of story. Yet she worried about that, too. So why did she worry so much?

"Why did I do this, Charlie?" she asked as she got the infant ready for his night out. "I invited him, which is bad enough, but then I accepted his invitation, which was even worse. I like the man, but not in the way I should be dating him. Or doing something that could vaguely be construed as a date."

One bad long-term relationship was enough to make her swear off all relationships for quite some time and concentrate on the only man in her life she truly loved—Charlie.

"Momma's going to get this right," she told her son, who was busy playing with a stuffed teddy bear as she tried to dress him. "I promise you, I'm not going to do anything stupid like get involved with Simon. You'd like him and, as a matter of fact, I like him, too, but now's not the right time for that. And I'm not sure if or when there's going to be a right time."

However, who said they couldn't be friends? She'd settle for that and be very happy with the outcome, as she didn't have that many friends on which to count—thanks to Eric, who had been so controlling she'd lost contact with most of her friends from medical school—and she felt as if she could count on Simon. But men always wanted to take it to the next level, and she surely wasn't ready for that. No way, no how.

"Your momma just wants an adult friendship," she said to Charlie, who'd tossed his teddy to the end of his crib and started squiggling around trying to get it. "Which you'll probably never understand since you're going to grow up to be a man. But the truth is, it's not always about sex. Sometimes it's about a close relationship that can include everything that goes along with a good friendship and nothing more. I like Simon that way."

Although, who was she kidding? He was her type, at least physically. In fact, she'd picked out a man with Simon's features to father her child... She liked her men dark, with broad shoulders and green eyes, which fit Simon to a T. A trait she noticed over and over throughout the evening.

"Your cooking's very good," she said as she ate her Chinese stir-fry. "I hope I can teach Charlie to cook when he's older. There's always something appealing about a man who can cook."

"I'm not that good, but I do have a few specialties, so after you've been here four or five times you're going to have to settle for reruns or eat some of my more dubious dishes."

Was he implying four or five more invitations? Suddenly, that gave her very cold feet as it sounded like a dating relationship to her. And just after she'd convinced herself she could be friends with him. Del sighed. What was she getting herself into? "You do realize I don't date, don't you?" she said, being brutally honest with him lest he got ideas about the two of them.

"Neither do I, so that makes us even," Simon replied, then took a bite of the chicken in the stir-fry. "Haven't since my divorce and I don't intend to for a good long time, at least not in the dating sense. It's too rough getting involved then uninvolved."

"So we're OK with this, whatever it is?"

He chewed, then swallowed. "A few meals here and there, maybe a walk in the park…I am if you are. I'm thirty-six and one marriage at my age is enough. I've still got the battle scars to prove it."

"I have some of those myself." She laughed. "So we're both at the same points in our lives, it seems."

"Friendship. No dating. That sounds about right to me."

"But can that work?" she asked. "Because I honestly don't know. I've never been in this position before."

"There's only one way to find out," he answered. "We'll try it until we know one way or another."

"And no one gets hurt?"

"No one gets hurt."

In an ideal world that could work, but she knew they weren't living in an ideal world. They'd both had bad breakups and were gun-shy. Neither one wanted permanence. Well, she'd see. She'd just see what happened. Nothing ventured…

* * *

The evening hung on nicely. They ate, Charlie dozed off, and Del and Simon talked about various medical issues, including FAS. Then all too soon it was over and it was time to take Charlie home and put him to bed.

"Let me walk you," Simon offered. "It's not that far and it is dark outside now."

"I'd appreciate that," she said as she slipped Charlie into his coat and hat.

"It's hard to imagine how close we live and yet we've never bumped into each other on the street."

"I haven't gone out much," she said. "My whole life's been tied up with taking care of Charlie. It hasn't been easy doing it alone so I don't get out too much." She shrugged. "I'm not complaining. Just telling you the facts. Single parenting is difficult and I wouldn't trade it for anything in the world. So if I passed you on the street, nine times out of ten I'd be preoccupied with Charlie and wouldn't even see you." She smiled. "That's just the way it goes."

"I suppose it is. But since I'm not a parent..."

"You'd make a great father," she said, slipping her hand into his. "To any child." As they walked in sync, she could hear him sigh.

"The problem is the one I *want* to be a parent to isn't available to me."

She stopped and held onto him. "You'll work it out. One way or another you'll work it out. I have all the confidence in the world in you, Simon. You're meant to be that little girl's daddy and it will happen."

"All the confidence in the world?"

"Since I've gotten to know you better I do. You're a strong man and a caring one and it will happen for you one of these days. I'm sure of it."

"I'm glad we get along now. You're the strong one, Del. And you say the right words—the words I need to hear to give me hope."

She started to walk again, her hand still in his. "We can be strong in this together for each other. I need someone there to be strong for Charlie and me, and you need someone there strong for you and Amy."

"Equal in strength," he said.

"And needy in a way. It's nice to have someone to rely on."

"You'll make a great parent to your own child one day," she said as she put Charlie in the baby carriage. "When the right woman comes along…"

"You didn't wait," he said to her.

"Biologically, men can produce children much longer than women can. And my time was running out. Besides, I always wanted a child. Eric promised me we'd have one when the time was right, but there was never a right time for him because then he backed out on his promise when he found someone else. So I just decided to do it on my own. No fuss, no muss, no bother. Have my baby by myself and skip all that came in between like the role of the father. Made it easy that way. At least for me."

"But what will you tell Charlie someday?"

"The truth. When he's old enough to understand it."

"Don't you think that will hurt him?" he asked as

they strolled down the street in the direction of Del's condo.

"Not if I do it the right way. He'll understand that he was my choice and not my obligation."

"You're sure of that?"

"If I raise my child the right way, I am. I'll just let him know he was a wanted child and not an accident."

"I hope that works out for you," he said as they stopped in front of her condo. "But you're a great mom, so I suppose it will."

"Thanks for the compliment. But I'll admit, I've thought about that more than once. It's not going to be easy telling him."

"You'll do the right thing when the time comes, Del. Anyone who loves her child as much as you do is bound to."

"Thanks again." She reached up and placed a tender kiss on his cheek. "Maybe you'll find the right woman soon and we can raise our kids together."

"I'm not looking for the right woman right now. Did that once and that was enough for this part of my life."

Del laughed. "Never say never."

"Well, I'm about as close to never as you can get."

"Don't be so pessimistic. You never know what's going to happen in your life."

"True. But I've pretty well put myself into the no-relationship category for now. And what about you?"

"I think I'm sitting right there next to you. I'm not really interested in finding someone right now. Charlie's enough for me."

"You're lucky to have him."

"I know I am. Which is why I don't want to mess things up and bring in someone else. We're good the way we are."

"But what if you met the *one*?"

"What if *you* met the one?"

He thought about it for a minute. "I suppose that's one of those bridges you cross when you get there."

"And keep your fingers crossed you don't get there."

"Come on now, it's not that bad."

"Oh, it was that bad. And toward the end it got worse when he was cheating on me. It caught me off guard."

"You never expected it?"

"At the time I didn't. But later, when I thought about it, I realized he'd been playing me for a fool for quite a while. Then talk about feeling stupid."

"I guess that's the way I felt, too. Pretty damned dumb. She didn't cheat on me but she sure had another life going. Lied about it, and went through my bank account to do it. But in her defense I was busy looking the other way so I can't blame her for that."

"You'd think they'd be honest about it, though. If you don't want to be in the marriage get out, don't bully your way through it like Eric did our relationship. He could have simply left."

Simon shrugged. "Who knows what goes on with people and why they do what they do?"

"One thing's for sure. I'm going to teach Charlie to be better."

"With you as his mother, Charlie's going to turn out fine."

Del blushed. "I appreciate the compliment. I hope I do well with him." She hoped to heaven she did well. Charlie deserved that from her.

CHAPTER SIX

"I'm going to see Charlie in a couple hours or so. Care to tag along and have lunch with us?" she asked the next day. "He sure does like you."

"Can't," Simon practically snarled. "Too busy."

Where did that come from? "Fine. But if you change your mind…good. I'll call you when I'm ready to go over." She glanced at the clock on the wall. "Charlie eats between eleven and twelve."

"And when do you eat?" he asked.

"Hardly ever when I'm on duty. Don't have enough time."

"Don't wait on my account. I have a lot to do." The sacrifices you make for your kids, he thought to himself. He remembered all the sacrifices he'd made for Amy—the missed meals, the days off work, adjusting his schedule to fit to hers as she got older—none of which had been appreciated by Yvette, yet he hadn't begrudged the child anything.

Charlie held his arms up to his momma and she picked him up and cradled him. As it turned out Simon wasn't able to make it, he was so busy. "He's fixed on some-thing and I don't know what it is, but it's work, and you know that work comes first." Charlie giggled then burped. "And you, of course. You're always first."

She did wish there were something...anything she could do to help Simon, though. She felt so bad for him and she could understand what it would be like ripping your child from your arms because she had Charlie.

Charlie snuggled his head against his mother's shoul-der, which indicated to Del that it was time for a nap. "I'll see you after work," she promised him, "or before if I can catch a break for fifteen or twenty minutes."

"He's doing splendidly," Mrs. Rogers said as she watched Del put Charlie down in his designated crib. "Plays with the other babies his age as much as a six-month-old can play, and he's caught on to his routine easily. No separation anxiety. He's really a good little boy, so there's really nothing to worry about."

Del breathed a sigh of relief. "I'm the one who has separation anxiety," she said. "And while you say there's nothing to worry about, I still worry."

"Because you're a good mother."

Maybe she was, but that didn't stop the pit in her stomach from growing every time she saw Charlie in day care. She wanted so badly to stay home with him it hurt. But there was nothing she could do. This was her life and she had to make all the pieces fit together. "Thank you," she said humbly. "But that doesn't make it any easier."

"Well, for what it's worth, it will get easier over time, once you've adjusted to *your* new routine. I've seen too many parents come in here and drop off their kids and be glad to get rid of them. It's refreshing to see a parent who frets so much. But I promise you, he's getting good care, as good as we can give him without being his mother."

"I appreciate that," Del said, bending over the crib to give Charlie a kiss on his chubby cheek even though he was already fast asleep. "And if I get in your way or start making a nuisance of myself, please let me know. I don't want to disrupt things here."

"We have fifty children, half that many workers and volunteer grandmas, and the presence of one more person here isn't going to disrupt a thing. In fact, it's good seeing a parent who wants to be so involved. Currently, we have only about a dozen or so parents who make an effort to have lunch with their children."

"That's surprising," Del said, quite stunned at the low percentage. How could a parent not want to spend as much time with his or her child as possible? "Look, I've got to be going," Del said, giving Charlie one last kiss. "I'll see you later, big boy," she whispered in his ear, then went off to find Simon, who was simply standing in the clinic hall, looking at the patient board.

"So many children, so little time." He gave her a sideways glance. "So how was your lunch with Charlie?"

"He slept through most of it. Seems he had a big morning."

"I'm glad someone did. I spent my lunch hour on the phone with the lawyer fighting for Amy. It seems like that's all I do lately."

"Any progress?"

"He said we can start from the beginning again but he wasn't very optimistic that anything would change. He said I'd need more evidence that Amy's being neglected or mistreated—something new that they haven't seen before."

"Is there anything new?"

"Not that I'm aware of. And since I never get to see her…" He shrugged. "It's hard to tell."

"Would Amy ever call you?"

"If she had access to a phone she might, but they make sure she doesn't have access."

"So you can't just call her?"

He shook his head. "That would only make it worse on her and I don't want to do that."

"Do you want to chat about it?" she said. "I've got fifteen minutes."

They went to the doctors' cafeteria, where they found a secluded corner and sat down, he with his coffee, she with her tea. "Let me make this long story short. Yvette took everything I had—my car, my money, my house. Everything. It was for Amy, she told me. She needed a way to support her, and I let her do it. But like an idiot I discovered she took it all for her new boyfriend. He was a gambler and he was tapped out at the time. I felt so stupid giving up everything, but that's what I did and when I came here I barely had enough money to start over. The condo isn't even mine—it's a rental. My life is practically a rental because I wanted to take care of Amy and as it turned out I was left with nothing. Talk about being stupid."

"That's not being stupid. That's loving someone more than you love yourself and you can't fault a person for that." She took hold of his hand. "If you need more hours…"

"More hours aren't going to fix what ails me, I'm afraid. And it's not the money. It's being gullible to my ex. I didn't expect her to do what she did, especially since it involved Amy. If anything happens to her I don't have the means to take care of her properly."

"I'm so sorry, Simon. I can't even imagine what you're going through."

"I moved back to Chicago, because I love it here, but I was perfectly happy in Boston and would be happy anywhere Amy was. But Yvette and Amy are here now, and I'd hoped…well, let's just say I'd hoped she'd come to her senses one of these days and give me visitation rights."

"And there's nothing else you can do?"

He shook his head. "Not a damned thing. The court has spoken and I suppose I could appeal again but I really don't have a legal leg to stand on since she's not my daughter and Yvette would never allow me to adopt her for fear she'd lose child support from Amy's real father."

"Does he have visitation rights?"

Simon shrugged. "I suppose he does, but all he is to Amy is a name attached to a bad connotation. To Yvette he's a monthly check in the mail, and that's it."

"Maybe her new stepfather is good? Although the fact he's a heavy gambler doesn't really put him in a very good light."

"I'm not judging him, because I haven't met the man, but it's hard for me to picture."

"Maybe if you talked to him he might come around."

"Like he did when he took everything I owned before."

Del sighed heavily. "Would either one of them listen to me?"

"I doubt it. Unless you ante up and pay them. Nothing comes cheap or free wherever they're concerned."

"So they wouldn't be amenable to a civil chat from one of your friends?"

"Nope. It's all about what they can get out of any deal and they know they can't get any more out of me...and there's no reason for you to be involved in this mess."

"And in the meantime?"

"I get by."

"Does this explain your mood?"

"I hope so. Because nothing else does. I was on the phone with my lawyer earlier looking for another way in and he wasn't encouraging. Told me straight up that he'd send me a bill first of the month so we could settle up and call it quits."

Del couldn't even imagine what she'd do if someone usurped her rights with Charlie and took him from her. Someone such as the sperm donor who had changed his mind and wanted visitation or, worse yet, custody. The thought of that made her queasy and she pushed her cup of tea away. "You've got to be kidding!"

"I'm afraid I'm not. He fired me."

"Can he do that?"

"Apparently he can."

"Is there anything I can do?" she asked. "Give you a letter of recommendation or appear somewhere on your behalf?"

"I'm afraid the fight is fought. As the judge so eloquently pointed out, I have no rights whatsoever when it comes to Amy. She's not my child, I didn't adopt her, and all I did was what any for-hire child-care worker would do for her."

"Seriously?" She was shocked by the judge's lack of sympathy for a man who loved a child as if she were his own.

"The hearing lasted ten minutes, the verdict came in instantly. Amy is lost to me forever."

"How old is she?"

"Seven."

"Then she'll have memories of you, so maybe someday…"

"After Yvette does a number on me the way she did on Amy's father, there's not going to be any someday. She trashed Amy's father every chance she could and Amy heard it. Yvette never took care to mind her words around her child and that has to have an effect. And I expect if I keep trying to get back into her life she'll do the same to me. Kids that age are so impressionable, too." He shrugged. "I've exhausted everything I know how to do without hurting Amy, or without involving her. Even my own attorney told me it was time to give up for the sake of the child."

"Why did you marry her if she's so vindictive?"

"I never saw that side of her until we'd been married awhile. Then when it came out, it came out ugly. She looked like a good mother. Amy had everything she needed, mostly thanks to me. But I wasn't enough and she reminded me of that every day. I couldn't provide the life she thought she deserved. And to be honest, I think she'd already set her sights on finding her next victim by the time we'd split, because she went directly into his arms three months later."

"With the man she married?"

Simon nodded. "One and the same."

"Oh, I am sorry."

"So am I. Which is why I thought I'd better tell you the rest of the reason why I get so grumpy sometimes. I miss my daughter and there's nothing I can do about it. I owed you that much. And I know all the psychology behind it, went to a shrink for a little while and got my head straightened around. But it still doesn't take away the sting." He shrugged. "Mixed moods is my diagnosis. The doctor said I'll just have to put up with it because there's nothing I can do to fight against it."

"And Yvette won't even let Amy talk to you on the phone? I can't believe that!"

Simon shook his head. "No. It's totally no contact."

"That's cruel for both you and Amy."

"I can't even imagine what Amy's going through right now."

She let go of his hand. Let go of the smooth feel of his skin and hated to do so, but anyone looking on might misconstrue their hand-holding as something more than lending comfort in a bad situation. "Maybe things will change for you. Be patient. Something will work out. It just has to."

"That's what I keep telling myself. But I'm not counting on it."

"Well, like I said, if there's anything I can do…"

"I appreciate that. But I'm afraid I've run out of options."

"You say they're here in Chicago, though."

He nodded. "Which is one of the reasons I was desperate to come back home. First, because I love it here, but also because I felt more steady fighting for Amy here. And I'm closer in case…well, just in case."

Del glanced at her watch and stood. "I think it's time we'd better be getting back. We're already twenty minutes late. Oh, and, Simon—thanks for telling me. I know it can't have been an easy thing to talk about." Not easy at all, and her heart did go out to him. No wonder he didn't want to get involved in a relationship. It was obvious his first marriage was horrible and he was now taking time out to sort things. That was something she understood well.

The afternoon was uneventful, with a waiting room full of sick kids, none of them serious. Some were the products of over-zealous mothers who thought sniffles equated to something bad, while others were sick with various colds, flu bugs and cuts and sprains. By all counts it was a nice afternoon—nice to not see anybody who was seriously ill, and Del was grateful for it as her mind was fixed on Simon and his mess of a life. Even after he'd told her, she still couldn't believe that a caring mother would completely turn him away from her child. Which meant only one thing. Yvette wasn't a very caring mother. She did everything out of her own selfish gain and didn't care about her daughter enough to reunite her with someone who truly loved her.

It was a very self-serving motive, especially since Simon had no financial obligation to the child. Yet Del bet that Simon had supported her for five years, glad to do so, and if he offered to continue that support now, even though his circumstances were dire, she'd probably let him back in. So devious. "What a rotten thing to do," she said to Charlie as she changed him out of his day-care clothes, gave him a bath and put him in his pajamas. "And there's nothing I can do to help him."

She gave Charlie his dinner and spread his play blanket on the floor, but tonight he was being fussy. Wouldn't eat, didn't want to play. Only wanted to sleep. So she took his temperature to make sure he wasn't coming down with anything, found it to be normal and simply sat in her antique Victorian rocker and rocked him to sleep. Just one of those fussy baby days and they did have them, as everybody did. So she didn't worry as he pulled up his knees, stuck his thumb in his mouth and drifted off into a fitful sleep.

After about fifteen minutes she put him down into his crib and leaned over to kiss him, but he shrugged away from her. "Tired from day care?" she asked. "Did you have a big day?"

He didn't respond to her voice, though. Instead, he simply shut his eyes and ignored her. So she checked him once again to make sure he wasn't sick, but he showed no symptoms of anything serious except being extremely tired, so she turned on the night-light and

turned off the overhead light and left the room, leaving
his door open a crack lest he should start to cry.

Her mother's intuition was instantly on alert, as was
her doctor's intuition since Charlie wasn't acting normal, but so far there was nothing to go on that pointed
to him being sick. So she settled down on the living-
room couch and picked up a medical journal to read. But
for some reason, she was too antsy to stay down so she
got back up to do some household chores like laundry
and dusting—things she barely had time for these days.
In fact, her time was so limited she was giving some
thought to hiring a housekeeper to come in a couple
days a week. She hadn't decided one way or another,
though, as she was still pretty adamant she could do it
all. Even though all of it was not getting done as much
as it had before she'd gone back to work.

On impulse, she called Simon's number and felt silly
when he picked up on the second ring. "You OK?" she
asked. "After our talk this afternoon I just thought you
might be down in the dumps."

"I am, but I'll get over it. I always do."

"Want to come over for a glass of wine or some coffee or something? Charlie went down early so I've got
some time to myself this evening."

"That's nice of you but you don't need to feel sorry
for me. I told you because you needed to know, not because I was looking for some sympathy."

"How could I not sympathize, though? That's my nature, why I became a pediatrician. I have great sympathy for children. Kids are great. They don't complain,
they're brave, they do what they need to do without

making a fuss over it. I fell in love with the field my first day in and that was that."

"Pretty much the same with me. I intended to be an anesthesiologist but this is what worked out for me and I'm glad it did. Kids are fun to treat most of the time. After my divorce and before I came to Lakeside Clinic I was doubting my choice a little, thinking maybe I should go back and become a pediatric anesthesiologist or specialist in something like pediatric oncology. Something to change my life. But that was all because I'd lost Amy and she was like my compass in a lot of ways. Then I came here and realized I'm where I belong. No turning back. No changing."

"Well, it's never too late to change, if you're thinking about it. Nothing wrong with shaking things up."

He chuckled. "I think I've got a little too much water under my bridge to change my field at this stage of the game. Besides, I like what I do. General care is good. It's what I want to do because I like the interactions as well as the dynamics of the whole field. And in a day and age when so many people are specializing, or where so many family-care practitioners are seeing children, I think the place of the general-practice pediatrician is more needed than ever. Besides, kids are fun."

"Give it some thought, though, since it's still obviously on your mind. Lakeside has a good anesthesiology program. Then there are other hospitals with equally good reputations, as well."

"I've given it a lot of thought, but I'm where I want to be. Either in a clinic or in the ER."

"Well, you're good at what you do, and if you're

happy there…" She quieted for a minute, then said, "Could you hang on for a second? I hear Charlie crying, and I'm not sure he's feeling so well this evening. I'll be back on in a minute."

"How about I let you go and I'll see you tomorrow?" he responded. "Charlie could take a little while, and I don't want to rush you."

"Tomorrow," she said, then hung up, smiling. It was nice having Simon for a friend. Although it did make her wish she had room in her life for something more.

For the first time in her motherhood experience, except for one brief exception, Charlie slept all the way through the night, which should have elated Del but actually it bothered her. He was restless, kept himself curled into a ball with his little legs drawn up to his chest, and didn't get the restful sleep she'd hoped he would. Then when by morning he was still fussy she knew he definitely wasn't feeling good. But another preliminary check showed him to be in good shape. No cough, no runny nose, no fever. Just grouchy again, and he definitely didn't want to be held, which was unusual. He also refused to eat. In fact, he threw his bowl of oatmeal on the floor, which was, perhaps, the most alarming thing of all as Charlie had a pretty hefty morning appetite and loved his oatmeal and bananas. So rather than taking him to day care first thing, she took him to the clinic to get an unbiased opinion of what could possibly be wrong since she had a suspicion she knew and it was best not to treat him herself. Not that she could, if she was right about this.

"Simon," she said on the way in, "would you mind looking at Charlie for me and seeing what you can come up with? He started acting fussy last night and, while I have my suspicions, I'd rather not be the one diagnosing him."

"Take him to Room One and I'll be right there," he said as he slung on his white lab coat and followed her into the exam room. "So what are his symptoms?" he asked, listening first to his chest, then his tummy.

"Fussy, won't eat, doesn't want to be held and he balls up in a fetal position when I put him down. He was fine last night. Slept all night, was a little fussy when I put him down but he didn't display any overt symptoms."

"Knees drawn up to his chest?" Simon asked.

Del nodded.

"Has he ever had an intussusception?" This was a condition where intestine folded into another section of intestine, much like the way a collapsing telescope folded up into the section in front of it. In and of itself the condition was not serious in the first couple days but it did carry with it a risk of surgery if not treated soon enough. Especially if an intestinal blockage occurred.

Del sighed out loud and her hands started to shake. "No. Did we catch it in time or will he need surgery?"

"If his symptoms just came on him last night or this morning, he's probably a good candidate for treatment without surgery."

Del brushed back a tear. "I didn't miss it, did I?"

Simon shook his head. "You brought him in as soon as he presented with symptoms. Don't second-guess yourself, Del. Babies have no way of telling us what's wrong and if he's not showing symptoms, you can't just guess there's something wrong or you'd drive yourself crazy. You were observant and you did the right thing as quickly as you knew."

She brushed back another tear. "It's so difficult sometimes. So many things could go wrong."

"And so many things could go right."

"I guess so, but when it's your child…" She shrugged.

"You're a normal mom, doctor or not. And most moms would be scared by the diagnosis."

"So how are you going to treat him?"

"Conservatively at first. I'd like to start with an ultrasound followed by an abdominal X-ray just to make sure that the bowel hasn't gone necrotic. And we'll go from there. But he does need to be hospitalized for the procedures and to be watched for a day or two. You do understand that, don't you?"

She nodded. "He's going to be so frightened."

"He may surprise you. One of the reasons I like kids so much is that they take things better than we do. If someone told me my intestine was twisted up I'd be in a panic, but Charlie will just accept things as they come his way."

"He will, won't he?" she said, trying to muster up some conviction in her voice even though she was scared to death.

"Look, Del. You've seen this before and treated it. It's usually not a complicated procedure once the diagnosis is confirmed." He prodded Charlie's belly for a mass and sure enough, there it was. "You know the outcome is good in most of these cases. And if he does need to have surgery, it's a relatively simple procedure."

"I've treated it, but never in my child. He's always been so healthy."

"And he still is healthy," Simon reassured her. He was thinking back to when Amy was sent home from school with the measles. He'd been on call and hadn't seen much of her for a couple of days, then to see his daughter all covered with a rash the way she was—at first he'd been angry that her mother had allowed her to go to school that way, then he'd turned his concern to Amy, who had been one mighty sick little girl for a few days. He'd felt so helpless and vulnerable because there really had been nothing to do for her except sit with Amy and help her ride out the illness. Because of that, he knew how Del was feeling and his heart went out to her because she, too, was feeling so helpless and vulnerable right now. And blaming herself.

"So here's what I propose," he said to Del. "First we get him admitted to the hospital and get the diagnosis over with, then we discuss the options. And even though you know, it falls down this way. He'll be treated with either a barium or water-soluble contrast enema or an air-contrast enema, which will confirm the intussusception, and in the best possible scenario reduce it. The success rate is pretty good—about eighty percent. If this does recur, it should happen in about twenty-four hours, and that's when a surgeon will open the abdomen and manually squeeze the part that has telescoped. Or the surgeon may choose to reduce the problem by laparoscopy. Any way you go, it's going to be more stressful on you than it will be on Charlie. Best case scenario puts him in the eighty percent category and he'll be home in a couple of days. Worst case is surgery, which means he'll be here a little longer than that."

"I appreciate you going over this with me. Of course I know it, but right now I'd be hard pressed to tell you my name let alone anything else."

"It's Del," he said, smiling.

She smiled. "Will you be there during the tests and/or surgery?"

"If they let me. And if you request it."

"I'll request it," she said, "because I don't want him to be alone, and I know they won't let me anywhere near him while they're doing whatever it is they've got to do." She looked at her little boy lying there on the exam table all drawn up in a ball, then bent and kissed him. "I'm trusting you with my son, Simon. He's the best thing in my life and I'm handing his care over to you."

Simon swallowed hard. He knew what it was like to surrender your child. "I'll take good care of him, like he's my own."

"I'm counting on that," Del said as she reached out and took hold of Simon's hand and held on for dear life. "I'm really counting on that."

CHAPTER SEVEN

THE PROCEDURE TOOK longer than she expected and it was nice having Simon sit there with her, holding her hand at first, then holding on to her when her nerves finally got the best of her and her whole body started shaking. "It's so much worse when it's your child," she said, fighting back tears of fear and anguish. "Even though I know he's getting good care."

He ran his thumb over the back of her soft hand. "He'll be fine," Simon reassured her, even though she didn't feel much as if reassurances were going to work.

"Sure. But still, suppose this doesn't work and he has to move on to the next step, which is surgery?" She grabbed hold of his hand and clung tightly to him. "I don't know if I could get through it, the thought of them having to remove a piece of his intestine. That's so serious. And the risks so great it scares me to death. I mean, what if...?"

He stroked her cheek. "One thing at a time, Del. That's what I always tell the parents of my patients. We'll deal with one thing at a time, get through it and hope for the best. That's all you can do."

She exhaled a big, wobbly breath. "Easy to say when the shoe is on the other foot. But when it's on your own…" She shut her eyes as the tears streamed down her cheeks. "When it's your own child it's different. He's my flesh and blood, Simon, and he's suffering. But there's nothing I can do to fix this. I'm the mother. I should be taking care of him."

"You can't just center your entire life around what he wants or needs. You need to have something in there for you, too, and that's your medical practice, no matter how hard it is to be a single parent as well as a full-time doctor. It's called balancing your life."

"But how did you do it?"

"It wasn't easy, and I'll be the first one to admit that. Amy came first, but my medical practice had its place in there, as well. I learned to balance it so we were both happy."

"How?"

"First, by realizing that I was happier having a life in medicine than I was without it. When I was happier, Amy was happier. I think by balancing myself I evened out everything for the both of us, which was difficult because the older she got, the more she recognized that her mother simply didn't care enough to be involved. Which made for some awfully moody moments. Except, she always had me and she counted on that. I just had to make sure I never missed out on the important things going on in her life. That was the tricky part, too, I'll admit. Amy needed me, my practice needed me and for a while even Yvette needed me. I suppose you can say I failed Yvette, but I think she set up the situation between us to fail." He shrugged. "There was nothing I could do about that, but I did have control over the rest of it, no matter how difficult it became. I just had to make sure that Amy never missed out because of anything else going on in my life."

"I admire that in you, Simon. I'm not sure my priorities are that clear yet. For me it's all Charlie and nothing else. Even my medical practice takes a backseat, which I know it shouldn't. But Charlie is so important to me that I'd love to retire and stay home with him. And I might for a while except I know I'd miss my practice and wouldn't be completely happy not working. It's a real dilemma."

"There were days I certainly hated walking away from Amy, so I understand."

"But you figured it out."

"After a while."

"When I had Charlie I was fiercely adamant that I could have it all, and I didn't count on the emotional turmoil I'm facing now. But there are days when I hand him over to day care that I'm literally so conflicted I don't know what to do."

"You do the best you can. That's all that can be expected from any of us. And the thing is, you can have it all. You already do...at least all that you want."

"What would I do if I did get involved with someone? Maybe even got married? There's not enough of me to go around. I couldn't do it."

"Sure you could, if that's what you wanted. You'd just have to marry the right person. The one who understands that you have this huge life going on already.

He'd certainly have to be patient. You'd choose wisely." He smiled. "Because you've had what you know you don't want, I'm willing to bet you've put some thinking into what you do want."

The surgery ward door pushed open and Del's heart doubled its rhythm, but it wasn't for her. Nothing to do with Charlie, but some other surgery waiters got a bit of good news judging from the round of cheers that went up.

After the noise of the happy waiters died down, she continued, "I've never really given it that much thought because I'm not sure anybody would want to handle my life, such as it is. It's so full already that I don't think I'd have room to add anything or anyone else. And I don't want to get involved when those are my expectations."

"But you could be missing out."

"Or not," she responded. "I mean, look at everything I've got. That's enough to keep me busy."

"But don't you get lonely when you go to bed alone every night?"

"Don't you?" she countered.

"I'd be lying if I said I didn't. But I've got different standards this time. And I'm going to be very careful if I get involved again."

"Let me guess. No women with children."

He arched his eyebrows. "I'm not opposed to children. In fact, I'd love to have a large family. But I don't want to be put in a position where the kids can be taken away from me. Next time I'm a dad, I want to be a dad for real."

"Poor child," Del said. "To count on someone so much then have him kicked out of her life."

Simon shrugged. "And not to know what she's doing. Sometimes I feel…lost.'

"But Amy lost, too, didn't she?"

"I hope not, but I can't help but think that she did. It keeps me up at nights sometimes wondering and worrying."

"I wouldn't do that to Charlie, which is why I'm happy just the way things are. But today…it's not what I bargained for, and that's stupid of me, considering how I'm a pediatrician. I mean, I know better. Kids get sick with all kinds of strange ailments and I guess I always thought I'd be exempt since I'm a professional in the field. But it doesn't work that way, does it?"

"Amy broke her arm once. She fell down a flight of stairs and the break was pretty substantial. Her mother was out of town, so that left me alone to deal with it and I don't know when I've ever felt more helpless than I did when she was getting it casted. But she came through it better than I did, just the way Charlie will come through this better than you do. I promise."

"Amy needs you as her father. Her mother did a really stupid thing taking her away from you."

"I agree with you on that. I would have done anything for that little girl." He shook his head. "Which is the reason I won't date another woman with a child because, if something should come of it, I stand a very good chance of having that child yanked away from me after I've formed an attachment."

"I can't blame you. If someone came and took Charlie away from me…" She brushed back a straying tear. "Just call me an overprotective mother. I know I am, and I'll admit it."

"Nothing wrong with that. Better to be overprotective than to be Amy's mother, who looks at her daughter as an inconvenience."

"Well, Charlie's not an inconvenience!" Del sniffed. "And I'd fight anybody who said he was."

Simon laughed. He liked that attitude of a mother lion, wished he'd seen it more in his own home with Amy. But Yvette had never cared that much and she was always glad to give up the chore of child care to someone else so she could have her life to herself. Honestly, had he seen that in her when they were married, they wouldn't have been married. But he'd been blinded by a great body and good looks, and back then he'd been too young to look any further. Now he knew, and he was on his guard against the type.

The thing was, Del could have been his type, as fierce as she was, but he wasn't about to put himself into that position again.

"You're a good mother," he told Del.

"With a sick son. I'm so worried, Simon. I know there was nothing I could do but it's still so easy to kick myself about it."

"If this is the worst he ever goes through you'll be one lucky lady. Kids get sick every day. If they didn't we'd have to find a new line of work."

She chuckled. "You're so good to me, Simon. You know exactly what to say and when to say it."

"Comes from practice. Years and years of practice.

Just doing my job," he said, letting up a little on his grip around her for fear he was cutting off her circulation. Either that or creating a dependence he could ill afford to develop.

"This is going above and beyond the call," she replied, snuggling back into him. "And I appreciate it."

He knew he should pull away from her right now, but he liked the feel of her pressed tight to him, and it wouldn't take much for him to ask her out on a rightful date when this crisis was over. Of course, he wouldn't. She was a single mom and he'd promised himself he wouldn't do that. So as much as he liked Del, even cared for her, he wasn't going back on his word. Friendship was as far as he was taking it. Although, he wasn't quite ready to define the level of that friendship yet.

Another snuggle and he'd be lost, he was sure. Yet he didn't have it in him to pull back from her, especially not now when she needed him so badly. So he tightened up a bit, braced his back as well as his resolve and endured the feeling passing through him, the one that told him it would be very easy to develop feelings for Del. Whether or not they'd turn out to be serious feelings, he didn't know, but there was some kind of feelings there nonetheless.

They sat there together like that for the next hour, with her clinging and him regretting until the pediatrician on call came out and told them that Charlie's barium enema seemed to have worked out the kink just fine.

"I want to keep him here for a couple days to watch

him," Dr. Knowles said. "But right now everything looks good."

"He's sleeping?" Del asked, pulling away from Simon and adjusting her white lab coat.

"Sound asleep, and I'd like to keep him that way for a few hours, if we can, so when you go in to see him try and be quiet."

Del nodded. Then looked at Simon, who'd backed away from the whole scene. "You coming with me?" she asked him.

"No, I don't think so. The more of us in the room, the more likely the odds of disturbing him are. So I think I'll go back over to the clinic for now and catch up with you later on."

"I'm grateful for your support, Simon," she said, reaching out to take his hand. It was soft and gentle and large the way he was. "I couldn't have gotten through this on my own."

"Call me if you need anything," Simon said, then nodded to Dr. Knowles. "Thank you for what you did to help Charlie," he said, then turned and left the waiting area.

Brian Knowles smiled. "You make a cute family," he said.

"We're not a family. Simon's just a friend."

"Couldn't tell that from where I was watching."

"Then you were watching from the wrong spot because Simon and I have nothing going between us." Even though she wanted to, her feelings were growing so strong for him.

"Well, I've seen families with a whole lot less going

on between them. All I can say is, you look good together, and Simon looks like he really cares."

There was no point in arguing the matter with the pediatrician. He'd already made up his mind and had her and Simon and Charlie posed together as a family. Of course, maybe that was what it looked like, the way she'd clung to Simon during the entire procedure. "When can I see him?" Del asked.

"Now. He's in Recovery, but you can go sit with him there, then after he's transferred to a regular room you can spend as much time with him as you want."

"Was there anything I could have done?" she asked nervously.

"Just what you did. It's a relatively rare condition and one that doesn't always get caught in time. I'd say, between you and Simon, you did an excellent job of catching and diagnosing it before it progressed too far. As for whether or not it's cured, time will tell, but I'm willing to bet it's probably a one-time incident. At least I hope it is." Dr. Knowles shook hands with Del and exited the room, leaving her standing there alone, feeling grateful and scared all at the same time. She didn't want to be alone just yet, but Simon had made it abundantly clear his involvement there was done. She was glad for as much of him as she'd gotten, but she wanted more just now. Wanted his comfort again, as she was still upset and his seemed to be the calming influence that had got her through.

It was three hours before Charlie was moved into a private room, and Del was right there with him every step of the way. Simon had called once, albeit a very brief and businesslike call. And Dr. Knowles had stepped in to have a look one time, pleased with the results so far. "It's looking good," he said to Del, as he hurried back out to see another patient. Leaving her and Charlie there virtually alone again, except for an occasional check by a nurse.

"You scared me to death," she told her son as she took hold of his hand and he gripped on for dear life. "But you're going to be fine. The doctor said you're making a good recovery so far."

"I understand you've arranged for more time off work," Simon said from the doorway. "I was going to put in the request for you, but you beat me to it."

"That's what I said I was going to do." She shrugged, secretly glad to see him, and trying to act aloof about her feelings all at the same time. "I'm used to doing things on my own."

"Well, I wasn't sure if that was you or a panic attack talking." He smiled as he walked over to the crib and looked down on Charlie. "Good-looking boy," he said. "He looks just like you."

She smiled. "I'm surprised you came back. I thought maybe I'd scared you off earlier, being so clingy."

"Your son was having a procedure. You were entitled to be clingy. So, what's the word?"

"So far it's all good. He can go home day after tomorrow if everything goes well."

"It will," Simon said confidently. "And in the meantime, I've ordered a pizza to be sent here to the hospital since I figured you haven't eaten all day."

"I hadn't," she admitted. "Too worried."

"Well, I ordered large because I thought I'd hang around and split it with you, if you don't mind."

"I'd welcome the company. And the pizza," she added, realizing how hungry she was now that the ordeal was over.

Dinner was neither fancy nor romantic, but she appreciated the gesture. In fact, had he not reminded her she hadn't eaten at all, she probably would have gone the rest of the day and maybe had some graham crackers from the nurses' station. But Simon had been so kind and thoughtful that she wondered why he was still single. Not every woman out there had a child and certainly he could have and probably should have attracted someone who liked him for all his endearing qualities. Maybe he just wasn't ready. Or he was mistrustful, which was certainly something she understood.

"This was awfully nice of you," she said, debating her second slice of pizza. "Does your ex-wife know what she let get away?"

"More like shoved out the door. She was all set for wealthy and I wasn't."

"Doctors aren't always wealthy," Del defended. "I'm comfortable, but you could hardly consider it wealthy."

"A lot of people don't understand that. Especially my ex. I had student loans to pay back, a family to support. It was a lot of responsibility."

"A lot of people don't count, but your ex should have in the manner in which she expected things from you. Personally, I'm not all that concerned with the material gains in my life. I want to make Charlie comfortable but I don't need to be wealthy to do that."

"So if the man you decided on was temporarily tapped out…"

"Wouldn't matter one way or another. I'm looking for character and integrity. Someone who'll be decent to my son and grow to love him. That's more important than anything else, at least in my opinion." Someone like Simon, she thought to herself. He would be the perfect man in her life, if he wanted to get involved. Of course, he didn't, which made her wary of her growing feelings for him.

"So would you ever find yourself in a relationship with someone who wasn't so tapped out as you are?"

"Depends on who she is, I suppose. My next go around, if there ever is another one, is going to be with someone who's down to earth, someone who values things other than financial gain."

"And her financial status wouldn't matter to you?"

He shrugged. "Get me to that point and we'll see. I'd like to think I'm more responsible than that but who knows? We all make our mistakes, I guess. Mine was thinking she'd change."

Del laughed. "That's what I thought, too. You know, you wake up one morning with the person you want who has magically changed overnight from the person you had."

"I stayed for Amy's sake and look where that got me." He sighed as he closed the pizza box. "None of it's predictable."

"Is that why you haven't gotten together with someone else?"

"Big mistrust factors on my part, and I'll admit it," Simon said. "I proved what kind of a bad choice I made the first time and I don't want to go there again. So for me it's easier being single."

"I get the mistrust factor. That's why I had Charlie with no one else involved. I wanted a baby but I didn't want someone else involved who might injure him the way I was injured during my relationship with Eric. Bringing up a baby alone was my choice and a good option for someone my age, I think."

"But don't you ever wish you had someone there to share parenting duties with? Another person who loves him as much as you do, who can help you when you need it?"

"I never thought I did, until today. But today was out of the ordinary."

"So what happens next time he gets sick and there's no one around to help you? I can tell you from experience it's easier raising a child with two parents than one. That's the kind of built-in support you need."

"But from the way you tell it, you had only you."

"I did. Yvette was more than happy to pass Amy off on me and it wasn't easy working and raising a child all at the same time. I really wanted things to be different, where she assumed part of the parenting chore, but she never did. I was the designated parent in the relationship and she was the one who was free and clear to do what she wanted without the involvement. In fact, if she hadn't met someone else I have an idea she would have still hung onto me because she knew how deep my feelings for Amy were."

"And you would have stayed?"

"Probably."

Del shook her head. "Sounds to me like I'm better off being a single parent than having someone else around who doesn't care as much as I do."

"The thing is, parenting is a tough job and the older they get, the tougher it gets. Charlie's just a baby right now, but what about when he's five or six and needs a man around?"

"What about when he's five or six and doesn't need a man around?" she asked him. "Not all kids have two parents and most of them turn out just fine."

"But how do the parents turn out? What happens when you don't have someone to lean on?"

"Then I don't lean. It's as simple as that."

"You needed me today, Del."

"Because I was scared and this was Charlie's first real sickness outside a cold. And it wasn't about Charlie anyway. It was about my weakness. But I'll get better as I get more used to being a single mother."

"Maybe you will. Personally, though, I never got over needing someone else to help me raise Amy, and she had a mother."

"We all make our choices, Simon. You chose to raise Amy the way you did and I chose to have Charlie and raise him the way I am. Initially, I didn't get any support from my parents. They thought it was crazy. But once they saw their grandson…" She shrugged. "They changed, I changed and everything in my life changed all because of my decision. If you'd been allowed to stay and raise Amy your life would have been different, too."

"Which is why I won't do that again. It rips your heart out when the child isn't yours and you've got no legal claim."

"So we've both exercised alternately good and poor judgment that got us where we are today. What can I say?"

"That we're human." He stood and picked up the pizza box. "Look, I've got to go. I'll be working for two for a couple of weeks and I need to get to bed early tonight. If you need anything, give me a call...I assume you're spending the night here."

"I am. And thanks, but I'll be fine."

"Need some clean clothes? I can drop them by in the morning?"

"I was thinking about running home once Charlie's down for the night, grabbing a shower and changing my clothes, then coming back here and sleeping." She pointed to the bed next to the crib. "Not comfortable, but it will do in a pinch."

"How about breakfast in the morning? Or coffee?"

"Coffee would be lovely, but you really don't have to take care of me, Simon. I'm good on my own."

"Which is why you hadn't eaten today?"

She smiled up at him. "It would have come up at some point. I'm not a martyr to the cause."

"I think you are, but that's an opinion we'll save for another day since I really do need to get home."

"Thanks for everything you've done today."

"My pleasure," he said, thinking it was his guilty

pleasure as he enjoyed his time with Del way more than he intended to.

"I'll…I'll see you around. Maybe I'll stop in the clinic when I know Charlie's one hundred percent."

"Or maybe I'll stop by your place one night and bring dinner. There's this great Chinese restaurant just down the street from me and…"

"Ming's?" she asked as her eyes lit up.

"Ming's," he answered. "Great—"

"Egg rolls!" she finished his sentence. "I like the vegetarian."

"And I like the pork."

"So we have a difference of opinion," she said, laughing as Charlie started to cry. He was strapped down with so many tubes and monitors it looked uncomfortable to her so she knew it had to be to him. She stood from her chair and picked him up gently so as not to disturb his IV or his NG tube.

"And on that note I'll say good-night and leave you two alone."

She'd gone home, taken her shower, changed her clothes and packed an overnight bag for both her and Charlie and headed right back to the hospital only to find him still sound asleep. It had been quite the ordeal for him today, and one for her, as well. Without Simon…well, she didn't even want to think how her day would have progressed without him. Going through all that alone just wasn't appealing. She had called her parents, who were on their way back from Costa Rica to help out, which she appreciated, but that help was a little too

late, and for the first time ever Simon, combined with
Charlie's illness, had showed her just how utterly alone
she was as a parent.

It had never scared her before but now it unsettled her
knowing she was in this all by herself without a nearby
shoulder to cry on. Truth was, she didn't have a lot of
friends—her job had taken care of that. And she had
no brothers or sisters. Not even any cousins she could
call on. So her backup plan was, well...no one. Which
was why she was so glad to have Simon there with her
for support. Not that she considered him her backup
plan or anything like that. In fact, she wasn't even sure
she considered him more than a casual friend yet. But
things seemed to be leaning in a different direction,
which made her glad he wasn't interested in anything
more than a casual friendship because that would signal the end of things between them, since casual was
all she wanted. Two peas in a pod, she decided. They
both wanted the same thing for different reasons. How
absurd was that?

He probably shouldn't have been so forthright with her
about the way she was bringing up Charlie, as it was
none of his business how she raised her child, whether
that be alone or with someone else to help her. But
he remembered how difficult it had been raising Amy
without any help and the older she'd got, the more help
he'd needed. It hadn't been easy, being a daddy without
much of a clue, but he wouldn't have changed a moment
of it because he'd loved that little girl. Still did. And he'd
take her back in a heartbeat if her mother ever cared to

give her up, which wasn't going to happen as Amy was a shining star who drew other people in. Yvette used that to her advantage. Took every chance she could to push Amy right on out there.

So he'd wanted to impart his wisdom, except his situation with Amy was nothing like Del's with Charlie. She'd made her choice and the one thing he knew for sure was that Del would never use Charlie as a pawn in her own schemes the way Yvette did with Amy. Del's love for her baby was true all the way.

Still, he didn't want to see things going so hard on Del and he knew they were right now, judging from the way she'd clung so desperately to him yesterday. It was as if he were the starch she needed to keep herself from collapsing, and if something ever happened to Charlie when he wasn't there to hold on to Del, he wondered how she'd manage to get through it. Her true colors as a caring mother had really shown through, but so had her frailties over being alone. Except, she wouldn't admit that was what he'd been seeing. One good, objective look was all it took, though. From him, even from her if she weren't so personally involved.

Admittedly, though, he'd liked being important for her in that time. Liked the way she'd held on to him, the feel of her hands grasping him, the way she wouldn't let go. It was nice being needed. Maybe even a little wanted. Especially by Del. But who was he kidding? It was a one-time event, born out of her need for comfort. That was all it had been, all it could be. After all, she had a child and he refused to put himself through that again. Once was too much. Probably for her, too, once she'd had time to think about it.

Simon sighed as he went to Exam Four to check out a youngster with type one diabetes. Both parents were there, both were equally concerned, even though they were newly divorced. That was the way a child should be raised, he thought as he knocked on the door then entered the room. Yes, that was definitely the way a child should be raised. Only he'd missed his chance and Del didn't want hers.

Weren't they the perfectly mismatched couple? he thought as he flipped on the computer screen in the room and took a look at the child's blood work. "Good job," he said to the little girl, who was about Amy's age. "Everything's in perfect order and it's all looking the way it should."

Everything but his life. And maybe a little bit of Del's life, as well.

CHAPTER EIGHT

IT WAS A week from the day of Charlie's successful procedure to the day when Del showed up at work. "Only a week off?" Simon asked her on his way in to examine a bug bite in Exam Three.

"My parents want some quality time with their grandson and that doesn't include me, I'm afraid. Besides, they're both retired doctors so who better to watch him for a few hours?"

"I talked to your dad on the phone the other night, when I was thinking about bringing dinner by. He's awfully protective of you. And of his grandson, too."

"So that's why you never came over?"

"They'd already eaten by the time I called. He seemed like a nice man, though. Reminded me a lot of you... straightforward, honest, overprotective of his child."

Del laughed out loud. "That's what a protective parent does. He watches after his kid even when his kid is thirty-five years old."

"And that will be you and Charlie in another few years. You won't exactly warn off the girls he'll want to date but you won't be overly friendly, either."

"Like father, like daughter, I suppose."

"Anyway, I'm glad you came back early. We're short staffed, as you already know. Dr. Kent went into early labor and Dr. Morgan is off with the flu. So we're really down on our numbers and we could use the help."

"Which is why I came in today. I'd intended to stay home with Charlie and my parents another week, but the clinic needs me even more than Charlie does since he adores his grandparents, so I was feeling a bit useless." She shrugged. "Meaning I'm back."

"How's Charlie?"

"Doing nicely. No flare-ups, no real disruption to his routine unless you could call grandparents a disruption. He had his incident and it was cured, and, even though the doctor wants to follow him for a couple of months, there don't seem to be any bad consequences."

"Good to hear that. Look, the board's full, and, even though you're one of the bosses and owners of the clinic, all I can do is tell you to take your pick of patients. We're busy today."

"And I was so looking forward to Ming's egg rolls," she teased as she took the first chart off the top of the stack then logged it into the computer. "At least now I know why you didn't bring them. My daddy scared you off." She almost strangled herself she laughed so hard.

"He didn't scare me. He just made it abundantly clear that my attention wasn't wanted or needed."

She reached up and ran her hand over his cheek. "I needed your attention."

"Well, just name the time and place and you've got it."

"Ming's tonight, after work. My parents won't mind. In fact, I think they'll be glad to have extra time alone with Charlie. They don't get much time with him and it will be good for all of them."

"Allows them their time," he said. "Makes for good luck all the way around. That's what your fortune cookie will tell you."

It was sometime midafternoon, after Charlie's lunch, when Simon caught up to Del. "You look like you could use a cup of coffee or tea," he told her.

"I lost a patient today," Del said. "Not as in dying but as in yanking her kid out of the clinic, and it drained me. And I got pretty indignant with the girl's mother. Child's anorexic and the mom was pretty disgusted with the girl and I, in turn, got pretty disgusted with the girl's mom. And of course I couldn't say anything."

"For what it's worth, I think your indignation toward that girl's mother was righteous in every way. I know what it's like to deal with a parent who thinks it's all about them."

"Amy's mother," she murmured.

He nodded. "Trust me, there were plenty of times when I had a whole string of things I wanted to say to Yvette, but didn't because it wasn't in Amy's best interest."

"Is there a day that goes by when you don't think about her?"

"Not a day. Some days it's worse than others, though."

"I'm so sorry."

"Me, too. And thanks."

* * *

As the rest of the day pressed on, things settled down into a normal routine. Del saw a few regular patients, helped with the overflow, and nothing was out of the ordinary. Not the ailments, not even the minor emergencies. It was the kind of day everyone wanted and drove you crazy when you got it. But as the day progressed, she found herself looking forward to her dinner date at Ming's, and it wasn't the egg rolls that were stirring her. Del was actually excited about her date with Simon. Just the two of them in a quaint little hole in the wall. It had all the earmarks of being romantic, even though romance wasn't what she wanted from him. But she did like his company, loved his conversation, enjoyed their alone time together. It was amazing how in just a few weeks he'd become so important to her. And dinner at Ming's was just the icing on the cake as far as she was concerned.

Was there potential in their relationship? Possibly? Maybe even probably. Except he'd made it pretty darned clear he wasn't interested in getting involved with a woman who had a child. Who could blame him for that? Certainly, she couldn't, after the way his last relationship had turned out. Couldn't they have a casual fling though? One without commitments? One that could even be platonic if that was what he wanted in order to keep himself safe. Certainly, she wanted that safety net, too, and she'd made up her mind not to get so deeply involved that intense emotions came into play.

They took a seat by the front window, where they could look out over the lake, and if there ever was something that called for romance, this was it. The restaurant itself was tiny and intimate and the decor was like stepping back into old-world China, where a jade Buddha sat on a shelf, and beaded curtains separated the front from the back room. The room was bathed in reds and black and the smells coming from the kitchen were enough to make her mouth water the instant Simon opened the front door and she heard the quaint, old-fashioned doorbell jingle on entry.

And the lake… Del loved the vastness of it. Ming's sat on the other side of the busy Lakeshore Drive, opposite the lake, but because the lake itself there was so beautiful she didn't even notice the traffic up and down that stretch of road in front of it. All she could see was the sun setting over the water, casting it in the glow of golds and navy blues. And all she could hear was the faint strain of Chinese music playing in the background.

"I haven't actually been in here since, well, it was a long time before Charlie was born. This place always seemed like it was for couples and being a single in an establishment for two just didn't feel right. So I ordered takeout, or had it delivered. Made it less pathetic that way, I think."

"You think of being single as pathetic?" he asked her as he took the menus from the server's hand.

"In a restaurant that caters to romance, yes. In my normal day-to-day life, no."

"I've come in here alone before and eaten."

"Then you're braver than I am, Simon, or at least less self-conscious."

"But you've got nothing to feel self-conscious about.

You made your choice and you don't regret it, so that should include dining out even if it is a romantic restaurant. Especially if you like the food."

"I love the food here. It's the best Chinese I've ever had. Everything prepared to order.'

"Like your life, where everything's prepared to order."

"And what's so different about your life?" she asked.

"I venture out of my comfort zone for one thing. I don't think you do."

"Maybe not so much, but I have Charlie to consider."

"And you couldn't bring him here with you?"

"Maybe when he's older." She looked up at the server, who was patiently awaiting drink orders. "I'll have unsweet iced tea," she said. "With a lot of lemon."

"And I'll have a beer. Whatever you have on tap is fine. And could you bring us a couple of egg rolls as appetizers, one pork and one vegetarian?"

The girl scrambled away to fetch the orders while Del and Simon continued talking. "I think the ambiance here would be lost on Charlie, anyway."

"But not on you, and you do count in the mother-son relationship. You can build your life around him to the point that you're suffocating him and I don't think that's your intent, is it?"

"Charlie goes out with me."

"Where?"

"To the park, and the grocery store. Sometimes we just go for a walk. He likes that."

"But where do you go for yourself?"

"Same places Charlie goes," she said, reaching

across the table for a packet of sweetener. He laid his hand atop hers for a moment. "How long has it been since you've been on a real date?"

She thought a minute. "It's been about eight years. I got tangled up with Eric for five, then I was recovering from that, then I got pregnant and next thing you know I had Charlie."

"Eight years? How could you deprive yourself for so long?"

"You were married, Simon. How long has it been for you?"

He winced. "About the same."

"So we're alike in that." She took the tea the server brought to the table and dumped the packet of sweetener in it while Simon took a swig of his beer, then sighed.

"We are alike in some ways, aren't we?"

"More than I like to think about," she said, pushing out her plate to take her oversized egg roll.

"So this is both our first dates in years."

"Except we're not dating," Del reminded him.

"Just having dinner for two in a romantic little hideaway. Sounds like a date to me."

Del shook her head as she cut off a bite of her egg roll and dipped it in sweet-and-sour sauce. "I accepted dinner, pure and simple. I wouldn't have accepted if you'd asked me out on a date. In fact, I'm fully prepared to pay for my own dinner, which makes this even more of a non-date."

"So I'm on a date and you're not. I suppose we could leave it at that."

"But I thought you didn't want to get involved with a woman with children."

"A date doesn't always mean an involvement. Sometimes a date's just a date and nothing more. Or less." He ate a large bite of his egg roll then picked up his menu. "So, do you want to order separately, or do you want to do the dinner for two, which starts with egg drop soup and goes from there?"

"They do have awfully good egg drop soup," she commented. "So if you want to go with the dinner for two..." She shrugged. "Why not? That could be my concession to our non-date date."

Simon chuckled. "You're stubborn. Did anybody ever tell you that before?"

"I wasn't for a lot of years. But when I broke clear of Eric that was one of the first things I worked on. I was in counseling and the doctor told me I had a lot of work to do on me and finding myself again. Which I did."

"You still in counseling, or is that too personal to ask?"

"Nope, not in counseling. I graduated from that when I decided I wanted a baby."

"How did that come up?"

"It didn't just come up. I've always wanted a baby and I thought—stupidly—Eric was the one. By the time I knew he wasn't I was in too deep. But that desire in me never changed. I still wanted a baby, just not his. So I jumped at the chance after we broke up. Actually, not jumped so much as gave it some long, hard thinking before I knew I could do it. And what about you and Amy?"

"I didn't know she was part of the picture when I married Yvette. Amy was never mentioned and at the time her father had custody. But he didn't want her so after we were married about six months there she was on the doorstep one day. A man with a toddler with a little suitcase of clothes, telling Yvette he was finished with the father things. Honest to God, that was the first time I knew of her existence and we'd been married for nearly six months. I suppose that's why I could never pin her down on having a family—she already had one she didn't want."

"That's rough."

"It was. But I think I grew into being a pretty good dad. Problem was, Yvette wanted someone more exciting than a dad, but Amy needed a parent." He sighed. "And life goes on."

"But you got hurt in the deal."

"Not as much as Amy did. That last day when I finally had to say goodbye she clung to me, crying, begging not to be taken from me." He sniffed. "I've never felt so helpless in all my life."

Their soup arrived before anything else could be said, followed by their chow mein, followed by deep-fried bananas and by the time they reached their fortune cookies, Del was almost too full to have the strength to open hers up. But she did.

You will have a lucky night.

Simon's said: *This will be a night to remember.*

"I think they have two different boxes of cookies—

one with regular fortunes, and ones they give to the couple they believe will find romance." Del wadded up her fortune and tossed it on the table. "So much for that," she said, taking a bite of the cookie, then leaving the rest on her plate. "The only luck I'm going to have tonight is if I didn't gain five pounds eating so much good food."

"Well, mine's coming true as we speak because this is definitely a night to remember."

"But for how long? And for what reason?"

"Probably until I get senile, and the reason...I'm enjoying the company of my first date in all these years."

"Married years don't count?"

"Says who?"

"Says me," Del replied, looking at her crumpled fortune. "And that's all that counts."

"Whoa. You're the only one who's entitled to an opinion?"

She nodded. "In my life I am."

"But this is my life, too."

"And you're entitled to your opinion, however wrong it may be."

"Spoken like someone who was in a marriage-like situation for five years."

"Close to marriage, but not marriage. So it doesn't count. And for what it's worth, after we became a couple he never *dated* me again." She took out her credit card to pay her portion of the bill and Simon rejected it. "You can pick up the whole tab next time."

"It's a deal," she said, realizing suddenly that he'd

taken the advantage here by getting her to commit to a second date. "If there is another time."

He arched wickedly provocative eyebrows. "There'll be a second time, if for no other reason than you owe me a dinner out."

"Aren't you the tricky one?" she said as they walked to her front door. It was a high-rise, its walkway lined with fall flowers and pumpkins. At the top of the five steps, she turned around and looked down at him. "Care to come in and meet my parents?"

"Um, no. They might think that we're...well, you know what I mean. And I don't want to give them any false hopes about their daughter."

"Coward!" She laughed. "They already know how I am, so there's no jeopardy involved."

"I've got an early morning," he finally conceded. "I promised to take early-morning duty at the clinic and work straight through to close."

"That's being quite the martyr, isn't it?"

"It gives a couple people the opportunity to be off and have the day with their families, including you, if you want it."

"But the clinic can be a madhouse on Saturdays because, outside the ER, we're the only practice that's open on the weekends."

Simon shrugged. "Weekday, weekend, it's all the same to me. Otherwise, I'd be spending my day at home, alone, which gets boring after the first hour."

"I might drop in, depending on my parents' plans," she said, then, standing on the top step while he was two below her, she gave him a gentle kiss on the lips.

Nothing demanding, nothing deep and delving at first. Just a kiss between friends was the way she looked at it. Although the second kiss was more. It probed, and was a real kiss, not just a friendly one. And it went on forever, grew in intensity until she was nearly breathless. Her face blushed and her hands trembled as she tried to bid him a nonchalant good-night, which was nearly impossible to do given her rising feelings for him. So, he didn't want a woman with a child but she couldn't help the way she felt when she was around him, either, so what was she going to do?

"See you t-tomorrow," she stammered as her knees trembled on her way in the door. But before she could get inside he gave her a long, hard kiss.

This one deep and abiding. The kind of kiss reserved for dates and special occasions. The one that set her heart on fire.

Even though it was mid-October the chill in the air turned into a fiery blaze and it was all she could do to keep from fanning herself. But that would be too much of a giveaway. Too obvious a reaction to what should have been a simple kiss. So, instead she buzzed herself in and turned back to face him. "Oh, and, Simon, thanks for the lovely evening. I really did enjoy the time out with you." And the kisses. So very much the kisses.

"Glad you did," he said, backing away. One step down and he turned and sprinted to the sidewalk. "See you tomorrow...maybe."

She waited until he was out of sight before she stepped in and, once she'd greeted the concierge, she went on upstairs, which was where her mother practically pounced on her.

"He's quite a good looker," Mrs. Carson said.

"Were you looking out the window, Mom?" Del asked.

"Maybe for a minute. With your binoculars."

Del shook her head. "He's a friend. That's all. *A friend.*" Even though tonight he felt like more—so much more. And that second kiss was certainly for more than friends.

"He's a colleague," she said, feeling the blush rise once again in her cheeks. "That's all." Except colleagues didn't kiss colleagues the way he'd kissed her, or the way she'd kissed him back. Especially the way she'd kissed him back!

CHAPTER NINE

SHE WAS QUIET around Simon for the next couple of days. In fact she avoided him—something that wasn't lost on him. When they did make contact it was about work and that was all. Nothing personal, no references to two nights before, definitely no small talk. But what had he expected from Del, anyway? She was the original no-contact girl, and he wasn't acting much differently himself. No contact, nothing personal. And there was nothing *not* personal about their kiss on her front step. In fact, as kisses went, it was right up there with the best he'd ever had. Which wasn't good at all as he didn't want the relationship to blossom. Of course, he was hanging on to the hope that she didn't want it, either. So that made it two against the odds, which he liked a lot. Except he was afraid that one more kiss and he'd fall hard, since he was already halfway down.

So the days went on and he alternately regretted and was glad for that moment of intimate contact because it showed him that he could move on. He was no longer so emotionally strung out from his previous marriage, which was a good thing. But the bad thing was the distance that kiss had put between Del and him and he regretted that enormously as he had to work with her, and he also enjoyed her friendship. But he was finding that he wanted more, and the more he resisted it, the more he wanted it and couldn't stop thinking about it. That wasn't to say he wanted some convoluted, drawn-out high-tension relationship that would lead him back to where he didn't want to go. But he liked the conversation, liked the companionship and most of all liked it with Del. Though, as it stood, that moment was done. They'd given in to the weakness and look where it had got them.

Simon sighed as he entered Exam Four to take a look at a little boy who had a bad cough and a runny nose. Cute kid with curly red hair and green eyes, and a look that told Simon he was in agony. "So, what can I do for you today?" he asked the boy, as he acknowledged the boy's mother.

"Can you make me better?" Billy asked. "I don't feel so good."

"And where do you feel bad?"

He pointed to his head then to his throat.

"How long you been feeling bad, Billy?" he asked the boy, who was about eight. He liked to make direct contact with his patients when he could as he found that they had great insight into their own ailments—insight outside what a parent might report.

"Since day before yesterday."

"So which came first? The runny nose or the sore throat?"

The child shrugged. "Runny nose, I think."

Now Simon deferred to the mother. "Is that right?"

"He was running a slight fever day before yesterday, and the sore throat came on last night."

Simon smiled. "Thank you for getting him here so quickly. You'd be amazed how long it takes some parents to react when their child is sick."

And so the conversation and exam went for the next fifteen minutes until Simon diagnosed Billy with a mild head cold, and prescribed something for the stuffiness as well as the sore throat. Then the exam was over. Just like that he was alone in the exam room thinking about Del again. So much for the power of a good distraction, he thought as he headed back to the hub to hand-deliver the applicable notes and prescriptions to the checkout clerk. In that brief lull he saw Del dash down the hall, white coat tails flying, and it all came back to him. The conflict, the resolve, everything.

Face it. He wasn't sure what he was going to do about Del yet and, so far, he hadn't given any thought to the fact that this might be the end of something that had never really got started. So he liked Del! More than liked her, cared for her! But as what? A friend, a possible lover? And what was the big deal anyway? They were two mature adults who knew exactly what they wanted. What was stopping them from taking their relationship to another level and evening it out there rather than leave it festering where it was?

Fear, that was what. They'd both spoken their minds, made their opinions, fears and vulnerabilities perfectly clear, and that was that. But why couldn't they work through those issues together? Or could they? It seemed a logical thing to do, having some help to get through. But Del was afraid of that help and, to be honest, so was he. Because there was no telling where it would go. Vulnerability was a strange thing. It caused people to do things they didn't want; caused them to break vows and promises and ignore the real heart. So maybe Del was correct in ignoring this whole thing.

But, damn it! Why did he want to pursue it anyway?

It wasn't the fact that it was awkward so much as that she was embarrassed by the whole episode. She'd kissed him. Started it, and welcomed the second and third kisses. Then she'd avoided him ever since because she didn't know where to go from there. They'd established some kind of chemistry, obviously. But it was nothing she wanted to admit. She wasn't ready. She had Charlie to think about. And a job. No time to be in a committed relationship. The list was long and she'd gone over and over it all weekend and hauled it out and went over it again each and every time she saw him. He had that irresistible charm she needed to keep away from or else next time the third kiss would lead to more, and she couldn't handle that. Didn't want to handle it. All she wanted in her life right now was her son. So it was time to back all the way away and simply be professional colleagues.

Except she remembered those kisses; they were on her mind all the time. So was the next thing and the thing that could come after that if she allowed it. Which she wouldn't. Of course. The kisses were it and no further. It was fixed in her mind like etched glass.

"Do you think talking about it would help us?" he finally asked her.

"Talk about what?"

"What we were leading up to."

She frowned. "We weren't leading up to anything. They were just simple kisses, that's all."

"But what they evoked wasn't so simple, was it? We've been avoiding each other like the plague for the past two days and I know it has everything to do with that last kiss."

"It was a mistake."

"You weren't acting that way Friday night."

"I was out of character for myself."

"Or maybe that was in character and now you're out of character," he returned. As they walked along the hall, each on his or her way to visit a patient, there was no way she could get away from him for the next thirty seconds, so he took hold of her arm, an intimate gesture in and of itself, and led her to Exam Three, to treat a rash. "You enjoyed the evening, Del, and there's no denying that."

"I'm not denying it," she said, looking around to make sure no one else could hear their private conversation. Luckily, that end of the hall was empty of employees, and all the patients back there were in their rooms and would have to have ears pressed to the door to hear them. "It was a nice evening and it was nice to get out and have some adult company."

"We could do it again."

"No," she snapped. "We can't. We both know where this thing could go if we let it, and neither of us want it."

"That's not what your lips were saying."

"Lying lips."

Simon chuckled. "Beautiful, kissable lips."

"And *that's* the problem. I don't want to be kissed. It can lead to, well…other things. And I don't want that in my life right now. I'm doing good to manage everything I've already got without adding anything more."

"Would you even admit it if you wanted more?"

"Have you changed your mind, Simon? Have you suddenly decided that it's time to go out on the hunt again?"

"Not the hunt so much as I've decided it's time to move on."

She laid her hand on the door handle. "Well, I'm happy right where I am. And that's the difference between us. You can change your mind easily enough, but I can't. I'm on the course I want to be on."

"And you've never heard of adjusting the course?"

"Not in my life. Not since Charlie."

"Too bad, because I think we could have something." He bent low and stole a quick kiss, then left her standing all flushed and confused at her patient's door. It took her a few seconds to regroup before she went inside and was greeted by a mild case of the chicken pox. "Hello, Miranda," she said as she saw the little girl scratching away at the pustules on her arms. "I think I've got a cream that will help relieve the itching."

Too bad she didn't have a cream to relieve her of her growing feelings for Simon.

"Hello, dear," Del's mother said, greeting her at the door when she got home. "Your father's out for a stroll with

Charlie. Oh, and those came for you a little while ago." Gloria pointed to the dozen long-stemmed red roses all bedded together in a spray of white baby's breath. "I don't know who he is—maybe the man on your doorstep the other night—but he has good taste."

"He's one of the doctors at the clinic. Just a colleague."

"Colleagues don't send colleagues red roses if there's not something more attached to it."

"This colleague wants to take our friendship to the next level."

"Well," said her mother. "It's about time. Is he the one you went out with Friday night?"

"That was just a dinner among friends. That's all." OK, so it was a bit of a lie. But there was no reason to let her mother in on something that wasn't meant to be. She'd only get her hopes up that her stubborn daughter was giving in, which wasn't the case.

"And these are red roses among friends, too? Is he why you've been so grumpy these past couple of days? Honestly, that's why your father took Charlie for a walk over to the park. We're both aware of how grumpy you are when you come home from work, and he didn't want to deal with it this evening."

"OK," Del said, sighing. "I thought I'd found the perfect companion—someone who didn't want to get involved as much as I don't want to get involved. But things have changed. Now he…well. Let's just say that he wants to be the whole package when I'm still not in the mood to unwrap it."

"Because of Eric?"

"Because of Charlie and me. We have a good life."

"That could be so much better if you opened yourself up to letting someone in."

"That's your marriage, and maybe someday I'll find something like what you and Daddy have. But not now."

"And you're not the slightest bit interested in Dr. Red Roses?" her mother asked.

"I'm not saying I'm not interested. It's just that Simon wants to take things faster than I'm ready for."

"He's a man who knows what he wants."

"He wants me to fill a void left by his ex-wife and stepdaughter."

Gloria Carson took a step backward. "You didn't even read the card that came with the flowers." She grabbed it and handed it over to Del.

Del hesitated before she took it from her mother's hand. Suppose it spelled out some kind of term of endearment, or said something she didn't want it to.

"You're being silly, Del," her mother accused. "It's just a simple card. A small one. How many words could he have squeezed on it?"

"It's not how many, Mom. It's what they might say."

Her mother grabbed the card back and sat it down next to the flowers. "You're too stubborn for your own good. You know that?"

"It's just that I'm trying to do what's best for Charlie and me, and I don't think squeezing in a relationship is what either of us needs right now."

"Don't go using my grandson as your excuse. At his age he doesn't care one way or another. If there's something about this Simon that doesn't interest you, that's fine. There'll be another one come along. But you don't need any kind of excuse. If you want to, then do it. If you don't want to, then don't do it. But quit trying to fool yourself into believing that your son needs only you because he's at a perfect age to welcome others into his life. In fact, he's open to it much more than you are. So I'm not saying it has to be this Simon you work with, but at least keep yourself a little more open to the possibility that there's someone out there for you."

"It could be Simon," she heard herself admit, then wanted to kick herself for saying the words out loud.

Gloria arched her perfectly sculpted eyebrows. She was a striking lady—short blond hair, petite figure, eyes that told the whole story. "When I met your father I knew right away. No denying it for me as he was such a good catch I didn't want him single out there in the world for fear someone else would snap him up. But that's just me. I've always known what I wanted and gone out and got it."

"I know what I want," Del defended, as her gaze went to the flowers and the note sitting next to the vase.

"Doesn't sound like it to me. In fact, you sound a little lost."

"I'm not lost." Words spoken tentatively. "It's just that I'm not…"

"Found." Gloria crossed over and hugged her daughter. "Speaking of which, I'm going across the street to the park to find your father and finish off the walk with him. You're welcome to come along, or you can stay here and relax. And think of more excuses why you don't want to go after the one who could be the one."

She patted her daughter on the cheek, then grabbed a light jacket and headed to the door. "And don't worry about dinner. Your father and Charlie and I will find something on our walk."

"Tell Daddy to make sure Charlie is warm enough."

"Your father doesn't need to be told how to take care of a child. The one he raised turned out just fine. Except for that little glitch…"

Del laughed. "I don't have a glitch."

"Then it's a blind spot. Call it what you want."

Del shook her head, and sighed impatiently. "How long will you be gone?"

"Long enough," her mother said, laughing. "And not a moment longer than that." With that she walked out the door, leaving Del alone in her condo. It was strange being there all by herself. She was used to having Charlie around, to talk to, to fuss over. "So it's just me," she said aloud, feeling silly for talking to the walls.

She looked at the card next to the roses, and it was getting larger and larger. Or maybe it was that her attention was becoming more and more fixed on it. Whatever the case, she picked it up, looked at it, then put it back down. Then picked it up again, and held it up to the light as if something were going to be revealed in the overhead studio lamp suspended from her ceiling. Talk about feeling silly. She was certainly going to teach Charlie to be more direct than she was.

"Charlie…" she murmured, as she picked up the envelope yet again and finally looked at the note Simon had enclosed. It simply read *thank you*. But that made her wonder what he was thanking her for. Was it dinner, or the kisses at the door? Was it for something on the job, or for listening to his plight with Amy? In fact, the card wasn't even signed so the flowers could have been from anyone, which left her feeling a little disappointed. No, she didn't want more sentiment, but she did want to know why he was thanking her. And if the flowers were, indeed, from Simon.

On impulse, she picked up her cell phone and called his number.

"Simon Michaels," he came on, sounding as if he was in a rush.

She found it strange he didn't identify her with the phone-number-recognition feature on his own phone but maybe he was in too much of a hurry to look at it. "It's me," she said, in a subdued voice.

"As in Del?" he asked.

She could hear the teasing tone in his voice. "As in Del."

"And what can I do for you this lovely evening, Del?"

Now he was toying with her, which caused her to relax a little.

"Were you the one who had the flowers delivered?"

"Flowers, you say?"

"Flowers, I said. Red roses, white baby's breath. Ring any bells?"

"Oh, *those* flowers. I seem to recall picking them out this afternoon on my lunch hour."

"Why, Simon?"

"I thought they were pretty."

"They're beautiful. But you're evading my question. Why did you send them?"

"I think the card says it all. You *did* read the card, didn't you?"

"You mean the one with the very vague thank-you?"

"I don't see that as vague. In fact, I think it's pretty direct. I was thanking you."

"But for what?"

"Ah, now comes the real reason for the phone call. The lady wants to know what I'm thankful for."

"The lady *is* curious."

"You're acting like nobody's ever sent you flowers before."

"I've had flowers before, even from you, but I usually know why they've been sent."

He chuckled. "Not knowing bothers you, does it?"

"Well, if it's for the kiss…"

"Which kiss, specifically, as we're beginning to develop a habit?"

"It's not a habit!" she exclaimed. "And the one this afternoon…"

"Stolen kisses are often the best, don't you think?"

"So that's what you're thanking me for?" She'd hoped it was for something more than a pure physical urge. Maybe in the grand scheme of things she did want him to admit that his feelings for her were growing stronger, and the roses signified that. But they were for that silly little kiss at the exam-room door? Yes, she was disappointed. The thing was, she seemed to be wanting some big romantic gesture on one hand, and on the other she didn't. Which clearly indicated she was confused by the whole prospect of the man called Simon Michaels.

"What I'm thanking you for is a whole conglomeration of things—your friendship, your kisses do have some play in there, for being a great colleague…"

"And for not firing you when you manhandled me in the hallway today?"

"You looked at that as manhandling?"

"I looked at it as inappropriate."

"Then you've never watched any of the medical shows on television because they're always doing inappropriate things in empty rooms, halls, supply closets. X-ray is a particular hotbed of activity of that sort," he continued, then laughed. "Were you a woman of the world, you'd know."

"I am a woman of the world. I just didn't appreciate—"

"And here I was thinking you were calling me to thank me for the flowers. How disappointing that you turned it into an argument."

"You didn't even sign your name to the card."

"You've got that many men calling on you that it required my name?"

"You know I don't have *any* men calling on me. So what's this about, Simon?"

"Dinner tonight?"

She huffed an exasperated sigh into the phone. "You think food will fix whatever's ailing us?"

"What's ailing us, Del, is you. You're too suspicious. I invited you out for a simple dinner, and all that requires is a yes or no. Yet look what you go and do. You blow it up into something that it's not."

"But you're the one making advances."

"And you're the one rebuffing them. All I did was ask you out to dinner."

"You sent me flowers," she reminded him.

"For a totally separate reason, not to be confused with anything in the future."

"So you consider dinner tonight the future?"

"Well, it's certainly not in the past, is it? Especially since the evening is young. Oh, and I know you're alone because I ran into two people pushing a baby carriage with a baby in it who bears a striking resemblance to Charlie. Nice people, by the way. They asked me to accompany them to dinner."

"So let me guess. You told them you hoped to have other plans in the near future."

"Actually, they told me to call you and ask you to come along."

"Which you didn't do."

"Which I'm doing now."

"Because you knew I'd call you."

"Something like that." He chuckled. "And for what it's worth, I'm willing to take romance off the table this evening, if that's what you want. In fact, since you're so darned suspicious of them, I'll even take the flowers back."

"I'm keeping the flowers. And I'm not going out with you to have dinner with my parents."

"Then where would you rather go? Over to Maria's Italian Kitchen? That's always good."

"What's always good is a night alone with Charlie."

"Which you can't have because he has other plans."

"So what are we fighting about, Simon?"

"Nothing, as far as I'm concerned. I sent you some flowers and asked you out to dinner. You didn't thank me for the flowers and you haven't accepted my invitation. Does that about sum it up?"

"Did anybody ever tell you that you can be frustrating?"

"I've heard that said a time or two."

"So then it's not just me who thinks that?"

"Why would I admit something like that to you? We all have our peculiarities, you know."

"Mine being?" she asked, not sure she wanted to hear the answer.

"Your attitude. You're so...evasive. And you're sure as hell one of the most doubting people I've ever known. I mean, I sent you flowers and look at the way you're acting about it. You'd think I'd sent you something toxic instead of roses."

"Yes," she said.

"Yes, what?"

"Yes, dinner."

"Seriously?"

"Didn't you ask me?"

"I asked, but I didn't expect you'd accept."

"Do you want me to turn you down? Because I can."

"No. No. I asked, and I wanted you to accept. But with the way we are..."

"How are we, Simon? Tell me, how, exactly, are we?"

"If you know, you tell me, because I don't have a clue."

"Well, then, should I have said no?"

"You should have said exactly what you said. But

without all the bickering in between the question and the answer."

"How about we don't bicker tonight?" she asked him.

"No bickering. No romance. Anything else?"

"No more flowers."

"Then next time I should send chocolates?"

"I thought I'd order out and bring it home," he said when she arrived at his door later that evening. "Didn't know what you'd want so I have a sampler of several different dishes. I recalled you like Italian."

"I love Italian," she said, stepping into his condo. It was a converted warehouse, huge on space, and lacking furniture. But very esthetically pleasing. Immediately she began to decorate it in her head. Some easy chairs, a dining-room set, some bookshelves, a sofa... Right now all he had were a couple of chairs, a coffee table and a coat tree. "And I love this condo."

"Like I said, it's too much for me. I bought it with the intention of fixing it up for Amy, but now, since that's a no-go, I just haven't gotten around to doing anything with it."

"You could fit two of my condos in it. Charlie would love all the space."

"Really, at six months old? He's an advanced kid if he's that cognizant of the amount of space around him. Of course, babies are amazing little people, but I doubt the size of this place would really impress your son one way or another."

"Maybe in a few years."

He took her jacket and showed her to the counter in

the kitchen, where he'd laid out his array of food. "You feeding an army?" she asked.

"Depends on how hungry you are."

"I can tell you right now that I'm not that hungry. Looks like you're going to be eating Italian leftovers for several days."

"You and Charlie can always drop by and help me."

"Or I can always stay at home and feed Charlie something less messy."

"At his age, is there anything less messy?"

She laughed. "He doesn't quite have his table manners down yet. But we're working on that."

Simon pulled two plates from the cupboard and handed one over to Del, who was busy deciding what she was going to eat. "I opted out of spaghetti because that's too messy. But if you want spaghetti I can run back over there and..."

She held up her hand to stop him. "What you have here is fine. I'm always good with penne and garlic bread." With that she dished up a plate then stood and looked at him. "Where do you propose we eat this?"

"On the floor at the coffee table." He held up a bottle of wine. "It's red. Hope that's OK with you. I know you don't drink much but you've got to have wine with a fine Italian meal."

"Red's fine. And I'll take half a glass."

"It really does affect you, doesn't it?" he asked, pouring the wine.

"When you've seen what I've seen..." She shrugged. "I spent my whole pregnancy being so careful, not eating or drinking anything that wasn't good for my baby, not engaging in risky activities. I know you can't prevent all the misfortunes that can happen in birth but I sure tried hard to be as good as I could be. And my resolve not to drink…well, let's just say that, while I'm not against it, I don't see enough people exercising wisdom when it comes to what goes into their bodies."

"I'm sensing all the carbs in the Italian might not be the best thing I could have done."

"Carbs are fine. We need them. But I saw a pregnant woman the other day and she was smoking and I really wanted to tell her what she could be doing to her unborn child, but I stopped myself before I caused a scene and remembered that it's her right to smoke if she wants. It's not a good choice, in fact it's a lousy choice if you ask me, but she wasn't asking me."

"And the kids with FAS you treat—they're the reason you don't drink much."

"I got used to it in med school. My parents were never heavy drinkers—they'd have the occasional glass of wine but that was all. And as for me, the first time I saw a child with FAS I was glad I didn't drink too often as I would have given it up on the spot."

"I like a woman with conviction."

"I like a woman who controls her impulses," she said, on her way back to the living room, where she set her plate on the coffee table then sat cross-legged on the floor. "Or a man."

"You're referring to the kisses?"

"I might be."

"They were natural. A perfectly nice way to end the evening."

"What about the one you stole today?"

"I'll admit. I should have done better."

"You're kidding, aren't you?" she asked, reaching out to take her paper cup of wine.

"What if I'm not?"

"Then I probably shouldn't have come here."

He laughed out loud. "You're safe here, Del. Short of my getting drunk and manhandling you, you're going to be just fine."

"OK, so maybe that was a pretty strong word for what you did. I'm sorry that's the way I phrased what I think you see as a little innocent mauling," she said, then took a bite of her pasta.

"Mauling?"

She shrugged. "What else would you call it?"

"A kiss, pure and simple. A short, nearly circumspect kiss."

"Not circumspect enough."

"So it left an impression?" he asked.

"Not an impression so much as chapped lips."

"Whoa now. I wasn't there that long. If I'd really kissed you hard enough to chap your lips you wouldn't be eating tomato sauce with such gusto tonight. You'd be wincing between bites."

"I'm wincing on the inside."

"All this over one little stolen kiss. I wish now I'd made a production out of it. Swooped you into my arms, parted your lips with my tongue, run my hands over your...well, anything of yours would do fine."

She took another bite of her penne and shook her

head. "You'd better not be running your hands over anything of mine," she said after she swallowed.

"Isn't that why you're here? To get a little adult stimulation?"

"Adult, yes. Stimulation, definitely not."

Simon held up his paper cup for a toast. "Here's to not stimulating you, even though you know you want it."

She pulled her cup back from his. "What I want is to eat my dinner without being verbally assaulted."

"But I'm not assaulting you."

"You said you weren't ready for a relationship. That's why I've been keeping company with you. Because I took you at your word. Thought you were safe." She tore off a corner of the garlic bread and popped it into her mouth.

"But I am safe. And whether or not I'm ready for a relationship…honestly, I don't know. I tell myself I'm not, but when I'm with you…"

Del thrust out her hand to stop him. "No! Don't say it."

"Say what? That I'm attracted to you? Because I am."

"And I have a child."

"Which I'm fully aware of. That's the reason I'm not in this to commit to a serious relationship because I still mean what I said. No women with children. Not in the long-term."

"But short- or long-term, I'm a package deal and nothing about that's going to change."

"So we can't play at a flirtation?"

"Why bother?"

He set his paper cup down hard, and some of the

wine splashed out on the hardwood floor. "Damn it," he grunted, jumping up to run to the kitchen to grab a rag to clean up his spill. When he got back, Del was shrugging into her jacket getting ready to leave. "What's this about?"

"We won't work. We can play at it, or play around it, but that's still not going to make it something it isn't."

"So that second kiss. When you kissed me back, and I might add it was pretty hard, it didn't mean *anything* to you."

"It meant we were getting too close."

"Which is your cue to run away. Right?"

"I'm not running. I'm just avoiding the inevitable."

"By walking out my door."

"Look, Simon. We haven't got our wires crossed here. We both know what the other wants, so why tempt fate and broken hearts?"

"Because we do know what the other one wants."

"How does that make sense?"

He shrugged. "I had it all worked out in my head before you came over tonight. Thought we could actually get through a semi-romantic evening and end our day on a good note."

"Well, the part you hadn't thought through is that you're getting too close. If and when I ever meet a man I want in my life, I don't want him conditionally, and that's all you can be—conditional. You don't want a woman who has children and that's a huge condition. And I'm not saying that I want to be alone for the rest of my life because that's certainly not true. But I want a man who wants Charlie in his life, too, and who'll love my son as much as I do. That won't be you. It's not your fault, though. The thing is, as much as you try to fool yourself into a relationship with me, it just won't work because I'm not who you ultimately want."

"Which makes me not who you ultimately want."

"Does that make sense?"

"You want to know what makes sense?" he asked, taking a step closer to her.

He was so close she could smell the tinge of garlic on his breath. "This won't make it right for us, Simon," she said breathlessly.

"Who the hell cares what's right or wrong?" he said, his voice so thick with need it was almost a growl.

Dear God, she wanted this, and she wanted him, too. Just one time. Like their stolen kiss, a stolen moment of intimacy. In that very moment all her resolve just melted away—she forgot all the reasons why this wasn't the sensible thing to do and just gave in to her desires. She wanted Simon. Now.

"Do you have a bed?" she asked, twining her fingers around his neck. So what if they hadn't defined their friendship in terms of how it was going to be? She was an adult and she could certainly be adult about a one-time fling. Or maybe it would be more than once. Who knew? Who even cared at this point? It wasn't as if they were a couple of kids groping around in the backseat for a fast slap and tickle. They could do this…she could do this without regrets because she genuinely cared for this man. Maybe she was even falling in love with the type she said she'd never have a relationship with. It didn't really matter, though. None of it did. She wanted him here and now and she could tell he wanted her just as much. So, all things considered, what was one night out of her life? Not much, that was what.

"King sized."

"With sheets?"

"Just put on clean ones because I was hoping…" He bowed his head down to hers and pried her mouth open with his tongue, and delved in urgently.

The kiss was rough and demanding, like the one she'd been waiting for and had never before had. It was so full of need as he explored the recesses of her mouth and pulled her so tightly to him she could feel his erection pushing against her belly.

"Are you sure?" he panted as he removed her jacket.

"One time only," she said as her own breaths started coming in short bursts. "Read nothing into it, Simon," she said, as he picked her up and carried her to the bedroom.

"Hell, reading is the furthest thing from my mind." He threw her down on the bed and landed on top of her. "Oh, and so you know, once is never enough."

CHAPTER TEN

DEL WAS NAKED, basking in the steamy spray of the shower with Simon, not anxious to leave his condo, torn between the knowledge that she wanted to stay and couldn't, when his cell phone went off.

"I should probably take this," he said, reaching over to the vanity top to grab it. "Simon Michaels speaking," he said, as he playfully rubbed the palm of his hand over her right breast.

He listened for a second then dropped his hand from her breast, and said, "When?" His voice was dead serious. "How is she doing?" He listened for a minute and finally said, "I'll be there in twenty minutes... No, you're not interrupting anything. I *said*, I'll be there." With that he clicked off his phone and stepped out of the shower abruptly, leaving the cold air to flutter in behind him.

Goose bumps raised on her body. "One of our patients?" she asked, grabbing a towel and wrapping it around her as she stepped out. Simon was already half-dressed.

"No. It's Amy. She was in an accident tonight and

she's on her way to Lakeside right now. Yvette had her rerouted halfway across town so I could take care of her. Which I can't because I don't work in the hospital."

"Is it serious?" Del asked, running into the bedroom and dropping the towel to pull on her clothes.

"She's not conscious, and that's all I know."

She wanted to ask him if he needed her there, but that didn't mesh well with their new relationship—dragging a lover along to visit an injured little girl. So she followed him out the door, and down the flight of steps to the outside door, then onto the sidewalk. "If there's anything I can do…"

Simon shook his head. "I'll call you later." Then he was off in an abrupt run, no goodbye, no goodbye kiss. Nothing. She stood there for a second and watched him until he turned the corner, then she turned and walked toward her condo feeling quite…unresolved. Although it wasn't his fault. Amy was in trouble and his place was with her and Yvette.

Still, it was unsettling having him practically jump out of bed and into the arms of his ex-wife, no matter what the circumstances. Oh, well, she thought as she keyed herself into the building and said hello to the night concierge, who was sitting at the front desk reading a mystery novel. It was good while it lasted.

Very good. And best of all, come morning she wasn't going to kick herself because she'd wanted it just as much as he had. *I am human*, she thought, as she took one final appraisal to make sure every piece of her clothing was in perfect array before she entered her condo and was forced to confront her parents. Straightening her hair a little, and making sure her blouse was buttoned properly, she glanced at her watch. Two hours, all in. Not bad. Not bad at all. Especially for someone who'd started out the evening not even wanting a minute of it.

Del puttered around her condo for a while, folding Charlie's clothing, talking to her parents, all of it very restless energy. She knew where she needed to be and it certainly wasn't here.

"Why don't you go to the hospital and help your friend through this?" Her mother's suggestion was very much at the forefront of her thoughts, especially when she considered how he'd been there to help her when Charlie was sick. Simon hadn't left her side, and she wouldn't have gotten through it without him. But the thought that held her back was Yvette. She wasn't sure she wanted to see him with his ex, as that would remind her that Simon was at one time part of a happy little family group, even though she knew that wasn't the case now. But a badly injured child had a way of making people grow closer and, having just been in his bed, she wasn't sure she could go that route this soon after.

"He was a big help to me," she told Gloria, who was getting Charlie ready for bed.

"Then go to him, dear. I'm sure he'll be glad to see you."

But she felt a little strange running after him when just an hour ago they'd forgotten for a few minutes there was an outside world for them to worry about. But she had to behave maturely about this, didn't she?

Simon might need her. And she was pulled toward him as she paced her condo, going back and forth from wall to wall. "Look, do you mind watching Charlie for the night? I think I need to be with Simon right now."

"Of course we don't mind watching Charlie, do we, Charles?"

Charles Carson smiled. "I'll walk you over to the hospital."

"I'll be fine on my own."

"You may be thirty-five, but you're still my little girl and my little girl gets her father's escort to the hospital even though it's only a couple blocks away."

Del nodded. Now wasn't the time to argue with her father. She just wanted to get to the hospital. So she threw on a lightweight jacket and waited for him at the front door. "I'm glad you're both here," she said, giving her mother a hug. "It makes life easier. And Charlie loves having you here."

"Not as much as we love being here with him," her mother said. "Now, you go on and take all the time you need. Charlie will be just fine with us."

Del's dad opened the door for her and took hold of her arm as they entered the hallway and went to the elevator to wait. "You like this fellow a lot, do you?" Charles asked her.

"We're friends."

"Last time we checked you were colleagues."

"Things change. And he's been a big support to me, especially when Charlie got sick."

The elevator door opened and they got in and rode

down to the first floor. "He was there for me every step of the way. I didn't even have to ask him."

"And the two of you are dating now?"

Dating and so much more, but that wasn't something she cared to discuss with her dad. "We've had a couple of dates. Nothing fancy. Just…nice."

"He's not like Eric, is he? Someone who'll string you along with his promises for years, and cheat on you every chance he gets."

"Simon and I don't have that kind of relationship. It's casual. If he dates someone else…" she tried to imagine Simon with another woman and her heartbeat increased a beat or two "…that's his business. Like I said, we're just casual friends."

"Well, casual or not, don't go getting yourself mixed up in another screwy situation like you had with Eric. He was no good for you."

That was putting it mildly. "What Simon and I have can hardly be called a relationship, Dad. So don't worry about me. I've got my head screwed on straight this time."

The rest of their two-block walk they talked about Charlie and the progress he was making. Then when they arrived at the hospital, Charles left Del at the admitting door and turned around and walked home, while Del's stomach knotted. This was where she got involved in a whole different way than she'd ever believed would happen and it scared her. But, this was about Simon and his stepdaughter, and they might need her help. At the least, Simon could use the support. So, turning toward the ward, she wandered down the hall, took a look at the admittance board in the emergency room and saw that Amy was in holding in Trauma Five. Which meant Yvette couldn't be too far away. Gulping, she slipped very quietly into Trauma Five and just stood pressed to the wall.

"Amy, honey, you're going to be just fine."

"I'll swear, that truck came out of nowhere," Yvette said. She was standing at the bathroom mirror fixing her hair.

Simon could smell the liquor on her breath and the stale cigarettes in her hair. So she'd picked up a new bad habit. Nothing like some secondhand smoke for Amy.

"What was she doing in the street in the first place? And at this time of night?"

"I was going to the store, and I had her run back to the house to get my purse. I'd forgotten my credit card."

"And she crossed the street alone?"

"She knows how to cross the street, Simon." Yvette slid into a chair and almost slid down to the floor, she was so *relaxed*. "I know you taught her."

"Of course I taught her, but I didn't teach her how to do it alone, after dark, on a busy street."

"It was an accident. And if that damn truck hadn't turned the corner when it did…" She waved a limp hand in the air. "It was all his fault. You should be talking to him."

"Did he stop after he hit her?"

"He stopped, and accused me of being a bad mother. Of all the nerve."

Simon shut his eyes for a moment. "Where's your husband?"

"Away on business," she said.

"Did you call him?"

"Why? Amy isn't *his* kid."

"And she's not my kid, either, but you called me."

"Because you can patch her up and see that she gets home."

"She's unconscious, Yvette. That's going to take a hell of a lot more than a patch."

"Maybe Yvette would like some coffee," Del said from the doorway.

Simon spun around to see her standing there with a paper cup full of coffee from the vending machine.

"I saw how she was and I thought…" She shrugged and held out the coffee. "Do you want anything, Simon?"

He shook his head no, then took the cup from Del and handed it to Yvette. "Drink it!" he ordered her.

"You know I like sugar in mine."

"I'll go get sugar," Del volunteered, and in a split second was out in the hall on her way to the bank of vending machines, with Simon on her heel.

"Why are you here?" he asked, his voice still hanging on to a shred of its accusatory tone.

"Thought you might need me. And I do have some clout here."

"What I need is information about Amy," he said, running a nervous hand through his still-mussed hair. He hadn't combed it after their shower together.

"She's going into X-ray right now. Still unconscious." She shrugged. "I looked at her chart before I came down here."

"She was hit by a truck."

"I know. And the police aren't holding the driver because it was an accident. Amy crossed against the light. Apparently her mother was across the street screaming at her."

"Damn," he muttered, fixing on the sugar packets in Del's hand. "She must have gotten confused."

"Or frightened, poor thing."

"Is Charlie OK?"

"He's with my folks. They'd put him to bed before I got home." She reached out and took his hand. "Look, Simon. She's in good hands here. It's a small hospital but the staff is top-notch all the way around and they'll take good care of Amy."

"I should have fought harder for her. Should have gone back to court another time."

"You did everything you could do. And when she's older I think Amy will understand that. But in the meantime, I think you'd better go take care of Yvette. She's not in very good shape." Del placed the sugar packets in Simon's hand and closed his hand around them. "I'll go see what I can find out and I'll be back to talk to you directly."

He bent down and kissed Del on the forehead. "Thank you for coming. I know I was a little abrupt when I left you on the sidewalk, but—"

"But nothing. You did what any good parent would do. And I don't blame you. We all have ups and downs, especially when your children are sick or injured." She turned and reentered the trauma wing while Simon went to the waiting area only to find Yvette sound asleep, her head on the shoulder of the stranger sitting next to her. He was drinking her coffee. No sugar.

"She's awake now and they said you can go in and see her for a minute," Del told Simon, who was standing out in the hall leaning against the wall.

"Did they give you her diagnosis?"

"No, I thought that it would be better if they talked to you *and* Yvette, since you can't make the decisions for Amy."

"Don't remind me," he grumbled as he walked through the trauma doors into the main hall, with Del walking shoulder to shoulder with him.

"She's in a serious condition, Simon," Del warned. "Pretty beat up on the outside with some internal injuries, as well."

He nodded, and greeted the doctor on call, who was looking at Amy's EKG tracing as Simon stepped into the cubicle.

"Daddy," Amy said weakly. "I'm scared."

"Daddy's here to take care of you now. No need to be afraid," Simon said gently, taking hold of Amy's hand. She was dwarfed by the chest tube, EKG leads, IV tubing and oxygen mask on her, and Simon's first reaction was to assess everything, including blood that was coming out of one of the tubes. "So what are we talking about here?"

"She needs emergency surgery," Dr. Ross said, "to remove her spleen. We also need to surgically repair her leg. Her head films are negative for brain damage and she's alert and reactive."

"Daddy?" Amy whimpered. "I don't feel so good. Is Mommy going to be mad at me for messing up her evening?"

"Mommy's not mad. She's worried."

"I didn't mean to get hit, and I didn't see that truck. Honest I didn't." Amy coughed and a little bit of blood trickled out her nose.

"I'll go wake up her mother and get permission for the surgery," Simon said.

"How about you stay here and I'll go wake her up?" Del offered.

"She can be pretty ugly when she wakes up from a drink."

"And I can be pretty insistent." Del smiled as she squeezed Simon's arm. "You stay here and comfort your little girl. She needs you more than Yvette does."

"Thanks," he said, hovering over Amy's bed as the child drifted off to sleep.

"Why's she drifting in and out?" Simon asked the attending physician.

"We gave her something for pain and she's pretty sensitive to it."

"So tell me the truth. Is she going to be OK?"

"I'd like to get her spleen out of her as soon as possible, to control the internal bleeding. We're not too worried about her leg. It should repair pretty easily once we get the orthopedics team in place."

"Will she be able to endure that much surgery all at once?"

"We'll have to evaluate that as we go along," Dr. Ross explained.

Damn, he felt helpless. He wasn't her real dad, and he didn't even feel much like a real doctor at the moment. The worst part was, he couldn't make the decisions. By all legal rights he shouldn't even be here since Yvette had a restraining order out on him. But he didn't care about that. If they rounded him up and threw him in jail for being at his daughter's bedside, so be it. This was about Amy now, and Amy needed him here. From the looks of Yvette, so did she.

Out in the hall, Del looked into the waiting room at the sleeping woman who was slumped all over the man sitting next to her. She knew they weren't together and could only surmise this was Yvette in her drunken-stupor, passed-out state. It wasn't going to be easy to shake her out of it. "Yvette," Del called from the doorway.

Yvette lifted her head for a moment, then crashed back down on the willing stranger, who didn't seem to mind having her there. Living vicariously, Del thought as she stepped inside the crowded room. "Yvette, wake up."

"I'm awake," she mumbled, opening her eyes.

"You need to get up and come back to Trauma with me. Amy needs you."

"Kid doesn't even understand a stupid traffic light," she said, her voice slurring.

"Amy needs you," Del repeated as all eyes in the room turned to her.

"Her dad is with her."

"No, Simon is with her and you made sure he's not her dad, so he can't sign off on what Amy needs."

The man next to Yvette pushed her upright. "Your kid needs you, lady," he said.

"Fine. Tell Simon to sign the papers for me."

"He can't!" Del crossed the room and physically pulled Yvette from her chair. "You have to do that."

"I faint at the sight of blood," she complained. "Never could understand Simon and his passion for medicine 'cause you get exposed to all kinds of nastiness."

Del steadied the wobbly woman, and pulled her out into the hall. "She's in Trauma Five. Go down to the nurses' hub and sign the papers then go down to see Amy in Room Five. She needs to see you."

"And just who are you?" Yvette asked, straightening herself up.

"I'm a friend of Simon's."

"So he's got a girlfriend." She laughed a shrill laugh that could be heard the entire length of the hall. "Well, what do you know about that?"

"What I know is that you're wasting precious minutes of Amy's life. You need to go down there and sign the surgery consent form."

"OK. OK. I'll sign it, but I expect Simon to stay here with the kid while I go home and make myself presentable for my husband. He's coming home tonight."

"Honestly," Del hissed, "I don't care what you do after you sign the papers. In fact, I'll be glad to call you a cab."

"I'll just bet you would." Yvette snorted as she bobbed and wove her way down the hall, where she stopped at the central hub to inquire about the paperwork.

The unit secretary handed her a consent form, on which she scrawled a signature halfway over the entire page, then she turned and staggered back to the trauma doors.

"Your cab will be here in five minutes," Del told her.

"I don't suppose you're paying for it, too, are you? See, I don't have enough cash on me right now to…"

Del huffed out an impatient sigh as she took hold of Yvette's arm and led her to the door. The cab was already there, waiting, so Del got Yvette inside and handed the driver a hundred-dollar bill. "That's to make sure you get her up to her door," she said. Whatever happened after that, Del didn't care.

"How did you manage with Yvette?" Simon asked Del after Amy was taken down to surgery.

"Let's just say that she probably won't even remember any of it tomorrow."

"I appreciate everything you've done, up to and including sending her home."

"Amy doesn't need a drunken mother here."

Simon smiled as he took Del's hand and led her back to the cubicle where Amy had been treated. "She's going to spend the night in the ICU and if all goes well be transferred to a pediatric bed in the morning."

"Well, for what it's worth, I can see why you didn't stay with Yvette."

"Yvette does have her bad moments but she's not always so...oblivious. And she's not so cruel that she'd want to see her daughter hurt."

"But she's drunk!"

"Which means something's going wrong in her life."

He was much more lenient with Yvette than Del expected him to be. Did he harbor leftover feelings for her? Maybe part of him still loved her in some odd, convoluted way. It was obvious that Yvette still counted on Simon to see her through and Del felt confused by the emotional interplay she saw. Simon should have been livid with Yvette yet he wasn't. In fact, he was being awfully kind.

"She's worse now than she used to be. For all her faults, Yvette was never a real drunk."

"This new marriage must not be agreeing with her too well, then."

He shook his head. "And Amy's trapped in the middle of it."

"Might be a good time to revisit the custody issue. You'll have the records from the hospital to back you up." Del smiled sadly as he put his arm around her shoulder. "I'm sorry it turned out this way."

"So am I. Amy doesn't deserve this."

"Look, Simon. Let's go up to the doctors' lounge and sit there until Amy's out of surgery. I'll tell them at the desk where we'll be. They need to clean up this cubicle for the next patient."

Simon nodded his agreement and they walked, clinging to each other, to the elevator, where they boarded and went up one floor to the doctors' lounge. It was blessedly quiet in there. A couple of the docs there were dozing, one was eating a meal and another one was reading, with his reading glasses poised on the end of his nose. All in all, it was a peaceful place and Simon was glad for the quiet as he didn't feel like talking, he was so numb with worry. So he and Del sat on the couch, arms wrapped around each other, with Simon's eyes glued to the clock.

Every now and again he sighed and shifted, but he didn't let go of Del. It was well into the first hour of surgery when he finally spoke. "If I went after custody now, wouldn't it seem like I'm taking advantage of a bad situation? I'm afraid that would eventually hurt Amy. I should have had her with me, but the court has been against me every step of the way," he whispered, so as not to disturb the tranquil atmosphere in there.

Del nodded. "Sometimes life's just not fair. Tonight it's not fair for Amy."

He looked down at her and smiled. "Charlie's a lucky little boy having you for his mother. You were meant to have children, Del. I'll admit, I wondered why you wanted to do it, but now I know. You're a natural."

"Thank you," she said. "I love being a mother. I never gave it much of a thought while I was in med school, and even in the beginning of my practice, but being around babies every day…it's how I define myself now, even more than I've always defined myself as being a doctor. But I think you're a natural, too."

"A father without a child."

"Because the child's mother doesn't care enough about her to do what's right. I can't believe she wanted to go home before Amy's surgery."

"Believe it. That's the way the last couple years of our marriage were. She was out playing while I was at home taking care of Amy."

"Yet you still defend her."

"Because for all her faults, I know she does love Amy. It's just difficult for her because she doesn't have that natural mommy instinct like you do."

There he was defending Yvette again. She'd just made love with this man and here he was defending the woman she'd thought he hated. Perhaps it was her own judgment that should be called into question here, getting involved with a man who was distanced from the relationship because he still had feelings for another woman. Could she overcome that? Or did she even want to try?

"I'm just amazed that she wanted custody, when she clearly doesn't care about being a mother."

He shrugged. "I think having a child makes her appear more stable than she is. Yvette's a total mess. Worse tonight than I've ever seen her before."

"I can only imagine what her husband's like," Del commented.

"I've tried not to think about it," Simon said, sounding so discouraged his voice barely broke through the air around them.

"Simon, Del…" A scrub nurse entered the room. "Her splenectomy went fine. They're in for the leg repair now and Dr. Ross said to tell you he'll be up here in a little while to have a talk with you."

Simon heaved a sigh of relief. One surgery down, one to go. Which meant it was still a long night ahead of them. "Thank you," he told the scrub nurse, then turned to Del. "If you want, you can go home now. I'm fine here by myself. And little Charlie may be waking up wanting his mommy anytime."

"How about I call home and if I'm not needed there I'll stay here with you?"

"I'm really OK being by myself here. Especially since you did my dirty work and dealt with Yvette."

"Do you think you should call her with a progress report?" Del asked.

"How about I wait until she calls me?" he snapped.

"Because you're better than that."

"I know. And something's obviously wrong in her life or she wouldn't be acting the way she did. But I'd sure like to treat her the way she deserves."

"Except you won't, and you know it."

Simon sighed. "I'm not looking forward to calling her, but maybe by now she'll be coherent enough to care a little."

While Del made her call, only to find out that everything was being managed quite well, Simon made his to a voice mail message, telling the caller to call back in the morning. *"If you're calling at night, call back in the morning when I'm awake. If you're calling during the day and I don't answer, leave a message and I'll get back to you as soon as I can."*

Damn, she sounded so sweet on the phone. He could see why he'd fallen for her. She had a way of turning it off and on to suit her needs.

"So, what did she say?" Del asked.

"Nothing. It rolled over to voice mail."

"Seriously? With her child in surgery? Maybe she didn't want to be here but you'd think she'd want to know what was going on."

"She doesn't care."

Del frowned. "I just don't understand it."

"And I hope you never do. People like that shouldn't have children, and Yvette certainly is one of those people."

"Well, for what it's worth, my parents said to tell you that Amy is in their thoughts and prayers tonight, and they're keeping a good thought for you, too."

"Are you going home?"

She shook her head. "I'm here for the duration. As long as you need me..."

"Daddy, where am I?" Amy asked.

"You're in the recovery room. The doctors had to operate on you tonight and you're going to be just fine."

"Is Mommy here?"

"Mommy had a headache and she had to go home."

"Oh," Amy replied, her speech thick with anesthesia. "I'm so sleepy."

"Then go back to sleep, sweetheart."

"Are you going to stay here with me?"

"I'm not going to leave your side," he promised. "And next time you wake up I'll be right here, holding your hand."

"Promise?"

"Promise." He bent over and gave her a kiss on her forehead, then looked at her tiny form lying under the blanket. The daughter he would choose...if the choice were his to make. Unfortunately, it wasn't and he was scared to death that once she was past this crisis Yvette would take Amy away from him again.

Simon didn't know how he'd survive that.

"She looks like an angel," Del said, stepping up behind Simon and putting her hand on his shoulder.

"She is an angel. Such a good child… Yvette doesn't know what she has or how lucky she is."

"Well, Yvette is out in the waiting room with a man I take to be her husband. He's older. Old enough to be her father, and he looks like a dude, with all his gold chains and rings. And he's wearing sunglasses even though he's inside the building at night."

"He brought her here?"

Del shrugged. "She seems more sober than she did when I sent her home several hours ago."

"I suppose I should go out and see her."

"Well, they won't let her in Recovery. I told her she'd have to wait until Amy went to the ICU, then she'd probably get ten minutes with her."

"Was she agreeable?"

"Her husband did all the talking for her. He wanted to know when that would be and I told him we have no way of knowing. He wasn't happy to hear that."

"I guess it has to be done." Frowning, Simon stood up and walked slowly to the door, then out to the surgery waiting room.

"How is she?" Yvette asked as she looked in a compact mirror and fiddled with her hair.

"Rough shape. She lost her spleen, and had to have orthopedic surgery. She'll probably be down about six weeks, and they'll get her up and start her on physical therapy as soon as possible so she won't get weak."

"Six weeks?" Yvette's husband shouted. "We can't have a sick kid hanging around that long. We've got things to do, and if she's laid up that means we'll have to get someone to watch her."

"You must be Mack Brighton," Simon said, without extending his hand to the man.

"Sure, this is my husband, Mack," Yvette said. "Mack, this is my ex, Simon. The one who was fighting me for Amy."

"So you're the one who wants the kid. Funny how that's going to work out for you, 'cause it looks like you're going to get her for a while, since we can't take care of her the way she needs. Or, I suppose we could put her in a nursing home of some sort if you don't want her the way she is now."

"Amy's not going to a nursing home," Simon said, fighting hard to hold his temper in check.

"Then you'll keep her?" Yvette asked hopefully.

"Of course I'll keep her. But you'll have to have the court revoke the restraining order against me."

"And you'll have to give him full custody so he can make all her medical decisions," Del said from behind Simon. She stepped around him and looked straight at Mack. "The way it stands now, Simon can't do anything to help Amy because of the way you've got him tied up. So untie him and give him a full-custody agreement, then you won't have to have him bothering you every time something has to be decided."

"Sure, whatever," Mack grunted. "I'll call the attorney first thing in the morning."

"You're taking my baby?" Yvette asked, as if she wasn't even paying attention to the conversation going on around her. "Does that mean you're going to pay for her, too?"

"Of course I'll pay for her."

"And he won't come after you at some time in the future if you agree to sever all ties to Amy now, and in the years to come."

"You mean you're just going to take my baby away from me forever?"

"That's exactly what he means," Del interjected.

"And I want to adopt her," Simon said. "Give her my name and become her legal father."

"That's being harsh," Yvette said. "Just because she had a little accident."

"An accident that almost killed her," Simon returned.

"Let him have the kid," Mack said. "If you don't she's going to cost you a fortune, and don't expect me to chip in for her care."

"Why do I feel like you're all trying to take advantage of me?" Yvette asked, putting on her pouty face.

"You think you can do better?" Mack asked.

"You know I can't do better than you, babe," Yvette answered him.

"Then give him the kid. You don't want her anyway. You told me so a dozen times."

"Yet you went after me and took a restraining order against me having any contact with her?" Simon almost shouted.

"That was purely a strategic move," Yvette said. "And you failed."

"You were going to extort money from him to see his stepdaughter?" Del asked. "Was that the plan?"

"Not extort money so much as just make him pay for the privilege."

"I sure as hell don't pay for that kid," Mack butted in. "And I made that perfectly clear when we got married that the kid was baggage."

"Baggage her mother thought she could make a buck on," Del argued.

"Who the hell are you anyway, lady?"

"She's the person who cares more about Amy than Amy's mother does," Simon told him.

"Your hook-up?" Mack asked.

"My friend."

With that Del stepped closer to Simon and slid her hand into his. "His very good friend."

"Then you tell your very good friend he can have the kid if he wants her, but it's going to cost him."

"It will cost me nothing," Simon said, squeezing Del's hand. "In fact it will save me another court battle where I go after child support from Yvette, which is what I could do since you're so willing to give Amy away. I'm sure the courts would agree with me that neither of you deserves to have her, and if it gets that far in the court system Yvette might be the one who ends up paying me child support."

"You wouldn't do that," Yvette said. "We were married five years and the one thing I know about you, Simon, is that Amy matters more than anything else to you. You wouldn't tie her up in a family court battle like one that is bound to hurt her."

"You're right. I wouldn't. But you would, and that's the difference between us, Yvette. You'd use Amy and I'd protect her."

Del smiled. "See, the thing is, Amy will be going where she's loved and wanted, and if you care for Amy at all, then you'd want that for her. Especially since you'll be getting Mack in the deal."

Yvette sighed. "Are you going to be around to help raise her?"

"I'll be around," Del said, then looked up at Simon. "One way or another."

"Could I at least see her sometimes, Simon?"

Del held her breath. This whole thing had been a gamble to start with, but it looked as if Yvette was about to give in to her husband's wishes. Here was hoping she had no more children in the bargain.

"Of course. Ideally, you'd even want to have a relationship with her."

"Except we're moving out of Chicago," Mack said.

"We are?" Yvette questioned.

"Yep. I've got a hot prospect coming up in Vegas and I need to be closer to my work. Ain't no place for no kid, either."

"I could call."

"You can call," Simon agreed.

"And video conference," Yvette suggested.

Simon agreed to that, too, knowing full well that once Amy was out of her sight she'd also be out of mind. "So, I'll get an attorney. For my side of it, and—"

"Got one already," Del interrupted. "He's my next-door neighbor."

"Then it's set. I'll adopt Amy." It seemed so simple and almost civilized. Of course, they were talking money at this juncture and Yvette didn't have a say in that, apparently.

"And we won't be paying for the kid one way or another," Mack said, smiling as if he'd just won a great victory.

"And you won't be paying for the kid," Simon agreed, nodding. "Oh, and in case you're interested, Yvette, she did ask for you."

Yvette looked shocked. "You tell her Mommy's moving, that she'll be calling her as soon as she's settled in."

"You could see her before you go," Del suggested.

"Don't have time," Mack said. "We've got packing to do. Just make a lawyer's appointment before we leave town next week, and we'll get this all wrapped up."

"Dr. Michaels," one of the recovery nurses said, tapping Simon on the shoulder. "Just thought you'd want to know that Amy's coming round again and if you want to keep your promise to her..."

Simon took one last look at Yvette and, while he didn't regret their marriage because it had given him Amy, he did regret that she'd let herself be trampled so low. But that was her life, and he had a brand-new life ahead of him. "Thanks," he whispered as Mack and Yvette walked away. Simon didn't know if it was his imagination, or if it was real, but as Yvette glanced back he thought he saw a look of regret on her face. He hoped, for Amy's sake, he did. But Yvette was pulled into Mack's embrace as they exited the hall, and she didn't look back again.

"Goodbye and good riddance," Simon said as he rushed back to the recovery room, pulling Del along with him. By the time Amy came around again, he was sitting next to her, holding her hand with his left, and holding on to Del for dear life with his right.

Things had worked out rather simply, Del thought as she stood there. But she still wondered about Simon. Would he commit to someone other than Amy? If, per chance, they got together, how would Charlie rate with him? Would Charlie always come in second? She pictured him adoring Amy while practically ignoring Charlie, and that bothered her. She couldn't be involved with a man who would do that. Time would tell, she supposed, and if there was one thing she had plenty of, it was time.

"That's all for the night," Del said as she and Simon walked away from the ICU viewing window. "You can see her again in the morning."

"This has been the longest night of my life," Simon said, stretching his arms as he turned and started down the hall. He reached over and took hold of Del's hand. "Congratulate me. I'm going to be a father."

"Since I've known you, you've never not been a father," she said.

"You got pretty feisty in the confrontation." They walked past the exit sign and on to the front door. "I've never seen that side of you before."

"That's the mother side of me fighting for a child. Tonight I was fighting for Amy."

"But you're not her mother."

"And you were in the position where you had to be more diplomatic than I was. One wrong word and Amy would have been chucked into a nursing home while Yvette and Mack went to Vegas. So as the innocent bystander…"

"You're not so innocent, Del. Let me tell you, I have a new appreciation for that side of your motherhood. Pity the poor idiots who try to get one over on Charlie, because you've got some wicked claws."

She laughed. "It's called a mother's defense mechanism."

They headed out into the parking lot and decided to spend the rest of the night next door in the clinic so they'd be close to the hospital in case Simon was called back. Not that there was much left of the night, as it was going on to four a.m.

"I wonder if I'll develop something like it."

"Oh, I think you already have. You stand up for Amy quite nicely. Nice enough that it got you a child tonight."

"I don't think that's sunk in yet. More than likely it won't until I see the signatures on the court document."

She stopped and pulled him over to her, and reached up and kissed him full on the lips. "That's for good luck."

"I've already had all the good luck I'll ever need," he said, putting his arm around her waist as they finished their walk over to the clinic. "And it's sure been one hell of a night, you know that?"

"I know," she said, remembering how it had started

in bed. Just for a quickie was what she'd promised herself, except somewhere in there that quickie had been extended into an emotional commitment. She realized then that she did love Simon, and she didn't regret that for a moment. Loved the way he took care of his child, loved the way he was with her. Too bad he still wouldn't commit to another woman with a child because she was suddenly in the mood to be committed to him. But that just wasn't to be and she knew that. Couldn't blame him, either, after what he'd gone through with Amy. Besides, Amy would be enough for him to deal with for a good, long time.

Del sighed. Their timing was sure off, she decided. Which didn't make them too much of a meant-to-be proposition. It was on that note that she decided to leave him alone at the clinic and go on home, where she was supposed to be. At least in the morning she could see Charlie, and he would renew her vitality. Because tonight she felt fully drained. Fully, completely drained.

"She's doing great," Simon said. "She's in physical therapy next door so I decided to run over here to the clinic to see how things were going." He was on an extended leave of absence, pending Amy's release from the hospital any day now. And although he was officially offf call, he'd managed to drop in on Del at least once a day for the past two weeks. Sometimes he had a legitimate excuse, sometimes he just came to loiter and be near. Either way, she always seemed glad to see him. Glad, yet back to the casual. So while they hadn't managed another night together yet, that connection was still there between them, ever clinging. But he felt it slipping away.

Besides, Del's parents had gone home to Costa Rica and she was back to her old schedule, which left her with very little time to herself. "I've checked in on her a few times when I've gone over to visit Charlie on my lunch hour and she's wonderful. So bright. So eager to work hard to get better because she wants to come home and live in her new daddy's condo."

Simon smiled. "I can see why you didn't want to leave Charlie. It's a hard adjustment to make."

"It's getting easier when I drop him off, but it's never totally easy."

"Have you ever thought about a child-care center here in the clinic? We've got a few parents here who could benefit from that."

"Actually, no. I'd never thought of it, but it might be worth considering."

"That would keep Charlie closer to you. And Amy closer to me before and after school."

"So you're really going to come back to us when she's better?"

"Yes. I'd never planned on quitting altogether. Somebody's got to support us. So unless I marry a rich woman who doesn't mind taking on all the responsibilities..."

"She can't have children," Del reminded him.

"About that. I think I've changed my mind."

"Changed your mind about what?"

"About someone with children. I think I could possibly manage to have a relationship like that in my life."

"How? When all I've ever heard from you is that you wouldn't get permanently involved with a woman who has a child. When did that change, or did it change?"

"It changed when I started using my head. And it's about finding the right relationship. Knowing that she would love Amy as much as I would love her child."

"So you mean a blended-family type of situation?"

"That's what they're calling it these days."

"But could you do that, Simon? Just walk into a family and love her children as much as you love Amy? Or would Amy always come first? Because that wouldn't be right. Children need love on their own terms, and they don't need it in a pecking order. Amy comes first, the other child comes second." She shook her head. "It wouldn't work."

"But what if I didn't have that pecking order? If I accepted all the children as they are and loved them in no particular order?"

"You've gone to hell and back for Amy. How could she not come first in your life? I mean, you bring with you, by default, a split family already."

"Not split. Just blended."

Del blinked hard. "Anybody in mind?"

"Just one person. But I'm not sure she wants a relationship with anybody other than her son."

"I think she does. Something tells me she had a change of heart somewhere along the way. But you scare her because of your close ties to your daughter. Can anyone else truly fit in or will there always be a division? And while we're on the subject, do you still have feelings for Yvette?"

"I'll always care about Yvette because she's Amy's mother. But does that mean I want her back? Hell, no! I want to stay as far away from the woman as I possibly can. As for that division, we wouldn't be divided, Del. I don't worry that you couldn't love Amy as much as I do because I know your heart. As I hope you know mine."

"It still scares me, Simon. I'd love to have a daughter and Amy's a wonderful little girl I've already grown to love. But you...you're the unknown to me. Could you ever love Charlie the way I do? Because you'd have to before I...committed to anything. And I just don't know."

"What tripped me up?" he asked.

"Your own words, that you won't have a woman who has a child. I know that's not playing fair using them against you at this stage of our relationship, and especially now that you have your daughter, but it scares me that Charlie will always run a distant second to Amy, and I can't have that."

"Yet you don't think that Amy will run a distant second to Charlie?"

Del shook her head. "I have room in my heart for many more children. Amy would just fill in one of those empty spaces."

"Yet you don't think I could do the same for Charlie?"

"Blending isn't easy, is it?"

"What if I were to adopt Charlie and give him my name as my legal son instead of my stepson?"

"You'd want to do that?"

"In a heartbeat, if you'd let me, and if it would prove to you that I could love him as much as I love Amy. Stop and think, Del. Amy is not my biological child, either, yet I'd defy anyone who said she's not my daughter. I fell for her just the way I'm falling for Charlie."

"Then that makes you a remarkable man," Del said.

"So if I'd ask you to move in to my much larger condo..."

"I might be willing to accept. Provided you really want to take on another woman's child again and maybe add two or three more to the mix."

"More kids?"

She shrugged. "I like being a mother."

"Well, Amy could use another child in the house. She'll make a super big sister, and I could certainly use a woman who would stand by me as staunchly as you do."

"That's a mighty tall order."

"From a man who's head over heels crazy in love with you?"

"And you're sure my having Charlie doesn't matter to you?"

"Oh, it matters a lot. I'd love to be the one to teach him to play ball when he's old enough."

"I think Charlie would love having a father."

"But would you love having a husband?"

"Depends on who it is, and since there's only one candidate on my list..."

"Want to go to Ming's tonight and discuss it?"

"I have a better idea. Let's go to your condo and discuss it. Because here's the thing. Now that I'm going to be the mother of two children, I'm dying to have another baby. So I could get a sitter and we could go to your condo and begin to work at making a baby of our own."

"Seriously?"

"You want to be a father, don't you? And I'm assuming it's to be a large family. So one or two more children should round us out nicely."

"Why, I'd love to make a baby with you, Del."

"And I'd love to make a baby with you, Simon." With that, she twined her fingers around his neck and pulled him closer for the kiss that sealed the deal. "I love you," she whispered to him, not caring that they were standing in the middle of the hall where anybody could see them."

"And I love you," he said back, his lips to hers.

"I love the family we have and the one we're going to make together, too," she continued, only this time in a whisper.

"Do we have to wait until tonight to start?"

"Just a minute," she said, then went to the doctors' board and wiped her name off it. "Now, we've got three hours until I have to pick Charlie up from day care."

"And I promised Amy I'd be back at the hospital to have dinner with her. This is our life now," he warned. "You do know that, don't you?"

"I know," she said, taking his hand as they hurried out the clinic door. "And I wouldn't trade it for anything."

As they walked hand in hand down the sidewalk to his condo, which was the closest by a block to the clinic, she looked out over the lake and smiled. Yes, this was her life now. The one she wanted. The one she needed. The one she loved.

* * * * *

JOIN US ON SOCIAL MEDIA!

Stay up to date with our latest releases, author news and gossip, special offers and discounts, and all the behind-the-scenes action from Mills & Boon...

 millsandboon

 millsandboonuk

 millsandboon

It might just be true love...

MILLS & BOON
A ROMANCE FOR EVERY READER

- **FREE** delivery direct to your door

- **EXCLUSIVE** offers every month

- **SAVE** up to 25% on pre-paid subscriptions

SUBSCRIBE AND SAVE

millsandboon.co.uk/Subscribe

LET'S TALK
Romance

For exclusive extracts, competitions
and special offers, find us online:

facebook.com/millsandboon

@MillsandBoon

@MillsandBoonUK

Get in touch on 01413 063232

For all the latest titles coming soon, visit
millsandboon.co.uk/nextmonth